The Dragon Dimension

CAUGHT

IN THE DRAGON COVE

1st Edition – Uncut

Ressa Empbra

Copyright and Legal Info:

Copyright © 2011 by Theressa M. Branham
Clifton, Colorado
http://ressaempbra.wordpress.com
ISBN-13: 978-0985941703
ISBN-10: 0985941707
Distributed by CreateSpace
1st Edition Release Date January 21, 2013

Ressa Empbra—Author
Theressa M. Branham—Editor
Monica Black—Co-editor
Dave J. Ford—Cover Art Designer

Dedication:

To my Grandma, Helen Hawley Thomas—March 18, 1929, to October 22, 2011—I dedicate this book. She was an educator, a mother, sister, wife, daughter, niece, aunt, granddaughter, grandmother, great-grandmother, and much more. Grandma only recently asked me when I was going to let her read one of my books. Well, since I wasn't done with either one, I couldn't yet. I thought it had to be perfect before she, of all people, read it; I was wrong. We're not promised any tomorrows, so don't wait. If someone dear to you asks something of you, give it to them now. Grandma passed away, and my deepest prayer is that she is reunited with my Grandpa, Hadley, and that they are both now and forever resting in peace with God....

I love and miss you already, Grandma~

Prologue

Thirty-four Years Ago
Date: December 25, 1977
Time: 04:48 Hours
Place: Virginia Hospital Center—Maternity Ward
601 South Carlin Springs Road, Arlington, Virginia, USA

To witness their stillborn baby girl being taken away as if she had never even been, made today the worst day of his entire life. His love, his reason for living, would have such a difficult time after this. He would too, yet he would cope. But with the whole 'maternal-instincts' thing and all, it had to be much harder for a mama. Especially one who'd been trying so hard, and patiently waiting like a Saint, for this very day. Now, he was unable to erase the last few moments from his mind's eye; probably never could....

"Oh, I can't. I–I...just...can't..." she quietly cried out, her weakened voice trailing off. Huffing and puffing, she was unable to bear down or endure the excruciating pain for another moment, as absolute exhaustion finally took its toll. Only moments later, she felt herself fading away and welcomed the heavy pull of a beautiful, unconscious state-of-oblivion.

For him, thirty-one-year old David Conifurr, the love of his life lay unmoving in her sterile hospital bed. He was amazed she had lasted even this long. Even at her young thirty-years of age, Elise Conifurr was frail and worn-out. Her pregnancy had been... complicated, to say the least. Even though they knew from experience the risk they'd be facing, they'd had to try again.

His still magnificent bride of just over ten-years had been looking forward to this life changing event; the moment when she would finally bring their perfect, precious bundle-of-love into the world. He knew she longed for the loving bond one has with their own child; they both did.

From their first meeting, that moment when he had gazed into her vivid, dazzling hazel-eyes, he knew without a doubt, she was the one for him. Not only was she his other or better half, but his everything; the air he breathed, and the sunshine in his darkest of times. He was a man blessed, and knew how fortunate he was to have her in his life. But he'd also always felt that he wasn't good enough for her, not by an extremely long shot.

Standing next to her bed, gazing sadly yet fondly down on her unconscious form in the unfeeling hospital room, he cried silent tears of the deepest sadness he had never known. And it hurt—literally—as if his heart and soul were being torn into two pieces. His chest was squeezing, iron fingers gripping around his heart, tighter and tighter to the point he felt the pain grow and worsen. Clutching at his chest with one hand, while still holding her petite, beautiful hand in his other, he willed his pain to subside, and hers, too.

Elise had done everything as right as anyone could, to ensure each pregnancy would be successful, only to suffer one miscarriage after another. Oh, of course, she would act as if it never hurt too badly, but he knew it had to hurt. It did for him, and he wasn't even the one who had to go through the physical parts of it all. However, he did feel each loss deeply.

And, when she had actually carried their child to eight and a half months this time around, nothing could have dampened her joy, her absolute, utter jubilation over her dream—their dream—coming true.

To see this happen, though, David was afraid for her and what she may, or may not do, as she dealt with their loss. Even more frightening, would she try something crazy, such as try to take her own life, or maybe even his? Or possibly even both of theirs?

David didn't, and couldn't know. But he could, and did pray; he prayed for God to comfort and get them through this together.

He knew that all-too-often, after a couple suffered this kind of loss they drifted apart or at least the majority of them did, eventually going through an ugly divorce. He couldn't live without her, he also knew.

So he continued to pray, it was really all he had left.

Chapter One

Ten-Years Later
Date: December 25, 1987
Place: The United States Pentagon, Arlington, Virginia, USA

The young, fresh, extremely ambitious Special Agent enjoyed working closely with his new partner, and newfound idol, the now forty-one-year old Special Agent David Conifurr, in Arlington, Virginia. All of their Operations were highly sensitive and Top-secret, even to the entire staff and anyone else who entered the massive, seven-story, over three-and-a-half-million square feet of office space that made up the United States Pentagon.

Although he couldn't see it, except for lunch breaks, and of course, coming and going, being located directly across the Potomac River from Washington D.C., was just another bonus. Not to mention all the other various Memorials and Landmarks in the vicinity, he had decided Arlington was a magnificent place to live and work.

He'd moved here only a few months ago from Missoula, Montana, which he missed almost like a phantom limb. Montana was spectacular in its own right. It was one of the most peaceful places he'd ever been to. And, when he'd said there were significant differences between the two places, he had meant to say that there was no comparison, whatsoever.

Bounding into the shared office space situated and cut off from the rest of the employees, buried in the storage areas in the bowels of the second-sub-level-story of the mammoth building, he loved it even though there were no windows or visible links to the outside world.

Although he didn't like to admit it, at first he had needed assistance navigating the beast-of-a-building. Everyone had been extremely warm, welcoming, and plenty helpful. As much of a nightmare as it'd been in the beginning, he was proud to say that it wasn't so bad now.

This specific day, he was practically vibrating with excitement. He was the newest, youngest employee in the O.W.O. Unit, or the Outer Worldly Operations Unit, and he reveled in the newness of it all. Being so green, he still had much to learn.

So far, he'd figured out that somehow, this division of the C.I.A. could communicate with their namesake: Outer Worldly Operations, also known as Dimensions and Realms apart from the only one widely known to humankind: Planet Earth.

They would receive Intel with just enough time to get a Special Agent or Agents into the Realm in whichever Dimension that was having problems. Said Agents, all of whom were highly trained, and extremely sharp at many tactical skills—along with other skill-sets which would blow one's mind—would have a set amount of time to locate, and then fix the problem.

Once their assignment was complete, whatever it was that had enabled them to 'go there' was the same way they 'got back' here. Weird stuff, to be sure, but he didn't work in that particular department. So, he figured, all in time. As long as he could hold on to this great job, he'd stay and all the while, he'd continue to learn.

Today, however, he had a wholly different reason for being so overly ecstatic. He had news to deliver; incredible news, in fact, for his new partner and friend, Mr., or rather, Special Agent David Conifurr.

I like the sound of that for me, too. Special Agent Fred Travett. He sighed.

He would always be grateful, and he had no idea just how true his pensive thoughts would one day prove.

He'd been told of some of Agent Conifurr's beginnings here, at the O.W.O. Unit, and how tragic things had been for him and his wife. All they had ever wanted, prayed night and day for, was to have a child of their own. They weren't even greedy, they only wanted one. More would have been an enormous blessing, but all they had ever wanted, needed so desperately, was simply one small healthy, happy bundle-of-joy to love, to call their own. Which they'd never had.

Though one would expect the couple to be somber, sullen, or possibly even rude, it just wasn't their way. All anyone ever said about the pair was accomplished and honorable things; they donated time and money to all causes related to babies and children.

And they had always made sure some their coworkers, along with a few of their Church members, even many of their own neighbors never went without anything. They preferred anonymity for as many of their generous acts of kindness as possible, and obviously, they'd been seen doing volunteer works, but the monetary side was hush-hush.

Everyone said the couple had never wanted any credit; they simply wanted others to be happy. And, since they didn't exactly have a whole brood of their own to raise and care for, they had the time, and even some extra funds to help cover some of the financial needs. But, it was never enough since there seemed to be no end to their giving—their true joy—to all of those in real need.

Mrs. Conifurr also held fundraisers, working in conjunction with their Church and other meaningful organizations to ensure the necessary funding to cover all of what they did. And they did a lot, she spent most of her time doing for, and taking care of others. She apparently lived for just that. They undoubtedly would have been the best parents ever.

Fred had never been so humbled than he was upon learning those things about his new partner and the man's wife. And, he was not surprised to hear that Mr. Conifurr worshiped and loved Mrs. Conifurr more than anything, anywhere.

He could be tough and gruff; born and bred on the mean streets of New York City, the man really was threatening, even had the accent to back it up. He could be terribly intimidating, but Fred mostly just saw 'him,' the extraordinary man underneath it all, and how deeply he seemed to care for others, just like his wife did.

This was the key reason Fred was flying so high on this particular, fine Monday morning. Even if it was below zero outside, and the power kept going out, and the generators kept leaping back and forth from life to off, life to off.

East Coast winters were brutal, and they were right in the middle of a nasty, classic December ice-storm. He thought Montana had insufferable winters, and they did, but still…this was downright frigid. In any case, Fred almost couldn't contain the joy flowing fast and free through his veins, warming him from the inside out.

This'll be the best Christmas gift he'd ever have the pleasure to deliver. Even if it wasn't from him, he was just so thrilled, elated even, to be delivering this specific, perfect gift to the most deserving couple he'd ever had the blessed honor of meeting.

Suddenly, he became nervous, his heart thudded heavily inside his chest, blood rushed loudly in his ears. "What if we're all being presumptuous? Oh, Lord! What if it's too late? They might think so. I hope not, but they are in their mid-forties," he worried quietly out loud.

After a few deep, cleansing breaths, and more of the inner-pep-talk, he was at Agent Conifurr's office door. *Breathe, it's fine. They'll be ecstatic, this is what they've always wanted–isn't it?* he tried to bolster himself.

Before he could square his shoulders and knock, the door swung open and Agent Conifurr ran right into Fred, practically knocking him over. "Whoa, there. Where's the fire? You okay, sir? I'm sorry, I–I was just gonna knock," Fred rushed out in one breath.

"You're fine, I'm fine. So, what did ya need, kid?" Fred smiled. Only Agent Conifurr standing in his office doorway as composed as he pleased, could get away with calling him 'kid,' he thought, amused.

Okay, Fred, you can do this, he told himself, a little more pep-talk. "Good, okay, um…" *Gah! Just do it, you big Nancy-ass! Big breath…. Ah, okay, I can do this.*

Mr. Conifurr, clearing his throat, brought Fred out of his head, and he realized he was standing there gawking at the man he so respected, sweating and blushing like a damn fool! A damn *female* fool, at that! Shaking his head, sneaking in a quick, *you're a jackass-loser,* to himself, he finally piped up and found his balls. "Yeah, sorry 'bout that. Guess I didn't get much sleep. Anyway, is the Misses still here? We…er, I have news that'll affect you both, and it'd be best if I could tell you. Together, that is," he finished. A relieved breath gushed from his lungs.

That wasn't so hard, Nancy-ass, he reprimanded himself a moment longer.

"Yeah, sure, Son. What's on your mind? Come on in, please, have a seat." He gestured to a chair for Fred to use, next to the lovely and beautiful Mrs. Conifurr.

He nodded as he politely brushed past her to claim the empty seat, asking, "How are you today, Mrs. Conifurr? Beautiful day, isn't it?" *What? Ugh! It's not a beautiful day, it's miserable outside! Damn fool!* He sighed.

"Yes, Fred, I am well. Thank you." Offering him a smile, he was grateful she didn't remark about the "beautiful day" he'd just assured her existed. Fred let it go, and sat down just as Agent Conifurr claimed his seat across from them behind his large, too-organized desk.

"Alright, son, ya got us here, ya got our attention. What's on your mind?" the older man asked, as the couple smiled pleasantly and expectantly at him.

You can do it, they'll be the happiest they've ever been, they'll have to be. He cleared his throat, wiped his still sweating brow on the back of his shirt sleeve, and smiled the best he could.

"Yes, and I thank you both for your time, I know how busy you both always are. Um, we have a, um…well, ya see, we have something. For you. A situation happened, and now we have it for you. If ya want it?" he finished, sweating even more while awaiting their reply. *When did it get so hot in here?* He couldn't stop sweating!

Obviously, they'd have to at least think about it. Maybe even take a little time and talk it over. As the thought hit him, he shot to his feet knocking his now-vacant chair over backwards, and he heard it hit the floor. *Ugh! You're a damn klutz now, too?* He huffed, frustrated.

"Got it. Sorry, just, this is a lot to take in. I get it if you'll need some time, a talk, or whichever. I'll give you more time. Just get back to me once you've decided, and we'll take it from there." He blushed. Again.

Busy trying to say the right things, keeping his brow wiped, and trying to get the fallen chair back into its original spot, he hadn't noticed the expressions on their faces. They were glancing back and forth from each other to him, eyes full of concern and confusion.

He wrinkled his brow, not sure of what the problem was. Before he could ask, Agent Conifurr spoke, "Ah, why don't ya sit back down a minute, ya don't look so good. And while you're at it, ya mind explainin' what you're ramblin' about? What exactly would you like us to think and speak about? You're not makin' much sense, Son. Ya okay?" Agent Conifurr questioned, concern clear in his observing gaze.

Suddenly, the problem dawned on him. *I've never been more humiliated in my life!* Fred chastised himself. *And by myself, even, what a jackass! You left out the whole thing! The actual 'surprise-gift' part!* Shaking his head at his own ineptness, he didn't think it was possible to get any redder in the face as he felt the heat radiating from his skin.

Lord, please strike me down now, I'm such a loser! he pleaded. If the floor would only open up and swallow him whole, he'd be grateful!

Alas, he was wrong. He *could*, and he *did* get redder when Mrs. Conifurr got up from her seat and leaned over to press her bare inner-forearm against his forehead. Her beautiful face was tight and serious, brows wrinkled in deep concern. He felt like a child. A dumb, clumsy, didn't-know-squat child.

Could this get any more embarrassing? he asked himself. *Well, sure, of course it could and it most likely would. Just give me a minute, I'm sure I can one-up myself a few more times.* He took a few deep breaths and tried to fix the disaster he'd just created. *And, of all the people to do it to and in front of? It's okay, just fix it.* He sighed.

"I'm fine, really. Thank you, Mrs. Conifurr, just tired and obviously my brain's not working properly. Really, I'm okay." He offered a kind smile, as she returned her own.

"Well, Son, what's goin' on? Ya need somethin'?" Agent Conifurr politely pressed, still eyeing him with too much knowledge behind that gaze. Fred felt a shudder go through him. As great a man as Agent Conifurr was, he truly never wanted to be on the man's unpleasant side. Ever.

"Yeah, okay. I'm sorry. I didn't mean to jumble things up. I've just been so excited I guess I lost my head for a minute. Of course, you want to know what I'm rambling about." He gave them both a sheepish, half-smile before continuing, "What I meant to say, was…is, um. Well, there's a situation, and from it came something I think the two of you would be very interested in. To keep, I mean." As he fumbled for the right words, he realized that seeing is believing. Besides, he was almost positive there would be no way they could say no once they saw and touched the surprise. He smiled again, feeling a little more confident.

He stood and gestured toward the office door. "Would you both mind coming with me? Then you can see for yourself. I think it'll make your decision much easier this way, too." The couple glanced at each other, then up at Fred, confusion written all over their faces, but he also picked up on their curiosity.

That's all I needed. His smile widened.

The area utilized by the O.W.O. Unit was large, and even though it should have, it didn't even make a dent on their level. There were also other back rooms where who-knew-what went on. Luckily for him, today Fred knew exactly what was going on in one room, and he knew it was all good. As he led Agent and Mrs. Conifurr down the corridor and across a space taken up by row after row of metal shelving, he couldn't help but smile. *This is just too perfect!* he agreed with himself.

Coming to another corridor lined with rooms, each door stood about twenty-five-feet apart from the next, Fred lightly knocked a definite code-knock on the door marked 'TOP-SECRET: HIGHEST CLEARANCE ONLY,' in bold red-letters. Even Agent Conifurr raised a questioning brow at Fred as he simply looked on waiting for the door to be opened from the other side.

Only moments later, though it felt like much longer to Fred, the door quietly, slowly opened to reveal a small, dark-haired woman wearing a black skirt-suit, big glasses, and her hair pulled back in a severe bun. Recognizing Fred at once, the small slip of a woman stood back to allow him and the couple to enter the room. Afterward, she re-closed and re-locked the door.

"Dana." Fred politely inclined his chin to her. She was so tiny, he couldn't believe she'd made it through the physical training and landed herself a job here.

Filing those random thoughts away, he focused on why they were all here, gathered in the hard-edged, cold-feeling room. He glanced over his shoulder by the back wall to make sure nothing had changed, and sure enough, there it was. He smiled again.

"Mrs. Conifurr, Agent Conifurr, if you would please, could you come over here and take a look at this and tell us what you think?" He wanted to jump out of his skin by now, the excitement was too much! He had a strong feeling they'd say yes, he felt it in his bones. *Please, let them say yes, this is what is best for all of them–let them say yes,* he silently prayed.

The moment Mrs. Conifurr's eyes found the small baby bassinet, her entire body stiffened just before she shot across the room to close the gap between them. She peered tentatively down into the bassinet, and then leaned over to get a better look-see. "Oh my, it's a baby. A newborn baby. What...I–I..." Mrs. Conifurr whispered, pressing the back of her right hand to her lips to stifle a small sob, as her left hand instinctively gravitated down to rest upon the newborn's back.

Agent Conifurr shot a strange look at Fred, which he mistook for anger. Fred swallowed the lump in his throat that had formed while he watched Mrs. Conifurr's initial reaction to the baby.

What have we done? What have I done? I thought they'd be thrilled for sure, and want this. He hung his head in shame, feeling utterly defeated.

A sharp, strong clap on the back made him stumble forward two steps. His eyes snapped up and Agent Conifurr was still standing where he had been, but now he wore an almost silly grin on his face.

What the hell? Fred puzzled. *I thought he was upset? This must be the most confusing day of my life.*

"Son, ya mind tellin' us what this is all about? The wife's gettin' herself worked up, and I think I know why. But I'd like to hear the words before this goes too far. Ya understand?" Agent Conifurr smirked, seemingly sure of his own thoughts.

Jackpot! Fred almost said out loud.

"Yes, sir. I believe it is just what you're thinking. You remember the file I was going over last week, the one about the Agent who came back from the Amethyst Faerie Dragon Dimension, dead?" Agent Conifurr nodded. "Yeah, well, when he reappeared to wherever it was that he usually made the transition, they found this little one strapped to his chest. Thank God he landed on his back, but yeah, she appeared with him."

"She? A baby girl? How…?" Agent Conifurr shook his head now, as if he could make sense of it quicker, but confusion flitted across his features again. Not so much in a bad way, but he was clearly confused. *Who wouldn't be?* This was a bit much, even for the O.W.O. Unit.

Fred needed to figure out something to say that would calm the couple. They were obviously highly emotional. He could hear the quiet cries from Mrs. Conifurr, and see it in Agent Conifurr's expression; they needed confirmation.

"Yes, Agent and Mrs. Conifurr, congratulations, it's a baby girl! Merry Christmas!" Fred beamed a bright smile. "For all intents and purposes, she appears to be healthy and normal. So far, there doesn't seem to be any outward-signs of any other type of 'being,' or anything. The Lab's been monitoring her since she arrived, almost two-weeks ago. They didn't find anything that would lead anyone to believe she wasn't human, but only time will tell." He shrugged a shoulder.

Agent Conifurr had made his way over to stand next to his wife, who was now holding and gently rocking the baby girl in her loving arms. It had to be the most tender, intimate thing Fred had ever eye-witnessed. He actually felt his eyes welling up with tears. Coughing into his hand, he quickly turned away, giving the couple a small measure of privacy while flicking away the silly tears falling from his own eyes. *Man, you really are a Nancy-ass today, aren't you?* he scolded himself. Though, he couldn't stop the smile from forming on his lips at the thought.

This was quite a day. He never would have guessed he'd get to be a part of something like this; bringing a family together, a new life with older lives. It was all the couple had ever wanted, and here it was. Finally. Literally, in their hands.

It was so quiet, he almost didn't catch Mrs. Conifurr's words when she spoke, "She's so beautiful, David. So…so perfect. Is this

sounds pretty normal. And, if you think about it, people combine family names all the time. Besides, it's not totally a lie; the Lab believes those were her birthparents' names. So yes, I think it's a perfect combination."

There can be no doubt that this baby, the unique Iax Sarvias Eluhyax Conifurr, was and always will be remarkable. World, you'd better watch out, remarkable doesn't even come close to covering this one. Not only that, but she'll be a true force to be reckoned with, Fred qualified, feeling like he was floating on cloud nine. He'd never been psychic or anything, but he had the strongest, strangest feeling about this baby girl; she would surpass any and everyone's expectations and then some.

He smiled, watching the overjoyed couple cooing and gently touching the baby girl's face, her golden hair, and of course, each of her perfect little fingers and toes.

Chapter Two

Present Day
Date: December 2011—Earth Calendar
Time: Unknown—Still Daylight
Place: Dragon Cove Realm
World: The Dragon Dimension
Superior Life Form: Dragon-Shifters (Maintain human-like forms unless provoked, senses a threat, and in planned or unavoidable battles).

Dragons, Dragons, and more Dragons. Every size, shape, and color of which the brain could conceive. *Beautiful. Scary. Amazing.* Only three of the words that came to mind instantaneously. Some with soft, leathery-looking hides, others were tough, almost steely-looking. And surprisingly, several even looked as if they might be 'friendly,' if a Dragon could be considered friendly. Many looked territorial, extremely dangerous.

Iax was grateful she hadn't caught their notice…yet. They'd most likely breathe fire and brimstone on her, incinerating her in mere seconds. That thought inspired the next three words that came to mind; *well, fu-uck me*. It was all so bizarre, yet somehow beautiful at the same time.

Dragons flying overhead, running, or maybe—as it was hard to tell from a distance—they were merely skimming over the surface of land charred beyond repair, only scant inches below them. Many were launching themselves at one another, furiously swiping at others with massive, dangerously strong tails. Others colliding, tangling in thunderous claps midair, rolling and diving as they fell hard to the ground landing in large heaps with loud, sickening *thuds*, sounding imminently final. There were so many, at least a couple hundred, and it seemed such a waste to maim, destroy, or even harm such beauty.

The land and vegetation all looked as if it would go up into flames at any moment now as lava lazily seeped and slowly rolled all around them, as far as the eye could see down through the valley. Tall mountain peaks proudly loomed like sentinels on either side of the vast valley floor.

Another waste of immeasurable proportions. It was a beautiful area; large copses of antique-looking trees in various types and sizes scattered over the mountainsides, uniquely attractive large and smaller bushes, wildflowers, and on and on. *Such a waste.*

How did I get here? she speculated. It had never been explained to her, other than some kind of weird 'link' thing. She'd be sure to corner Fred when she got back and find out exactly how, or what made these fun little 'trips' even possible. For now, there wasn't time to worry about it.

She'd visited many different places while 'hop-scotching-it-through-time,' as she called it, in just under a year. Different time periods, people, shifters, animals, and alternate Realms from many of the different Dimensions. Everything had always seemed so surreal, possibly imagined, but not. This wasn't her first rodeo; everything here was all-too-real.

The scene was breathtaking, both beautiful and dismal. The sky, which seemed to run forever in either direction of the seemingly enormous valley, was painted in vibrant swaths of purples, oranges, pinkish-corals, as well as different hues of greens and blues.

All the visuals were totally at odds with the sounds and explosions blasting all around her. Carrying on the wind with it all were the putrid, noxious odors, worse than the charred vegetation; charred hide. Everything on and including parts of the actual ground itself, was melted to oblivion.

Iax wanted to retch at the smells and sights—it truly was disheartening—but that would give away her presence, something she most definitely did not want to happen. The massive explosions rocked her entire body, her throbbing head was begging for relief.

She needed to know where she was, what was happening, and why the hell she'd ended up here. Well, truth tell, she knew the *here*; The Dragon Dimension. *But in which Realm?* There were several: Each Realm consisted of various groups made up of a specific type of Dragon-shifter, all of whom inhabited their own territory; the claim they staked upon their creation. Each group, a family or village of shifters, was called a Weyr; much like a Clan, Tribe, or some other such grouping. It was almost unheard of for a Dragon-shifter from one Realm to visit another, as they usually kept to themselves.

Although Iax had been to a few of the different Realms, she still didn't know exactly how many there were. She could be wrong, but she thought this one in particular was the Dragon Cove Realm. The inhabitants were essentially your typical human-like beings who just so happened to be able to shape-shift into their Dragon-forms.

That covered the here part, but the *why*? She had no clue. Something she knew for certain was, one minute, she'd been sippin' a vente mocha latte, trying on some killer heels, and the next…she was here. *Fucking awesome. Not!* She quietly snorted.

Iax learned on her previous 'vacays,' she had to remain focused, concentrate on every detail.

If only she could've landed somewhere poolside, appletini and a great book in hand. Oh, and maybe even one of those hot cabana boys massaging her feet, fanning her while feeding her grapes and berries. Not that she drank; Iax never enjoyed it after watching peeps she truly cared for fall apart—and worse—because of their drinking problem. Still, it sure sounded sensational, and would've made a much better vacay; so worth her time and trouble. Shoulders slumping, she sighed again.

I wish I had my Zune, all this noise is driving me nuts, she grumbled inwardly as a groovy tune was running through her mind, bringing up questions about her mental state; *what's wrong with me? Why do I feel like this? I'm going crazy,* just to name a few. *How àpropos.*

Alas, fun was not meant to be had, at least not yet, and not here. Convincing herself that one of these times she'd certainly make the other trip happen. At least she'd give it one helluva shot, anyway.

Meanwhile, she was here, it was hot, dry, nasty, and she had a job to do. It was obvious that she was here due to the flame-throwers who evidently didn't know how to channel their anger in a healthy way. Now, she needed to figure out exactly what was going on, and what she should do about it.

Hmm, she thought dryly, *better check my bod and see what kind of goods I brought forth this time. Please let there be a canteen of cold water somewhere on my person.*

Night's darkness was closing in quickly, and the charred air around her was cooling just a tad as she hid under the cover of boulders and burnt trees. Her continual sweating could spell grim news for her, and soon.

Iax wasn't fooled for even a second to think hiding would save her ass for long, these kinds of creatures always sniffed out anyone or anything different from themselves, all-too-soon.

Also, if she died here, she actually died, *for real.* Not an option, even though her real life wasn't going quite her way, she still wasn't ready to die.

She needed to reach Gemma, her 'tour guide,' as she called her. Gemma always knew what to do, where to go, and why the hell Iax was brought to, well, wherever it was she always ended up. Gemma was impressive like that, always had all the answers and knew just what to do.

To be honest, Gemma was more like a giant jigsaw puzzle; all the pieces were there and they were fascinating pieces, it was just hard to fit them all together sometimes. But, in the end, they always got the job done, even if the puzzle didn't always come out perfect, it did come out done.

And, Iax got to continue living, *for real.*

Although she was frustrated enough to scream, she knew better. Screaming wasn't necessary anyway, she could simply use mental projection, and Gemma would magically appear.

Here's lookin' at you, Gemma. Iax hoped fervently. Closing her eyes, she sent her thoughts out in a wide arc to summon her buddy. After the third try, Iax started getting pissed. She was hot, sweating, tired, a little hungry and, even though she shouldn't —'cause it seemed rather inappropriate—she had a deep craving for BBQ food.

Shaking her head to clear the random thoughts, she peered around hoping to see Gemma wandering somewhere close by, as always in a daze with a beautiful smile on her even more beautiful face.

Gemma always appeared clueless, but man, the sister should never be underestimated; she's brilliant, and not one to be fucked with.

Still waiting, looking about again…nothing. *Where is she? Dammit, I hate when this happens and she doesn't show up right away!* she grumbled inwardly, then using the same method, she shouted for Gemma. Big mistake! All that did was amplify her already hellacious headache. *Ugh! Smooth doin', Ace!*

Iax started at the reply that came right next to her ear!

"Oh, bother, dear, do not have a hit-attack, I am here already. I am here."

Like a welcomed flood, relief flowed through Iax's veins cooling her overheated system at hearing the voice, but it did nothing good for her newfound headache or her nerves. Without thinking first, she snapped, "Gemma! Why do you always have to scare me? Shit! And, how many times I gotta ask you to please not sneak up on me, yet you keep doing it?" Iax hissed out.

Perfectly arched brows raised, Gemma replied, "Well, it seems that someone's panties are in a wait. Really, Iax, you need to chill. Is this not what you have advised me to do so many times?

And, look, I have. You, on the other hand, are so pumpy. Humph. You are welcome for me showing up, as I always do!" She sat down on a large rock, elbows on her knees, chin resting in her upraised palms.

Trying for patience, Iax didn't want to start things out on a bad note, but she never could help herself from correcting people, either. "Okay, Gemma, A; it's panties in a *wad* not a *wait,* and two; it's *jumpy* not *pumpy,* okay? And, you're right, thank you for always showing up and helping me. I really do appreciate it." She let out a long, slow breath before continuing, "I'm sorry, I'm just pissed. I was having a great day, drooling over a hottie at the mall, having a coffee…thing, fixin' to buy some kick-ass heels, and all of a sudden, I'm here." She opened her arms wide and turned in a half-circle to encompass the scene unfolding all around them.

"And, it's *heart* attack, not *hit* attack—which by the way—I am not having. If you're going to use my stuff, please try to get it right." She waved a negligent hand toward the fiery scene in front of them, and asked, "Now, what's the scoop on all this?"

"Well, my dear, you must not have a potty-party, we shall see you through this as we always do." Gemma smiled innocently, knowing very well that she was riding on Iax's last nerve.

Iax knew the woman thought it was entertaining to poke at her from time to time, but now was not good. Gritting her teeth, she tried to calm down and not blow a gasket. "Gemma, it's *pity*-party, not *potty*-party, and I am not having one of those, either," she finished, offering her friend a fake smile. *Breathe, just breathe slowly. She's here to help, ya gotta be more patient,* Iax attempted to calm her hot-tired-self. *Ah…better.*

She was more than grateful to Gemma, since after all, the woman had saved her ass in more than one scrape, but she always got her aphorisms wrong. Sometimes it was truly funny, but others were a waste of precious time. Still, *potty-party?* She almost laughed out loud upon reflection, it was damn hilarious! *Snap out of it, Iax, and focus! It's go-time!*

"Okay, Gemma, what do we know about what's going on here? Obviously the flame-throwers are pissed off, attacking each other and—" Squinting to see better, Iax tried to get a better visual on what was doin' further up, and back down both ends of the valley, as well as on the mountains standing tall on either side. Trying to discern any possible other creatures or *whatevers*, she was unable to detect anything other than the huge, colorful dudes making jerky of each other and everything else in sight.

"Well, Iax. Gordell—a master-beastie whom is most likely picking his teeth with the bones of the much smaller-beasties as we speak—is very *pissed off,* as you say. It would seem his Truemate, Yoren, was stolen by another beastie-pack. Mind you, I am explaining this in a way you will understand better. These are the unofficial terms, you see." She beamed a proud smile.

"Alrighty, then. So, who's the other pack that stole what's-her-name, and why'd they even do it to begin with?" Iax asked.

She'd done a quick, not-so-thorough inventory of herself. Every time she hop-scotched-it-through-time, she always had several supplies and was dressed in appropriate attire pertaining to the situation she'd be facing. And, though her supplies were always somewhat meager, they had saved her ass before. It was far better than nothing at all.

Rummaging around inside the large, lightweight pack that was strapped on her back upon her arrival, she found familiar, yet equally disgusting packets of 'puke-powder'—*Yum!*—ick, was more like it. They were the kind of 'meals' where you simply add-water-and-eat. The nutritional value was unmatched. The taste? Not so much. Again, they'd saved her life in the past and were kind of better than nothing. Still, it was some of the most rank, nastiest shit Iax had ever consumed, which was saying a lot considering the woman had traveled the world many times over, and had vacayed in several Realms of the various alternate Dimensions.

As always, she also found pre-filled vitamin packets ready to go. Some of the buggers were huge, but they kept a person healthy.

Who knew what you'd come across in a place like this? Health was all important.

The pack also held your basic, standard-issue military eating utensils; a metal plate, cup, fork, knife, and spoon. And there was a Swiss Army Knife with so many goodies in it, she couldn't wait to play with them all.

There were two canteens shaped sort of like a small laptop, about two-inches deep and made of a flexible, seemingly indestructible material. They could be stored in several different compartments in the backpack, even folded to fit into a pocket when empty, if necessary. She decided the pack had too many little pockets and compartments to mess with at the moment, but she was pretty sure it held clothing, and everything else she'd need to eat, clean, even first-aid herself when need be. And it would be needed, that was a given.

One of the coolest things about these vacays was, all the battle-wounds she received while she was there, disappeared when she finally got home. *Ah, home...*Iax already wanted to go back. *Focus!*

Some claim that scars on men are sexy—so why not on women as well?—she had often wondered. To be honest, she had loved a few of her battle-wounds; they were like mementos, little reminders of what she'd done while saving the world and beyond. Some of her missions, though grueling and often deadly, left her filled with pride at the end of the day. A few of her scars could've told some kick-ass tales. Others? Not so much, as most were nasty and awful, so ultimately, she hadn't minded losing them.

Realizing Gemma was speaking in her proper, singsong voice, Iax decided it would be a good idea to pay attention. Although, at least a third of what the woman said made not one lick of sense, the other two-thirds was usually imperative.

Taking a long pull from her canteen, pleasantly surprised to find it was still cold, she turned to face a decidedly flustered Gemma. "Sorry, chicka, ya lost me back there. What was that?"

Smiling brightly, Iax stifled a laugh at the expression on Gemma's face. *Poor thing,* Iax thought, *I seriously should stop being rude to her.* "I'm sorry. I was going through my bag-o-goodies, guess I got distracted. I'm all ears now, so please, carry on." Saluting Gemma with a straight face, Iax clicked her booted-heels together, giving the woman her full attention, in earnest.

"I–I was relaying to you the answer to your previous question, Iax. You asked me why Yoren was taken. I was explaining that I do not know the whole of it, yet. If you could simply pay me the courtesy of listening, you would have some knowledge by this time. I do not speak for my own self, you know." With a resigned sigh, Gemma glanced around, taking in the hot-pocket they had landed themselves in.

"I am sure it has something to do with the fact that Yoren is young and beautiful, therefore, the boss of the bad-beasties wanted her for himself. Such typical male behavior, do you not think?"

Gemma wore a faraway, thoughtful expression that wrinkled her face brought out a few lines in her forehead, and around her pursed lips. She looked rather upset, in general, about 'typical male behavior,' yet none of it took away from her beauty.

"You're on the money honey, men pull some pretty lame shit to get women. I don't know what the hell they're thinking. If some jackass decided he wanted me and I was already taken, he wouldn't stand a chance. What a dick-move. Stealing me would only serve to piss me off, not to mention my own man, if I had one…" mumbling the last part under her breath, Iax continued, "Look around. Obviously, Yoren's dude is highly pissed, and I don't blame him a bit. But all this destruction is a bit extreme. Oh well, I guess to each his or her own–right?"

Checking the scenery once more, Iax shook her head in disgust. Thank God, men on Earth don't go quite this postal or the entire planet would be disintegrated in mere days over 'their women'!

She pictured a group of caveman-dudes pounding their hairy, dirty chests, chanting and spewing lame, degrading shit about 'their women' while pulling said women around camp by their long hair. *Jeesh!* To think, those things actually happened, and to some point they still do to this day. *Loons, all a bunch of loony-tards!* Iax huffed in exasperation.

"Lemme get this straight; Gordell and Yoren went up the hill to fetch a…? Pail of something. They turned around, to see on the ground, other badass-beastie dude thinking; Yo, bitch, you don't need him 'cause now ya got me, and I'm better. Gordell rebelled, and then decided he'd rather his enemy be dead–er." *Okay, lame, but still some funny shit.* Giggling to herself, Iax was unquestionably delirious.

Staring at Iax as if she had totally lost her grip on reality, which maybe she was correct, Gemma slowly shook her head, her expression one of utter disbelief. "Oh, Iax, are you well? There was something wrong with what you just said. Do you not agree?" Her overlarge, violet-eyes looked a bit too concerned as they rested on Iax, clearly feeling sympathetic for her.

Laughing quietly, Iax replied. "Ah Gemma, I'm fine, really. I'm just tired and being a smart-ass. I'm an expert, do you not agree?" Lips twitching, Iax wanted to laugh again but she suppressed the urge for fear of drawing unwanted attention their way.

"Anyhoo, don't you think we'd best get out of here? Don't get me wrong, I love what they've done with the place and all, but it's a smidgen hot, I'm tired, hungry, and we need to go somewhere safe so we can make a plan. What say, let's boot-scoot and get the hell outta here? Or maybe 'let's get outta hell' would be more àpropos." Iax did laugh at herself then, quietly as possible.

Gemma shook her head again, her long, silky, molasses-colored tresses gliding over her shoulders and bouncing softly around her face. She even wore a half-smile on her mug, finally. There was no doubt for even a moment that this job could and most likely would get dangerous, but there was no rule saying they couldn't at least try to keep up their lively spirits during the interim.

"Perhaps you are correct, Iax. And, yes I agree, you are quite the expert smart-ass." Gemma quietly laughed at herself.

Iax thought those words just sounded wrong coming from the exotic, proper, ladylike Gemma, whose looks totally belied her persona. She could kick ass, and never pulled any punches.

After re-strapping her pack onto her back and glancing one last time at their surroundings, Iax took another swallow of the heavenly water before re-stashing it. Helping Gemma up off her rock, they started out in the direction behind them, toward the nearest mountain.

The entire mountain terrain was covered in thick trees, most of which were still intact; only a few here and there had become collateral damage in the fire-throw-down.

Iax was thankful when the temps dropped enough so she wasn't sweating any longer while they continued to climb. Then once it became noticeably cooler, she was thankful again as she pulled out a lightweight, yet warm jacket from her pack. Shrugging into it, they took a much needed break.

After drinking from her cool canteen, she wiped her refreshed mouth on the back of her sleeve—no one ever insulted Iax by accusing her of being a lady—then she reached out and offered her canteen to Gemma.

All in all, it took two solid hours to complete their trek up through the densely populated forest to the mountaintop. From there, the view was astonishing. The Dragons had settled, at least for now, probably temporarily out of fire. *Too bad they couldn't just plug-in somewhere for a quick recharge,* Iax thought with a chuckle. She was in desperate need of sleep. Her thoughts were just too silly especially for her, and her brain kept taking timeouts.

"Gemma, how much further are we going? I'm so tired I think I could sleep standing up. And these new steel-toed boots are kickin' my ass. I've got some killer blisters on my heels and a few on my toes. Cool kicks and all, but owe! Please, tell me we're close?"

Gazing out around them as she whined, which bothered her 'cause *Iax don't do whining,* she suddenly recalled another question she had for Gemma. "This is probably a stupid question, but are the Dragons all shifters? I know in the past all the 'creatures' we've encountered have been, but those guys are enormous! How in the hell does a mere body transform into something that big, then back into a regular body without it killing them?"

She sat on a fallen log, removed the offending boots from her much abused feet, and waited for Gemma's answer.

Gemma was, as usual, already gathering flowers and things sprouting from the ground. Experience reminded Iax of the stuff Gemma could make from the natural habitat wherever they were, and how much better it tasted than the nasty ass puke-powder. Always smelled better, too.

After a few moments of silence, Gemma joined Iax on the log, procuring her finds into a leather pouch secured at her waist. Gemma wore all leather, and not that modern-day, treated crap, but the roughhewn, real stuff from way back *before* 'back in the day.' Not to mention, she was a knockout; rockin' bod, all that thick, silky hair, gorgeous features, beautiful voice, and her eyes! Violet freakin' eyes! Gemma was a five-feet-ten-inch-tall package of perfection.

Iax wasn't lacking, not in the least. Standing a proud six-feet-tall with long, wavy, golden-blonde hair, bright green, almond-shaped eyes, and a flawless complexion. Her thick, pouty, raspberry-shaded lips accented her heart-shaped face.

As for her body, well she'd always been proud of that. Iax worked hard to attain and maintain her form. She wasn't heavily muscled, but exceptionally strong, nonetheless. Her long, shapely legs and arms were smooth, sculpted from perfect muscle tone.

She tried to keep a good tan; one never knew where they would be from one minute to the next, so it was only wise in case you ended up in a place with no protection from the sun. Getting sunburned always put a damper on one's mood and ability to keep oneself alert and alive.

Together, they equated two super-smokin-hot-babes. Iax smiled to herself, she'd have some serious competition if Gemma lived in the modern world with her. Not that she ever minded some healthy competition, but still.

Gemma's voice brought her back to reality. "Yes, all the beings here are Dragons and shifters. I do not know the makeup of their genetics, nor do I pretend to know how they do it, as you said, being so large as their Dragon, then regular sized in their human-like form." She shrugged a shoulder. "We shall arrive at a small building soon, it is not far now. We can make our plan, and eat, drink, sleep, or whatever else we may require. I studied the area before you arrived, and I believe I have an accurate account of the landscape. Also, I believe I may know where Yoren has been taken to. If we can get her back, it will halt this warring."

She smiled at Iax for a moment before noticing the blisters on her feet. "Oh, my! Here, let me help you. I have just the thing to give your poor feet some relief. I am sorry, I did not realize you were in so much pain." *How sweet,* Iax thought. They did hurt, but nothing she couldn't handle. Still, the relief was a welcome offer.

"Thanks Gemma, I'd appreciate anything you could do." Iax watched Gemma pull out a short, rounded, corked jar from her pack. Removing the cork, Gemma reached three fingers in and scooped out a large amount of some pasty-looking ointment. Iax reached over to take it into her own palm, but Gemma gestured for her to turn around, indicating that she preferred to apply the stuff on Iax's sorely blistered feet. With a shrug, Iax complied.

"Ah, thanks a bazillion times over, Gemma. Whatever's in your stuff took away all the pain and the blisters even look better. You're awesome." Only minutes after Gemma had applied her gunk to Iax's blisters, it was as if they had never even been. Iax excitedly re-donned her socks, pushed her now happy-feet back into her boots, and they headed off to find the small building.

Chapter Three

Another thirty or so minutes went by and just as Iax was about to have a shit-fit, they rounded a corner, and there it was! *Finally! Wait. This can't be right.* With a small frown, she decided to make sure Gemma hadn't taken a mental detour and gotten them lost and taken them to the wrong 'small building.'

"Gemma, I thought you said a 'small building,' so what the hell is this? Not a small building, that's for damn sure." Continually scanning their surroundings while trying to check out what Iax could only call a large and beautiful *cabin,* which stood right before them, she couldn't wait to get inside, if this was even the right place. A soothing, hot bath sounded heavenly at the moment. Iax sighed.

"Yes, Iax, of course this is the correct place, and it is small, look at it. Another thing, we are going to work on this language you insist upon using all the time. It is not proper for a lady to speak in such a manner." She lifted her chin in a dignified fashion and walked straight toward the cabin.

Opening the front door and entering the place, Iax was awestruck. Open structured, vaulted ceilings adorned with massive, wooden-beams; everything was the epitome of luxury.

"Well, girlfriend, you git 'r dun and lemme know how it works out for ya," she replied absently to Gemma's declaration about her language. *Knock yourself out trying, and good fucking luck while you're at it,* she thought, amused. "Better women and men have tried, all have failed. I tells 'em like I sees 'em, and I sees 'em in my own way." She couldn't help chuckling at her friend's perturbed expression.

Looking sadly defeated, Gemma shook her head as she walked over to a long hallway. Figuring the bedrooms were in that direction, Iax, still slack-jawed and only paying half attention to where she was walking, followed Gemma's lead hoping to spot a bathroom with a nice Jacuzzi tub along the way.

There were old, crude-like tiles where woodwork was absent, and where those two were missing there were rough, clean rocks; both in all different sizes, shapes and colors. Everything was rustic such as an old wood-burning cookstove, hand-pumps for water, and stuff like that. But it was still luxurious, especially compared to the alternative of sleeping outside.

It's such a gorgeous place, I could live here! Well, except for those flame-thrower dudes who would find and destroy me in no time, Iax conceded.

"Here are our bedchambers; we can each have our own. I hope you like this place. As I said, it is small but quite nice," Gemma said.

Shaking her head, Iax was in disbelief over the woman thinking this place was small. *Crazy broad must be used to a damn palace.* Iax sighed, missing her own place, or rather, *places.* She didn't realize she'd made the rather rude remark out loud until Gemma turned and scowled at her. "Sorry, just kidding," Iax attempted to appease her friend; her much too *sensitive* friend.

Iax had been making bank since right out of high school. Somehow, someone had told someone else, and on down the line about Iax's 'mad-skillz' in hand-to-hand fighting, as well as strategic combat, tactical planning, and her unnatural abilities with every weapon known to man. She had this nasty little habit of never missing her mark. Ever. After a few so-and-so's had learned of her talents, they tracked her down and hooked her up lickety-split. Of course, it hadn't hurt any to have Dear Old Dad working there, too.

She'd completed the required training everyone else had, which nearly killed most of the others also vying for positions in the C.I.A., causing a large number of them to dropout or be relieved during the process. It had been like watching flies drop.

But not Iax. She'd kept up, no problem, and excelled in each new trial much to the dismay of *most* the women, and *all* of the men. She hadn't exactly made many friends—not that she cared—that's not why she had been there.

It probably hadn't helped when she openly laughed at those who were rudest to her, when their own exercises would go south. They would make utter asses of themselves on the daily, and sometimes even hourly. Which, or course, never failed to make her giddy and impossible for her to *not* poke, prod, and just in general, make fun of them. Quite openly. It had made for great fun, at least for her. So who cared?

She had passed every test and graduated top of her class, and with the highest marks anyone had ever scored. Man or woman. Oh yeah, Iax was quite pleased with herself over that accomplishment.

Since then, she'd traveled the world many times over, even traveled to other Realms in the various Dimensions multiple times. Any time she traveled in her own place and time; Planet Earth—the here and now—she did it like anyone else, but in high style. Fancy helicopters, private leer jets, things like that. First-class all the way, baby.

She'd always been drawn to certain things, so that and her OCD issues had turned into high-dollar habits. Iax truly spent a hefty, or if she were to be honest with herself—but on this front she preferred to tell herself one white lie after another—an absurdly, asinine amount of her boodle to pay for her expensive fun and taste.

The important things in her life when, or if, work allowed her any time to enjoy them were things such as hi-tech toys, home decor, badass clothes, all the accessories to match; shoes, handbags, jackets, jewelry, etc. Of course, there was also her all-important coffee habit, Iax was always discovering and trying new gourmet coffees she found in shops and online. Can you say a-d-d-i-c-t-i-o-n? Iax certainly could, and in twenty-four different languages, too. Something else she was damn proud of.

However, when it came down to her away work—jobs away from Earth—things weren't always so posh or fancy, nor were they easy since she didn't get a single damn clue about the job before taking off through that weird link thing.

Traveling to Realms and Dimensions was a surprise-a-fucking-minute. Her bosses, the bastards, knew she'd dig deep and do as much research as possible to make a game plan well in advance. Problem was she would leave a trail, a digital footprint at the very least. Nobody could ever know we had peeps slipping in and out of alternate Dimensions and unknown Planes. Or so that was always the excuse they used for never giving her advanced notice. She would just find herself in a new location on another lovely O.W.O. vacay.

What-eve, no skin off my ass, Iax mused. She undoubtedly was one of, if not the best in the biz. Fast, smart, tough, along with a few other talents nobody else knew about. She even discovered a new one occasionally. Hey, a girl's gotta have at least a few secrets–right? And Iax had secrets aplenty.

The O.W.O. Unit, aka: Outer Worldly Operations Unit, was a branch of the C.I.A. dedicated to intervene in any war already taking place, or prevent wars of an imminent nature, if possible. Somehow, they had found a way to communicate with the other Realms and Dimensions, but unfortunately, technology didn't work in any of them. It would've been fantastic to have some tech-help each time.

Iax always wondered how she got to all the places she'd wound up in, especially since tech-goodies were of no assistance in any of them, but she still had no clue. She just simply 'appeared' and then 'disappeared.'

The O.W.O. Unit had treated her very well, and Iax had always painted herself with a patriotic, loyal, proud American brush. Yet this 'Outer-Worldly-Shiz,' fun as it was, still chapped her ass.

Wasn't like the trusty old U.S. of A. didn't have enough of their own troubles without always going balls-to-the-wall to help out so many other countries and causes. When, instead, they should be cleaning out their own closet first, *before* jumping ass-deep into every Tom, Dick and Harry's problems.

There wasn't much that pissed Iax off beyond all reason. *Okay, that's a lie,* but this was one of her biggest hotspots.

Everything was just so ass-backwards, not to mention the financial burdens; the entire situation made Iax a little bat-shit-crazy. It also never assuaged the deep guilt she harbored over her substantial personal wealth, even though she had earned every red cent, and then some.

Still, it made her feel guilty, her strong feelings about wanting, or rather, needing to be able to help her own country before running to the rescue of everyone else. This was why she anonymously donated large chunks of cash to many deserving, American organizations. How could she not? Someone had to.

She didn't require much in her personal life—if you could even call it that—other than her little secrets and wants. And she had more junk than anyone needed, so she'd slowed down on buying stupid things she didn't need. Then she'd also found an incredible investment broker to manage her funds. With her employers covering all her expenses, she was financially able to help, so why not?

Women needed to run everything, Iax had long decided. Everything in the world would go so much smoother; people could hold their heads higher and stand taller because women would make it a much better place. It would be a life of all people thriving and being rightfully proud of their accomplishments, instead of how it had all become. *What a shame. Aggravating,* Iax owned.

Again, it always led back to those loony-tards, otherwise known as; typical men. The whole reason—or maybe the excuse?—she used and blamed for the kibosh always weighing heavily on her so-called social life. *Okay, another lie.* She'd never had one of those. Not really. She had a few awesome girlfriends in both of her places of residence.

Her particular bff group in Manhattan, New York, was the kind who gathered once or twice a month for their girls' night, which was always hosted by a different person in their little group. Iax wouldn't mind having them at her place, but she'd rather they be elsewhere. She never knew when she may disappear, and that would be impossible to explain to her friends. Thank God it hadn't happened yet.

Still, she wished she could host the gatherings, her place was hella-cool, and it had cost her a pretty penny. She had written a check—payment in full—at the closing, and garnered a whole a lot of strange looks from everyone in the room. It was more than rare for a woman so young to do such a thing, and all on her own. But she had, and owned her pad outright. Something she wouldn't give up for any amount of anything.

At the thought of ever losing her family, friends, and her cool places and stuff, she vowed, *I'll be one of those flame-throwing-Dragon-fuckers before that day ever comes.* Momentarily in the present, Iax quietly chuckled to herself.

Iax's family had lived all over the U.S. due to her dad's C.I.A. job. It had been difficult especially for her poor mama who hated moving, but knew going into the marriage that relocation was inevitable. Still, you didn't have to 'like' something even though you knew what you were signing up for. They loved each other immeasurably, and that was enough.

At the ripe, yet still firm age of twenty-four, Iax had already lived more than most. She currently resided part-time in her stunning Manhattan pad in New York, USA, and spent the rest of her time in her cozy cabin in the small Colorado Mountain town of Pitkin. The place of her fondest childhood memories. No matter where her family lived, they had always taken the time to visit every summer for at least a week, sometimes two. That was, until it had to be sold when shit got tight after her dad's health had declined.

His health insurance was topnotch, but not enough for all the expenses he incurred. He was collecting his pension now and Iax's folks lived a comfortable life, but the loss of the family cabin was a sadness. At least the money they got for the sale covered what his insurance didn't, so they weren't in debt. Still, Iax had always wanted to repurchase it, but either she didn't have the funds, the time, or whatever; something always stood in the way.

Fortunately, after her first two-years of being employed by the C.I.A., she'd finally made enough green to buy the cabin back. She loved it there more than anywhere else; the summers were better than most, and she would know. Winters, on the other hand, were harsh and almost unbearable, and when she did much of her traveling.

When she wasn't traveling, she lived in her fancy, plush, sickly expensive Manhattan Brownstone after having it entirely renovated. She had spared no expense on either place, each having the latest of everything. The best of the best. She could afford it, so why the hell not? Being in the position of either knowing 'the man' to fix things, or able to hire 'the best' for her security and electronic needs. She had a 'station'—she called them—in each of her digs which made her feel more professional at home.

Iax had become so regimented and self-disciplined over the years, structure had become a large part of her life. If she didn't have something to do, she made stuff up.

Her stations consisted of six separate computers with large screen monitors, stacked in two rows of three which hung over large, handmade desks. All of her stuff was state-of-the-art and allowed her to do anything one could ever imagine, tech-wise. She was also a tech-genius, which always came in handy.

She loved staying up nights just to check out things like weather patterns all over the world, or learn about different foods and things in different cultures. It boggled the mind, the many differences there were just in the basics such as how people dressed; something she always indulged in wherever she went.

Being excessively anal and a total perfectionist, her coworkers, friends, even her family had always given her shit about it. *But really, what's wrong with being organized?* She never had quite understood their main malfunction regarding that.

Losers, they're just jealous, she always told herself with a laugh, knowing her love for them couldn't run deeper.

She hated downtime, one of the worst 'four-letter-words' in her opinion, and did everything in her power to stay busy. "Idle hands are the devil's workshop," her mama had always told her, so her hands were only idle if she slept. Even then, she'd always been a fitful sleeper, so maybe her hands were on the move then, too.

That was another thing, she didn't sleep much, just couldn't, she always had too much on her mind. When one travels as much as Iax, even though all the travel plans, hotels, rental vehicles, and anything else one needed was already taken care of by some unseen entity, it still leaves one to worry over stupid shit: *Are the flights all correct? What kind of room will I get once I arrive? Will I arrive at the correct location? And, on time? Will I like the food there? What about the language?*

She'd found out firsthand how easy it was for an itinerary to go south when some dumb-fuck had made even the tiniest mistake in booking. Or through language barriers; sometimes words incorrectly interpreted could make for an extremely bunk travel plan. You never knew if you were going to end up where you were actually supposed to be.

Traveling as she did, she learned something new everywhere and every day. Some places were five-star resorts, and some were flee-ridden, half-fallen down shacks. *Ya just never knew till ya got there.*

She'd found herself sleeping on sidewalks pretending to be a street-bum more than once. A couple times she'd even had to take refuge in a park inside one of those jungle-gym do-dads. Not real comfy, but out of sight and doable. Anything to remain invisible.

And, the food? Seriously, she could not believe what some people considered 'food,' 'delicacies' even. It was easy to locate food vendors in the small, dusty, overcrowded foreign streets when she needed to. She would happily load up on fresh fruits and veggies before she'd even consider putting some of that nasty shit inside her body. Our body is our temple, or so she'd been told.

Language was never an issue, either. Since junior high school, Iax had always been extremely interested in other languages. She had taken a variety of available courses and after graduation when the C.I.A. had contacted her, they required her to learn more. Not a problem, since she loved learning new ones, anyway. She'd become fluent in twenty-four languages, including her own, English, and it was one of her most pride-filled accomplishments.

Well, that and all her mad-skillz, which she was more than thrilled to possess. Especially, since she'd started this whole hop-scotching-through-time thing about a year ago. Apparently, the C.I.A. had enough faith in her abilities to send her on the weirdest, most high-risk assignments they came across. *Who-da-thunk there were actually whole other Dimensions out there?* It had never crossed her mind.

Every time she would show up somewhere, Gemma was already there to guide, help, and keep her ass alive. She owed much to the woman and genuinely cared for her. Too bad she didn't live in Iax's real time and place; what a trip that would be for everyone. Although Gemma was somewhat of an anomaly, she definitely had powers and a vast knowledge of times, places, and histories pertaining to the various creatures, Realms, and Dimensions. Luckily, all the odd languages were covered in the woman's arsenal, too. Even though Iax was wholly fluent on Earth, she knew they didn't teach any *other* languages anywhere. Another awesome asset in having Gemma on her side.

The first time Iax had gone to another Dimension, upon her return she 'landed' on her own couch in her Manhattan pad in front of her superiors. She'd been frantic to locate Gemma, searching each room, under every piece of furniture, hoping and praying she'd find her. The woman had saved Iax's ass and she wanted to thank and introduce her to her superiors. But she hadn't been there, not a single sign of her was to be found.

Her main boss, Fred Travett, thought Iax had lost her mind. He'd even ordered her to see the company shrink to verify that she was still mentally stable. He feared that she'd been so traumatized by the whole thing, she may be useless to them after the incident. Thank God he had been wrong.

Fred was a close friend of her parents, and like an uncle to Iax. He'd always been extremely protective, always worrying and fussing over this and that. She knew he and her dad worked together for several years and even though he was at least twenty-years younger than her dad, they'd always been super close so she trusted him. But, in this particular case, she had to keep Gemma to herself even if the lie, or rather, the omission made her feel bad.

Iax had finally calmed down and realized that Gemma was from the other Dimension, and had obviously remained back in her own time and place. She had convinced Fred she'd just been so rattled upon returning home, she was simply confused. She never brought up Gemma around anyone ever again. Well, except for her folks; she knew she could trust them, and besides, they seemed to be genuinely interested in her O.W.O. work—more so than she ever understood—and were able to keep her secrets.

When Iax had gone on her second trip, which was to the Amethyst Faerie Dragon Realm—one of her favorites so far—of course Gemma had been there waiting again. Iax had asked about her origins, abilities, and how and why she'd happened upon her both times. Gemma had brightly expressed that she was somewhat of a "Guardian Angel" for Iax. Stating wholeheartedly to Iax, "Someone has to do it, as you are far too careless for your own good." They had already worked together eight times, and Iax had come to trust Gemma with her very life; would trust anyone or anything she held dear to the woman.

Iax wasn't exactly supposed to be out making friends on her away jobs so, in theory, that meant Gemma could be considered the enemy, or at least in league with them. No one was supposed to have knowledge of Iax, and since Gemma had plenty, it made her a target. By existing in the often unstable and dangerous alternate Dimensions during such tenuous times, such knowledge could be used against Iax. Another reason she still kept Gemma a secret; in case she was ever given the order to kill Gemma, taking her friend out was not an option.

Leaning back against the doorframe, Iax watched as Gemma drew the curtains back in the bedchamber she'd claimed. Always one to gravitate to all-things-nature, it didn't surprise Iax that Gemma would want the curtains open so she could look outside often to see everything outdoors. Iax suspected it was a built-in mechanism to aid the woman in continually scanning their surroundings and always knowing what was doin' and where.

Gemma reminded Iax of the mythical fey. She could picture her as a tree sprite, albeit an unusually large one, she was just so elegant, gorgeous, and lethal all at the same time. Having those magical powers may have added to the illusion a bit, too.

"So, where's the bathroom, and what're we gonna eat? I'm still starving," Iax pointed out again. Her stomach was growling and starting to cramp. She hadn't eaten since dinner the night before this little trip, and it was also contributing to her feeling almost out-of-body-like. She didn't like not being in complete control of her body and mind. In this weakened state, mistakes could be made, accidents could happen.

"Of course you are hungry; it has been quite a long day for you. I have just the thing to bring you back around. Cop a squirt in the dining area and I shall be right there to fix you up." Gemma beamed proudly.

Shaking her head with a small laugh, as she didn't have the energy to do anything else, Iax was amused by Gemma slip-up again. "Babe, it's cop a *squat,* but you're trying and I respect that." Still laughing, Iax turned back and went to find the 'dining area.'

Iax was also always amused by Gemma's old-world way of speaking and what she called things. At least here and now they didn't have to whisper, although that was always a bucket-o-fun, it didn't always cut it for her.

After eating a large bowl of tasty herbal-something-or-other soup, fresh bread Gemma had effortlessly and quickly whipped up, along with several kinds of fruits and nuts, Iax's previously empty stomach was pleasantly full. The two cleaned the kitchen and then parted ways, going to their respective bedchambers.

Soaking in a steaming hot bath, Iax reflected on the day's events and tried to figure out first, why the 'bad-beastie' had stolen Yoren from the Gordell-Dragon-Dude. It could be, just like at home, the dude was simply jealous and wanted the female for his own. Or, there could be a more nefarious plot afoot. Next, what was she supposed to do about any of it, in either case?

One thing Iax had learned well and at a very young age was, there were politics in every race, religion, age, country, time, and Dimension. Another thing she'd learned well was, politics always brought out the sheer worst in people. Since the Dragons were shifters, they obviously had a 'people' side, at least in some capacity, so there could be any number of reasons for this incident.

Now, she just had to find out if any of her thoughts were factual; tomorrow, after this decadent bath, and after a full night's sleep. Both of which she felt she thoroughly deserved.

Chapter Four

I. Want. Her. Back. *Now!*" Gordell roared in the cave where his warriors had gathered. His deep, parched voice boomed in all of their ears, and practically made the stone walls vibrate. Over two-hundred of his warriors sat around the raging campfire, gaping at him as if they were scared to even breathe.

Gordell Rhaumonesthius, Chief of Weyr Rhaumonesthius, was a formidable male. Standing an intimidating six-feet-ten-inches-tall with broad, bronzed-shoulders as wide and solid as a medium-sized boulder; anyone would have to be insane to court his wrath.

Thick, raven-black hair hung straight reaching the lower part of his back. Long, thin warrior braids trailed down both sides of his unusually handsome face, which was currently formed of rigid planes and stressed angles. Though he was covered in black soot from that morn's battle, his perfect bone structure was ever-present, lending to his looks that every female always took notice of.

Gordell's usual demeanor was a pleasant one; almost everyone enjoyed his wit, charm, and humor, but at present, anyone whom would attempt to approach him would be a fool. He darted his cold, deep-blue gaze around the cave, daring anyone to say anything wrong. Simply one wrong word, and sadly, it would most likely be their last as such a brazen fool would not live much longer.

This was a side of Gordell almost no one had ever encountered. He had never had any reason to be so riled, so thoroughly angered, before this day. Sure, he had a temper and, yes, most certainly they had all seen it before. But this? This was downright terrifying. Then again, this was about his Truemate, his beautiful, loving Yoren.

Gordell and Yoren had known each other all of their lives; grew up together, had the same friends, even their families had gathered for fun as well as fought at each other's backs. They always knew they were meant for one another, and just had their official

Mating Ritual less than one-year ago. Also, though none had yet been told, Yoren was carrying his youngling.

If any harm came to either of them…he did not even want to contemplate such a thought. May *Meynix*—their Goddess—have mercy on the fool and any of his conspirators for their unforgivable actions against his Yoren and their youngling! His fury ratcheted up another notch. Anger, resentment, and fear were all eating at his insides like acid dripping through his veins. Not fear of the situation —never that—fear *for* them; his female and their youngling.

He had never experienced such potent emotions, and Gordell found he did not particularly care for them, either. He was too angry, too emotional. Such feelings would only serve to complicate things. But, how was he supposed to tamp them down? If he did not, he knew all-too-well he could become reckless, a terribly dangerous thing for a warrior.

Is that what the bastard wants from me? Did Mazar want Gordell so out of his mind, so crazed with emotions that he would fail due to his own madness? That could not happen. If it did, he would never see them again, alive or… no! No more thinking along those lines.

He would construct a plan of action; not just attack, but action. One that would ensure the safe and swift return of his female and youngling back into his life, his care. He shook his head at himself. *'His care'?* Apparently, he had not done a highly commendable job of caring for and keeping her safe, or this would have never happened to begin with.

Shaking his head again, this time trying to dispel those thoughts, this was the worst position Gordell had ever found himself in. Again, he did not particularly care for it.

As High Commander of his troupes, he had orchestrated countless battles, never losing a single one. He had never been bested. He had taken some hits, of course, even some near fatal blows, but he always bounced back. Even on his almost-death bed, he had never felt as helpless, as vulnerable as he did at this moment.

No, this should not have happened and now it was up to him to fix, and see that it never happened again. If only he and his warriors had been faster. The other Weyr warriors had been plenty quick as they went about the business of taking his Yoren. It was only due to Gordell's First and his unerringly accurate senses that they even knew what was happening when they did.

The abducting cowards had fled but many of them had fallen back, ordered to watch for anyone attempting to cease their efforts. Only problem was, his Yoren was long gone, way ahead of the Dragon-shifters he and his warriors had battled with. *And right here, in my own territory!*

The firm, always calm voice of his First brought Gordell back to the present. "Gordell, might I speak freely?" He probably should say no. Gordell was certain Darkan would say all the right things; things he, himself, should be thinking right now. Of course, he had never been this far gone, either, so anyone else would probably make considerable sense at this point.

Heaving out a long sigh, Gordell replied, "Yes, Darkan. Help me see reason or anything which may help make sense of this atrocity, if you can." Taking a seat on the cave's hard dirt-packed floor, he grabbed a wooden mug of fire-brew; he and his warriors all needed some after this day's events. The brew burned a fine path all the way through your body beginning in your throat, not ending till it hit your toes. He could think of nothing better at the moment, so he drank long and deep, waving his other hand toward Darkan in a gesture for him to speak freely.

Darkan cleared his throat. "Let me begin by offering my apologies for allowi–"

"Do *not* blame yourself for this! If anyone is to shoulder the blame, let it be known here and now in front of everyone, it is *me* who carries this burden. No one but myself. And I may as well put it out there now, my Truemate is carrying our first youngling. Proceed, but be warned; no more of that," Gordell bellowed.

Collective grunts and gasps of disbelief resounded from all around the cave. Gordell knew this would happen and now all of them would go crazed, just as he had. But it was best for them to know.

Gordell raked them all with one sharp glare, his goal achieved by the warriors immediately toning their voices, quietly chattering to and over each other for a moment. After another moment, everyone realized Gordell and Darkan were both glaring daggers at them. A few roughly mumbled apologies were voiced before silence ensued once more.

"My thanks for your attention. This news changes much. It has been an unwritten code for all of time that no harm will ever come to a female unless she has been taken for law breaking, or some other type of punishable offense. Now that the youngling has been announced, this is even more serious. To harm a youngling, especially while it is still in the mother's womb, is ever allowed. I believe it is safe to assume that Yoren and the youngling are whole and hale as we speak, and will remain thus. Mazar may as well have forged his own death order just by taking Yoren with the youngling growing inside her." Scrubbing a large, soot-blackened hand down his tired, equally grimy face, Darkan took a few deep breaths in attempt to calm himself. "We know where they are, or at least the general area. Do any of you know specific details of their claim?"

Every Dragon Weyr had a large territory, whereupon, they may choose any part of it to stake their main claim; the village area and where their Chief's holdings would be available to all. Whoever did not wish to reside in or near the main claim had the option to choose another area, as long as it was within the borders of the overall territory.

Much of the outer-territory—the parts where nobody settled —was where livestock grazed alongside other animals. Many were used for continual breeding, but the majority were slaughtered and used to feed the entire Weyr no matter where they were, as long as they remained within the main territory borders.

No matter where they live out their overlong lives, most remained with their family and other Weyr members in the same area. Dragon-shifters lived for at least one-thousand-years, but some —the extremely strong—lived even longer. Many fell in battle, as there always seemed to be one raging somewhere in the Dragon Cove Realm.

Most males were fierce warriors, having cut their teeth on the practice field. Being a warrior was the highest, most coveted and respected position one could have bestowed upon him. If they were fated to fall in battle, that was also highly respectable.

There were accidents, nobody could fully avoid them, but it did not happen often to a Dragon-shifter. Beside the fact that there was no honor, whatsoever, in death-by-accident, it was also possible merely to be marred, crippled, or worse; death would be a welcome alternative to certain ill-fates.

When an unmated male was not engaged in battle, he was helping his father and mother to care for their homes and families, hunting to keep the Weyr fed, and doing necessary repairs and such around their homes.

Hunting was always a pleasurable sport. Any male worth his scales as a warrior was an exceptional hunter. Not only did it keep their families and Weyr members fed, it also kept their fighting skills sharply honed while they were not battling. A win-win for all.

Darkan was recalled to earlier years, back when Gordell and Yoren had been younglings and grown into their adolescent stages, then into adulthood. They were birthed in the same year, a particularly telling sign and rare happening. He was older than them by merely fifty-four-years, but it certainly felt much longer at times. Especially times like these.

He had always felt protective of all his Weyr members, but those two had niched out a special place deep inside Darkan's heart. That was why he had no reservations when Gordell had called upon him to be his First, his right-hand warrior, brethren to their Weyr. To fight directly at Gordell's back in battle, help draw up battle plans, even simply to spend time around the two, and help keep the entire Weyr in check.

They needed someone to do it, and Darkan was the best. Having served Gordell's own father before him for a time, he was the ideal candidate for the position. Now, with the abduction of Yoren and the coming youngling he would be expected, and rightly so, to come up with the best plan, and then carry it out to perfection. He knew by the expression Gordell had been sporting on his puss since this all began two-days ago, his expertise would make or break Gordell. He was more than up for the task.

"No replies? Has no one anything to add? I was certain at least a few of you would know something of their territory. All right, let me think." Darkan raked his hand through his hair a few times, tousling it more with each pass. The male looked awful, he needed sleep, food, and time to think clearly. But, he did not have time for such luxuries at present, there was too much yet to do. He was surprised when his Chief next spoke, and at what the male said.

"Darkan is right, no harm should dare come to Yoren or our youngling. Without rest and food, none of us will be any good for anything, only liabilities to ourselves. Everyone go home, clean and rest up, then let us all meet back here at sunrise. Gratitude to you all, as those two mean everything to me." With one sharp nod of his head, Gordell left the massive cave to seek his quiet, lonely, overlarge home.

****

"You are not stupid enough to believe you will truly live through this, are you, Mazar?" Yoren had been throwing those kinds of words at him since they abducted her. Two. Days. Thence. His head was throbbing and he was seriously considering begging Gordell to take her back, to forget the entire, blasted event had ever happened.

No harm had, nor would come to the female. She was beautiful and smart, all the things a strong male looks for in a

Truemate. But, her mouth needed to learn how not to work itself so! She had aggravated him more than anyone he had ever known, and that was the truth. He had no idea she would be such a chore to have around. In fact, he had thought she would be pleasant to look at, maybe even a little fun to tease. He could not have been more wrong.

"Do you always speak so, Yoren? Does Gordell allow you such verbal freedoms? If so, he is a fool!" Mazar shook his head in disgust.

He and all his fellow-warriors who had gone with him arrived back at their territory only moments ago. The other warrior's females—*quiet* and *obedient females*—had readied baths, prepared foods, and were not bothering any of the males. Exactly how good females *should* behave.

In reply, Yoren merely gave him a scathing glare, shook her head, and grumbled words under her breath. Though he could not make them out, he was positive they were not things any female should ever be allowed to even hear, let alone repeat! She vexed him, and if he didn't make his way away from her, he feared he may explode!

Although he did not understand nor believe how she acted, Mazar had to admit she was tough. She had been dragged along through rough terrain, and braved the heat without a single complaint about either circumstance. But she was still impossible.

He and his fellow-warriors had secreted Yoren away into a small, empty shack near the back of their village. He wondered now, why she was not being louder, wailing and squawking as she had on the journey back here, ensuring her grievance was clearly known to all.

Has the female figured out that I did this whole thing in secret, and merely awaits the perfect moment to take someone unawares and scream? Or cause a disturbance knowing she would be saved and sent back to her Weyr and Truemate? he puzzled. *What will I do now?* He should have never entertained the idiotic notion of abducting the female. His and Gordell's Weyr had never been especially fond of one another, but they had never battled, either. They simply had left each other alone. *What have I done?*

During trading and other necessary Weyr business that had him traveling to other territories, he had seen Yoren from a distance many times over the years. He always noticed a radiance about her, a smile which sparkled in the light. Her long, flowing, silky tresses looked as if they had been spun of the purest gold. Her soft laugh echoed and bounced off the mountains framing the valley her Weyr lived in.

After hearing the news that she and Gordell's official Mating Ritual had taken place less than a year ago, Mazar was peeved beyond measure. *Why should Gordell have her?* He already had the best territory, the finest warriors, and the most faithful, loyal Weyr members. *Why did he get her, too?* Even knowing how wrong it was, Mazar had snapped and decided to take Yoren to have for his own.

Females always did as they were told even if they did not like it. They did not have to like it; they only had to do it. Or so he thought. He cursed a string of self-loathing words in his native tongue. Yoren's head shot up and she glared at him as if he had personally insulted her. *What is the matter with her? And for her to think she has any rights? Surely she errs and is not allowed to behave so at home? Surely! Females never acted out thusly!*

Grumbling under his breath, Mazar got up and walked at a fast clip, seriously reconsidering what he had done as he kicked rocks all the way to his home. He knew it was wrong while the plan was being carried out, but could not help himself. He was beyond tired of waiting.

Male-Dragons sometimes had to wait many lifetimes to find their Truemate. Until they did, after reaching full adult maturity, there was a horrible, constant buzzing noise inside their heads, and they could rarely sleep. Even if they did, it was always a fitful, terror-filled sleep.

A male had to kiss a female to know if she was his or not. If she was, the buzzing would cease, and they could start sleeping at their next bedtime. *What would one not do to attain such an elusive peace? What would a male not give for such a blessing?* Although Yoren was Mated to Gordell, Mazar simply could not accept it. He was older than them, had waited longer, he deserved happiness and a certain measure of peace.

The worst part of this atrocity was, Gordell never suffered any of the discomforts of having to wait. He and Yoren had been born the same year, and grew up together. Mazar had been told that Gordell placed a chaste kiss on Yoren's lips when they were still very young. The buzzing did not even begin until a male was full-grown. *The bastard had not suffered a single day!*

Upon entering his humble home, he expelled some of his frustrations by kicking the entry-door harder than he probably should have. Trying to quell his rage before it thoroughly consumed him, Mazar went directly to the counter and poured himself a cup of fire-brew. Drinking it all down without stopping, he slammed the wooden cup down on the counter hard enough to crack its surface, making him even angrier at himself. He did not have much, but this was his home and he was proud of it.

It seemed that he was most definitely losing his mind and had been for a long time now. He just needed the buzzing to stop, and some real sleep. *Was that asking too much? Have I not always been an asset to this Weyr and always treated them all well?* He was not the Chief, but he did rank higher than most—*did*—being the operative word. After the Chief found out what he had done, he would be punished, stripped of his position, and most likely become an outcast; a laughingstock. *And who even knows what else?* He may end up dead, too. Along with his fellow-warriors and closest friends who had gone along with his stupid idea.

Mazar flung himself down into a wooden chair at his table. *Was there a way to get Yoren back to Gordell and forget this whole thing happened?* Shaking his head at his own ineptness, that was a joke. This news, if it had not already, would spread quickly throughout the Realm. There would be other Weyr backing Gordell in a massive hunt for Mazar's head. Maybe he should just give it to them.

What a way to live...he had to think. After another drink. It would help quiet the buzzing in his head, calm his thoughts, and tame his inner-animal. It had to. He got up so fast he knocked his chair over backwards and snorted in self-disgust. He went back to the counter and upended the jug of fire-brew, not stopping until it was empty.

****

Sighing, Yoren lay back on the filthy fur a male had flung at her from the door of the sparse, one-room shack they had just placed her in. Her wrists throbbed and burned from the rough-rope Mazar had bound them with. The dried blood itched, and being in her carrying state, her wounds would take longer to heal; pity, that. Something she had always taken for granted–until now. She tried to find comfort in several positions, but it was no use. One of the males had at least retied her hands in front of her, as they had been behind her back since she had been abducted.

"Oh, Gordell, how did this happen? Where are you? You must hurry! I know you are coming for me, but hurry. Our youngling will not survive much of this abuse," she said aloud. She could take it, but not their innocent unborn-youngling. She had been fed, but not much nor well. Their kind had exceptionally healthy appetites and now that she was carrying, it had almost doubled. Her stomach tighten and growled loudly just at the thought of food.

Fighting back the tears threatening to break her spirit, she closed her eyes, willing herself to sleep. It did not work.

What was Mazar thinking? He had to know he would never get away with abducting her. Perhaps he had gone quite mad; she had heard tales of male Dragons doing just that if they never found their Truemate. She had never witnessed or even given it much thought, but if this is what their madness caused, she felt a small twinge of sympathy for them. She knew she was getting under Mazar's skin and most likely driving him even madder. What did he expect?

She neither had, nor would ever do anything to harm another soul, and she most assuredly did not deserve this. And now that she was carrying her and Gordell's youngling, she was afraid for the first time in her life.

****

Yoren was on a footpath which ran from the back of their holdings to the small village where many traveling vendors had set up their wares just the day prior. She knew of a female who traveled a long way to hock her silks and other fine fabrics, said to be the most beautiful in the Realm. She wanted to purchase a variety of them to sew blankets and clothing for her youngling. The nursery had been coming along quite nicely, and Yoren could not wait to decorate the walls and furniture her father had already been building. This was supposed to be the happiest time of her life.

As she walked along the footpath singing quietly to herself, she heard the sound of twigs snapping, but did not give it any real thought. There were always harmless animals in the woods minding to themselves. Younglings played in the woods oft, too. She thought that was all it was.

She turned her attention back to the path she traveled on when suddenly, and completely unexpectedly, all the breath was knocked from her lungs in a rush, as something large and heavy hit her from behind. She found herself lying face down on the footpath surrounded by several rough-looking males, not from her Weyr.

"So finally, she leaves the safe, protected walls of her holdings. *Alone*. Not a very smart thing to do, now is it, Yoren?" Mazar sneered the words from behind her, then reached down and roughly yanked on her arm to turn her over so he could see her face.

She was shocked at what she saw; he looked crazed, filthy, and quite scary.

She had seen Mazar before but never up close. She was also told of his name, but never gave him any thought. *Why would I?* She had Gordell, the love of her life. She did not want, nor did she need to be thinking of other males. She simply never did. *Mazar has to have a Truemate of his own. What is he doing here attacking me?* she wondered. *How could he have known Gordell and his warriors would be gone this day?*

Stiffening her spine and letting her temper flare, she spat back, "How dare you attack me? What do you want? You must know Gordell will skin you alive and roast you on a spit when he hears of this!" Yoren was usually mild-mannered and friendly but this was going too far, she felt this warranted unleashing her always well-controlled temper.

"Ah, yes…your precious Gordell. And where is he now? Should your almighty male not guard his female better? Obviously he is so overly confident, he feels no harm would ever come here to his own territory. Would he not at least set a guard around you, his 'Truemate'? Perhaps he does not love you as much as you thought."

Yoren shuddered inside at the hate she felt coming off of Mazar in thick, hot waves. *What has anyone here done to rile him?* She had not heard of any grudges or problems which would precipitate such blatant disregard and animosity toward her Weyr.

She realized quickly she would be unable to fight her way out of this situation. There were too many of them, and she was carrying. It would be best to keep that bit private for now, she decided. Furthermore, she would do anything to protect her family, including letting this crazed-male abduct her, if it would keep him from harming her and in the end, their youngling.

Feeling sick to her stomach, she wanted to retch. But that would show weakness, and she was not weak. Gordell would come for her; he would kill for her…for their youngling.

****

Bringing her mind back to the present, Yoren stifled a moan as she rolled from her back onto her side. There were no windows in the shack where she was being held prisoner. If there was, she could at least see the stars which always soothed her. She knew if she could only relax a bit, she could sleep. She also knew if she could sleep, she would be stronger and this ordeal would not be so hard on her body.

Why did I not pay more attention to my surroundings? She should have known when her instincts made her stop at hearing the twigs snap, something was amiss. Dragon-shifters had exceptional instincts and they were raised never to ignore them. Since she had been carrying their youngling, however, her mind seemed to go its own way oft. Her current decision making abilities left much to be desired. She simply could not concentrate well of late, and that had been her downfall.

The only thing keeping her together now was, she knew with all she had that Gordell would come for her...*them.* If it was only her, she would have already fought back—most likely to her own death—but she would have at least made the attempt. Alas, she would never do anything to put herself and their youngling in danger, not more than they already were, so she had succumbed to Mazar's madness.

What does this all have to do with me? She did not truly believe he would let real harm come to her. He had to know her abduction was already severe enough, but harming an innocent female and an unborn innocent was the lowest of lows. Until now, only she and Gordell knew of their coming youngling. Her and her Truemate had wanted the announcement to be a private affair, a celebration with only family and close friends. *Too late now. Surely everyone knows now, since the abduction?*

Only a few youngling were born into each Weyr every year, and some mated-pairs waited lifetimes to create new life. Females were treated extremely well, as if they were as fragile as the younglings they carried. They were pampered and taken exceptional care of by all, even their enemies. Therefore, just from the injuries on her wrists—cuts, rope-burns, and bruises—Mazar was already begging for death.

Deciding to reflect upon treasured memories, times when she and Gordell were younger and he was always near, Yoren closed her eyes once more. She was exhausted and kept minding herself that she must sleep, or she would have a much harder time of it here; away from her Weyr, her home, and her Gordell. And it helped, as she finally dozed off and allowed darkness to envelop her.

Chapter Five

"Wake up sleepy head, it is time to shine the rise! There now, you must awaken, Iax. We have much to do this day!" Gemma nearly floated as she skimmed around Iax's bedchambers straightening things, opening curtains, and trying to get the female to rise. She knew from experience Iax did not sleep well, but when she did, it was difficult to wake her. Wanting to allow the poor thing to sleep a bit longer, Gemma almost left the chamber to allow Iax to do just that.

That is, until she suddenly remembered the lone-female who was out there in need of their help. Most likely a terrified, hungry, and exhausted lone-female, the whole reason for her and Iax to be gathering now. And though only Gordell had been privy to the news until last night, she carries his youngling. This revelation just brought the stakes up on their job.

With a sigh and a heavy heart, Gemma walked back over to the bed and shook Iax again. The female only rolled over, the covers falling away and exposing her bare form for all to see. "Oh, my! Iax, you must not...I–I–how can you behave so? You must rise, and please cover yourself!" she pleaded with the female who was still sleeping like the dead.

Iax executed an undignified snort. "What? Is five more minutes too much to ask for? A girl needs her beauty sleep, dammit. Go away," Iax mumbled. Still uncovered and not shy whatsoever about her body. "Wait, 'time to shine the rise'? What the..." she slurred, not sure what she wanted say in response. She shook her head at Gemma's antics; the woman was funny, usually unbeknownst to herself, but not when Iax was in such a deep and comfortable sleep. Something that never happens, and of course when it does, someone rattles her cage. "You'd best have coffee. I cannot and will not open my peepers till there's coffee. Period." Iax rolled back over taking the blanket with her, snoring almost the second she resettled herself.

Gemma shook her head, but had to admit to herself that she honestly cared for this female. She was the closest thing Gemma had to a real friend in so long, she could not even recall. She also admitted to herself that she wished to be a bit more unabashed as Iax usually was. Smiling at the snoring madwoman in the bed, Gemma turned and left the chamber.

"I should have recalled this. *Coffee,* she says," Gemma murmured to herself. "Well, Iax, I have a surprise for you. Though I have no idea of your world or your ways, I have knowledge of what you mean. I have improved my morning-brew since our last time together, so this will be the best you have ever tasted." Giggling like a youngling, Gemma practically danced her way to the cooking-quarters.

She was still a bit confused as to how Iax could even remotely consider this small building such a wonder. Gemma was used to living in a castle that had much in common with Iax's ideal of the palace she had referred to upon their arrival here. She must take Iax to her real home. One of these days. "Do not start dribbling, Gemma," she reprimanded herself. With age, she was becoming increasingly emotional and sentimental, and did not know the first thing to do about it.

Deep down, Gemma knew she probably would never be able to take Iax to her home because of their differences. Gemma was independent and never had to answer to anyone, except their Leader, who also happened to be her older brother. A brother who was not a particularly pleasant soul; he was bossy, grumpy, and simply rude to everyone. No one ever looked forward to going to him for any reason, including Gemma. If she did want to bring Iax home, she would first have to get approval from him. *Ugh.* Just the thought made her tired. The male was impossible.

Why did their parents have to pass? She truly, with every fiber of herself, wished they had never left. She desperately missed and wished them still alive and running the family holdings.

Thinking about her brother…she shook her head and forced her eyes not to leak. She was not certain what else there was to think regarding him, anyway. He was who and how he was, and no amount of thinking would ever change him.

Wait, leaky eyes…what is this? It had never happened to her before. She sighed.

She understood the process, the protocol, and how things worked; when the parents passed, the oldest son and family heir was bequeathed all the family's holdings. Literally from the most precious gems hidden deep in the family vault, down to the drying towels everyone used for bathing, and of course, all the decision making.

Standing over the wood-burning cookstove making her delightful, tasty new brew for Iax, her thoughts continued to wander. If only Maxiur would relax, breathe, and simply calm himself, not only would he feel better, he may even behave better, too. Obviously, when one feels good it comes through in everything they do and deal with.

If she had a bff group, as Iax called her friends from home, she would certainly match them up, or at least try, anyway. Gemma was afraid for Maxiur's soul, for his very sanity. If he did not shake this attitude soon, well, she did not even want to think of the repercussions. But perhaps a good female in his life would be helpful? She would think on that later, along with other issues regarding her personal life. More things to add to the list of the extremely unusual sadness she had felt of late.

As it was now, the majority of their Clan members had already called upon The House Council demanding Maxiur to step down, and to allow Gemma the highly coveted only-to-be-filled-by-a-male position. She did not want it, but she thought she could most certainly keep their people much happier and better under control than her older, especially grumpy brother.

Finished with her morning-brew, Gemma poured a mug-full for Iax and returned to the bedchamber to see if the female had even moved since she left her for 'five more minutes'.

She needed to calm herself; *breathe in, breathe out,* another thing Iax had taught her a while back and it was surprisingly helpful. With her own powers and knowledge, Gemma should have known of something this easy to relax.

Another reason she was grateful for having Iax around, even if their time never lasted long, Iax was like the sister Gemma never had.

Peeking around the corner through the half-opened door into Iax's sleeping chamber, Gemma was not surprised to find the female still sleeping. She hadn't moved a single muscle as far as Gemma could tell.

Smiling and feeling a little better already, she padded on bare feet to Iax's bedside. "I have your *coffee,* only this is better. I do believe you will love it, but you will never know if you do not waken. Please, Iax, we truly must rise now." Gemma set the brew on the bedside table and reached over to rub large circles on Iax's back. She lay on her side now, and to Gemma's relief, was completely covered.

"It came to me in my slumber that Yoren is with youngling, her and Gordell's first. She must be so frightened, we must find her soon, Iax. She cannot handle the rough ways of males, especially those whom are mad enough to abduct her. Come, now, please rise."

Iax didn't know what it was, but Gemma's 'improved' morning-brew smelled to die for. She decided to lie there for a few moments and listen to Gemma, getting lost for a second to the wonderful aroma. Suddenly, she stiffened at Gemma's announcement of Yoren being pregnant. *Is that what's bothering her?* The woman sounded so sad, Iax had never seen or heard her friend like this.

It took a minute for Gemma's words to fully hit Iax and when they did, she rolled over so fast she almost knocked Gemma off the side of the bed. Then she whirled around into a sitting position while trying to keep herself covered; she knew Gemma didn't understand why she slept in the nude, but she didn't usually care. As far as she was concerned it was the only way. She was exceedingly proud of her body, Lord knows she worked hard to attain it, so why not? But she would try to spare her friends feelings where she could and when she seemed so upset, so up the covers stayed, and up her ire rose over the news about Yoren.

"Yoren is pregnant? Or, sorry, I mean, 'carrying a youngling.' Those rotten, lousy, sons-a-bitches! How dare they? I don't imagine the dudes who stole her are being even somewhat gentle. Dammit! Okay, fine, what's the plan? We have to go. Where —" Anxiety was getting the best of Iax as it usually did when she was pissed. *What were those stupid fuckers thinking? Apparently nothing.*

"I'm sorry, Gemma. I didn't mean to go off on you. I just get really pissed when it comes to shit like this. It's not enough for them to take her, terrify her, but now there's a youngling involved? I'm not from here and I don't know all the rules, but I do know from other Realms and Dimensions that women are hands-off. And babies? Shit, the stupid moronic idiot'll be dead before we ever even find him!"

She reached over and grabbed the cup of brew, after giving it a *sniff* she had to close her eyes. It instantly affected her mood and somehow relaxed her right away. The smell.... *Oh. My. God.* It smelled better than any coffee she'd ever drank, and Iax was a *serious* coffee drinker. 'Caffeine Addicts R-Us' was one of her mottos at home. Taking a sip to test its heat level, it was hot but not so much that she couldn't handle it. She took a couple long pulls. "Oh, Gemma! This is sooo good! You outdid yourself, what a nice surprise. Thank you!"

Reaching out with her free arm, she encircled Gemma for a quick hug of appreciation, then set the mug down and jumped out of the bed before she'd even released the woman. "Well, what's the plan? Do we know where Yoren is now, the name of the 'bad-beastie' who took her, or what their deal is? Come on, let's go already! What are you waiting for?" She scrambled around the chamber like a madwoman, jerking clothes from her pack, squirming into a pair of jeans while hopping madly from one foot to the other, roughly pulling a brush through her hair, and trying to brush her teeth all at the same time.

"There is no need to be shit-bat-mad, Iax, we have time for you to properly ready yourself. Please, relax before you harm yourself." Gemma got up and brought the morning-brew to Iax, who was now standing in front of the bureau washing her face from a basin of fresh water Gemma had placed there earlier.

"Here is a cloth and your brew. I am pleased that you like it, and there is plenty more. I will be in the cooking-quarters when you are ready. Slow down a little bit, a few more moments will not be a problem."

Iax accepted the cloth, dried her face, and then chugged the rest of her brew. "Ahhh, this's some good shit!" *What the hell's in it, though? I don't usually get this hyper so fast,* Iax pondered, then laughed out loud when she realized Gemma's latest; *'shit-bat-mad'?* Shaking her head in amusement, she finished dressing, pulled on her boots, grabbed her pack, and left the room. She continued to laugh all the way to the 'cooking-quarters.' "The woman is hilarious sometimes, 'shit-bat-mad,' that's gotta be one of her funniest yet," she mumbled to herself.

"What are you finding so amusing, Iax?" Gemma asked with a smile when Iax joined her by the cookstove. "Laughter is wonderful; it is pleasant to hear it from you so soon after just waking up. Here, let me fill your mug again before we depart. Sit for a moment, I do have a plan to go over with you. Please, sit." She waved an elegant hand toward an empty wooden chair at the table.

"Thanks, Gemma. This is the best coffee, or whatever you call it, that I've ever had, but I'm sure hyper. What's in it?" Iax accepted the refill and settled into the chair. "Oh, and I was laughing at what you said. You know I can't help correcting you, and I'm not trying to now, but if you really want to know why I'm laughing, I'll have to. Please, don't take it wrong, but you crack me up." Smiling and awaiting Gemma's go-ahead, she sipped the brew. This time she drank it slower; maybe she wouldn't be bouncing off the walls, and then the trees once they got on their way.

"It was something about the bats, was it not? I do try to say things correctly as I find much humor in your words. I know you get upset at times, but I only mean to poke some fun. What should I have said?"

Oh no, not with the sad face, Iax thought.

"It's really no biggie. You said, 'shit-bat-mad' but I say it as 'bat-shit-crazy.' See? Nothing major, just funny. And I know you're only trying to have fun, you always make me laugh, too. So thank you, and no worries. I don't mean to get upset and I'm not right now, but I know I can be impatient at times. I'm rested now and feeling good. Again, I'm sorry when I snap, I don't mean to."

Gemma burst into a delightful sounding laughter, and to Iax's surprise, her own returned in force. After a few moments they sobered, and felt lighter and more relaxed. Iax had to agree then, laughter was wonderful; a perfect way to start the day.

"I can see why you would laugh at that, I really did mess it up. It also sounds funny the way you say it. Perhaps we should start mixing our words, imagine the humor in that!" Gemma proudly declared.

Iax felt much better seeing Gemma's eyes sparkling, unlike only moments ago when she had seemed so sad. She was certain Gemma was upset about something more than the kidnapped Dragon-chick and her baby, but she wouldn't push her on it. If Gemma wanted her to know, she'd tell her in her own time. Nuff said.

"Right now, our primary concern is to get this ship a rollin'. Show me what ya got first, and then we'll figure out what we need to do about Yoren and company." Still seated, she scooted her chair closer to the table, and got serious when Gemma started rolling a couple scrolls out over the tabletop. *Scrolls, really?* Cool, but positively ancient at the same time.

"It would seem that Mazar, the bad-beastie, was overtired of waiting to find his own Truemate. You see, after a male reaches full maturity, about thirty or so years old, he has a constant buzzing sound in his head. It never quiets, and they are unable to slumber well. It sounds frightfully miserable, and only goes away when they find their own Truemate. Mazar must have gone mad, perhaps completely, or only for a short time. Nobody yet knows. He took some of his warriors to Gordell's territory, and abducted Yoren from a path they use to walk from their holdings to the village. She was unattended, and on her way to purchase some fine fabrics for her nursery from a traveling band of vendors who had set up only one day prior," Gemma explained.

Unattended? A high profile, pregnant female. *Why the hell was she walking around alone?* It made no sense. By nature, all the 'Outer-Worldly-Peeps' were highly predatory creatures, and that was an enormous no-no. "Where was Gordell? As far as I remember, none of the females, especially while pregnant, are allowed to go anywhere alone. Or has that changed?" Iax asked.

Tapping out a rhythm on the tabletop with her fingertips, Gemma frowned down upon the scrolls and then turned her head both ways, as if something was happening that only she could see. Gemma was different like that; able to see things no one else saw and know things no one else knew. When the woman acted like this, Iax kept her pie-hole shut and paid attention. Gemma was always right, and able to come up with the best, fail proof plans.

Iax looked at the scrolls, but didn't notice anything out of the ordinary. She leaned back in her chair and continued to sip the divine brew, while Gemma puzzled out whatever was doin' with her crazy-cool scrolls.

"Mazar's emotions keep...changing, as if he does not know what he wants to do. I would venture to guess that he regrets his decision, wishes time back to before he took Yoren. How odd...for this to happen. I have never before seen this, Iax, and I am unsure now of how to proceed. These are heavy emotions and if Mazar truly regrets his actions, this will have to be handled much differently, in deed, much differently," Gemma mumbled the last part, more to herself than to Iax.

Regretting his actions? Iax had never seen or heard that before, either, in any of the alternate Dimensions she'd ever been to. What the hell did this mean now? Was she here for nothing? Would it even matter, like, say to Gordell, whose *pregnant* Truemate had already been abducted? *Doubtful.*

"What's supposed to happen now? I mean, regret is pretty and all, but the dude still messed up. He stole a pregnant woman and, correct me if I'm wrong, but isn't she kinda up-there, as in her status? What difference will it make to her Weyr that what's-his-fuck is 'regretting' what's already been done? I say too little, too late, asshole." Shrugging a shoulder, Iax smugly crossed her arms over her chest.

It was almost comical to her. And wouldn't it just figure that the male 'changes his mind' and ends up getting away with pulling such a jacked up stunt? *Bullshit,* is what Iax thought. *Bull-fucking-shit.* The more she stewed over it, the more pissed off she got to the point that if she didn't get up and go outside for some fresh air, she thought she just might explode. "I'm sorry, Gemma, I need to go outside for a minute. Is it safe? I need fresh air to clear my head. I'm so pissed at Mazar, I'd break his damn neck with my bare hands if I saw him right now," sneering his name in disgust, Iax spit out the rest of her thoughts, and then sailed out the door without waiting for Gemma's answer.

Gemma heard only parts of what Iax had said, or rather, the string of confusing words she had spat out in one breath. Standing and leaning over the scrolls on the table, what Gemma saw frightened her. Having read the scrolls all of her life, this had never happened. It was as if she was actually *seeing* Mazar's brain activity, watching the male's very thought process. She was not exactly sure what she could do with…whatever this was.

Only a moment had passed since an extremely agitated Iax had slammed out of the front door. Apparently just enough time for Gemma's brain to register what Iax had said, and what she was doing right now. "Oh, my, Iax. I must go after her before it is too late," she mumbled to herself as she made her way to the door through which Iax had just exited.

"Iax, you must not go! Please, wait for me!" Gemma bellowed. Rather undignified for her, but she did not want her friend to be in harm's way. She had an all-too-familiar feeling that harm was, indeed, nearby. "Please, where are you? It is not safe, Iax, you must return!" she yelled even louder.

Cautiously peering at her surroundings with her exceptional sight, she went further into the out of doors, the woods were merely a few paces from the building; Iax must already be in there. "Oh, no! This cannot be good," Gemma said in a rushed whisper, already at a dead run toward the woods. "Iax! Iax! Please, where are you? You must return! Please, Iax?" Sadly, Gemma was unable to spot Iax's form yet, but she did pick up on her scent which was helpful. She took off to her right vaulting over fallen logs and quickly, expertly darting around standing trees without missing a beat. She knew if she did not make it to Iax and find her soon, something terrible could happen.

Just as Gemma rounded a corner to her left, there in the thick of the woods she thought she caught a glimpse of the bright purple shirt Iax had been wearing. Relief flooded through her at finding her friend, but only momentarily, because at the same time Gemma realized if Iax had gone in that direction, she could still be in danger.

There was a sheer cliff just beyond the point of where Gemma could see, and Iax would not. It was completely out of Iax's view due to the dense forest, and because Iax has no knowledge area or of cliff's existence. "Oh, no! Iax! Please, stop, do not take another step! You may fall! I am here, I am right here, wait for me!"

Though she had been running lightning fast for several moments already, Gemma was not even winded. Another nifty thing about her 'abilities,' she could run faster than most, only a blur to anyone else's eyes, and each breath she drew only made her go faster. In this case, the case of her friend, she was going faster than she ever had before.

Coming to a perfectly executed halt, Gemma's toes rested right at the precipice of the sheer cliff. There was no Iax in sight. Fear gripped her insides, twisting them into vicious, painful knots. "*No!* Not Iax! She cannot have fallen!" she screamed, her eyes leaking once more. *What is happening to me?* This was the most unusual behavior Gemma had ever experienced. Putting away those thoughts for now, she launched herself over the cliff.

Chapter Six

Iax heard voices. Several deep, concerned voices coming from all around her. Normally, her first reaction would be to jump up into a fighting stance and size up her foes. But were these her foes? She wasn't quite sure.

Her head throbbed in time with her right leg, and she could not open her eyes no matter how hard she tried. *What the hell now? This shit's getting old,* she thought, angry and confused.

Feeling large, strong hands carefully running over her legs, her back, her arms, then her head, she deduced that she was lying on her stomach, which also hurt like a bitch. An agonized groan escaped her mouth when she tried to move her right arm. *Did that come from me? Only pussies groan, seriously, this must be a fucking nightmare. I. Don't. Groan. At least not from pain. Furthermore, who the hell are these…beings, and where the hell is Gemma?*

She vaguely remembered hearing Gemma calling, even yelling for her in the woods, but she was so caught up in thought, she hadn't been paying attention. Her mind was thick and fuzzy, but Iax kind of recalled that she was finally getting herself under control, just before taking a step onto nothingness….

She'd never hurt this bad in her life. She had been run through with swords, run over by horse wagons and cars, and had her ass flat handed to her by all types and sizes of people and creatures. But, this…this really took the blue ribbon. *Damn! How far did I fall? Again, where is Gemma? Shit! If she fell, too, and because of me? No! No way!*

Trying to clear her extremely dry throat, Iax winced inwardly at the pain even there. *Suck it up, bitch! You have to speak and find out about Gemma.* After another try, she dryly managed to croak out the words, "G-Gemma? Where is Gemma?"

A deep voice from over her back rumbled a reply in a language Iax didn't recognize. If this was Earth she probably wouldn't have a problem interpreting, however, it wasn't, so Inte heller förstå in Swedish, Non comprendere in Italian, không thấu hiểu in Vietnamese, Ärge näima in Estonian, не разумею in Belorussian, não compreender in Portuguese, nav saprast in Latvian, or in simple English; she didn't comprehend.

Dammit, this is so not working for me. Maybe if I could roll over and see their faces then I could...not sure what, but I'm sure I could do something. Here goes; think Band-Aid, just do it all in one, smooth move. No hesitation, just go! Like, right now! Completely and momentarily forgetting all the pain she was in, Iax used a move she'd learned early on in her training. 'Flippin' the pancake,' she called it, and it worked! She found herself lying on her back, and then she heard foreign noises coming from her own pitiful-sounding self. "Ahhh! I–I..." *why the hell did I do that? Holy....* Again, she wasn't sure what; there had been a thought, but now it was gone.

Mentally shaking her head—'cause there was no way in hell she could move a single muscle—the pain was too intense. *This is what'cha call pain. Hells, yeah, good old fashioned pain. It sucks like a bitch, but hey, it also lets you know you're undeniably still alive.* For that, Iax would take it.

Now, she had flopped over for a reason...something important. *Think. Think.* Accessing her thoughts was kind of like wading through a thick, dense fog; not easy. *Oh, that's right, Gemma.* She needed to will her achy, sticky eyelids to open, then she could surely figure out and fix any problem life had just thrown her way, if only she could open her eyes. *Okay, again, just like the Band-Aid. Breathe. Again. One. Two. Three.* Shit, it didn't work for this dilemma. Maybe relaxing, trying to open them slowly might work best. *Slowly?* Mental snort, *Iax don't do slowly.*

It took a few moments of some serious find-your-center-bullshit, but at least now her eyes were finally opening. Albeit exceedingly slowly and they, too, hurt and burned like a bitch as if someone had poured acid in them, but she did accomplish the feat.

Squinting, eyes watering like a broken faucet, she was at least able to make out shapes and sizes.

There appeared to be several beings in human-form gathered around where her fucked up form lay on the ground. As Iax's vision started to clear by only infinitesimal degrees, she was grateful for it. It was now clear that two extremely large dudes sat on either side of her upper body. She thought there may also be another one behind her, but there was no way she would even think about moving to confirm it.

Her still somewhat fuzzy-gaze roamed downward to find more peeps, she noticed the rest of the beings were females. There were two on each side of her legs, and one at her feet. All of them were tall with long, muscular limbs and solid, athletic builds. Being Dragon-shifters would explain their size, she supposed. *Wouldn't they have to be kinda big to accommodate shifting into a Dragon? Focus, Iax!* chastising herself; wrong time, and certainly the wrong place.

Realizing all the peeps were simply looking on as if in expectation for a response to whatever the dude had said to her, she had forgotten all about that. *Ugh. This is quickly becoming a colossal pain in the ass. Think! Making hand gestures may help. Riiight.* In order to do so, one would have to be able to actually lift one's arms and use one's hands, or fingers. *Not happenin' just yet.*

After two more attempts to clear her parched, burning throat, one of the females left and returned in a blur offering Iax a drink. Who knew what it was, and right now, who the hell cared? She was extremely thirsty and would maybe even drink camel piss at the moment; or not. Either way, she was still immensely thankful.

Whoever was sitting behind her head gently began lifting her, supporting her head and shoulders so she could take a drink and not choke. That's all she needed; survive the fall, then choke to death on a drink. She almost wanted to laugh at the thought. Almost.

The female brought a wooden cup to Iax's chapped lips, peering at her with a small smile, and what Iax took to be sympathy along with much confusion in her expression. Accepting the proffered drink, Iax was pleasantly surprised at her discovery; it seemed to be just pure, ordinary water. Nice. *Cold.* Water. Refreshing and instantly soothing her sore throat.

The dude behind her lowered her head and shoulders back down with extreme care. Iax was slowly beginning to realize, if she had to have an accident—like jumping off a fucking cliff—these were the kinds of peeps you'd want to find you. Thank God she hadn't been found by a group of crazy, mean, demented…whatevers. She still needed to find a way to communicate, though.

Iax closed her still achy eyes to think for a minute. She quickly felt hands working, doing something to her right leg, and it hurt…bad. Another someone was messing with her noggin, while yet another was working on her stomach; all of which also hurt, more so than anything she'd ever felt in her life.

What were they doing to her, and where the hell was Gemma? She needed to figure it all out. She *needed* Gemma. For the woman not to be at Iax's side after such an injury was rather discomfiting, Gemma was always there at such times.

Just as she was going to open her eyes to check out who was doing what and why, she felt herself slip away into a cozy, inviting darkness.

****

As Gemma floated through the time and space separating her and Iax, she put on a burst of speed. Iax had never seen all of Gemma's powers at their fullest, such as this one where she could fly, float, gravitate, or whatever else the occasion called for. She could also perform these talents with whatever speed, agility, or grace was needed.

She had vaulted herself off the top of the sheer cliff already knowing Iax accidentally fell; Iax had been running, not walking, and would not have known about the cliff.

Deep in thought, Iax obviously had not heard Gemma's pleas for her to halt. Oh, she felt horrible for Iax. *This is all my fault,* she thought, her chest tight and achy. Odd, that.

If only she had been paying better attention, listening to what Iax had been saying to her in the building, she could and would have warned her of this specific danger, as well as others. Although, at the moment Gemma could not bring to memory anything worse than what she was witnessing now.

She did think it rather odd, however, that not only had Iax not screamed—a common reaction to falling—but she had not made any sound, whatsoever. People, namely humans, had built in reactions, and Iax should have made some kind of noise. *Oh, no! What if something else had happened? What if there were other things at play involving Iax's fall, and it had not simply been a fall?* she worried inwardly.

Gemma knew firsthand of things such as compulsion, bindings, spells, and even trickery which could muffle one's voice, dulling or muting it out altogether, so nobody could hear one calling for help. *If* one had even made an attempt, to begin with.

What if some of Gemma's *feelings* were portentous of an evil presence in the area? One who had compelled Iax simply to jump off the cliff and think nothing of it?

At the last possible second, Gemma was able to swoop under Iax's body as the female was still making her descent to certain death, had Gemma not gotten to her as quickly as she had. It was nothing more than a buffer, a quick jolt with her own body to slow Iax just enough so when she hit the ground, she would not be killed upon impact. She would be injured, that was a certainty, but Gemma had not made a clear plan in advance.

The rate of speed at which Iax's body was falling, Gemma did not have enough time or room to get underneath and catch her to safely take them both to the ground without harm. Such an impact would most certainly kill Iax, and feasibly disable Gemma for the rest of her time, which is why she had chosen to buffer Iax's fall, instead.

As she had once heard Iax say, "Pick the lesser of the two evils." Or at least Gemma thought that was how the saying went. She genuinely enjoyed Iax's sayings, even if she did jumble them up more oft than not. While that random thought skated across her mind, she glanced down just in time to see Iax's limp body hit the hard dirt-packed ground with a sickening *thud.*

Distracted as she was at the scene before her, Gemma fell the remaining distance to the ground, landing a good ways away from where Iax now lay unmoving. The fall hurt, but it was nothing she could not handle. Taking a few deep breaths, she briefly wondered once more about her leaky eyes.

When she got to her feet, she immediately realized they had at least ended up on the grounds of a friendly Weyr, for which she was grateful. Equally, she was grateful for being able to buffer Iax's fall the little bit she had, in hopes of keep her friend's injuries to a minimum.

Gemma pushed all thought aside and ran most of the distance between them. When she was only a few yards from where Iax lay, she noticed that one of her friend's legs was positioned at an unnatural angle; her stomach lurch.

Iax appeared so helpless and much smaller than Gemma had ever seen her. And broken; her friend most certainly had a few broken bones. Fear, guilt, and another strange, unfamiliar emotion in the pit of her stomach quickly banished any feelings of relief Gemma may have had only moments ago.

There were several shifters perched around Iax, encircling her broken body. They were quickly yet calmly speaking to each other in their own native language. Luckily, Gemma could interpret any language and instantly concluded that she needed to stay back, leave them alone, and allow them room to work, which they were, fervently.

From all outward appearances, two of the females were attempting to heal what must have been a broken bone in Iax's right leg. A male and female were doing the same over her stomach. And three males worked calmly yet nervously on her head.

"Oh, Iax…I am so sorry, this should have never happened to you. It is all my fault," she cried out in a whisper. Gemma shook as she sunk to the ground, suddenly feeling her body giving out beneath her. Kneeling on the ground and seemingly frozen in time and rooted in place, the Weyr members who were so diligently working on Iax turned their heads when they must have heard her speak.

They did not look angry, nor did they look happy; simply sad and not terribly confident of their abilities. The largest male who sat behind Iax's head, waved Gemma over to join them with one large arm. She wanted to go to her friend, and was even certain she could aid in the healing, but she could not make her body move. Not a single muscle. Other than a slight breeze bringing to her notice a coolness upon her cheeks—obviously more of the leaky eyes—she felt utterly useless. A heavy numbness blanketed her outwardly.

Her insides, however, were churning, grinding, and making her want to retch. She had seen Iax do such a thing a few times before, but she had never retched in her own long life. Her kind simply did not have to deal with most of the bodily things she had noticed Iax do. She also felt a tightness gripping at the inside of her chest again. *What is this?* Another oddity. Gemma had no idea of what she should do. Still unable to make herself move, she remained in the same spot, her eyes heavily leaking.

Unsure of how long she had sat unmoved, Gemma started at a hand coming to rest on each of her slumped shoulders. Two of the females had joined her in an attempt to comfort her. How strange this all was; she had never needed comforting, either. Her kind had always been able to master their feelings and emotions, so there was never such a need.

Large, sad, tear-filled violet-eyes peered up at the two females. Their expressions held sincere concern; unsure of how to help a stranger—obviously not of their own kind—to feel better. They were beautiful female-shifters, Gemma noticed. Her mind was fuzzy, hazy; she was unable to hold a clear thought. Confusion clouded her entire being as the females knelt down to sit on either side of her, one placing an arm around her back, the other around her shoulders.

Gemma's gaze moved to where she was sure Iax had been lying on the ground, but not now. *Where is she?* She had short flickering thoughts, images in her mind of Iax's body falling over a cliff and landing hard on the ground. She saw broken bones, and then Iax had gone unconscious. She found herself wondering if she had imagined it all. The whole thing was too horrible and awful, she did not want it to be true. Yet, when she turned first to look at the female on her left, then the one on her right, she could see it in their expressions. It had happened, it was real, Iax was badly injured.

Why, then, was Gemma sitting on the ground feeling helpless? Why was she not with Iax, her friend, helping to care for and aid her in any way possible?

****

Iax awoke in a cold sweat fully encompassed in darkness, making it impossible to check her surroundings to see anything that may give her the slightest clue as to where she was and why. *What the hell happened, and where am I? Furthermore, who the fuck kicked my ass and left me for dead?* she wondered to herself.

Hurting in places she didn't even know she had, something she'd heard others say before and had always thought it was ridiculous, she totally understood it now. "This totally fucking bites," she mumbled out loud, confident she was alone. Even if not, so what? She'd never curbed her tongue for anyone, and wasn't about to start now.

Think! You must remember something. Anything? Iax closed her eyes to concentrate and tried to pull up her memories. Any memories at all that could aid her in puzzling out the conundrum she currently found herself in.

One: *My name is Iax. Good to know.* B: *I distinctively know I'm clearly not in Kansas anymore, but on a job for the O.W.O., where there are Dragon-shifters.* And, three: *I hurt like a bitch from the tips of my toes to the end of my longest strand of golden hair. Even my teeth hurt! Ugh! This is the worst pain ever, and I would know. But hey, I've survived worse injuries, I'll be just fine,* she tried to bolster herself. She still had too many missing memories and thoughts, and it scared her. Suddenly, she recalled Gemma. *Where is that woman?* She was always with Iax on all of her O.W.O. jobs no matter what. *So, why isn't she here? Where the hell else would she be?*

Gemma had saved her ass many times over and had never left her alone, anywhere, ever. The realization bothered Iax as panic swelled her insides. An emotion she wasn't all that familiar with, and she knew it could be detrimental if she didn't quash it, and fast.

Eyes still closed, she took several deep, cleansing breaths. It always helped and it had to now, 'cause she had nothing else. She got a flash of a memory, at least that's what it felt like: Her and Gemma in the kitchen of a beautiful house, or more like a log cabin. They were going over some scrolls Gemma had laid out on the table, discussing a plan of action for, well…something. *Why can't I remember?* she pondered, frustrated. Relaxing, or trying to, she took more deep breaths and focused, determined to get inside her own head and stay there as long as it took to figure this shit out.

She'd been upset about…still unsure of the what or the why, but recalled needing fresh air. She'd gone outside and for some reason, she was hauling ass—faster than normal even for her— through a densely wooded area. Not in the same direction from which they had originally approached the cabin, but behind it. *Why was I running?* It didn't make any sense; usually when she needed to cool off, she certainly never ran like a damn crazed animal into territory unknown.

Gemma's voice. She vaguely remembered hearing that familiar, beautiful voice. Gemma was crying and calling out to her, even yelling; for Gemma to raise her voice, something serious had to be horribly wrong. *And, why didn't I answer her?* That wasn't like Iax, either. Shaking her thickly fogged head, she couldn't get anything to make sense. She would never purposely ignore Gemma, and again, she most certainly would have never ran all-out while trying to relax.

A soft clicking sound brought Iax back to the present. Instantly on alert—habitual instincts she couldn't help kicked in— although she didn't know what the hell she could do, since moving was impossible due to the pain she was in. Her eyes opened wide as she heard and smelled the striking of a match, just before a soft orb of light flickered over a candle several feet in front of her bed. The room was pitch-black before the candle had been lit, and who knew how long she'd been lying there? It took a few moments for her eyes to adjust as the candle slowly moved toward her, until she was finally able to make out who was carrying it.

"Gemma! Oh, thank God! Wh–where—" She didn't know what to say or ask first. *How frustrating!*

"Please, Iax, do not speak if it pains you. I shall explain everything. All is well, and not as bad as it may seem. Relax, and I will begin." Gemma carefully settled herself on Iax's bedside.

Similar to a twin-sized bed, thought a tad wider, it was the most comfy mattress Iax had ever slept on; supremely thick and soft, obviously made of some high-dollar stuff for the Dragon-peeps. Iax settled her throbbing head and body back on the mattress and pillows, grateful for their comfort.

Gemma reached over and placed the candle on a bedside table, then turned back to face Iax as she gently clasped one of her friend's hands with one of her own. "You see, we were in the small building where we slept last eve. Do you recall that?" With a wan smile, Gemma waited patiently for Iax's reply.

"Yes, I do remember the 'small building,' but as a large, gorgeous cabin. And, I just envisioned us sitting at the table discussing a plan, right before I went outside to get some fresh air. Still not sure why, but I was pissed and for some strange reason I was running–I mean, hauling-ass through the forest." She took a few breaths and continued, "What's going on? Why would I run if I was trying to calm down? It doesn't make any sense. I also heard you calling out to me, but I couldn't respond. What the hell is happening? Please, Gemma, tell me you know something, anything?" she pleaded.

Tears threatened to be Iax's undoing, 'cause *Iax don't do tears.* She was deeply scared, but *Iax had never done scared*, at least not to this degree. She was hoping with everything in her that Gemma would have some answers, an explanation as to what the hell was going on, and why she hurt so damn bad. This was beyond ridiculous – she had done pain a thousand times over, but never like this.

"There now, I will explain, but please, try to relax and let me do what I can to help. Oh, look, your eyes are leaking. Mine have been, too, though I do not know why. What does it mean? Mine have never done so before." Studying Iax with an intense observation, Gemma was surprised and thorough unhappy with what she saw in her friend's expression. She only hoped her explanation would not further upset Iax.

Iax laughed, then stopped herself when the small action hurt too badly. "Leaky eyes? Oh, Gemma, you really are funny…thanks for that. Okay, it's called crying, a thing my people do when we're sad, in pain, and even when we're happy. It's an emotional thing, although I can't say why I'm doing it, 'cause I never cry. This little jaunt-through-the-Dimension-track so far has been different all the way around from previous trips. I'm not sure but maybe due to all that's happened, you're just experiencing and feeling things differently? I don't really know. Sorry I can't explain it better, but that's about all I know on the subject."

Gemma stared thoughtfully at their joined hands, a small, sincere smile on her lips. "Emotions? Hmm, yes, I have heard of those. Though, my kind does not normally have difficulties with such things. We are always able to control and not let them show. It is all so rare and new for me, it feels quite odd. My eyes do not hurt, but it does pain me here." She touched her chest with a sad smile. "Perhaps I am becoming more like you and your kind, which is alright—unexpected—but all right. I like you, so I think I would like most of your kind as well. Now, about what is happening." Scrunching up her forehead, she searched for the correct words for her friend who was lying there in so much pain.

She felt that she and the other healers had done a tremendous job with Iax's injuries, that is, once she was finally able to get herself under control to aid them. There were no longer any broken bones, nor were the cuts and scrapes visible. However, that did not mean she was not bruised on the inside.

Gemma wished she could do more for her friend, and decided that simple conversation may help get Iax's mind off her pain, at least for a time. But, she did not want to disclose the full spectrum of injuries her friend had suffered; both bones in her lower right leg had been broken, and the lining in her stomach had been torn—most likely as a result of the impact from Gemma's body jolting Iax's from underneath, during the fall—which made her feel even worse. Iax had also suffered three skull-fractures, all of which had been the most worrisome. The worst of everything had been healed, and Gemma was grateful to the shifter-healers for what they had done.

"I must apologize, Iax. I was so deep in thought over the scrolls when you spoke of going outside, I fear I did not hear all of what you said. I vaguely recalled, after you had already gone outside, you asking if it was safe. Apparently, it was not, and I should have been paying better attention. But the scrolls were moving, the words and diagrams reshaping as I looked on. I have never seen such."

Iax wasn't about to let Gemma take the blame for what she had done to herself. "*You* have nothing to apologize for, Gemma. *I'm* the fucking idiot who rushed out and should've paid better attention. Only now do I have snippets of a memory that something weird was going on with your scrolls. I felt a strong need to get some fresh air, and I was so angry and it felt like my head would explode if I didn't. So don't you dare blame yourself for me being in such a rush, it was entirely *my* fault. I wasn't thinking rationally...*not* your fault," she finished, deeply breathing through more bits of memories quickly rushing through her brain.

"In any case, I should have listened better. It is, after all, why I am here for you. No matter, here is what I have concluded," Gemma explained. "Obviously, there is something strange going on in this Realm. Since Mazar abducted Yoren, there have been a few similar events. When you were running through the woods, I was calling for you, even *yelling*—" she broke off and glanced away from Iax, blushing at the admission. Gemma honestly never yelled for any reason. She had always thought it undignified, and simply just didn't. She sighed.

"It would seem as though all these events are related to females in their carrying season, which only happens every few years. However, it can also be mistaken when a female is already carrying a youngling. This may explain why Mazar took Yoren when he did, as it can be confusing when the youngling does not yet show on her physical form. The males who are doing the abducting do not even know the females are in their seasons. They are simply taking females whom they desire to possess for their own." She glanced at Iax for a response, but did not see one.

"Do you recall when I spoke of the torments the male-shifters suffer while awaiting their Truemates?" Iax nodded. "Well, it has always been a horrible affliction, and we suspect that for some unknown reason the torments have worsened. The shifters I have spoken with told me some of the males in their own Weyr have also been behaving erratic and bizarre, and obviously there is a collective concern about them and what they might do. Some of the males seemingly believe that if they simply go out and take a female, their torments will cease. Of course, they are mistaken, but they are virtually crazed and not thinking clearly. They have become desperate."

That's a lot to ponder, Iax thought. Still, it didn't explain what had happened to her. She certainly wasn't in her 'carrying season,' although…*no. No damn way!* She was getting ready to have her monthly cycle, but she wasn't a Dragon-shifter, or even the same fucking species! *What the hell would they want me for, and what am I thinking, anyway?* She was jumping the gun; this had nothing to do with her. Needing to slow her mental-roll and hear the rest of Gemma's theory, she nodded.

"You are correct. I believe having your cycle would make you able to carry–yes? We think a nearby male must have scented you and attempted to compel you into going to him. But with your mind being so strong, you were able to fight back. Unfortunately, it caused you to go in the opposite direction, and right over a one-hundred and fifty-foot sheer cliff. You fell, and I–I…" Gemma broke off in a small sob. Something Iax had never witnessed.

Shit, this is bad. Iax garnered up a little strength, and gently squeezed Gemma's hand. Then, it suddenly dawned on her that Gemma had just sensed her own thoughts about her cycle. She recalled the mental projection and how allowed her to summon Gemma whenever she arrived in any of the 'away' locations. For Iax, there was nothing to it beyond their initial meeting, it was just a temporary telepathic link. She decided to let it go, because she couldn't bear seeing her friend this upset. That was her main concern for the moment.

"Gemma, look at me, please? I'm kinda remembering little bits and pieces as you go, and I also remember—just barely, but it's there—when you somehow got underneath me, breaking my fall and making my impact much less than it would have been otherwise. You saved my ass again, didn't you?" Trying for a smile to affect Gemma and hopefully soothe her sadness, Iax was using her go-to;

being a smart-ass. And it worked, a little. Gemma smiled back, even hiccuped a laugh. *Much better,* Iax thought.

"Okay, so the flame-throwers are going after females in heat, even though they don't realize it, and somehow I was lumped into that batch. Then I fell a long way, but of course, you saved me. Now we have more females in distress, yet here I lay hurting more than I ever have in my life, and we're both having this 'eye leaking' problem. Sooo, what should we do now?" Iax contemplated out loud. "I can't move much, but I certainly can't just lie here, either. Don't these peeps have, like, some magical pain shit, or something? Oh, wait, I have something that'll fix me right up! Where's my pack? Where are we? Shit! I need my pack!"

Iax grumbled a few more swear words and random questions as she watched Gemma reach down under the bed and pull something out. Placing it on Iax's stomach, thank God it wasn't heavy or she probably would have screamed. "What? How'd you know? This is my pack! Thank you, Gemma! Thank you so much!" Without thought, Iax sprung into a sitting position and threw her arms around Gemma's neck, tightly hugging her while both of their eyes started leaking again. Regretting the spontaneous movement immediately, but not the reason for doing so, she let out a loud groan and Gemma helped settle her back on the bed.

Iax slowly dug through her pack until she found the white box with the big, bright-red plus sign on it and breathed a massive sigh of relief.

Chapter Seven

After taking a couple Tylenol, then waiting over an hour for them to kick in, Iax took two more. Finally, almost an hour and forty-five-minutes after the first dose, she was able to move more freely, and with much less pain.

Gemma had explained to Iax, her fall and all her subsequent injuries, yet she felt her friend had held back on some of the details, and maybe even some of the injuries, too. Then she had listened to, and been grateful for, how the worst of them had been healed by the Weyr members who had found Iax at their feet. They had been out hunting. One minute they were walking along, and the next, a female had literally dropped out of the sky and landed in the middle of their path. They had rushed to her aid.

Of course, Iax didn't remember any of it, but then, she couldn't think about much of anything at the moment. Four extra strength Tylenol later, she was lucky to still be awake at all. She had never been much for medications of any kind, so this was new to her system. Even though they were hitting her rather hard, she didn't mind one bit. Truly, she felt pretty damn good, almost giddy. A few achy spots still lingered, but nothing compared to how she'd felt before taking them.

She genuinely liked the people who invented Tylenol, and would personally write them a thank you letter when she returned home. Who knew? The shit was awesome! So much so, that Gemma had taken the little Tylenol packets out of Iax's first-aid kit and hidden them. Deep down Iax knew it was the right thing to do, but still. They were *her* new little 'buddies,' and they should not be kept from her.

Iax sighed, loudly and dramatically; very unlike her but she didn't care. "Oh, Iax. For the sake of Pete's shit, stop your driveling! You do not need to take any more of your 'buddies' because you are feeling better. In fact, I would venture to say almost too much better. And you said yourself, the instructions are to wait a *few* hours before taking more. I will administer them when the time is appropriate." With a disgusted, unlike-Gemma snort, she turned on her heel and quickly walked away before Iax could draw her into another discussion about those stupid white pills. Relieved as she was at Iax's comfort, enough was enough!

Iax's brows shot up and she started laughing so hard she could barely speak. "What? 'For the sake of Pete's shit'? Gemma, Gemma, Gemma, way off, and you swore! You never swear! What are we gonna do with you? But that is some funny shit, I must admit. Haha, I even rhymed! I am hilarious! Who knew? Hmm, aaand," drawing out the word for dramatic affect, "it's for *Pete's sake,* or for *shit's sake,* in case you wanted to know."

Gemma turned just in time to see Iax sticking her tongue out at her! *The female had lost any wits she had ever possessed. No. More. White. Pills!* Shaking her head, Gemma was somewhat amused, but she dared not let Iax see it or they would never move forward. And, forward they must move, as soon as possible.

A while later, Gemma decided it was time for introductions. Iax would not stop insisting on meeting her 'heroes' and 'heroines,' so Gemma obliged her extremely addled-friend. Although she was a bit apprehensive—given the way Iax had been behaving—there was simply no way of knowing what the female would say or do to the Weyr members who had saved her life. But she understood Iax was a particularly proud female, so she went along with it; praying to any Gods or Goddesses who might listen that it would not end up disastrous.

The introductions to all the shifters who had found her went pretty well, considering. Iax was so grateful and emotional, not to mention weirded out on those pills, she cried like a little baby as she shook the hand of each shifter. Her brain kept telling her, *Knock your shit off,* but she couldn't seem to stop for anything. Once the intro's were finished, she had broken out into semi-hysterical laughter. The most confusing thing was, she had wanted to tell them jokes. *Iax don't do jokes.* Yet, as she tried thinking of something, anything, but luckily nothing had come to mind. Not that she could understand a word they had said to her and vice-versa. *Still–jokes?* The mere thought was laughable.

Gemma had sat in a chair next to Iax's bed. Every time Iax shook another hand to greet each of the shifters, her eyes leaked heavily, and Gemma felt a heated blush rise up to cover her face. The female had gone mad! Gemma had never seen such a display, especially not from Iax. She had known many proud, tough females in her years, but Iax was by far the best, so this confused her. Those pills. *Ugh,* she groaned inwardly. Hopefully, Iax would not require more. They addled her brain to such a degree, Gemma was beginning to fear they may have already caused permanent damage.

She sighed, resigned to stick by her friend no matter what happened.

After the shifters had left the room, Iax felt drained, almost lethargic. She needed to sleep it off, that was all. She always had energy abound, but this was different in every way. *Those damn Tylenol, and my stupid fucking 'let's see if I can fly' stunt. Ugh!* Gently shaking her throbbing-again head at her own stupidity, she was humiliated at how she had acted in front of those shifters. *What the hell were you thinking, dumb-ass?* she chastised herself. She never acted like that. *Whatever.* It wasn't her fault the pills messed up her brain and turned her into a total fucking lack-wit.

"Thanks, Gemma, for everything. I'm also sorry for how I've been acting. I don't know what the hell's come over me. I don't do that kinda shit." Resting her head back on the pillows, Iax closed her eyes. She sure hoped her body would hurry up and get its shit together, this was ridiculous.

Even though the pills had taken away most of the pain, she decided she didn't want any more. Not if that's what they were going to do to her. She couldn't be acting like a mushy-gushy-Nancy-ass. No thank you, very much.

Gemma got up from her chair and came to stand next to Iax's bed. "I know it is from the pills, do not worry so. These are good shifters, and they could not understand your words, anyway." Gemma laughed softly at the whole incident now that it was over, "And the leaky eyes were alright. You have been through much and your body is still healing. Even Dragon-shifters understand pain. They also understand gratitude, which is what your actions showed them. They were happy to see you looking so much better." She smiled and patted Iax's hand.

"I hope so. I feel like a fool now, but I guess you're right, you usually are. What did they say about finding me falling from the sky and all?" Iax could almost laugh about it now, trying to imagine the whole thing from someone else's point of view.

Before her imagination went very far, and before Gemma answered her question, she felt the comfort of sleep's cozy arms enticing her to surrender. Grateful for the pull, Iax was more than happy to acquiescent as she drifted off into a deep sleep. She hoped to wake up feeling more like her normal self, even though nothing about Iax could be considered 'normal,' she could still hope.

****

Mazar was awoken by the loud throbbing in his head. It felt as though he had been in a great brawl, but unfortunately had lost and now felt the effects of being pummeled. Well, he supposed, if he had whether he remembered it or not, he probably deserved it. He felt as if he was losing his mind of late, going fully mad, and perhaps he was.

Even slight movements were painful, and he was almost positive his head would fall from his shoulders at each attempt. Finally, he got his large, aching body rolled over from his stomach to his back. Eventually, he was able to peel his sticky eyelids open. Surveying his surroundings, he was relieved to see that at least he was in his own home, even if he was lying on the hard, dirt-packed floor, he was still pleased.

"Why am I sleeping on my floor?" he croaked out. *Was that my voice?* He winced at the pain he had never before felt from simply trying to speak. This was not good. As he started to push himself up into a sitting position, the room wildly spun around him making him want to retch. Quickly, he settled back down onto the floor. *Perhaps I should remain here a bit longer.* He thought that would be the best, safest plan for now.

It took a few moments for the events of the previous few days to come rushing back to him at a dizzying speed. He groaned inwardly, knowing it would have also hurt had he done it aloud. *What have I done to her, them, my own Weyr?* he asked himself. Perhaps it was possible for him to simply lie here until death claimed his useless, ashamed, no-good-self. That would be a welcome boon, but he could never be so lucky.

Knowing he had no other choice than to get up, get moving, and go check on her, he forced his body into compliance. She would *hate* him. She *should* hate him. Oh, wait, she already *did* hate him, if he recalled her words correctly. Yoren had most certainly made herself more than clear on that point many, many times during their journey to this territory.

It took much longer than it should have, longer than it had ever taken in his long, useless life to ready himself for this day. Still, he was pleased to be done with it. He opened his front door to make his way to the shack Yoren was being secretly held in, hoping it was still a secret. As he pulled the door inward to open it, he noticed the large crack running from the middle of the door, all the way to its bottom.

Trying to recall how it got there, he scrunched up his forehead in thought. *Ah...that is it. You kicked in your own door, you stupid fool!* he scolded himself. Speaking aloud would still cause too much pain, so why risk it? He thought for a moment and then clearly recalled how it had happened; he had come home in a rage, and kicked the door so hard it had splintered. It would also explain the extra amount of pain residing in his right foot. And here was yet another repair which would cost him. Even doing repairs himself, they were becoming spendy. *I must get my temper under control.*

Leaving those problems for later, he stepped outside into what must have been one of the brightest days ever beheld by his sore and weakened eyes. Squeezing his watery eyes shut, he closed the fractured door behind him and started walking in the direction of the shack. *Let her be all right and well,* he prayed to *Meynix,* knowing what he must do next. It was too bad death had refused his plea as he had lain on his floor. This would be an extremely long, trying, difficult day, to say the least.

"Ho! Hold up, Mazar!" a male gruffly called out to him only steps from his front door. He quietly groaned and winced before forcing his watery eyes open a mere crack, just enough to see who approached him. He already knew he would be called upon by their Weyr Chief at any time, but this was not the Chief; a blessing, and one for which he was grateful.

Mazar turned to face the male who had called his name, and saw Frayier, a longtime friend of his, and one who had gone with him on his fool's errand. Memories of his deceit and the lies he had made up to get them all to go, made him feel like retching again. For his conduct, for his sheer stupidity, all of which would certainly land all of them in a load of trouble. He fought back the bile rising in the back of his throat to address his friend.

"Ah, Frayier. How are you this morn?" Frayier stopped only inches away from Mazar, anger oozed from him, heavy and sizzling. Mazar had never seen the like from him. Guilt, even more than moments ago, rose up in Mazar again, nearly choking him as he awaited the male's reply.

"You dare to pretend all is well? Are you mad? Word is spreading like fire that we abducted Gordell's female. You said our

Chief wanted her for bargaining purposes, but you lied to all of us! My own Truemate would not even allow me the comfort of her warmth, nor to lie in my own bed last eve! And she only knows a small portion of this story. How can you even show your face now? The Chief never knew, did he? Do not think to lie to me once more!" he hissed out.

What to say to that? I have made trouble for many innocent, decent warriors and to what end? Did I truly think any benefit would come of my stupidity? Stop grumbling to yourself and pay the male the answer to which he is due! Mazar tried to square his shoulders, wishing he had at least thought ahead and came up with a good story. Or even a bad story. Nothing, he had precisely nothing...but the truth. "You are correct in what you say, Frayier. I do not have an explanation for my actions. I can give you an apology, but I know it will not begin to make up for what I have done. I believe I am going fully mad, though. I cannot sleep without the aid of large amounts of fire-brew; the buzzing in my head makes me conjure up thoughts better left unspoken; my head throbs and pains me night and day. I need my Truemate more than the air I breathe, and I do not know how much longer I can go on this way. I–I..." Mazar trailed off with a sigh, deeply regretting his actions.

Frayier's shoulders loosened as some tension visibly left his large, tightly coiled frame. He knew the torments of which Mazar spoke, he had also tolerated them for many years. However, he had finally been blessed with finding his Truemate, and they had produced two fine male-younglings. He felt for the messy, poor excuse of a warrior looking like death who stood before him. It still did not make things alright, not by far, but at least he now knew what had motivated the male and he wanted to help him–but how?

Clapping Mazar on the back with a large hand hard enough to make the male stagger forward, Frayier gave him a half-smile. "Why have you not spoken of this sooner? Most of us know how you feel. I went lifetimes with no Truemate, and I know I am blessed beyond measure with the one I now have. There may be a way out of this, if you will allow me to do the talking. Can you keep your jaw clenched and allow an old friend to help you?" Frayier's smile reached both sides of his lips.

"*Help* me? How do you intend to do that? There is no excuse for what I have done, for what I have gotten all of you into. I will take my punishments as the Chief sees fit to deal them to me. It is the least I can do. You need not become further involved in my stupidity, but I offer you my gratitude, old friend." Mazar tried to smile, but it did not quite reach his eyes. He was beyond help, beyond sad, and beyond worth. Mazar deserved any and everything that was coming his way. Resigned to his darkened fate, he turned on his heel to march directly to the Chief's holdings; time to face-up and take his due, no matter what it may end up being.

****

Yoren was still lying on the hard, dirt-packed floor on the same filthy fur she had finally fallen asleep on mere hours ago. Her entire body pained her, she felt and heard her empty belly rumbling, and it made her want to weep. All of which only made her anger return tenfold. She did *not* weep. She was the proud, tough Truemate of Gordell, as well as daughter to one of the eldest and most respected Royal families of her Weyr, making her Royalty twice-over.

Clamping down hard on her emotions, she overcame the urge to weep and allowed her ire to take hold and wrap around her like a well-worn blanket. She would not weep! Wishing she could at least see outside, she struggled and scooted about until she was able to rise upon her knees. After taking a few deep breaths, she was unable to believe how much work the small chore had been, but she finally gained her feet.

She would find a way out of here, she had to. Her very life was at stake, and the life of their youngling. It was up to her to save them both, to make her way safely home this very day. She could not go through any more of this torture and abuse. To be fair, sleeping on the hard floor of this shack had been the worst of the ordeal. She had not been physically harmed or even threatened. *That is untrue, and you know it!* she scolded herself, recalling when she had poked at and spat unladylike insults and more at Mazar until he had made threats; many subtle, empty threats. She almost laughed at the memories when every time he tried to speak to her, he started out being exceedingly polite. But before the male could even finish his first sentence, Yoren had thrown an ugly comment at him. She had even kicked dirt into his face, more than once. Shaking her head in amusement at herself, she almost felt guilty. Almost.

"Oh, Gordell, where are you? I know you are coming, but do hurry. I will try to behave a while longer. I promise I will, if only you hurry," she spoke her plea into the stagnant air in the tiny, dirty shack.

Rethinking the idea of making her escape, she knew it would not happen. Even if she tried and actually managed to get out of this place, she would have difficulties making it home alone. She was not altogether positive of the exact direction in which they had traveled. Escaping would be a ruinous idea so she abandoned the notion. *Just be patient and behave, Gordell will come soon,* she reaffirmed her resolve.

With a firm nod of her head, she walked over to the only door in the shack to see if she could attempt to get outside. Yoren felt as if she would suffocate if she had to stay locked up in the musky, filthy shack another moment.

Just as she had reached down, both hands still bound together in front of her, she leapt back as the door swung in, startling her. Sailing backwards, she knew this would not end well as she landed hard on her rear. Feeling the impact reverberate throughout her entire body made her wince and mumble a few ill-mannered words under her breath. Now her rear most likely was bruised to match her pride.

She peered up at whoever had just caused this latest bit of brutality upon her person. *Ugh! It was all simply too much!* she grumbled to herself. In a burst of speed, a tall, beautiful female rushed forward and tried to grab Yoren before she hit the floor. She obviously did not make it, but the fact that she had tried made Yoren look upon the female in a different light.

She wondered if perhaps this was a friendly shifter, as she longed for a kind face and possibly a bit of female conversation. Even if she had been abducted by this Weyr, she knew not all members were to be held accountable for the actions of a specific few. She decided to chance it.

"Oh, apologies, forgive me! I was not expecting you to be at the door!" the female supplied in one quick breath. She looked sincerely shaken and upset that Yoren had fallen. She rushed to assist the female into a sitting position, her hands remaining on Yoren's back while she spoke too fast for Yoren to reply. "I am Jolsynn. I only meant to check on you and then I was to bring you to my home for nourishment and to bathe, if you would like to do so?" Leaving a question mark hanging between them with a small smile, she was visibly anxious and perhaps in a hurry.

The female appeared to be quite young, Yoren would guess her to be only about in her seventeen age. She was impressed by such a young female-shifter already being so tall, built so solidly, and returned Jolsynn's smile, happy for her company, in any case. A meal and a bath sounded better than anything else she could think of at the moment, so she jumped on the kind offer.

"Both of those things sound wonderful, Jolsynn. I am Yoren, and many thanks for your thoughtfulness and kindness. I was just now wishing to leave this shack even if only for some fresh air. I cannot bear being cramped up as I have, any longer. Again, my thanks. Oh, and it is not your fault that I was behind the door. You could not have known, and I will be all right," she finished as Jolsynn helped her to stand. Her wrists bled anew from reflexively trying to throw her hands behind herself to prevent hitting the ground. Another reason she had gone down so hard, it was impossible to use her hands and she now felt the folly of her failed attempt.

"Oh, you are bleeding! Upon my shame and sorrow, let us be away from here quickly. My mother is wonderful with herbs and healing, at least on smaller injuries. She will be able to tend you quite well in our home. Again, my apologies," the female-young offered a bit more anxiously. "Here now, allow me to unbind your hands. That cannot be comfortable." Yoren felt a sudden need to hug the female-young and weep again, but out of happiness and gratitude this time. There was something about her that called to Yoren; innocence and a hunger to learn all things. She had a positive feeling regarding the female's future.

"My thanks, Jolsynn. You are very kind. My wrists do pain me and I would welcome any aid from your mother." Holding her swollen, stinging wrists out in front of her, she winced and drew in a quick breath of relief when the female-young effortlessly and efficiently sliced through the rough-rope, and the remnants fell to the floor. Yoren quirked a brow at the small, extremely sharp knife the female had retrieved from a well-hidden pocket in the folds of her skirts. Noticing Yoren's humorous, questioning expression, Jolsynn shrugged a shoulder and tried to hide her smile as her cheeks bloomed into two pink blotches.

Emotions swelled Yoren's insides and she reached out to pull the female-young into a tight embrace. She knew immediately that she could trust the female and before she could stop herself, words poured from her mouth. "Oh, many thanks. I am forever in your debt. You see, I am carrying our first youngling and I am worried for its health, and my own. The males were not overly rough with me but I am fatigued, sore, hungry, and do not feel well. I am grateful for your assistance." With a small squeeze, Yoren released the female.

Standing back, she caught the expression on Jolsynn's face and instantly felt remorseful for her ramblings; the type she had suffered much, of late, since she was carrying. The female-young looked frightened for Yoren and her youngling, yet she wasted no time in gently grasping Yoren by the arm and quickly tugging her out and away from the small shack.

The brightness of the beautiful day blinded Yoren as they quickly fled the shack. She flinched and flung up her free arm to cover her watery eyes while squeezing them tightly shut. Jolsynn turned and noticed her discomfort from the overly bright day. Pulling off her waist apron, she quickly secured it around Yoren's head hoping to help block some of the brightness so they could make it to her home faster.

The poor female was not looking at all well and the news that she was carrying made Jolsynn's stomach churn. She began to feel anger such as she never had before. *How could those males, the supposedly worthy males do such a thing? And to a carrying female? This could be a death order for them all. Or at least for the one who led them...Mazar.* Subtly shaking her head in disgust, Jolsynn had known him the whole of her life and had always thought well of him. *Why, then, would a male of honor abduct such a female and callously throw her into that awful, filthy little shack to sleep on the hard floor?* The more thought Jolsynn gave to the scenario, the more upset she became. She was shaking with anger by the time they made it to her home.

"Please, enter our home. My mother is expecting you and has already prepared your nourishment. Here, have a seat and she will be out directly." Gently settling Yoren into a wooden chair at a wooden eating table, Jolsynn hurried from their main room to find her mother. The need to speak with her before she saw to Yoren burned hot in her veins. *How could he?* Again, the more she allowed herself to ponder it, the more her ire rose. The unwanted, unfamiliar feelings were scalding, coursing through her and she did not know what to do with, nor did she have any experience dealing with them. The intensity was such; she truly needed to speak to her mother who would know how to calm her.

Chapter Eight

Gordell had not slept a wink since the day he returned home from scoping out their territory with his warriors. Three long days ago. Of all the idiotic, fool moves! Why had their personal guard allowed Yoren such a dangerous freedom? To walk alone all the way to the village for fabrics and materials? He thought this had to be the singular most stupid thing he had ever heard of in his entire, long life. Especially for his Yoren; it was confounding and wholly unlike her.

Unwilling to even contemplate on their youngling, he wanted to thrash Yoren, and then fiercely pull her into his strong arms and hold onto her for the rest of their days. Always, she had thought kindly of almost everyone. Always, she had carried on with her fanciful and whimsical ways of thinking. Look at what it was costing all of them now. Her, their youngling, and himself. He had never been such a wreck.

All the females had been trying, to no avail, to make him eat. Even several of his warriors had given it a shot, too. How could he possibly eat, sleep, or any of the things they all took for granted not knowing at all what his Yoren, the love of his life, and their unborn youngling were being subjected to at the same time? He did not truly believe she would be harmed, not physically, anyway. But, he knew all-too-well how the mental and emotional games warriors played could cause far more damage than one would expect.

If there was even so much as a damaged hair on her beautiful head, a scratch—accidentally or not—marring her perfect, silky skin, he would personally detach Mazar's head from his shoulders with his bare hands. This, he would do with glee in his heart and a smile upon his lips. The bastard! *Breathe. That is it, breathe, and try to stay under control.* He had already been over this with himself multiple times. He must stay calm, at least attempt to care for himself. He could not go weak in any fashion, or he may never get his Yoren and their youngling back. That was unacceptable. He would see them home safe and soon. Very, very soon.

He had been informed of the precarious situation Mazar had found himself in. *Losing his wits?* Even temporarily, that was still no excuse for stealing Gordell's Truemate. There could be no excuse for anyone, in any way to do such a foolish, dangerous thing.

Perhaps they should have made the official announcement of their youngling upon their own discovery of the fact. Every member of every Weyr knew as a code of honor, none must ever lay hands on a female to begin with. And if she was carrying a youngling, one essentially was signing their own death order just to think of nearing her.

Darkan and several of their best warriors—which would be any of them—as they were all the best, had already set their retrieval plan into motion: There were ten groups with twenty warriors in each, all of which had headed out early the previous morn in different directions. They had pinpointed the exact location of where Mazar's own home was. The plan would bring Gordell's warriors from ten different directions to surround the bastard's living-quarters, and if the male had not already breathed his last, it was only a matter of time. A short amount of time.

Gordell had also been informed that several of Mazar's fellow-warriors and friends had aided him under the guise that their Chief wanted Yoren to be captured for some sort of bargaining purposes. However, the two Weyr had never had a grievance with one another, so there was no need for bargaining of any kind. The bastard had lied to all of those other males. Gordell could not blame or hold the others responsible, if that part was fact. He was, after all, reasonable.

Darkan, along with all of his other warriors had fully agreed it best for Gordell to stay home, certain that if he traveled with them, there was a very real possibility he would go off the deep end and make an even bigger mess of things. He had to agree with them, that was not how he wanted the situation to go.

Latest word was, Mazar had been placed in his Chief's dungeon, or would be soon, to await the decision on his fate. Gordell almost had a small amount of sympathy for the male. Almost. He had heard horror stories of many a worthy male going mad from the incessant buzzing in their heads, the sleepless nights, and other symptoms they developed if they never found their own Truemate.

Likewise, he knew how blessed he was to have found Yoren as a youngling, and to grow up with and be around her almost every day of his life. The chaste kiss Gordell had placed on her lips, simply being a playful youngling himself, had sealed their fates to be together and belong to each other for all of their days.

Now, with their youngling on its way, he had never been happier, yet due to the twisted irony they were currently dealing with, he had never been so upset, either. This type of worry was entirely new to Gordell. Certainly, he had seen things, been through emotional and unsettling situations. Those things, however, were nothing compared to what this was doing to him.

Having been reduced to staying home and waiting, something he never was very skilled at, especially not when he was so personally invested in the outcome as he was now, was driving him past his own limits. "Curse Mazar! I will kill the fool myself!" he bellowed out the window of their bedchamber. He was exhausted and knew he needed nourishment, but his heart and mind would not afford him those basic necessities. Even though he had not slept, he had attempted to do so, but one could not make sleep happen simply because it was needed.

Moving his gaze around the scenery outside, he was taken by the beauty of the landscape. He had always known this particular territory of the Dragon Cove was breathtaking and even more so from the air. Unfortunately, he was always far too busy to stop and take notice simply for the sake of appreciation. As he did so now, he wished his Yoren was right there next to him. She would have been beaming with happiness at his willingness to stand still long enough to actually look around and truly take notice of the beauty which surrounded them every day.

They had been fully blessed growing up and living in this territory and by having always been together. Blessings are ofttimes not realized until tragedy struck; perhaps this would be an eye-opener for him. Perhaps.

Ah, what would he not give to have her back right now? He would take her mouthwatering, tantalizing, soft yet still firm body to their bed where upon he would have already sprinkled a great variety of fresh flower petals. Knowing how much Yoren cherished all types of flowers, she would love it. The mixed scents would be a strong aphrodisiac, not that they ever needed one, but it would harm nothing.

After gently lying her bare, beautiful body down he would plant soft, slow kisses over all of her beginning with her perfect, adorable little toes. He could almost hear her heartwarming laughter filling the air, spilling out their window for all to hear. Gordell did not mind that at all; their entire Weyr knew how in love they were and always had been, since they were mere younglings.

She would not fight his ministrations and, indeed, she had always encouraged him to dabble in new fleshy delights, lifting their lovemaking to new levels and higher peaks. Taking particular care as he spent a few extra moments tending her dainty yet strong ankles, his female, who always seemed so soft and yielding, was much stronger and tougher than most would guess. She had always been of a pleasing size to him; Gordell towered over six and a half feet tall, she was only scant inches shorter. He knew how blessed he was for her to be built so solid and rather close to himself in height. She had long, lean muscles, shapely hips and thighs, all of which would aid her in birthing plenty of large, healthy younglings for them.

It had never been necessary to be gentle with her, although he simply was because it seemed to make their internal temperatures rise at an alarming rate, bringing them both more pleasure. That is how he would always tend her, as he would next work his way up her long, smooth, strong legs, possibly pausing to kiss and lick the overly sensitive backs of her knees. Those two particular spots were among his favorites on her scrumptious body. He loved the way she always wiggled and laughed, all the while begging him not to cease as he paid them special attention with his mouth. *Special attention every inch of her deserved.*

Then, he would work his way up her strong, supple thighs. Ah, those thighs, two more of his favorite spots on her body. Skipping the best, saving his most favored region for last, he would almost certainly have to stop to run his wet, hot tongue oh-so-slowly and lovingly over her slightly ever-rounding belly. He loved watching her writhe and hearing her tinkling laughter—ticklish as she was—would not allow him to cease in that bit of love-play. Ever squirming and undulating, unable to still herself, his Yoren was not one to simply lie like a wet cloth as her male took to her making maddeningly slow love to her with his mouth.

Unable to wait any longer, he would cease the tickling and begin paying homage to her creamy skin and the perfectly weighted, plump bosom they encased. They deserved to be worshiped, and he certainly did not mind performing such a task to the best of his abilities. According to her words, he did a quite thorough job every time they would join as a Mated pair.

Cupping a breast in each of his large, work and battle-callused hands, he would gently squeeze and knead them until she made the most irresistible sounds as she let her pleasure be known. Leaving his hands free to roam where they would, his mouth would eagerly take over their task of slowly, torturously licking each side of one breast, then the other. Eventually, he would work his way around the succulent orb, until she became a trembling mass beneath him.

By then, his Yoren would be all but begging him to cease his torture and begin their lovemaking in earnest. She was never inhibited; one more thing on a long list that he loved and even adored about his Truemate, the love of his life. In a blur, he would take her mouth, swallowing her moans and the sweet, mewling sounds escaping her luscious, perfect lips. Lips made just for his own. Beginning with sweet kisses and soft caresses all over her body, he would work them both into a frenzied, intoxicated state of arousal.

They would both need—more than life itself—their hot, heavily aroused bodies to be joined. The joining was always best when it was done slowly; not only because it spiraled their need even higher, but he always preferred his female to be truly ready for him. After a lengthy bout of love-play, she was always more than ready for his large, heavily muscled body to be against her own decidedly feminine, more lithe form. Both would be taut, slick with sweat from holding themselves back for so long.

Next, he would settle himself over her glorious body, her female arousal a thick, pungent aroma hanging in the air all around them. He would breathe deeply of his favored scent, until he was unable to stay his deepest desires any longer. Alas, he would guide his thick, hard, heavily swollen length into her sweet, honey-slick core where he would gently—considering her carrying state—slowly enter her hot, tight, welcoming sheath. As they made long, passionate love, they would gaze into one another's eyes, and they would find what the other felt; the irrefutable proof of their emotions running deeper than either of them had ever thought possible. Their love for each other, and now, for their youngling.

Those thoughts snapped him back into reality faster than he would have expected, but it was probably for the best. He was supposed to be doing things, but he could not recall any of them now. A *problem* was making it almost impossible to conjure clear, necessary thought. The problem being, his entire groin region was swelled, throbbing, and so hard he had to undo his leather belt and untie the strings securing his breeches at his waist.

Ah, now I can breathe. Yoren, if you are not home before much longer, I will come for you, myself. I cannot abide this worrying, nor can I be without you even for one more day. I love you so, I hope you know that, he vowed. He wanted his female back, and their youngling she was carrying. He *needed* them back, unharmed.

Then, he would give her a set down, unlike anything she had never known. Admittedly, much of her carefree ways were his fault also, but she had always done whatever she pleased. She had never been one with the patience to wait for anyone to keep up with her, be it her own personal guard, or even Gordell. Then again, there had never been any cause for real concern before.

Without realizing it, he suddenly began to laugh; a real, humorous laugh which felt good, yet wrong at the same time. Though, he could not have stopped it for anything as he found himself hoping his Yoren had sliced Mazar a few times with her sharp tongue. The female could keep up with his fiercest warriors, when it came to the things she said in anger. Mazar probably regretted he had taken her soon after they had made haste to be away from here. Most likely, the fool wished he had found a quieter, much more malleable female. Two characteristics his Yoren did not possess, and likewise, two more things Gordell positively loved about her. He loved everything about her.

His humor died off quickly with the thought. "They are on their way, my love. You shall be home soon and in my arms. After a well-deserved and long overdue tongue lashing," he declared aloud. A promise, an oath, a nonnegotiable fact. Never again would either of them be so careless, and never again would he let her out of his own sight. Even if he had to tie her and their youngling to his belt, which he was more than willing to do.

****

After three long days of feeling more useless than she'd ever felt in her entire life, Iax had finally been given the all-clear by the master healer of their Weyr host. Being laid-up in bed and only getting liquids and small amounts of fruits and breads wasn't cutting it; she needed food! Like, real sink-your-teeth-into-it food. And a real bath, 'cause sponges only go so far and can only do so much cleaning on one's body. She needed a big, steaming-hot bathtub to soak in for a good hour. Even if it got cold, she'd still welcome and relish every second of it.

That was only a small portion of why she was so tightly coiled, afraid she may just unwind like a spinning top and explode. Everything was getting on her nerves, she'd been biting her abused lips hard and wearing holes into them to prevent the verbal diarrhea she knew would commence if she stopped. Truth tell, Iax truly was comforted by her friend's presence while she slept, and enjoyed the familiar company during her waking hours, too. But the need to cut loose and give her tongue free reign was almost too much. She'd been behaving herself, of course, after all these shifters had done for her, but she was feeling cramped and smothered.

Gemma had been staying in the same room with her since the 'accident,' even while Iax slept. There was absolutely no way she would allow herself to be rude to the woman. *Not cool, even you know that,* she admitted. Someone had considerately hauled a cot into the room for Gemma's use, and even though the woman didn't need much sleep, she did require some. Iax had told Gemma it wasn't necessary, but once she got something into her head, it stayed.

"Thank God!" Iax sighed after the head-honcho-healer dude had left the room. "If I had to spend one more minute in this damn bed, I think I'da gone completely nuts! I wanted to thank you again for staying in here with me. You didn't have to, but I appreciate it," she offered to her friend. Iax wasn't a shrew, but she had never been all that comfortable with pleasantries; 'please' and 'thank you,' shit like that were things she didn't have to say often. Working on your own most of the time kinda changes a person. Of course she'd been raised with manners, but they were a bit rusty, to say the least.

"You are quite welcome, my dear. I am still terribly sorry about your fall. And, yes, I know–I know before you even begin, 'it is not your fault, Gemma, so shut the hell up,' is what you keep saying, yet I still cannot help myself at times. I am pleased to see you back in good health and better spirits." She smiled. "I know this was not part of our plan, but since we have been here I have discovered extremely useful information. I believe, other than your fall, us being here was meant to be. I also think you will be happy with the new intelligence these shifters so freely offered." Her smile brightened.

Tamping down the urge to laugh at Gemma's surprising willingness to say the 'h-word,' Iax pounced on the other topic. "Intelligence, you say? What, pray tell, have you discovered? While you're at it, would ya please shut the door and hand me my pack? If I don't get dressed and outta here soon, I still may explode." Gemma did, and Iax thanked her.

Hmm, I'm getting way too mushy-fucking-gushy, I'll be knocking this shit off, now, Iax chastised herself, wanting to laugh at the whole situation. She'd never had a problem using her manners around Gemma, but it seemed like she was doing it increasingly more all the time. Shaking it off, she leapt up more excited than a kid on Christmas morning, at the prospect of getting out of the bed and the room. She barely realized Gemma was speaking.

"Apparently, a male only knows for certain whom his Truemate is by placing a kiss upon her lips. I recall explaining the buzzing and how the males cannot sleep properly; those things all cease when he has kissed the correct female. I suppose a male can, and most likely has to kiss many females before chancing upon his own, if he ever finds her. I feel it is a sad existence, but it also makes me happy to be a female and *not* of this species. It would be a horrible way to go through one's life…" she trailed off, a glum expression on her face.

"True dat. It would really suck but there's nothing we can do about it, so don't be so sad. I can't stand it when you're all sad and shit. C'mon, braid my hair, would ya, please?" she asked, trying to get her friend's mind off all the sadness that was clearly visible in her violet-eyes. Out of all Gemma's considerably wondrous assets, Iax had never been jealous but she'd probably give at least an arm, or something similar, for eyes like that. In any case, it bothered her to see her friend in such a state. Gemma was an upbeat, positive person, and she didn't need to allow things like that to get to her; it was just a waste of thinking, anyway. All they could do was the job they were there for, then Iax would go home, Gemma would go, well, to wherever her home was, and they'd all have to move on.

Easy, breezy, peasy–right? Yeah, keep telling yourself that, Iax thought dryly.

Braiding Iax's long hair, Gemma continued to fill her in, "I have also discovered that within a one-week cycle of their first kiss an image will appear, or more precisely, it will burn itself into the flesh of both the female and male-shifter. Hers, a butterfly and his, a Dragon. Her Dragon-form, to be more precise. I do not yet know why his Dragon is not the image burnt into her flesh, but that is what happens. It is similar to a branding perhaps, though, I am not exactly certain. The strange yet chilly part is, his Dragon image matches her shifter coloring, and her Butterfly image matches his," she explained, finishing an intricate, beautiful braid. One Iax had never seen.

"Gemma, this is gorgeous! Thank you! What do you call it, and how come I've never seen it on you?" Iax gushed. *Again, with the girly shit!* Still, it was stunning. She'd have to learn how to do it before she went home. All of her girlfriends would love this.

"Oh, it is simply a warrior's braid from my kind. When a female goes into battle, she plaits her hair just so, as it holds well and for long periods of time, which will come in handy for us, soon," she almost whispered the last part, making the hairs on Iax's nape neck stand up.

"Um, what the hell does that mean, and what aren't you telling me?" Tapping the toe of one booted-foot on the floor, Iax fisted her hands on her hips with one brow raised waiting for Gemma to stop fidgeting and fess-up. "Well? Any day now. I'm not gettin' any younger here. Why would we 'need' warrior braids, and why are you stalling, woman?" she snapped. This was highly unusual behavior for Gemma and it was starting to make Iax nervous. Another emotion she wasn't all that familiar with, nor fond of.

"Alright, all right, settle yourself. It is not all as bad as it may seem. I have had plenty of time in which to make a plan where we will be traveling this day. And, um, well…that is all for now…" she trailed off, again.

What the fuck's the deal? Iax wondered. The 'traveling' was welcomed news, the B.S., however, sure as hell was not. Did she need to shake the woman? And she'd do it; Gemma should know that about her by now! *Dammit, this is ridiculous! What is Gemma hiding, and why? I'm a pretty tough bitch. Why's she acting like I can't handle whatever kinda shit she's planned?* Iax speculated, the infinitude of her frustration and suspicion peaking to alarmingly high levels.

"I now have the coordinates of Mazar, the one who abducted Yoren. In fact, I have directions to his very home. I suspect it should take us approximately one full day of steady travel on foot to reach the territory. Then we can spy on him, and work out the rest of the plan. I think it should be easy because, as I have already relayed to you, he is regretting his actions. By now he is most likely arranging for someone to take Yoren back to her home, and get her off his hands…" Gemma quietly trailed off.

"If you do that one, more, time, I will shake you!" Iax emphasized her warning. "Whispering the end of your sentences and the trailing off thing, stop it! Ya got any idea how frustrating that is? Seriously Gemma, it's me. Just me. We've worked together many times and we usually get along great, so why are you acting freaked out? What, you think I'm gonna snap, do something crazy? What? What is it with you?" she tried to tone it down a bit. Rattling Gemma more would only prolong everything, and apparently they needed to get a move-on.

Still, Iax honestly wanted to scream, just for the sake of screaming!

"Sit and I shall explain. And I am sorry, but this is difficult. I do not know why but it is. For some reason, things are becoming increasingly difficult for me, of late. I do not like, nor can I control it. I am growing tired of my eyes leaking, my chest painfully tightening, and feeling sad. I never have these…these emotions! There! Are you happy now? That is what my problem is! We must go. Now!" Gemma snapped back.

Wow, good for you! Iax wanted to praise her friend. Holding everything in all the time was the making of a ticking time bomb. Iax noticed since her arrival, Gemma was undoubtedly exhibiting an increasing amount unfamiliar emotions. It was obviously unnerving the poor woman to the point of distraction, which can and probably would become dangerous. Iax needed to come up with the correct verbiage to help calm her friend, before something awful happened as a direct result of her new emotional state.

Chapter Nine

It was not polite, nor was it fair how Gemma continued to act out in such extremes. And, taking it out on her friend? It was simply rude and unacceptable. She needed to figure out what was the matter with her, and why she was acting out as she had been. It was such unfamiliar territory, Gemma had no idea of what to do or how to fix her problem, and it was quite clear that she had a problem.

She was extremely pleased with Iax's recovery; the female always recovered and healed abnormally fast, even by the standards of shifters in the Dragon Dimension. It truly was quite odd. Gemma had never given it much thought before but something about it had been giving her pause, of late.

Besides that anomaly, Iax also had an uncanny ability to think similarly to most of the beings in any time or place, and to puzzle out much of the problems practically on her own, and in a short amount of time. Her natural instincts—recent events notwithstanding—were becoming increasingly sharper. And her abilities with weapons? It was a highly necessary skill-set to possess for one such as Iax. But again, how? What made Iax unique in so many ways?

The female spoke oft of her family and her beloved Earth. Gemma was filled to bursting with happiness and joy for the life Iax had led; the obviously shared respect and love Iax's human family had for one another. What Gemma would give for such blessings. She was not jealous of Iax—never that—she simply wondered why some had it so well, while so many others dealt with such struggles. Not that Iax did not work hard and deserve what she had, but it still made Gemma wonder.

She had never gone without anything. In truth, she had always been taken care of, and the females who helped raise her and her brother after they lost the parents she had so loved and desperately missed, had shown her what felt like a level of love. At the very least, they did have a true affection for her, which was undoubtedly something to hold on to and be thankful for. Why, then, did she feel so alone? So empty inside? She had lived with these painful yet hollow feeling emotions for so long, perhaps they were just now taking their toll on her. But, she had to put her emotions away for now, or she could end up getting her and Iax seriously injured, or worse.

"I don't quite know what to say, Gemma, other than I'm sorry. I've experienced a few of those feelings myself, from time to time. Yet, just like the 'eye leaking' thing, I just don't have much to offer in the way of explanations. I don't know why, but I've never been good at this stuff; the mushy-girly stuff. I don't know, it's just not my thing, I guess." She shrugged. "If it helps, I'll think on it and try to come up with something to help you out. But I think for now, the best thing for us is to get going. That'll keep us occupied and give us both time to think. What say we blow this pop stand?"

****

Iax and Gemma set out on their journey about fifteen-hours ago. The whole time Iax had been praying and wishing for the O.W.O. Unit to figure out a way for her to at least bring a few tech-gadgets with her. *At least some damn tunes!* She'd sang every song she could think of in her head, after Gemma had so politely asked her to stop singing out loud.

"I know I can't sing worth a shit, but I'm more bored than ever, and I love music! Maybe you ought to come to where I live and I'll play you all kinds of stuff. I love different music from all genres, or most, and different decades. Oh, you'll love this one!" she declared excitedly. Then she began to belt out another tune about motorcycles revving their engines, being like the noise in her head, people hating faster than they love, and essentially spinning out of control.

Pulling up short, Iax was startled when Gemma jumped in front of her and held her hands over her ears as if she were actually in pain! Wanting to yell at the madwoman, she started to go off on her. "What the…? Bullshit!" Then realized, her best move would be to keep on going, so she did; launching into more of the same tune. The singer was pleading for help, wondering how to save herself from a world-gone-mad. *If people on Earth only knew*. She laughed to herself, problems there were peanuts, compared to where she was now.

Realizing her efforts weren't helping anything, including herself, she huffed and spoke her mind. "What-fucking-ever, jeesh! I was only trying to have some fun, you know? Lighten things up? Break up some of this never-ending quiet?" Shaking her own head, Iax stalked, or rather, stomped away.

Now Gemma felt guilty, and it was written all over her beautiful face, which in turn, made Iax feel kinda bad. Only just a little bit. *Great, guess I messed that up!* she scolded herself. "I'm sorry Gemma. I'm about to lose my mind, I only wanted to have fun. I know I don't sing well, but you sure know how to make a girl feel even worse. Thanks a lot. And don't worry, I won't do it again. Your loss." She let out a loud huff and resumed her stomping through the woods.

A couple more hours passed before they'd both finally calmed down, and were sitting on fallen logs getting ready to have something to eat and drink. At this point, they were tired, grumpy, hungry, and just downright not-good-company even to themselves. Food and drink usually helped, and they both dug in as if they hadn't eaten in days.

As per usual, Gemma had taken care of their food and drink requirements. Always something taste-a-liscious appearing from, well, Iax wasn't quite sure where. Probably the woman's own pack. It was simple yet always highly satisfying fare, when it came from Gemma. Iax was always thrilled at how fabulous everything tasted. So many things seemed to just 'be' when it came to Gemma. Always finding things along their travels, every path seemed to have something new and unique from the previous one, such as berries and other various fruits, nuts, and a few things she had no clue of what they were.

Being surrounded by so much beauty and nature, they had quite a selection from which to choose, and both women were grateful for it. Even many of the ginormous flowers and such were edible, so they partook of those as well. Everything was superb, so far. Neither of them had ever been through this area or, obviously, to the destination they were working toward. Iax had to admit everything was breathtaking, gorgeous, and just plain stunning. She'd never in her entire life on any of her trips anywhere, seen what she had in the past several hours since they'd began their quest.

There must have been fifty different kinds of trees growing everywhere, so thick it was hard to make their way through them. It was an unbelievable sight to behold, like something straight out of a fantasy world. Other than the charred remains of that big section of the valley floor where Iax had originally 'popped in,' all the other landscape and scenery had left her awestruck. She'd been to many beautiful places, but this was way beyond any of them. Having seen everything she had in the last couple years, she could honestly say that with a rock solid conviction.

"Gemma, this is…I can't even describe it. I mean, looket around! You're seeing the same things I am–can you believe this shit? It's extraordinary, I love this place! Well, I mean minus all the warring, the huge predatory animals, the territorial males, and we can't leave out those ever-lovely, well thought-out abductions; they can kinda give a girl pause. Otherwise, this is seriously almost too amazing!" Iax excitedly exclaimed.

"It is quite sightly. Even more so than my own homelands, and that is saying something. Things are not as large where I am from, but it is still beautiful. Oh, watch out above you!" Gemma warned.

As the words were coming out of Gemma's mouth, Iax thanked God she hadn't let her guard drop. Beauty didn't always equal safety as they both well knew, and of course, this beautiful place would have hidden dangers, and some that weren't quite so hidden.

Quickly turning her gaze upward to check whatever Gemma was warning her of, she almost screamed, and then thought better of possibly startling all kinds of critters and such. It wasn't like this place was normal, not by a long shot. Even the bugs were enormous, iridescent, and all made of vivid, bright colors, magnificent in their beauty. Gemma had warned her that they also could be terribly dangerous, and many of them even poisonous. Neither of them felt like being bitten, or anything else, for that matter.

Leaping backwards about three-feet, Iax barely made it out of the way of what appeared to her to be an overgrown, or rather, a ridiculously large Katydid-looking thing looming over her. "What the fuck is that, and where the hell did it come from? I know you warned me of these huge…mutations. But this? Totally unexpected and beyond huge. Now what?" she squeaked out. Iax could have stared at the thing for hours, but she also realized somewhere in the back of her mind that she needed to know if this particular thing was friend or foe, poisonous or non. It was so mesmerizing, a person could be hypnotized just staring at it. She'd always been drawn to sparkly, shiny things, and this was no exception.

"Iax, no! You must not stay too close, nor should you look directly at it. Please, look at me or anything, just not at it. Yes, it is very pretty, but it can and will enthrall you. They do that to any prey which may be difficult to transport back to their pods. You must fight it and step away. And no, it is not poisonous, it does not have to be since it can easily enthrall you." A long moment stretched between them as Iax's attention was stuck on the creature. Gemma worried over this behavior she had noticed before; Iax was always taken with all-things-shimmery, much like the Amethyst Faerie Dragons. With no time to further contemplate that subject, she had to get Iax's attention off of the creature, and on to herself.

Iax heard Gemma's pleas, but there was something about this thing that wouldn't allow her to *not* stare at it. "Iax! Come to me now!" She heard Gemma snap, attempting to capture her attention from the beautiful yet somewhat scary-looking thing crouching a mere couple feet in front of her. Every inch of its body was the same green as the regular Katydids from back home, only much larger. The wings were the same, too, but almost transparent. The more Iax checked it out, the more details she noticed. Every bit of it sparkled, much like if it had rolled in a mighty large pile of fine silver glitter. It was thickest on all the edges and lines connecting one body part to another, like it was outlined with the shimmery, mind-melding stuff.

"Wow, this shit's wild," Iax murmured, transfixed by the natural, raw beauty of this freakishly large insect. Feeling like she could simply stare, or worse, follow it anywhere, she tried to shake her gaze away. Now she understood how it could enthrall its prey; just checking out its body was mesmerizing. She knew she needed to stop staring, and get her shit together before she fell into those large, deep, dark eyes which were currently roaming up and down her form. Maybe trying to figure out how many meals she'd make? Or, perhaps how many critters she could sate in one shared setting?

That did it, spell broken! "Oh, *hell* no, dude, and fuck you very much. Really, no thanks. How 'bout this, Mr. Green-Thing: I'll go this a'way, and you go that a'way." Iax hiked a thumb over her shoulder in Gemma's direction, then pointed behind Mr. Green-Thing, speaking quietly as she could when she needed to, 'cause stirring this bad-boy was the last thing she wanted to do. Unsure of what her next move should be, she consulted her friend, "Gemma, should I turn and run, or slowly continue to back away? Big guy, here, looks like he or she may just tackle my ass and end it, or better yet, end *me,* real quick-like. What should I do?" Iax entreated. Now, and for the second time since her arrival, she seriously was afraid. This time, of being eaten by the big-ass green critter-dude staring her down.

"You are doing exactly what you should, Iax. Simply back away as you are, but do not look directly into its eyes; that is how they are able to enthrall one. I know they *appear* innocent, but that is their guise. Most beings find them sightly enough, so they stand a fair chance of winning one over. When that happens, the being usually is never be seen or heard from again." she explained. "Yes, good. Keep backing toward me. You are almost here now," she encouraged. "And Iax…?"

Backing away as unnoticeably as she could, Iax barely heard all of what Gemma said she spoke in hushed tones. And, when she'd said, "And Iax…?" in the form of a question, it gave Iax goosebumps and reminded her to pay better attention to her friend. She hesitantly replied, "Yes, Gemma?"

Gemma cleared her throat. "Um, yes. Well, I do believe our critter has either brought or beckoned friends. Do not panic or become overly alarmed; if you pay attention to me, I can quickly get us out of this, and most likely without incident. Very slowly, you may now turn toward me but I repeat, do *not* panic. I have a solution, and panicking would only serve to agitate them. Alright?" she squeaked.

"Kay, I'm down with ya sista. Lemme guess; when I turn around I'm gonna see several new Mr. Green-Things–right? And, by several, we're probably talking oh, I don't know, a dozen or so? And surely your *solution* will fix everything–right? I hope you know I trust you, so whatever ya got up your sleeve, please make sure it's all ready to go right when we need it, okay?" Iax replied, her voice only a tiny bit shaky. Hearing Gemma take a deep, steadying breath, Iax turned slowly, not wanting to piss off any of their new friends. Feeling that her own eyes were as wide as saucers, she willed herself to relax and even them out, and to significantly slow her heartbeat. It didn't take a Ph-fucking-D to know these things were highly intelligent, predatory, and most likely could sense one's fear. That's the last thing they needed in their precarious situation.

Noticing at least eight more Mr. Green-Things, Iax settled her gaze on Gemma. The plead for help clear in her expression and her unusually large eyes must've made her discomfort obvious to Gemma. That's when everything suddenly seemed to go into slow-mo, then it all sped up so fast, everything became a blur.

She had been impressed by Gemma and her abilities, magic, or whatever it was, many times. Now, she was in shock at what the woman had just done. They'd been standing in the middle of a Mr. Green-Thing feast one minute, and the next thing she knew, they were in an entirely different place. It felt as if hours had passed since their little run-in, but Gemma told her that it had only been a few minutes.

"How come you never told me you could do that? It was…I don't know *what* that was, but…I just don't know," Iax mumbled. She was confused and disoriented as she shook her head in disbelief, unable to comprehend what just happened. The only thing she clearly recalled was, Gemma had slowly reached over and firmly gripped her upper arm, and then they were gone. Just gone.

Now they were in an equally stunning place, yet everything was totally different. There were trees, but not such a large variety and they were more thinned out. Also, she spotted countless types of flowers in different colors and sizes, nearby where they now stood. Everything here was also extra-large which Iax was becoming accustomed to, but she was still in awe. This Realm was undeniably one of the most beautiful one she'd ever had the pleasure of visiting. And that was saying a lot, as she had been to some outrageously gorgeous places.

Gemma had somehow managed to take control of everything, including Iax. Normally that would have bothered her, but she knew without Gemma's help and guidance, her ass would probably still be sitting on a rock or a tree stump, where she'd be gawking around like an idiot, and not knowing what to do or where to go next. Better yet, she'd either *be* a grand feast for all those Mr. Green-Things, or they would have already digested her.

Thankfully, Gemma saved the day once more, and in the end, saved Iax's ass…again. Although she'd never admit how much, Iax genuinely loved the woman. She was perfectly fine with their relationship, as she'd always been fully secure in her own sexuality. There had never been any kind of attraction between them, merely a deep rooted respect for one another; just close friends, or more like sisters. Having fought to help keep each other alive multiple times, how could they not be?

Of all the different types of debts one can owe another, having your ass saved multiple times by the same person, definitely topped the charts. What does one do to cover such a payment? Iax didn't know, but she was sure of one thing; she owed Gemma more than she could even comprehend, and now she could only hope and pray for a time when Gemma needed something huge, that only Iax could do for her. It would be a whopper, and Iax was more than up for that challenge. Well, really, it may take a few incidents to cover the totality of what she owed the woman. *One of these days…*she thought. *One of these days.*

As for attraction, Iax likes men. She really, really likes men. So what, that she'd never clicked with a single one? So what, if she had yet to land her own hottie due to a lack of chemistry? *My turn will come–right? Surely it will.* Those thoughts made her analyze her own so called 'love life,' or lack thereof. Sure; she always had all kinds of dudes hitting on her, asking her out, and all the normal bullshit. She'd even gone out on a date with a few of them.

One. Date. Per. Man.

She'd just never quite clicked with any of them; never felt like any of them would be a good fit for her. Not that they had been creepy or had done anything wrong. Quite the opposite; they had, indeed, been extremely polite and always good looking. A couple were downright hot, smart, and a few were even loaded—as in sickeningly rich—but there was never any of that 'chemistry' shit she'd heard about. Her girlfriends had all spewed on and on about the chemistry in their own lives and experiences, but it all made Iax feel a bit nauseous. Just the notion that a man could make her feel like she had 'butterflies in her stomach,' or some other kind of love-sick bullshit. *Ugh! Hell no,* was all she'd said to that. *No thanks.*

Iax would find her own man, her own way, and in her own time. He'd love and respect her for who she was, and wouldn't freak out over her 'job,' even though she'd probably never be able to divulge much, if any, of that info. But her man would be down with it, and even understanding about what she could share. He'd put her above all else and love her no matter what. *Yeah, right...dream on, bitch. Dream on,* she scolded herself. One has to get close to another before one will ever know, which meant letting one's guard down. *But a girl still hasta dream–right?* Of course, but that's where she differed from almost everyone else; she didn't have time, nor did she possess the patience, to nurture a relationship. The closest thing Iax ever got to one was with a cute kid in high school. The moment he saw how advanced she was, not only academically, but also in physical sports, he got butt-hurt and bailed. They'd never even made out, let alone *done the deed.* Nope, 'cause she always freaked out members of the opposite sex, without meaning to or even trying.

She may have a dream or maybe even two, but that's where she drew the line, like several large, bright-red lines drawn in the blinding-white sand in the form of: 'TRUST ME, YOU DON'T WANT ME! RUN FAST AND FAR THE OTHER WAY!' Shaking that off, she turned to give her full attention to the woman who continually saved her ass.

Chapter Ten

"S'up, Gemma? Where are we, and what're we doing here?" Gemma turned her dazzling, joy-filled gaze on Iax, obviously proud of having the right answers. Iax had to return a real smile, and that single moment helped her snap out of the shock, funk, or whatever it was she'd been in. She already felt like she could breathe easier, and she pulled in a full, satisfying breath.

Iax's mouth and throat were parched, so she reached down to extract her canteen from her pack where it lay on the ground nearby the tree stump where she sat. After taking a couple long swigs, amazed anew at how cold and refreshing the water tasted every time she drank it, she then offered it to Gemma. Once they'd both taken their fill of the life-giving liquid, they got down to business.

Facing each other with serious expressions and sitting on matching tree stumps, Gemma appeared ready to do biz. The woman never wasted time getting right down to it. Another quality Iax respected about her friend, she didn't fuck around, but jumped in with both feet, and got down to the bones of the matter at hand. This particular matter wasn't good, in fact, it was enormous and fucked up, to be precise.

"All right. This is the territory where Mazar and his Weyr reside. Just over there behind where you are sitting, and several yards beyond your line of vision is a cliff. Do *not* go near that cliff without me. Am I clear on this, Iax?" Determined to see to Iax's safety, she patiently waited for the vow.

"Yes, of course, Gemma. I will not even *think* about going near it by myself, trust me. I promise you this," Iax said immediately.

Surprised, Gemma went on, "Well, that really was quite easier than I expected. I appreciate your cooperation, Iax," she said smiling. "Now, my senses and sources have told me Mazar is to be placed in their Chief's dungeon until a decision can be made regarding his actions. There are those who believe he should be given leniency, and of course, those who feel he should be executed immediately. It will become a very ugly situation either way. Our mission is to slip in and get Yoren out, of before Mazar's fate has been decided upon, then be well on our way and out of reach before anyone knows we were ever here. How does that sound? Easy as bread?"

Despite the tenuous position they were in, a laugh escaped Iax before she could stifle it. "Sounds like a great plan to me, Gemma. And, yes, easy as *bread, pie,* or whichever," Iax returned, not really wanting to correct the woman. They hadn't laughed for a while so it was a pleasant and unexpected moment of humor they both needed. "So, where do we begin? I wanna get this done with already. Please, say I get to do something to that punk-bitch, Mazar? Pretty please?" Iax batted her lashes, innocently smiling.

"I would prefer you not, but I already know how you are. Once you get an idea into your head, you do not let it go. I suppose we shall have to wait and see what happens," Gemma chided. "We are going over to the cliff I just mentioned, staying back from the ledge a safe distance, and we shall spy on the area first. We need to figure out who goes where, when, for how long, and what they do. Once we know their routines, we will make our move. Can you do that?" Lifting her chin, she gave Iax a proud smile, knowing her plan was a sound one.

After taking in their surroundings for a few moments, Iax slowly nodded her head, surprised that her 'warrior braid' was, in fact, still holding quite well. Why she took that particular moment to think about her hair, she honestly didn't know. Since her 'fall,' it was still difficult to concentrate from time to time. Perplexed by the random thoughts running unbidden through her mind, Iax shrugged, more to herself than anyone else, *I'm so tired, I wish I could sleep for a few hours. Where the hell did that come from?* It was so unlike her. She had a hard enough time sleeping the night through, let alone contemplating a nap. She realized Gemma was expecting her to reply. "Yeah, sounds great. Let's get a move on, then. I seriously wanna get this damn thing done. I don't feel bad, or altogether good, but not quite like my regular self, and I just wanna do this and go home," she murmured.

Gemma raised a questioning brow at her, as if she didn't like what she was seeing and hearing. Iax thought she might be more of a liability in her present state of mind, and she didn't like the way that made her feel. She needed to get moving, shake it off, and then everything would work itself out. At least, she sure as hell hoped so. "This really sucks," she grumbled.

****

Tired, bored, and frustrated at having to stay in the same uncomfortable lie-on-your-belly position for so long, she'd had it. *Iax don't do boring.* Action was her gig, and she was currently in severe need of some damn action. "Let's just go in and get the dick-weed!" she hissed out in a loud whispered to her cohort. Her mood and implacable need to do something was driving her nuts. When Gemma gave her the evil-eye, she tossed the woman an innocent 'what did I do?' look.

They had been hunkered down for at least a couple hours in the same exact spot, lying on the ground at the edge of the wooded area. Iax needed to move; even just a small stretching of her arms and legs would be gratifying. Her plan was to just roll over, knowing if she sat or stood, it might draw unwanted attention to them from the various peeps milling around in the village below them.

Just as she was rolling over onto her back, she suddenly felt a strong pull—or more like compulsion as it had been explained to her—to sit up. *What the fuck is this?* she wondered. Not thrilled at the prospect of some suck-ass trying to hole-up rent free in her head, she tried to shake it off. The more she tried, the more she couldn't form any real thoughts; she could think, but nothing that made any sense.

All of a sudden, she felt her heart slam almost painfully inside her chest. *Holy shit!* Not liking whatever was happening, Iax willed herself to remain on her belly. It was an effort, but she managed. Sharply shaking her head and trying to dispel whatever the hell was going on, she slid a sideways glance to her left, needing visual confirmation that Gemma was alright. Thankfully, she was, so Iax turned her gaze back to the direction in which she was supposed to be paying attention.

Scooting on her elbows to keep herself low, she used her upper body strength to slowly pull herself forward, still trying to avoid being noticed. Creeping to the edge of the cliff to peer down into the valley below, short flickers of memories came rushing back at Iax like a tidal wave, assailing her physically and emotionally. Gasping, she pressed her body flat on the ground again and squeezed her eyes tightly shut.

She envisioned the cabin her and Gemma had stayed in that first night, and then the vision changed to when she'd been running through the thick forest, faster than she should have been able. Even though she hadn't heard anything at the time, she could now detect a strange, strong pull telling her to go the other way. Sensing that the pull was evil, or at least ugly, she had fought and pushed through.

Suddenly, she saw herself falling from the cliff-top as if she was watching from above; she was spinning, arms and legs flailing like she could somehow find purchase midair. Then, she seemed to be closing in way too fast on the ground when she felt a sharp *bump* underneath her body, just before the lights went out. That must have been when Gemma buffered her fall, as she'd told Iax. It had hurt like a bitch, but it also had saved her life so she couldn't get too upset. Her entire body shuddered at those painful memories, and even though seeing it hadn't been fun, at least now she better understood what had happened. Iax always liked to see things for herself; the good, the bad, and the ugly.

Breathe, you can do this. That's in the past and Gemma's right here. You're safe so breathe, bitch, just breathe. You're trained to get past this kinda shit, she tried to reassure herself. Although her trepidation would be considered valid by pretty much anyone, she didn't especially enjoy it. Fear and anxiety weren't things she'd ever played well with, or experienced on a regular basis.

Grateful that she didn't remember most of her horrible fall, just the thought itself still bothered her far more than she'd ever admit out loud. Besides, she was still a respectable two-feet clear of the ledge, she was fine. She took another deep breath. After a few mental slaps to bolster herself, Iax reopened her eyes and swallowed the lump in her throat. Lines of sweat trickle down several areas of her suddenly overheated body, but she needed to concentrate on the scene below, so she pushed those things aside.

The compulsion thing was finally gone, but she couldn't have changed the direction of her gaze any more than she could have changed the weather. Just then, her heart slammed painfully inside her chest at the exact moment her eyes locked onto a man. *Dude's fucking hot!* Needing to shake *it* off before *it* even started, Iax tried, she truly did, to look away hoping to find something, anything else to stare at or focus on—not drool over—since she was on a jay-oh-bee, and all. Try as she might, there was no tearing her gaze from the perfection of his form. She sighed.

Clipping along at a ground eating pace in long, purposeful strides, he walked down the middle of a dirt road lined with small, tidy homes on either side. Whoever he was, his large, muscular frame was difficult to *not* look at. Such confidence, his body exuded a sangfroid-air making it even harder to look away.

Hottie suddenly stopped, staggered, and lifted his head. And all she could do was gawk at him like an utter fucking idiot. Iax was captured, mesmerized by his every sleek move. Her breath hitched, his eyes slowly drew themselves directly to hers. Even the one-hundred or so yards separating them were not enough to extinguish the hot, magnetic pull that was bouncing back and forth between them. His eyes, haunted and sad as they now appeared, were still the most beautiful, shade of deep emerald-green Iax had ever seen. He was breathtaking and enormous. Everything from his long, wavy, dark-golden hair to the tips of his leather-clad feet was incredible and to-die-for hot.

Every. Single. Inch. Licking her dry lips, she audibly groaned.

Suddenly warming more, much beyond what the climate warranted, she thought she might melt on the spot like a candle burning itself down to nothing; a pool of Iax was all that would be left, if something didn't change. If she didn't find a way to stop staring, ogling, and flat-out, blatantly drooling over this man. *And, now. Now would be peachy, idiot!* she chastised herself.

She shook her head and closed her eyes again, an attempt to refocus and try to force his image from her mind. Who was he, and why the hell was she reacting like this? Furthermore, where had he been all her life? *Ugh! Knock it the fuck off, hoe-bag! We're not even the same species. But does it even matter? Seriously, enough's-a-fucking-nuff, already!*

This is insane! She shouldn't be here. Suddenly, and for the first time in her life Iax felt a strong urge to leave. To run as fast and far away from this place as her legs would carry her from *him,* to go home…to *her* home. But her legs took on a consistency oddly similar to Jello. Still, she *could* try. She certainly *should* try.

She couldn't keep her eyes closed, and of course when she reopened them, her sights honed in on him again. *You've got to be kidding me!* she reprimanded herself. Everything inside of her was screaming, warning bells rang loudly inside her head. She actually saw red flags popping up in her mind's eye. The only thing that stayed her from bolting, was the gentle hand Gemma placed upon her left forearm. She hadn't even been aware of her friend's movement.

Iax's eyes still refused to cooperate and not settle on the dude, who was once again in motion below them. Even hearing Gemma's voice laced with sincere concern, didn't help her to look away from him.

"What is this, Iax? You are shaking and sweating. Why? What are you feeling?" Narrowing a worried, suspicious gaze on Iax, Gemma did not know *what,* only that something of a considerable nature was undoubtedly happening to her friend. *What could be the matter?* she wondered, deeply concerned.

Giving Iax the time she obviously needed to gather herself and her thoughts, Gemma let her own gaze roam over the village below their perch. At once, she saw the problem, or rather, the male. *Oh, no!* Before Iax was able to form an answer, Gemma spoke quickly knowing she must take control of this situation before it was too late. "Iax, look at me now, please! Me! Over here!" she cried out in a hushed whisper, completely baffled and unsure of what to do even if she could draw Iax's attention away from the male. *Nothing.* Iax's continued to stare him. She must save her friend.

Never one to give up, Gemma gave it another try. "You must not look upon that male! Can you hear me? Pay heed to my words, please!" Panic filled Gemma's oddly tight voice as she shook Iax's arm with more strength than she normally would have, attempting to get her attention, thought still with no response, at all. "Iax! Please, come away from here now! We must depart! We should have never come here! Let us go now!" she was pleading, beseeching, even begging her friend to look away from the male, for Iax to come away before it was too late. Sadly, her fervent entreaty heeded nothing.

Gemma was not fully certain, though she had a good enough idea—even if it should be impossible—Iax and the male appeared to be Bonding. She already felt a strong connection forming, fairly crackling in the air around them. Even more bothersome, was what she detected with her overly sensitive hearing; she clearly detected her friend's rapid heartbeat, and the male's, as well as the syncopation taking place between the two. However, neither Iax nor the male seemed capable of thought, in deed, they seemed to be entirely oblivious as to what was taking place between them. Discomfort was overwhelming them both, neither was able to focus or fight whatever was happening.

The male's heartbeat was unusually strong, compared to Iax's much softer one. Yet, the rhythm, the very beating of their hearts now took on the same pace and strength. Perfect synchronization; Iax's heartbeat slightly softened the male's, as his subtly strengthened hers, until it was as if they shared only one heart between them.

Oh no, this is not good! I must get Iax out of this place, now! Unless is it already too late.... What does it all mean, anyway? Was this yet another symptom of this shifter species, when they found their Truemates, one we have not yet heard of? Gemma forlornly speculated.

Iax was not from here; she was of another species and this simply could not be…impossible. Why, then, was Gemma already sinking back down onto her stomach feeling as though she had just failed the biggest, most crucial task ever given to her in her entire, long life? Pain burned deep in the pit of her belly and the center of her heart. Gemma knew her appeals would do no good now. It was too late. She was too late.

****

Mazar quickly walked to his Chief's holdings, hoping to make it there as unnoticed as possible. Fairly certain his days were at an end, he felt a bit relieved; almost happy, even. Finally, no more of the torments, no more pain or sleepless nights. He should have felt sad, or at least guiltier than he currently did. He had misused his position, lied to his fellow warriors, his lifelong friends – yet here he was feeling better and more confident than he had in… so long, he could not even recall the last time he felt this good.

Deep down, he felt a strong need to search out each male who had gone with and aided him in his selfish, stupid plan. Then, he would apologize to them, and invite them to witness his rightful, long overdue death. Thus, he knew it would be wrong. He knew they would all be furious with him, and rightly so. He also knew, just as with Frayier, they would most likely show him understanding and possibly even forgiveness. He did not deserve such things. Not from any of them.

As he walked down the road he lived on, the exact road he grew up on, memories assailed him; playing, running, laughing, and enjoying the freedom and fun of younglings. Though he still had to practice his battle skills every day, he had been granted playtime each day, too. He and his playmates—many of his current fellow-warriors—would play long into the night, chasing each other and kicking rocks for the sport of distance, endurance, and aim. A favorite memory of his was when they all gathered to swim in the large, calm areas which pooled in many places along the side of the river they lived near.

A laugh escaped him at those memories, the clean fun of his youth. Letting that feeling wrap around him, it warmed him as did the loving, comforting hugs he used to get treated to by his long-passed mother when he had been so much younger; apparently much smarter, as well. Never would he have done something as foolhardy and unforgivable as what he had just done; abducting an innocent, worthy, *Mated* female.

Perhaps Meynix *will see fit to have the Chief finalize my execution before Gordell arrives.* But there would be no circumvention regarding his fate; something which would have to be earned, something he was obviously not capable or deserving of. Execution at the hands of your own warriors was far preferable over what the undoubtedly enraged and—if he must be honest with himself, now would be the right time for such reconciliations—worthy male would order to have done to him. Or worse, yet still understandably well-deserved, what the male would do to him with his own bare hands.

After a bit of clear thought, Mazar concluded that had he ever been blessed to find his own Truemate and anyone did the same to him, he would insist upon something grueling, inducing the worst sort of pain. Pain he would make certain lasted, possibly by slowly —very slowly—ripping their head off with his bare hands. A shudder ran through him at the thought. Simultaneously, something else, an unfamiliar feeling ran through his body, and its strength made him stagger. Instinctively, he lifted his head. *What is this I feel?* he wondered. It felt like a jolt of some sort, strong enough to lift the hairs all over his body that made them tingle.

Just then up on top of the cliff overlooking his Weyr territory, he spotted something strange. A female. A stunning, *unfamiliar* female. Their eyes locked upon each other's and he felt a strong, sudden urge to run as fast as he could to reach her. *Lying on her belly on the ground, and so close to the ledge? The female looks as stunned as I feel. Who is she, and what is she doing on that cliff? Does she not realize how dangerous such a position can be?* were his initial thoughts.

His next thoughts were far different yet still welcome, even if they were also a bit disconcerting. His entire body stiffened, and his blood roared in his ears as he lengthened uncomfortably inside his breeches. *What is this?* As alarm began to overtake and cloud his mind, his heart thudded dangerously hard inside of him, making it ache so that he reached up to clutch at his chest.

Is she a witchling here to be-spell me? Was she sent here by Gordell to punish me for my actions? he pondered. Unsure as he was about that, he knew he deserved whatever was to be meted out to him. Still, he could not shake the uneasy feeling the thought gave him, because of her; that female. He needed to reach her, find out who she was and what she was doing here. He may also give her a much needed, stern set-down about the dangers of lurking high upon cliff-tops, as she was doing in such a careless manner at the moment.

If only his chest would cease paining him, and his body would uncoil. His breeches were now stretched even more tightly over his painfully swelling groin. A molten, sizzling, almost unbearable heat lay heavily over his entire lower region, stirring feelings of which he had never experienced, to this degree. Mazar had been with many beautiful females in his long life. And though he would not admit this, it had been quite some time since he had allowed himself the pleasures of losing himself inside of a soft, giving female body.

Carnal thoughts were racing through his mind at a dizzying speed; he did not understand what was happening to him. The unfamiliar depths of these emotions were altogether foreign, and he unsure of what to do with, or about, them. He was supposed to be going to see his Chief, most likely to be imprisoned and then executed. *That* was the honorable thing to do. That *was* the plan. Why, then, was he suddenly feeling an overwhelming urge to bolt?

The want, no, the *need* to be near this female whom he was already certain would be as no other before her in all of his time, was overwhelming. Not only that, but Mazar also needed to *touch* this female, to *feel* her warm, bare skin against his own, all of which was becoming almost unbearably hot under his clothing. He must find a way to run his fingers through her hair. Even though it was plaited, he could still see how the sunlight glistened off its shiny length as it would were it spun gold. He imagined it most certainly had to be softer than silk, and would even bet everything he had—though it was not much—that it smelled like flowers and sunshine. He had to go to her. He *should* go see his Chief, but how could he follow through with that now?

Unable as he was to force his feet to move the direction in which they should, before he could stop himself, his traitorous feet and legs were moving toward the path which would lead him to the cliff-top. To *her.*

Chapter Eleven

As Yoren sat in the humble home of two of the nicest shifters she had ever had the privilege to meet, she began to feel shame and embarrassment, for how she had always taken everything in her blessed life for granted. *Meynix* had always answered her prayers. Her family had never gone without anything, indeed, they had always had much of everything. They had been wasteful when she had not even realized it.

She had eaten ravenously from the plate a quiet, shy female had placed in front of her on the family's eating table. Tearing into the meat, vegetables, and soup as though she had never eaten before, she rather felt that she had not. It had been a few days, in truth, since she had eaten anything of real substance. The meager fare was surprisingly exceptional, and very tasty. Everything had been perfectly prepared.

The drink strain they had served her was one she had never before tasted. She had quickly drank several servings, or rather, gulped would be a more appropriate description of how she had tackled the absolutely delicious liquid. Unable to resist as she was, its crisp, fruity flavor was simply that good. Already, she was planning to find out the mixing-plan.

She had finished her foods and drink, and was almost tempted to lick her cup dry when Jolsynn came back into the room. Seating herself in the chair across the small wooden table from Yoren, she noticed that the female-young appeared somewhat more relaxed than she had been upon their arrival. Yet, there was something…else, something Yoren could not place. The female was attempting hard to hide her feelings. She must still be upset over her own Weyr being involved in the abduction, and that Yoren was carrying.

Before Yoren could voice her worrisome thoughts, another female came from the bedchambers area to join them in the small eating-quarters. This one looked to be older, wiser, and obviously mother to the female-young. Yoren could see striking similarities in the two; equally beautiful, and a mutually intuitive trait of being able to easily puzzle things out and read one in many ways; was her immediate sense. *This is the 'simple healer'?* Yoren questioned silently.

"Mother, this be Lady Yoren. She is Royalty and the female that nasty, rotten—" She was abruptly cut off.

The mother came to Yoren and clasped her hands into both of her own. "It is a pleasure to meet you, Lady Yoren. I am Toralynn, and I am pleased to have you in our home." The female bowed low over their clasped hands, to pay her respects to Yoren. This humbled and made her feel unworthy, after how they were receiving and caring for her as a female and a fellow-shifter. "Would you kindly allow me the honor of tending your wounds, Lady Yoren? I am well-adept at simple healings here in my home, as I have the supplies necessary on hand. I am able to do more serious healings, but not here. Do you have any serious injuries?"

She was well-spoken, a worthy female, Yoren realized. Not a typical villager and obviously from a strong lineage. *Why would she be here, living as a villager?* Yoren asked herself. The more time she spent in the presence of these females, the more her curiosity mounted; questions were piling up in her mind, but for now she would give them the honor and courtesy of doing what they were evidently so proud to do. "If it pleases you, Toralynn, there is no need for formalities, you must call me Yoren. I welcome your offer to tend me, as you can see, my wrists are the worst of my injuries. They were bound with a length of rough-rope for the whole of our journey, until your young freed me from the restraints. They obviously feel better now, but they still pain me somewhat. My thanks for everything, I appreciate your kindness. All the foods and drink were very appetizing, and I feel much better now," Yoren finished, then stood and returned the female's bow as a sign of her own respect.

In a moment of shared female companionship and mutual respect, Toralynn beamed a bright, proud smile, which lit up her face. It made her look even younger and more beautiful. Yoren could not help but return a smile. Something else passed between them, and Yoren felt that she would forever know this family who had befriended her. She felt welcome, safe, and comfortable in their home, almost as if there was some kind of connection between them.

Why would I fell that with these strangers? she briefly pondered.

Before she could think further, the females each took an arm and gently guided her toward the back of their home. "We shall get you bathed first. I cannot imagine those brutes allowed you even that simple courtesy! No matter, you shall feel back to rights in no time, with a lovely hot bath and mother's healing herbs!" Jolsynn exclaimed. Her pride of caring for 'Royalty' shone bright on her comely, youthful face.

"A bath would be most welcome. And you are correct, Jolsynn, I certainly did not get such a luxury on our travels," Yoren softly laughed in sarcasm. She knew she could speak freely here, and even though she always had such a freedom, it somehow seemed different with them. She felt as if a massive weight had been lifted from her recently heavily-burdened shoulders. As if she could even breathe better, more fully. Such an easy, peaceful thing, for which she was most grateful, as both females joined in her laughter.

****

It felt like hours had passed, maybe even days, since Iax first spotted Hot-Dude. Still lying on her belly and feeling like she was in a trance, she kinda felt like a peeping-fucking-Tammy but she couldn't move a muscle. She could hear Gemma's pleas, and she wanted to turn and acknowledge the woman, she honestly did, but how does one do that when one can't move? *What's wrong with me, who is he, and why the hell do I feel like cement? This is stupid!*

Total bullshit! At least she hadn't lost her edge, her armor; her tongue. Mentally, anyway.

All of a sudden, and of their own volition, her hands moved to wipe at her sweaty face. *It's about time,* she thought, annoyed and relieved. Then she noticed Hot-Dude still on the move. Only now, he was moving toward the side of the mountain they were perched upon. *Where's he going?* She had the strongest urge to yell out to him and ask who he was. She really wanted—*needed*—to know. Then, just as fast as she had noticed him, he was out of her sight. *Where'd he go?* She sighed.

Iax had never, not once in her life, had this kind of reaction to any man. Ever. *Why now, and why him? What was so remarkable about him?* It was painfully clear that something about him was remarkable. He was what these shifters called a 'warrior' through and through, and she suddenly had a new, profound respect for warriors. Well, more accurately, for *this* particular warrior.

Of course, she'd seen hot dudes, many and maybe even a few hotter than him. Wait, no way. Impossible. *Never mind,* she scolded herself. It didn't matter. This…situation had been weird from the get-go, but now it had escalated to alarmingly out-there. Get in, do the job, then get the fuck outta Dodge. It had always been that easy. They were already running way behind. They should've had Yoren out of there and home, before Gordell's warriors even had time to come for her. That was the plan, and nobody from either camp—other than Yoren—would ever know they had even been there.

And now this; never, ever had she come across a man, or 'male' who had tempted her like this. Not even on Earth. This was totally outside her field of expertise, so many questions swirled around inside her brain, so many things she wanted to do, things she needed to know. Shaking her head, she was in serious need of some self-control. What had happened to that? Iax always had self-control. Nobody had ever rattled her cage or shook her up like this.

Hoping she could at least speak now, she turned to make sure Gemma was still there and that she wasn't still freaking out. Not that she blamed her. She attempted to clear her throat to speak, hoping to get a better grip on things. "Hey, Gemma, I–I…. What the hell's going on? I don't know what's happening, you got anything to offer that could maybe help me, like, how long we've been up here, and who Hot-Dude is–you know, the male who was down there a minute ago?" Brows raised, she tilted her head in the direction of where he'd just been walking. "How long has this…*thing* been going on? And why do I have this burning feeling down here?" She reached down to touch the right-front side of her hip. It burned and had for a while now. It wasn't especially painful, but it smarted some.

She didn't realize she'd been rambling, and wasn't even sure what all she had just said or asked. Gemma was staring slack-jawed at her as if she wasn't sure what to do, or say. *Strange…really fucking strange,* she thought. The woman had an odd look in her eyes; one that said she wanted to grab Iax and run fast and far away with her. She looked scared. *Gemma, scared? This is new.* Iax had never seen such a fearful and confusing expression on her friend before. It didn't take away from her beautiful countenance, but it did make her look older and worn out, which was also new. All of it worried Iax; this was not how things were supposed to go.

Feeling guilty, Iax wanted to soothe Gemma. But how? Pondering it for a moment, she realized the need to remain hidden was kind of moot, now. Nobody else was wandering around down in the village, and Hot-Dude was out of sight, so Iax stood up. It took a minute—tight as her muscles had become—being in the same position for so long had cramped her entire body. She stretched, bent, and leaned over to each side, then to her front, and backward. Her spine popped and cracked, instantly relieving some of the pressure.

Taking a few deep, cleansing breaths she walked the couple of feet to stand next to where Gemma still lay on the ground. She hadn't moved at all, just remained lying there watching every move Iax made as if she were expecting her to do something crazy. "Hey, you. Come on, get up." She offered a hand to help Gemma rise. Surely Gemma was at least a little stiff, too.

****

Eyeing Iax as if she were a fascinating yet venomous snake, Gemma slowly, tentatively took the female's proffered hand and accepted the aid to gain her feet. She was a bit stiff, but not in pain. Thankfully, Gemma did not suffer the normal aches and pains most beings did, especially those of Iax's kind. Although, of late it seemed that Iax was different from even her own kind, as she had just been contemplating. She pushed the thought aside, for now.

She slowly, cautiously stood and released her friend's hand to dust off her front side. She had heard each concern and question Iax had voiced moments ago, yet she still was not fully certain she had the answers her friend was seeking. Still in shock over what she had witnessed, Gemma was almost afraid to verbalize any of her own thoughts. In reality, it was obvious that the nature of whatever had just passed between Iax and her 'Hot-Dude' was of the utmost importance, and something Gemma was not comfortable even speaking about.

Wanting to approach the delicate matter carefully, Gemma needed to comfort Iax, yet she did not believe what she had to say would accomplish that. The female had a feral look in her eyes, as if she wanted to be away from here with all due haste. She did not blame her friend, she felt the same way. Her primary concern was the male who was making his way to them now, or more specifically, making his way to Iax; it was a discomfiting thought. She wanted to get Iax out of here. But how, and where could they go? He would reach them soon, in a matter of moments, to be sure. She had used up a large amount of the energy that fueled her abilities, when she got herself and Iax away from those large, green creatures in the other woods. There would be no way to move in that manner again for quite some time.

"Ah, well, I am…I have—" Gemma was stammering, which never happened. Clearing her throat, she made another attempt. *Clearing my throat? I never do that, either.* She frowned. "I believe the male we saw is coming our, or rather, *your* way as we speak, Iax.

I am afraid to voice my thoughts to you. Are you sure you are prepared to hear what I have to say? I could be mistaken, but I do not believe so," she finished, giving Iax a moment to be certain she truly wanted to hear her out.

"I'm sure. I need to know something so if you have any ideas, I'm all ears. Please, spill." Having heard the expression before, Gemma knew what it meant, so she would oblige her. But Iax was suddenly behaving even more oddly, pulling the right-front side of her breeches down to look at something under the garment. Gemma's breath caught in her throat.

Slowly, Iax revealed a mark upon her flesh. *A butterfly… burnt into her flesh?* Gemma's heart plummeted, just before her body collapsed to the ground she had just risen from.

"What the *fuck?* This is…is it? Is this what you were talking about, Gemma? Why the hell do I have a butterfly *burnt* into my flesh?" Iax was in shock, outraged, and thoroughly taken aback at this revelation. How could this even be possible? *It can't be, I'm not from here! I'm not one of them!* Iax couldn't think. She was under the impression that the image would burn into the flesh of a *shifter,* and that it didn't even happen until *after* the whole 'kiss' thing. Like, *days* after.

Shaking her head back and forth in total denial and shock, she was backing up, moving away from Gemma, from the cliff, wanting to remove herself from everyone and everything. *How…?* All she had now was questions. Her head suddenly snapped up as she felt the air moving, shifting all around her. There was a heavy presence crackling in the air, filling and heating it up. Iax sweating renewed and began to pour off her body, which had suddenly become even hotter than before. Her skin felt like it was wrapped too tightly over her bones and muscles. *Him…*it had to be. He was almost here–he'd come for her.

What the hell was she supposed to do now? She felt like a deer trapped in the headlights of a Mac truck. This couldn't be happening, not to her. She had to go and leave this place. She started running with no real direction in mind, since she didn't know her way around here, anyway. All she knew was that she had to go. *Now. Run fast, and far away!*

The butterfly that had burnt itself into her flesh was heating more painfully now. She could barely pull in a full breath and her side was cramping, which was new for her. With each step it felt like her feet were struggling through mud, water, or something thick and sludge-like. Out of nowhere, she ran smack dab into a tree-trunk—a damn big one—and it hurt, too! *Where the hell did that come from?* she wondered, lying on her back on the ground and unable to get up, due to the whole not-able-to-breathe thing. Oh, and she couldn't leave out the lovely side cramps. "What's wrong with me?" she asked out loud.

Twigs and leaves crunched a short distance behind where her head lay on the ground. Startled as she was, Iax still couldn't raise her head to see who or what was coming. Praying to everything Holy that it was Gemma, she squeezed her eyes tightly shut, willing away the hot tears already streaming from them. A laugh bubbled up inside her at the memory of Gemma's 'eye leaking' thing. There was no real humor in the action, maybe more resignation than anything else.

What difference did it make now, anyway? Almost positive she was already fucked, and not in a good way, she didn't try to move or take in her surroundings. *Lying down feels pretty good, I think I'll stay right here. Maybe I'll get lucky and just die,* was her last thought before the inky darkness enfolded her in its arms, and everything around her faded away.

Chapter Twelve

Darkan and his troupes had finally reached the territory to where Chief Gordell's Truemate had been secreted away. They would have shifted into their Dragon-forms and simply taken flight, but this was intended to be a surprise attack. Other Weyr along the way could have sent word ahead, tipping off the other Weyr to their imminent arrival. Word always traveled much faster than one would expect in the Dragon Cove Realm.

It would have been impossible to miss over two-hundred highly colorful, fully-shifted Dragons inflight from various views. Thus, choosing this specific route had enabled them to make the journey they all had agreed upon, even though it was a long, hot, tiring one. It had also allowed them to carry provisions all the way on foot, for the sake of self-preservation and to remain hidden. If they had been found by an unfriendly Weyr, it could have been difficult, or worse, to explain away their presence and intentions.

They had received word of that fool Mazar, and his stupendously idiotic plan to abduct Yoren, thinking he could somehow quiet the torments he had long suffered from not yet finding his own Truemate. *What a heap of shite! The male was insane, and most likely in the literal sense,* Darkan fumed to himself.

Darkan's original plan was to come at Mazar from all sides, and force him to surrender and hand Yoren over to Darkan and his warriors. But since discovering how he had tricked his own fellow warriors and even friends, into helping him carry out his ridiculous scheme, Darkan had changed his plan, as well. They had sent word ahead a couple hours ago to Chief Zarckael of Weyr Treuamarias, notifying him of their impending arrival, not wanting any surprises on either side since the game plan had changed. Now, they could walk directly to the Chief's holdings and demand Mazar be turned over to them. After all the formalities, they would find Yoren and everyone could return to their own territory.

An eye for an eye, or something of that nature; the fool male cannot be allowed to go unpunished for his crimes. The well-known fact that Yoren was Royalty, and the not-so-well-known fact that she was carrying Gordell's youngling; both in the forefront of Darkan's mind, made Mazar's crimes all the worse. For all practical purposes as Darkan had previously surmised, Mazar had already signed his own death order. They could rightfully kill him on sight, even right here in this territory. But Darkan had other plans; he would bring the male back to their territory, and allow Gordell to have a crack at him. Of course, as long as Yoren was all right Gordell would not kill the male, although Darkan would not blame him, if he did.

Perhaps they would play with him and drive him truly insane, then send him on his way. Gordell was not certain yet which path they would take, his duty and primary concern now was to find a whole and hale Yoren. If her skin was marred with even a scratch, Darkan would kill the male on the spot.

"Let us go to this Chief Zarckael, he should be expecting us," he prodded his warriors. "Too bad, is it not, that our plan had to change? It would have been much more fun and rewarding to come in here from all directions and cause a real stir!" he declared to the males closest to him. All he received were a few grunts of agreement and head nods. Wanting to laugh at the lot of these surly, battle-hardened warriors and their communication abilities—or lack thereof—Darkan resisted the urge. No hardened warrior ever took well to being laughed at, or about. Inside, however, he was rolling with laughter. "Madmen! All of you!" he voiced aloud mostly to himself, shaking his head in amusement.

They would never change. Even the Mated ones who mutually flirted with their Truemates, unable to stay their hands from one another as they laughed and carried on, much like younglings when they were home. Not in this, nor in any serious situation, though. You could never find a more feral, loyal, and dangerous pack of warriors. They had more honor than anyone Darkan had ever met. Even though he had lived with the same Weyr most of his long life, he was not born nor was he raised there.

He had come across plenty of drifters, grifters, and shady beings in his time, which made him all the more grateful for these males with whom he now banded together. They always had, and forever would, fight at each other's backs. No exceptions. In truth, he was a bit relieved that they would not be fighting this day. Even though they possessed the endurance and longevity to live for so long, he was beginning to feel older in his bones. It did not mean he could *not* fight; it merely meant that given a choice, he would *wait* and fight another day, saving his strength and energy for future physical demands. And they would come as they never ceased for long, which meant a male must take his rest when and where he could.

Reaching the gatehouse, he announced himself and his troupes. The Chief must have received their message, as they were granted passage without delay. As they entered the bailey, several rough and capable warriors escorted Darkan and his warriors inside Chief Zarckael's large, opulent holdings. After climbing a wooden staircase, they were led through a massive set of heavy-wooden doors. Inside was a sizable Great Hall, obviously much used.

A few comely maidens rushed about with drinks and various foods, for a long overdue repast, of which his warriors were in need and fully appreciated. Offering his thanks, Darkan dismissed them with a wave of his hand as they awaited the Chief. They were not the type to steal, nor did they require the companionship.

Hoping the Chief would not make them wait overlong; Darkan was a patient male, but not in these settings. They had just made a long, arduous journey, and needed to head back as soon as possible, and of course, with Mazar and Yoren in-tow.

By the time the Chief finally saw fit to make his appearance, Darkan and his warriors had eaten and drank everything that had been set out. During the Chief's lengthy lapse in punctuality, Darkan heard some of the plans the others were itching to carry out, and he was grateful for the male's arrival. Darkan took several deep, calming breaths hoping his males would also calm, and for this meeting to be advantageous for both sides.

The Chief marched up to Darkan and extended his right arm in a warrior's greeting. Reaching out, Darkan accepted the proffered honor, clasping the Chief's forearm near his elbow. Their shake was firm; always a telling sign and a strong first impression. The male's demeanor seemed to be respectful and honorable, both traits went a long way with someone like Darkan, and would aid them in dealing with their unpleasant business.

"Darkan, I take it?" the Chief asked, still clasping Darkan's arm.

"Yes, that is correct. How shall I address you?" Darkan returned.

The formidable warriors released each other, and took a step back to appraise one another in a non-threatening manner; it was the warrior way to always size up a potential opponent. Although Darkan did not truly believe that was the case, old habits were impossible to quash, especially for their kind, living as long as they did.

Chief Zarckael was a large male, all muscle, wide shoulders, and taller than Darkan, who was usually one of the tallest amongst males. His eyes were an almost eerie shade of hazel-green. His dark, golden-brown hair was pulled back and neatly bound at his nape. All outward appearances told his tale: The male liked cleanliness and neatness. *A good, respectable trait, and one I practice myself,* Darkan thoughtfully admired momentarily. They had much bigger issues to work out.

"I am Chief Zarckael Treuamarias, of Weyr Treuamarias. But you must simply address me as Zarckael, no need for formalities. I am not your Chief, and it would be nonsense for you all to address me as such. If it pleases you, let us sit so we can eat, drink, and discuss matters. Hopefully all will be well with the outcome of the precarious situation we seem to be in." He waved a hand toward the long-benches, a gesture for Darkan's warriors to reclaim their seats.

Busy with the Chief as Darkan had been, it had escaped his noticed when, to a man, his warriors had risen upon Zarckael's entry. He was most proud of their honorable display of respect, one that could go a long way for them all. Fighting a smile, he knew they were awaiting *him* to give the go-ahead. With a small nod, they all settled back onto their benches.

"Many thanks for your hospitality, Zarckael. We appreciate your meeting with us here in your grand holdings, but we were already served while awaiting your arrival," Darkan countered. "Now, let us not tarry as we have a long journey home. We should deal with this matter swiftly so we can return." His expression darkened. "With Yoren, and of course, your Mazar," he finished resolutely.

Zarckael eyed him for long moments, obviously contemplating their situation. He had not expected such a showing, though he was not surprised. He had never heard an ill word spoken about Gordell or any of his Weyr, and most certainly not about any of these warriors. He immediately respected Gordell's choice of his First; the male was a worthy one, anyone could see that.

He had given the serious matter much thought, and yes, he had expected them to demand he hand Mazar over to them. However, he was of a mind that they could reach a fair, reasonable compromise both sides could agree upon and live with; one which allowed Mazar to remain here, where he belonged. Whether the male was wrong, which he was, or crazed, as was now suspected, whichever the case, Zarckael was not willing to sway on the matter. As Chief to this Weyr he had always dealt swiftly and effectively with his own warriors himself, here within his own territory.

As time stretched on, Darkan began to think the Chief may not answer him. Or worse, would not hand over the criminal who had stolen Yoren, which was not optional. It was a matter of honor, an unwritten code. Mazar had crossed a line which could not be uncrossed and there would be no debating, it simply was what it was.

Just as Darkan was about to speak, Zarckael replied, "I understand your position. Mazar was most definitely in the wrong and needs to be punished appropriately, but how do I know you will even allow him to live?" he asked, his hazel-green eyes darkening more by the moment at their weighty predicament.

"I cannot promise you that he *will* live. However, I do not believe killing him is the plan. You do not seek to protect him and stand up for his criminally negligent actions, do you?" Darkan challenged, raising a firm brow.

Zarckael scrubbed a large, meaty hand back and forth over his cleanly shaved chin as he pondered his options. There were not many, he surmised. He had not changed his mind, and was not going to allow anyone to intimidate him into handing Mazar over to anyone else, for any reason. After listening to Frayier's explanation, although he did not want to nor would he admit it aloud, he understood how Mazar felt. It had taken multiple lifetimes for Zarckael to find his own Truemate. The torments had eaten at him for so long, there were times he thought he would go mad, too. *The male deserves punishment, but to what degree?* he asked himself.

"Why did Gordell not join you and your warriors for this journey? Is it not his Truemate who Mazar abducted?" Zarckael prodded, trying to gain a bit more time to consider things, and to cease their conversations from turning more grave. He gave Darkan a half-smile, attempting to interject some humor he did not feel into the air which had grown too thick with anger and emotions. He knew exactly what the male's answer would be; his Chief would most likely wish to kill Mazar upon sight.

Darkan's expression became grave as Zarckael looked on. The male had a wild, fierce look in his eyes.

What am I missing? he wondered. *Of course the matter is serious, but did his warrior have to die? Could they not come to terms with a fair punishment, then everyone move on?* He had not yet laid eyes upon this Yoren, himself, but he was fully certain she was unharmed. None of his warriors—crazed or no—would dare to harm a female of her ilk. He would never condone what Mazar had done, but he also did not want to condone the male's execution, either. His temper slid into place, and that was when it clicked; he had not been told the whole of the situation. "What have I not been informed of, concerning Gordell's Truemate? I mean no disrespect, nor am I making light of anything, but the expression you wear says things are far more serious than I had imagined. What else goes here, Darkan?" he asked, his own expression growing darker.

"You do not know where your Mazar is now? Is he not being held in your dungeons, as we were told? And as for his punishment; yes, I would say abducting a *Royal, innocent, carrying Truemate to our Chief* would be a very serious matter, indeed. Would you not?" he finished through gritted teeth, enunciating each word. He was becoming highly frustrated with the lolly-gagging.

"Sh–she is carrying?" the Chief sputtered in shock. "No, I was not aware of this. Torkquin, go retrieve Mazar and bring him up, now!" Zarckael snapped to one of his guards in a low, deep, almost too-calm voice. His frustration was quickly turning to fury, threatening to get the better of him if he did not control his emotions. He felt like a fool! That small bit of information had not been mentioned to him. *I will be punishing more than only Mazar, for this deceit,* he vowed.

"Truly? When you learned that Yoren was here, you did not know this?" Darkan asked, visibly relaxing. He even felt a bit bad for the Chief, and knew there would certainly be bigger troubles around here now, not only for Mazar.

"I had already retired last eve before Mazar and the other warriors returned. They were supposed to be scouting our territory, or so I was told, but I was only made aware of Mazar's perfidy this morn. And no, there was no mentioned of Yoren carrying. I offer my sincere regrets and apologies, as this should have never happened," Zarckael expressed. All color had drained from his face after grasping the seriousness of what his warrior had done.

"Well, it seems you are correct in that you were only told portions of the story. Now, what are you going to do since you have learned the whole of it?" Darkan asked, still feeling pity for this Chief. Too bad his own warriors had deceived him, such a thing would cut deeply and was unacceptable.

Before either of them could speak further, Torkquin came rushing back to his Chief's side where he leaned down and whispered something into Zarckael's ear. Suddenly, the Chief sat ramrod-straight, and his expression turned cold, hard as stone. Darkan had an inauspicious feeling in the pit of his stomach. Something had obviously gone wrong, and he could not hold his tongue.

"What goes here now, and where is your male?" he roughly demanded of the Chief. Rising from the bench he and his warriors had been seated upon, Darkan knew without a backward glance that all of his warriors had risen with him, which filled him with pride anew. He would reward their loyalty later, as he had bigger troubles at the moment.

Zarckael lifted a hand as show of peace, and his voice was both hard and peaceful when he spoke, "Hold, Darkan. Mazar has not been brought here yet, but not to worry. Several of my guards have already set out to retrieve and bring him here. They shall return promptly with Mazar and your Yoren. Do sit, and we will work this all out," Zarckael attempted to reassured him.

He did not want to sit, Darkan wanted to bash heads together! This was beginning to feel like a trap; he did not like games and he liked traps even less. Much less. "I do not wish to sit. If you cannot find your own warrior, then perhaps we can," he spat at Zarckael, completely fed up with all the foolery. "In fact, while you sit and wait, I say my warriors and I go find Yoren ourselves. I need to see to her and make certain there is not one single mark upon her flesh. If there is..." Darkan finished, leaving Zarckael to use his imagination for what may be done if Yoren was scathed in any way.

As one, he and his warriors turned and marched out of the double-wooden doors through which they had entered. Their mission; find Yoren, as she was the biggest concern at the moment. He would undoubtedly deal with Mazar, later.

Chapter Thirteen

Yoren's entire body felt light, free, and simply delightful after soaking in a hot, fresh bathtub. It had been filled with many of Toralynn's soothing, healing herbs which had worked their magic, as all of her previous aches and pains were merely distant, unwanted memories. She sighed. Her wrists now felt as if they had never been injured. Although there were mere traces of their former markings, they did not pain her in the least. Toralynn had applied a soothing, lovely-smelling salve on them, and bandaged her wounds once Yoren had finished her bath.

Feeling fresh and clean always helped one to think more clearly, and Yoren was doing just that, possibly a bit too much. *What will happen now?* she wondered. *And, why has Gordell not yet arrived to take me home?* She knew deep down help was on the way, she did not understand what was taking so long, though. *Had something gone awry? Did Gordell's plan run into some other type of troubles?* she worried.

It was difficult to feel this good, yet to worry so, as she was. All she wanted was to be held by her Truemate, in their bedchamber, in their holdings. *Was that too much to ask for? Am I being selfish?* she questioned herself. Although she felt much better at the moment, she was quickly and constantly tiring, of late. With the youngling growing more each day inside of her, it was taking a toll on her body. Female-shifters were not supposed to shift while they were carrying, as it could obviously be dangerous to the youngling and the mother. She would have already shifted and left this place by now if it were an option, however, it was not.

Crazed as it may be, she had enjoyed being here with the females whom had taken such excellent care of her. Still, she was missing Gordell and her home so badly, she wanted to weep at every turn. And now, she could not stop the tears flowing like rivers from her stinging eyes. Sniffling, she took in her surroundings, only now realizing she was alone.

The females had given her a small yet lovely bedchamber to get some much needed sleep. Yoren eyed the bed as one might a boon from her Goddess *Meynix*. "Dare I?" she questioned, challenging the bed. "Or will help arrive the moment sleep claims me?" That would most likely be the way of it; she would finally fall into a well-needed, peaceful slumber, then Gordell and his warriors would storm this village.

"Oh, no!" she gasped aloud. "They would not take the time to find out if these female-shifters were peaceful. I must warn them, tell them what to say and how to handle the warriors should they come knocking on this door, or kicking it in! I will tell them to come directly to me so I can deal with the brutes." She fled the chamber as if it was on fire. "Toralynn, Jolsynn! Where are you? I must have words with you!" she bellowed. "I cannot allow harm to come to these females, they are too good and kind," she murmured to herself as she quickly made her way from chamber to chamber. Not finding either of them, she worried about stepping foot outside, afraid of who may spot her and what they may do.

The females had told her of the trickery their own Weyr-males had used, and that Jolsynn had relied upon her stealth and unnatural speed to fetch Yoren this morn to rescue her from that shack. They were all of a mind that Mazar would go even more mad upon discovering that she was no longer there.

Deciding it was significant enough to chance, Yoren opened the front door. Carefully peeking her head out and hoping to find at least one of the females nearby, she let her gaze roam over the area out front. Nothing. Neither of the females were in sight. Ducking back inside, she closed the door and leaned back against it. As she glanced up at the ceiling, she did not know what to do. *Had they already been found and taken? Had harm already come to them?* She could not—*would not*—allow such a thing.

Stiffening her spine, she straightened to her fullest height, lifted her chin, squared her shoulders, and cleared her throat before she opened the door again. This time she stepped outside, intent on finding the females and needing to make certain they were well. Pulling the door closed behind her, Yoren breathed in the fresh air, relishing the beautiful day but only for a brief moment. There were several trees and shrubs in front of the home, all giving off a calming fragrance.

She heard voices and much loud shuffling coming from down the dirt road to her right. Bracing her back against the small home, and even more grateful for the trees now helping to conceal her, she peered around as best she could without being spotted, to discern what all the noise was. "Oh, no! It is them!" she whispered. *Wait, this is what you wanted,* she reminded herself.

In the lead, she spotted Darkan, Gordell's First. He did not look happy at all, in fact, he looked more deadly than she had ever seen him. This did not bode well. *Has something more happened?* she worried, her dilemma weighing heavily upon her heart. *Do I hide and search out the females? Or step out and let Darkan know I am well?* "Oh! Why do such things have to happen?" she grumbled low, angrily stomping one foot and slumping her shoulders.

Darkan's intimidation only served to strengthen her resolve; she knew what she must do. Straightening again, she walked out to meet Darkan in the road. "Ho! Darkan, you finally came! Where is Gordell?" She smiled, leaning this way and that way, trying to spot him in the large group of familiar warriors who were unerringly following Darkan. Only then did she realize that if Gordell was here, he would be leading the warriors next to Darkan, not following him.

Knitting her brows in confusion, she felt a lump suddenly form in her throat. "Darkan, where is he?" she asked, her voice wobbly as she continued to glance around and catch him in her sights.

Suddenly, she felt a large, strong hand gently grasp her upper arm. "Yoren, I am relieved to find you. Are you well? Has any harm come to—" Darkan's words ceased as his eyes tracked the bandaging on her other wrist, the one he wasn't holding.

He knew, and she could have kicked herself. *Oh! Why did I not think first? He sees my bandaged wrists, and now he will become overly crazed.* "I am well, Darkan, truly I am. Do not bother over this." Attempting to appease him, she wiggled her arm free from him and negligently waved her hand at her bandaged wrist. "These are of no consequence, I assure you."

He grasped her arm again and gently encircled it in his large hand as she spoke, and she felt it tighten a fraction at her words. She now knew the females and Gordell were the least of her worries. She tentatively peered into his eyes and found a murderous glint in their depths; one that she had only seen a couple of times in her life. *Oh, no!* She panicked, trying to come up with a story to explain the injuries, and not get anyone else in trouble.

Think! You fell! Yes, you fell and threw your hands forward to stop yourself! It was partly truth and she would tell him, then he would think no more on the matter. "Look at me, Darkan, please, and hear me. I fell, it was my own fault. Nobody harmed me." She waved a hand back toward the small home and continued, "The females who live here aided me. They fed me, bathed me, and then tended my silly injuries." Yoren tried to laugh in hopes of affecting his thunderous-looking expression; her giggle sounded a bit strangled, even to her own ears.

Yoren was beginning to believe the male would never look her in the eye, just as he finally lifted his gaze from her wrist to do so. "You say you did this–to yourself? Why would you defend the actions of the crazed fool who abducted you, Yoren?" his voice was so final; so calm. A lifetime of experience told her that when Darkan became this calm, his anger was deeply churning on the inside.

She would have to be more convincing, and could not allow another war to break out over this. Mazar had clearly lost his wits, but he did not treat her ill; none of the males had harmed her. She had even come to feel a bit of sympathy for the mad male. A small bit, but there it was. As far as the only others she had seen here—the females—she would never allow harm to come to them. They had shown her kindness, and they had all made a true connection which she felt would always exist between them, even though she still did not fully understand it.

Shaking her head to clear her thoughts, she could revisit that another time. Now, she had a disaster to avert. Grabbing his free arm with her own, she squeezed and shook it at the same time trying to capture his full attention. She had to be stern and put some weight behind her words. "Darkan, listen to my words, and do *not* say me a liar! I know what happened to my own self! I fell..." she drew out the last word as if he was a dolt.

Her ire was quickly rising. Had she even convinced herself of her own lie? Shaking her head once more, she released Darkan's arm and shook out of his hold. Taking a large step back, she pointedly glared at him.

After a long moment, he shook his own head as if he had just now heard her. "Apologies, Yoren." He bowed his head, unsure whether he believed her. At this point she cared not, she only wanted to find the females and ensure their well-being.

"Well enough. Now, have you or any of your warriors... *harmed* anyone–yet?" her voice squeaked on the last three words. She nervously nibbled on her bottom lip in anticipation of his answer; a lifelong nervous habit of hers of which Darkan knew all-too-well. *Let them be well,* she silently prayed.

When Darkan straightened to his fullest height, they stood almost eye-to-eye. He was just enough taller that she had to look up, which she could tell he quite enjoyed. "What do you mean 'harmed anyone,' Yoren? We only arrived here not long ago. Do you not think this entire village would have heard us, had we been 'harming' anyone"? he questioned, one brow raised in speculation.

Appraising the male in front of her with a touch of scorn and easily sensing his rudeness, Yoren wanted to lash out at him. *Who did he think he was? Furthermore, to whom did he think he was speaking?* "I do believe I meant my exact words, Darkan. Yes or no? It is a simple answer I seek." Her nervousness long gone, the situation she found herself in would have been one to laugh about any other time or place. However, this was neither the time, nor the place.

A resounding "No," was his full reply, as he continued to regard her with a suspicious gaze.

Well, Yoren thought, *he had better get his head on straight.* She did not appreciate the manner in which he was treating her. She had done nothing wrong. *You know quite well that is untrue,* she snapped back at herself. She had lied. *Ugh, I am awful and horrible. I deserve several lashings with a whip,* she reprimanded her lying-self.

Mentally shaking away those self-incriminating notions for now, she must find out the whereabouts of those females. She was humming with nerves and worry over their well-being, and could not allow her body language to deceive her. She stood tall and proud before speaking again, "My thanks, Darkan. Now, have you seen two females? Perhaps they may have been out walking about. They would be mother and her female-young, both tall and beautiful with dark plaited hair." She had yet to see any of the other females here, so who was to say the description she had just given would not fit all females in this Weyr? *Ugh! This was becoming increasingly complicated!* She fumed.

All of a sudden, she felt a prickling sensation at her nape. Smoothing a hand over it, she made a half-turn and noticed two beautiful sets of eyes peeking through a small portion of the window coverings. Relief flooded through her body with such a force, she almost collapsed. The only thing to stay her was Darkan grasping her upper arm to steady her.

"Are you quite certain you are well, Yoren? You almost collapsed. What really goes here?" he demanded, his gaze scanning her from toe to hair trying to find anything amiss, besides her wrists.

Head down and body fully relaxed, she was shaking. Darkan mistook it to mean the female was weeping. In one quick, smooth move, he had her carefully scooped up into his strong arms. He would personally carry her back to Gordell this moment, if need be. He leaned closer to her head, trying to figure out something soothing to say. All he could come up with was a few words and sounds he had seen mothers use on their younglings. He would give it a go. "Shhh, all will be well, Yoren. All will be well. Shhh, relax," he went on, and almost dropped her when he caught an elbow hard in his side. From her!

"Darkan! What are you doing? Put me down!" She jumped as he half-tossed her down. They stood there eyeing each other as if they had both lost all of their wits.

"What are you about?" Darkan demanded, still rubbing his abused side. She was strong and the jab hurt. A little bit.

"I should be asking the same of you! What were you doing picking me up and cooing to me?" She almost broke into laughter at his incredulous expression. The male was obviously beyond confused. She had also hurt him, which she did not mean to do, it was simply a reaction. *I must get myself under control. First when I fell on my rear in the shack, and now this?* Mentally shaking her head at her own actions. *I have never behaved this way in my life. What is the matter with me?*

"I–I thought you were weeping, so I merely meant to calm you. And, *cooing?* I do not coo! I was simply trying to soothe you. I thought you were in need of such." He looked ashamed, almost youngling-like.

Oh, no–this is not what she wanted. "Alright, let us settle this all now. Apologies, I was not weeping, I was laughing with relief. You see, there?" She pointed to the window to show him the two females peeping out at them. When his gaze moved toward them, they quickly closed their window coverings to hide. Laughter full of joy bubbled up inside her over their reactions, and it felt quite good.

"You—" he broke off, his voice full of exasperation, then sighed deeply before continuing, "What are you pointing at, and what makes you laugh so?" Darkan scowled, looking more confused and frustrated than ever. His face was flushed, his handsome features pinched, and it only made Yoren laugh harder.

"There, the females I have so worried over are back inside their home!" Unable to stop her laughter, she spoke through it. Bent over at this point, her hysteria stole the rest of her breath and words. Nobody spoke or moved until she finally sobered, though, she would have preferred to continue, but these males obviously did not understand anything. She cleared her throat with no shame, whatsoever.

"I am going back inside this home…and *no!*" she spoke sharply and clearly as the warriors moved to walk with her. "I will go inside, *alone,* and I will be *well,*" she emphasized the two words. "I owe much to those females, and would like to gather their contact information to keep in touch with them. Worry not, old Darkan, they have only been kind to me. You have nothing to worry about, here. I will be back out, anon." Finishing on a rather haughty note while trying to hide a smirk, she pinched her skirts on both sides, raised them, twirled on one heel, and practically floated back inside the small, humble home, leaving Darkan and his warriors scratching their heads in confusion.

Turning to face his warriors, all of whom were looking on in expectation of the inevitable speech, Darkan's mind reeled but no words came. In the end, he could only shake his own head as he glanced back at the small home, and awaited their Chief's strange, and apparently moody Truemate's return.

****

Gordell had performed many chores, several of which were usually done by the servants, but he was bored and going stir crazy. He had to keep busy or he would lose his own wits.

As he sat to partake of a small repast consisting of meat, cheese, bread, and a bit of fire-brew, he still could not cease his worry over Yoren's condition. His gut told him that she had sustained some sort of injuries, whether they were serious, remained to be seen. He was fully confident in Darkan, and if his feeling was factual, whoever had been fool enough to harm his Truemate would most likely not live to see another morn. Or at least wish they had been put out of their misery, after Darkan was finished with them.

Suddenly, he was yanked back from his thoughts as a lanky male-young came charging up to him, practically falling over his own ever-growing feet. The young was all legs and arms, and it made Gordell laugh as it brought to mind when he was in the same stage of growth. It was a welcome and needed break from the monotony of his darker thoughts.

The young accidentally sprayed dirt all over Gordell and his foods as he skidded to an abrupt halt. *Ah, I was not particularly hungered to begin with,* Gordell admitted to himself. Reaching out a strong arm to steady the young, while still laughing, Gordell gave him a moment to collect himself. "What goes, and why are you running as if something is trying to catch and eat you?" he questioned.

Panting, trying to force his breath to slow and smooth itself out, the young finally pulled himself up, straightened his shoulders, and attempted to appear under control. "Chief Gordell, I have a message for you. Darkan sent word, they arrived, and they spoke with the other Chief, and they ate, and they—"

Shaking his head in amusement, Gordell had to cut the young off. He was speaking far too fast and babbling. "Ho, slow yourself. I cannot understand what you are trying to say. Breathe for a moment and try to relax. Here, sit." Gordell scooted over on the bench he was occupying, giving the young room to join him.

Detecting that Gordell was not—for the moment—in one of his latest, ever-present foul moods, the young visibly relaxed. From his apparent worry over that, to his own clumsy foot-flight, and the awkward tangle of his own skin and bones, the male-young was a mess. After a few deep breaths he was finally able to speak more calmly. "Yes, and apologies, I got excited. The warriors made it to the other Weyr territory, they had a repast, and then Darkan spoke with their Chief. When he sent one of his males to retrieve Mazar from the dungeons, he was not there." Noticing when Gordell flinched at his words, he worried over how to proceed.

"You are doing well, finish the message," Gordell strove to soothe the young, but inside he felt as if he might explode. He was legendary for his calm and how he handled intense situations, yet as he turned the young's words over and over in his mind, it was difficult to hide his rage. *How could the male not be in custody?* Managing to hold his temper in check for now, he stewed over the message, as he suddenly realized the young was still speaking.

"The other Chief had no answer. Darkan became angry and took your warriors out to find Mazar, and their Chief sent his warriors to aid in their search. He had been told Mazar was coming to turn himself in after realizing how wrong his actions were, and the Chief assumed he was already in the dungeons awaiting his punishment." The young was well-spoken after he had calmed down.

Gordell thought it made clear enough sense, but he was still angry. A male who had lost his wits as Mazar had, should have been apprehended at once. Not left to his own devices, and allowed to roam freely and turn himself in whenever he felt the time was right. Taking a few deep breaths, he knew letting his temper flair, especially with the male-young sitting next to him, was not wise. "I see, and you have my thanks for delivering the message. Now, sit here and have some of my foods. The dirt will not harm you." Gordell humorously smirked at the expression on the young's face, obviously knowing whose fault it was that Gordell's foods were now inedible from the generous sprinkling of dirt.

"My thanks as well, but I have already eaten my midday fill." Color bloomed over the male-young's face as he rose from the bench. He inclined his chin, and waited for Gordell's formal dismissal.

Shaking his head again, he flicked a large hand in the direction from which the young had approached him, and then laughed as he watched him flee in much the same hazardous manner he had arrived. *Youngs, they bring much joy into our lives and sometimes dangerous Realm,* he thought almost painfully, as he and Yoren's youngling came to mind again.

Gordell could barely wait for the birthing, and he truly hoped for a male-youngling; one he could and would play with, as well as train and teach all the male ways to. He simply could not wait. This time he did not allow those thoughts to darken his mind, but rather, they lifted his heart. This was a joyous time and nothing would change it. *Nothing.* He would see to it.

Once the male-young disappeared, Gordell turned the message over in his mind. His warriors made the journey safely, which was always good news. They obviously had met and discussed the situation with the Chief without any bloodshed; also good news.

He knew Darkan had wanted to execute the original plan of coming at Mazar from ten sides, and it would have surely been a sight to behold! With a smile that held little humor, Gordell envisioned what such an attack would have been like, to the one who it was being launched upon. The male likely would have shite his breeches, which also would have been great fun to witness.

After gathering his inedible foods, he made his way to one of the many fire-pits strewn about the grounds of his holdings, and tossed everything into the flames which would burn the whole eve. He had personally seen to it that all the pits burned brightly, and would continue to do so until his Yoren was safely back in his holdings, and his arms. This entire debacle had taken far longer than anyone had anticipated, yet he still felt confident the outcome would be a desired one, where all were home safe and unharmed. But with one clear exception; Mazar. The fool would most certainly not enjoy his own outcome or his end. Whichever fate the male met truly made no difference to Gordell, as long as he was properly tortured physically and emotionally.

With a wicked-grin, he strode off to check on his animals, only to pull himself up to a quick stop. *I could shift, complete the flight in a couple hours, and be there to make sure things are going as they should be. What would I not give to witness the fool's end? Nothing. What would I not give to see and hold my Yoren even sooner? Again, nothing,* he concluded. There was positively nothing he would not give for both of those things.

Making mental notes of preparations needed for his journey, Gordell's footfalls were lighter and easier. He felt more eager than he had since before this fiasco had begun, even his heart felt lighter as it beat inside his chest. He would see his Yoren this eve! Just the thought made him feel as if he were already inflight.

It had been decided that he would stay home, to which he had even agreed, but as restless as he had become, he could wait no longer. Besides, was *he* not Chief? Could *he* not simply do as *he* deemed fit? Yes, he could, whether anyone else liked it. And he was certain they would not, especially Darkan. Alas, *he* was Chief, not his First, and everyone including that male, would have to abide *his* every decision. It was settled; of course he could go, and he would, once he readied everything.

Chapter Fourteen

Gemma was unaware of how long she had been lying upon the ground. All she knew for certain was, the ground had grown much cooler, and it was no longer daylight. She awoke to find a female gazing down at her through large, questioning turquoise-eyes; eyes which were almost hypnotic...enthralling.

It was an effort, but Gemma forced her own gaze away, not knowing who the female was or...*what* she was, for that matter. Although she felt a sense of peace, she could not be certain just yet. For obvious reasons, she knew she must not allow the female to enthrall her, if that was her intention. Even though Gemma was all but immune to any type of enthrallment by any being, she felt a bit of panic at the realization that if anyone could succeed, it was most likely this female.

Slowly, Gemma dragged her oddly achy and fatigued body up into a sitting position, and then glanced around to discern her whereabouts, hoping she was still in the same place she had been before. *Oh, no! Iax! Where is she now? I must find her–surely she would have need of me?* Without further thought she jumped up, her eyes darting around in every direction. Suddenly, Gemma felt another odd sensation...*dizziness?* She had never experienced it, and as it was happening to her now, she decided she most certainly did not enjoy it. Iax had been dizzy and described it to her before, which was the only reason she even knew what it was.

It was an intense feeling, she noted, as her body began leaning to one side. Just then, the female, who until now had only observed Gemma with a rather confused expression, reached out and gently grasped her arm to steady her so she would not fall. She appreciated the assistance, but as she began to offer her thanks, her voice did not want to cooperate. *I have grown tired of these many unfamiliar...things happening to me,* she chided her new emotions and sensations. Since it had worked before, she thought clearing her throat would help, and was relieved when, albeit not very smoothly, it did so she spoke to the stranger, "Thank you. Who are you, and… *what* are you?" she hedged suspiciously. Not wanting to seem rude, she regarded the female with a kind smile; one she actually felt, even though it also seemed odd.

The female was more beautiful than any being Gemma had ever laid eyes on. And she had seen more beings than most. She was taller than Gemma, which was saying much, as she stood five-feet and ten-inches in height. Most of the shifters in this Realm were of a great height for females, but the one standing before her was even taller than Iax, who stood exactly six-feet tall. *Astounding,* she conceded.

Letting her gaze travel up the female's full height, Gemma guessed she must be seven-feet tall, or close to it. Her long, wavy, golden blonde hair was much like Iax's only lighter and a bit sparkly, hanging well past her bare knees. Her facial features were simply too perfect to be real, in Gemma's opinion. As out-of-any-world beautiful as the female was, her eyes were what most caught Gemma's notice. She almost felt the sense of enthrallment return yet she did not feel it was an intentional act on the female's behalf. Her eyes were simply gorgeous, and impossible not to stare at. They were the deepest, most beautiful shade of turquoise Gemma had ever encountered; beyond compare.

Still openly gawking, Gemma did not know what to make of the female. She had an ethereal quality about her, yet Gemma instinctively knew without doubt that this female was anything but delicate. She exuded an absolute sense of power, strength, and knowledge even beyond Gemma's. The female's aura was quite odd and unique; the purest kinds of peace and tranquility. Gemma had most certainly never come across such a being anywhere. The easiest thing to figure out about her was, she clearly was not from this Dragon Realm.

Even though it was dark, heightened eyesight allowed her to see that the stranger's very flesh appeared to slightly shimmer and sparkle. She could also see—*wings?*—yes, wings, which also sparkled and much like with her skin, lent them a beautiful, gossamer appearance, as they slightly fluttered behind her back. She reminded Gemma of a giant butterfly; a perfect Goddess figure with large, semitransparent, turquoise wings, almost the same shade as her incredible eyes.

Small strips of an odd leather type of material only barely covered her female places. *Iax would likely appreciate this,* she thought, remembering how her friend enjoyed being unclothed and was even proud of it. This brought her mind back to her previous worries regarding Iax, and she suddenly realized she was standing with her mouth agape. Feeling her face aflame, she was embarrassed by her own behavior. Suddenly, Gemma felt another new emotion; *awkwardness?* This was another of the emotions Iax had explained to her in the past. She did not exactly enjoy this one, either.

After a few stretched-out moments of the two females respectfully sizing each other up, the stranger released Gemma's arm after making certain she was steady. As the female began to speak, Gemma was awestruck by a language she was barely able to comprehend, and only parts, at that. A first for her, and the revelation was confusing.

Apparently sensing that Gemma was not understanding her tongue, the stranger re-spoke, but this time her words came out in the Universal Dragon Dimension language; the one every shifter in the Dragon Dimension understood practically from birth. The language barrier now solved, Gemma still took notice of the female's voice; it sounded as if it was fading in and out, and seemed as if it came from afar, even though she stood mere inches in front of Gemma. "My name is Skenyah, sistair of Eluhyax. I come in peace to aid you and your female. Where is she, and why did you lie on the ground? Are you not well?"

Gemma rolled the female's words over in her mind a couple times before realizing what she had said. *My female? I do not have a...oh, she means Iax.* And that name, *Skenyah,* there was something about it and, though Gemma could not yet place it, she would in time. "I do not know why I was lying on the ground." Gemma hated to deceive, but truly, it had not been an outright lie; she did not know exactly what had happened. "I do not fully recall what took place before I apparently slept, though I feel well now. As for the female, do you refer to my friend, the female with whom I travel?" Skenyah took in her every move with those intense eyes, paying full attention to Gemma's words.

Gemma was pleasantly surprised when Skenyah nodded her head, but then stood stock-still for a moment, obviously in deep thought. When Skenyah finally spoke, Gemma's skin prickled and when she looked at her arms, the tiny hairs were standing up. *More odd emotions.* She frowned and rubbed her hands over her arms. *I should be getting use to this by now, but I am not, and I still do not like any of it.*

"Yes, I speak of the female with whom you travel. Iax, is your…*friend?*" Skenyah warily questioned, obviously unsure of what 'friend' meant. Then it struck Gemma; *The Amethyst Faerie Dragon Realm! But, how?* She was shocked anew. Come to think of it, the more she observed the female, the more she reminded her of Iax. *What could it all mean? Certainly nothing, there could not be any connection between them. Or could there? No, that is absurd.*

As she tried hard to convince herself such a connection was impossible, she recalled what had happened to Iax regarding the male from the village; none would have ever expected that, either. But she needed to put those thoughts away for a more appropriate time. She had several weighty issues to figure out; issues such as the strange female in front of her who made no sense whatsoever. *Who is she, and how did she get here? Furthermore, why is she asking about Iax?* Gemma puzzled, a small thread of fear, and a larger one of concern raced down her spine.

What is this, and how does she know Iax by name? This cannot be good, she worried, using one of Iax's sayings. "Iax is my friend. In truth, she is one of my only friends. Could you please answer a few questions for me, such as how you have come to know her name? You must understand how confusing this is?" she ventured. Neither of them had moved at all during their 'visit,' yet it was as if Skenyah's shimmering form was in constant motion.

Then another anomaly struck Gemma; Skenyah was not actually *here,* she was using astral projection. It was the only thing she could ascribe to the female's form, her strange in-and-out appearance, as well as the wavering, fading affects of her voice. She had certainly heard of it, but had never personally witnessed such a thing. It was incredible and absolutely wild! She stifled a giggle at another of Iax's quips, but it could not be helped. It was the most accurate term to describe this experience.

"You must sequester me. I understand, and I am pleased to comply. What do you wish to know?"

Gemma was unable to stop her giggle this time, which earned her a surprised and rather stern expression from Skenyah. Quickly sobering herself, she did not want to offend Skenyah as they had critical issues to discuss. Moreover, there were Iax issues of the utmost import to resolve. "Please, forgive me, I meant no offense. I would simply like to *question,* not *sequester* you. That would mean for me to take you, as in, um…never mind." She shook her head, unsure of how to explain the difference between the two words in a way Skenyah would understand. There was no time, anyway, because they needed to find Iax.

"Yes, you need to question me, I understand. What do you wish to know?" Skenyah kindly conceded, which brought a smile to Gemma's lips. She suddenly felt a strong sense of peace and belonging, almost as if Skenyah was somehow controlling Gemma's emotions. It made no sense, much like the feeling of enthrallment from a few minutes ago. In any case, she was grateful for the calmness, and certain it would make communications easier.

"Correct. Now, if you do not mind, please, tell me how you know Iax and where you are from?" Gemma asked as she recalled Iax fleeing from the male who had been quickly making his way to her. She was still nervous and worried over Iax's whereabouts, and what condition she may be in. She needed answers, and then hopefully Skenyah would be able to aid her as she had offered.

After staring at Gemma for several moments, Skenyah nodded her head as if answering something to herself. *Or, perhaps in communications with someone else?* Gemma considered. A possibility she had not given any thought to, until now. Hearing Skenyah's odd voice brought Gemma out of her musings.

"Yes, I know of your...*friend,* Iax. I am half-sistair to Iax's mathair, Eluhyax. As well as her likeness sistair, Eallaha. Do you truly not know of their history? And if it pleases, what may I call you?"

Iax's mathair, and her 'likeness sistair'? What could she be speaking of? Iax is from Earth, she is of 'human' parentage. None of this makes sense, Gemma puzzled. "No, I'm afraid I do not know of what you speak, nor do I understand. Iax is a human from Earth, not from any other Realm or Dimension. There must be a mistake, there has to be. This is not possible. Are you quite certain? Oh, and please, call me Gemma," she finished more confused by the moment.

"Yes, Gemma, I am certain. Why would I not be? She is not from her Earth, she is of the Amethyst Faerie Dragon Realm, as am I and all of our family. As a new-youngling, she was taken to Earth and raised there. But she is most assuredly blood of my blood, although she is not supposed to know this until her twenty-fifth age, which is soon." Skenyah cocked her head to one side as if she heard something in the distance.

Gemma, with her sensitive hearing, picked up on nothing. *Strange,* she thought. *All of this was quite strange.* Too many questions swirled inside her head and almost pained her, but she needed answers. "Why was she taken, and by whom? I still do not understand." Her brows furrowed, Gemma gazed expectantly at the female. Suddenly, Skenyah stiffened as some of the peacefulness they had been surrounded by slowly began to seep away from where they stood.

"Her mathair and fathair were slain in battle when their holdings were attacked without warning. There was a male at their side who had somehow journeyed there through a portal, with both of their knowledge. They liked and even trusted the male, and when they realized they would fall, they insisted he take Iax far away. They knew his world would provide the safety and security needed to keep the new-youngling well and alive, as they could not allow her to fall, too." Skenyah sighed and a sadness seemed to blanket the area where they stood.

At the same time Gemma noticed Skenyah's body, her wings were now flittering as though she was nervous or anxious relaying the tale. She could not blame the female.

"He took her and the prophecy I helped scribe. You see, it was necessary for Iax to be kept safe and far away from her birthplace until her twenty-fifth age. Around that time, she must return to fulfill her birthright. She is of Royalty, the same lineage of the Weyr who have always presided over the entire Amethyst Faerie Dragon Realm." Skenyah's chin went up a bit, her face colored with pride at the proclamation.

"Upon her twenty-fifth age, her powers and other strengths will be very strong, in fact, they should already be surfacing. She must be around her blood, her Weyr, so we can teach her of our heritage. It is her prophecy, not a choice, that she return to claim her proper position and take on her responsibilities. We have waited all this time to have her back, and I was chosen to retrieve her from the world the male had taken her to." She wavered a bit, seeming a little nervous before continuing her fantastical yet unbelievable tale.

"Yet, as I prepared for my journey I sensed her presence here. I did not understand, but this is where our Goddess, *Famista,* sent me. My other half-sistair, Eallaha, who awaits my return and Iax's arrival, will be most pleased that Iax was closer, as it will take far less time. Still, I sense trouble within her. Why are you not with her? Where is she?" She raised a brow, her radiance was almost blinding, growing with her excitement.

Iax, Royalty? Gemma could not have been more shocked! This would be humorous if she did not believe Skenyah. As it was, she felt her own sense of sadness at the prospect of never seeing her friend again. *What then? What would I do without Iax, since we have made such a connection? How would Iax take this news?* Not well, she knew for certain. First things first, though. "I am most surprised at your revelations, and I am certain Iax will be even more so. As for her whereabouts, I do not know. As for why I am not with her now? I am afraid I do not know that, either. We were..." Gemma almost revealed what they had been doing; spying on Mazar's village, then she thought better of it. It would take too long and be too difficult to explain.

"We were walking through here and suddenly, she felt ill. Then I began feeling odd, I suppose you could say. I do not get ill, yet I fainted right here where you found me. I remember Iax running off as if something was after her, but I could not follow since I fainted..." she admitted, trailing off as heat burned her face from embarrassment over letting her charge down. She, or rather, *they,* needed to find Iax and soon. Gemma had a strange feeling, and it was not good.

The formidable female who had stood—or floated—in place, since Gemma had awakened, simply stared at her; she began to feel uncomfortable under the scrutiny. As if she did not already feel miserable enough for not knowing what had happened to Iax. They must get moving and find her, she knew for certain.

"Why do I sense such a strong bond between yourself and Iax? I do not understand this," Skenyah inquired. Everyone who encountered them always felt their seemingly unbreakable bond, but never understood it. Not since Iax had been raised on Earth, and Gemma was from an altogether different world. Gemma could feel Skenyah's curiosity and just like Iax's, it always took precedence; they truly *needed* to know.

"I met Iax within the last year. She is a part of a group who helps to avert battles in various Realms from all the Dimensions. She does not know of her lineage, I am certain she believes herself to be a natural human. Though, I must admit, I have recently questioned some of her…abilities, some of the things that have happened. What you say makes sense, but I do not know how she will take this news. She very much enjoys her Earth, her family there, and most likely will not simply up and leave it," Gemma stated matter-of-factly.

"I understand your meaning and I do not blame her. However, her body is most likely undergoing many physical changes now. She will not understand this, which is why I must find and bring her back to her birthplace. She may well already be experiencing some of the transformation and is likely frightened. Where would we begin searching for her? I felt her presence right here, and it is highly unusual for my senses to mislead me," Skenyah finished, her patience waning and agitation mounting.

Should I mention the butterfly image burned into Iax's flesh? This all makes sense now, all of her oddities. Gemma had recently puzzled over some of them, such as Iax's faster than normal healing times, her physical speed, her skills with weapons, the butterfly image, and more. *This would be why, and I was not letting my imagination go too far. She truly is…different,* Gemma realized, knowing what she must do now. "These…*changes* you speak of, I believe you are correct. This day, Iax had an odd experience, one which I was told should only happen to a being of this Dragon Realm. A butterfly image burnt itself into her flesh as it would had she been kissed by her Truemate, yet I thought she was human so I was confused. I fear that is why she fled, and I suspect it stunned me so greatly that my mind and body shut down, and I fainted. I know she went in that direction." Gemma pointed off into the dense woods to her right, Skenyah's left.

Skenyah frowned. "A butterfly, you say? Yes, it would only happen if the Bonding with her Truemate was taking place. I neither see nor sense a male here, so how it that possible? Our kind do not have to kiss, they need only be within proximity of one another, and the image takes form in our flesh. This is…unsettling news," she finished. Her expression spoke of her mind, obviously assailing her with many troublesome thoughts.

It should not be possible, but then, Gemma had sensed that Iax was different. And, she pondered, what of Iax's issue with all-things shiny, sparkly, and glittery? She had always loved them to the point she had been drawn in, almost enthralled, or so it had seemed. It was from her Amethyst Faerie genetic makeup. Knowing what Gemma now knew, it all made great sense yet it was still farfetched and bizarre, to say the least.

The worry in Skenyah's voice caught Gemma's notice, "We must go now and find her. She is most assuredly upset, confused, and possibly in harm's way. Perhaps this is why I feel the way I do. Are you able to go with me now?" Gemma nodded. "Let us be gone, we must find her now." As Skenyah took off, or rather, floated away, her wings flitting nervously, as Gemma walked in long strides to keep up with her. The whole situation was so surreal, she truly hoped to find Iax whole and hale.

Chapter Fifteen

Great, here we go again. I cannot stand waking up in strange places, and not knowing what the hell has happened, Iax fumed to herself. And, of course, she hurt all over. Not like when she tried to fly, but she was pretty damn sore. Lying still, she caught the homey scent of a campfire, and faintly heard a rustling sound. *Is that a fire I smell?* This intrigued her, she loved a campfire, but didn't remember her and Gemma setting one up.

Scootchin' around to get more comfy, another more foreign scent wafted to her nose. Oh, and it smelled delicious. Sexy, even. *What the hell? I've lost it for sure this time,* she conceded, not at all surprised. *Wait, back the truck up. Why would I smell* sexy *here?* Gemma didn't normally stink, but she sure as hell never smelled sexy, at least not to Iax. *That would be too weird, but then, why should this be any different from the rest of this little trip?* she pondered.

Realizing she'd probably better get her ass up and in gear, didn't make her feel happy like it normally did. She'd always loved working, being on the move. *I've turned into a loser. A lazy, good-for-nothing loser. Ugh, I need a break. That's it, I've just been working too much.* What? *Working too much?* Shaking her head, she'd *never* had such an absurd thought in her life. Work was a great thing; productivity, fulfillment, the results good, bad, or even so-so, were always worth the effort. *What the hell is happening to me?* She frowned.

"Yo, Gemma! Are you sure I didn't bang my head up more than you told me? I swear, the way I've felt and the thoughts I've had are *not* right. Not for me, anyway. Seriously, what happened to my brain?" she prodded, eyes still closed and not wanting to move. Giving up on the comfy thing—it wasn't gonna happen while lying on the hard ground—she sat up and opened her eyes...and was absolutely, no other way to put it, shocked. *What the fuck is* this? *And, who the fuck is* that? she puzzled, sitting directly across a campfire from the best looking dude she'd ever seen in her life! *Whoa! This can't be real!* She shook her head hard, something was undoubtedly way off.

The man spoke, but damned if Iax could understand a word he said. Did it really matter? He was so hot, and his voice was so, so...she wasn't sure what to call it, but she could listen to it all night long. Good thing she had no shame or she'd be embarrassed by her own behavior, because she couldn't *not* gawk at him. A small amount of good sense crept into her brain, and made her realize she really *should* try to communicate with him. After all, he was making an attempt; it was only polite–wasn't it? Well, yeah, of course it was.

She glanced around hoping to spot Gemma, who she really needed since she didn't do Dragon-speak. "Gemma? Where are you, babe? I kinda need your expertise. Think you could come over here and help me out?" she belted out in case the woman was too far away to hear her.

The man's expression became confused and, if she wasn't mistaken, a bit...upset. *What in the world does he have to be upset about?* "What's going on now? I'm sick of surprises!" she loudly declared.

When he next spoke—this time moving his hands in the air—probably trying to make hand gestures like she'd wanted to with the shifters who had healed her. It hit her. *Oh. My. God! It's him, Hot-Dude! What the...? Holy shit! What's* he *doing here? Better yet, what am* I *doing here? Where's Gemma, and why hasn't she answered me yet?* Goosebumps spiked up all over her body. She bolted up to her feet while scanning her surroundings. Instantly, she knew Gemma wasn't there. *Come on! What have you done now, idiot?* she chastised herself. *Think, dumb-ass! You have to recall something!* This was all just too much for her. Every time she turned around she was in this kind of situation, and it was beyond pissing her off, it was seriously making her crazy!

Hot-Dude stood as quickly as her, darting his own gaze in every direction as if there was some kind of threat. She almost laughed out loud, but this wasn't funny, it was all-too-serious. She had to attempt communication–but how? Making hand gestures? She rolled her eyes at herself. *This is stupid, but what other choice do I have?* She at least had to try. *Here goes nothing.* Slowly, using her arms and hands, palms facing the ground, she pushed in a downward motion in an attempt to calm him, and let him know she wasn't feeling any threat; only confusion over...*him*, though that last part was her little secret. "Me, Iax. My name is—" *Shit, this is harder than it looks!* She sighed.

Sounding it out seemed like a good idea. "Eye–Axe...is me," she supplied, pointing to herself. "Who are you?" speaking clearly, she pointed at him and sounded everything out the best she could. This was gonna take a while, she decided. What else did she have to do? Shrugging that away, she focused on Hot-Dude.

"Eeeyyyee–Aaaxxxss, yooo," he slowly drew out the name with a wicked hiss at the end as he pointed to her, and it made her shiver. *This man is too hot, and he's taking an interest in me?* Se suddenly became suspicious; it was just Iax's way.

Yes! This wasn't so bad, she could do it. Nodding her head, she smiled. "Yes! Me Iaxsss. You, what is your name?" she hedged, still speaking slowly and pointing at him.

Furrowing his handsome brows, he glanced down at his hands, at the ground, then back up at her. He seemed intelligent and like he desperately wanted to communicate, but wasn't quite sure how to go about it. Iax *could* be patient, she just didn't usually *care* for it, but for now she would try.

After a few long moments he grunted, and she had to stifle a giggle as he shook his arms out to give it another shot. "Meeee–M–M," his mouth popped as he tried to make the 'M' sound, and it reminded her of a Blowfish, or maybe a Guppy. She couldn't stop her laughter from bubbling up.

He frowned, and she immediately sobered. *That wasn't nice, Iax, behave,* she scolded herself. Pressing her lips into a straight line, she nodded once.

She had to give him this much, he was persistent. "Mmmmaaaa–zzz," he drew out each letter, then stopped and shook his head. Her jaw dropped. *What the…? Mazar?* She knew without him even finishing, he was Mazar. The dick-wad who had abducted Yoren. The fucker who was responsible for every damnable thing she'd gone through. The whole reason for her even being here!

"Mazar? Oh, you son-of-a-bitch, you! Who the *fuck* do you think you are? How *dare* you–you—" What was the use? He couldn't even understand her! *Dammit!* She stormed around the campfire and got right up into his baffled-looking, too-handsome face. Not accustomed to having to look *up* to see anyone eye-to-eye, it pissed her off even more that she had to with him, of all people… er, Dragon-shifter. *Whatever! This really blows!*

Poking at his hard-as-a-rock, heavily-muscled chest—though it somehow didn't seem like such a terrible thing at the moment—he allowed her to be brash as she continued to poke and rant. Each syllable accompanied by another poke with a force that made him take a couple steps back, before he firmly yet gently grasped her finger in his hand at lightning speed. And unless she was mistaken again, his gorgeous, emerald green-eyes sparkled with amusement. *Bastard! I'll show you amusement!* she fumed to herself.

"Let go of me, you piece of shit! I'll kick your fucking ass, you low-down, demented loser-mother-fucker! You have *no* idea who you're messing with! Let! Go! *Now!*" she snapped, feeling heat rise up to cover her face from the anger boiling her insides. She couldn't recall ever being so angry!

He stumbled one more time, had the balls to grin, and finally let go of her finger. Then he was on the other side of the campfire in a blur, leaving Iax standing alone, confused, and even more pissed off. *Is it even possible to be more pissed off?* she seriously wondered. Speechless; Iax was utterly speechless. *Mama and Dad would love this.* She almost laughed out loud at the thought. She had been many things, but speechless had never been one of them.

Now what? She had no idea where to go from here. Obviously Hot-Dude, or better yet, *Mazar,* was getting a kick out of their confrontation. Hell, he didn't even realize it was a confrontation! He was obviously having a swell time! "Asshole," she grumbled. "All right, listen; I'm *here* because you took a female named Yoren. Ring a bell?"

He stiffened at the name.

Good, fucker. She grinned.

****

Mazar hurried as quickly as his feet would propel him forward, to reach the female on the ledge of the cliff-top. He did not know why, but he felt if he did not find her, he would die. Even though dying had been part of his plan this day, for some reason it simply felt different now, as he contemplated *her.*

Once he finally reached the top of the mountain, he veered off the well-worn path, sensing her presence in a different direction. *Why would I sense anything about her? I do not even know her,* he speculated. Whatever the reason, it did not seem important; all that mattered to him at the moment was reaching her. Slowing as he made his way through the thickly forested terrain, he caught a scent which had to be her. Following the scent, his heart wildly hammered inside his chest, it felt like nothing he had ever experienced in his overlong-lifetime.

What will happen when I reach her, and what am I supposed to do with her? he worried, suddenly feeling a strange awkwardness. He frowned as he slowed to a walking pace when a burning sensation he had felt earlier—though it had only been minor—started to heat to such a degree, it felt as if it was scalding his flesh on the right-front side of his hip area. He had dismissed all the heat he felt in that area since first spotting the female, assuming it to be a scrape or some such thing. He could have easily received it either from the long journey he had just been on, from the battle, or possibly even from abusing himself the previous eve after draining his fire-brew.

Slowing his trek even more, he needed to inspect the spot which grew increasingly hotter the further he ventured into the woods, as he searched for...*her. It cannot be.* Mazar stopped dead in his tracks. This was only possible when...*no.* He had to be mistaken or imagining things.

Whenever a male and female were Truemates, as the Mating Bond occurred, one's image would burn itself into the other's flesh. Hers, a butterfly in his Dragon colors. His, a Dragon in her Dragon colors. *Impossible,* he wanted to claim. There could be no denying it, however, as he peeled open the front of his breeches and saw the irrefutable proof. There it was, a stunning female-Dragon image burnt into his very flesh.

Mazar was so shocked, he sunk to his knees there on the forest floor where he remained for several moments, until he suddenly felt a strong urge to get to her. Jumping up, he fixed his breeches back together and ran all-out. It did not take long, and his heart sank when he finally happened upon her. There she lay seemingly—*sleeping?*—yes, sleeping on the forest floor. He slowly walked to her side, where he knelt to inspect her for injuries. *Please, do not let her be injured,* he silently prayed. He could not take it if he finally found his Truemate, and something untoward had happened to her.

Her beauty was such, it stole his breath; long, golden hair which he could not stop himself from reaching out and touching. As he had thought earlier, it was softer than silk. He smiled. She had a steady heartbeat which matched his own. *None of this makes sense. We have not yet kissed. How did we Bond?* He had never heard anything about their heartbeats matching. He frowned. His senses did not detect that she was a shifter of any kind, and this made his frown deepen. Baffled as he was, this discovery also made him sad, for obvious reasons. He was absolutely positive she was not a Dragon-shifter, at least not one from his Realm.

Her breaths came heavier and he worried at the cause. *Was she suffering from terror-dreams?* He did not care for the feelings welling up inside of him. She quietly murmured words he did not recognize, adding to the overall sense of confusion he already felt regarding her, troubling him further. *At least she does not seem to be injured.* He heaved a sigh of relief. If only she would open her lovely eyes—he instinctively knew they were lovely—and if only they could speak to one another. He was confident she would have the same pleasurable feelings he did.

Gently brushing a few stray tendrils of hair away from her face with a shaky hand, he quietly chuckled at how large his hand was next to her face; her mesmerizing, achingly gorgeous face. "Ah, my female. You are perfect," he whispered into the soft breeze.

Glancing around their location, he realized the sun would soon set, and he needed to care for her. *My Truemate.* Shaking his head in bewilderment, he smiled and sighed. "My Truemate. Finally, you arrive in my life." Only then did he realize...*the buzzing is gone!* Meynix, *I am more thankful than mere words can express!* He had never been so happy, nor had he ever felt such peace and quiet. The peace he found within the blessed quiet had hot tears of disbelief and gratitude stinging the backs of his eyes.

His smile faded as he recalled the gravity of his other situation; the one where he would most likely be executed. Life had never been easy, nor was anyone promised fairness. *But this is beyond unfair,* he steamed inside, his blood rushed and began to boil at the injustice of everything. *How could I have been so stupid? If only I had stayed here and been patient for what—a few more days? This cannot happen!* he roared to himself, but he truly wanted to bellow it aloud! He wanted to beat something, or someone. He wanted...he wanted.

Hanging his head in shame; this seemed to be his biggest problem, of late. He wanted. It was apparently all about him nowadays. *When did I become so selfish? I do not think I have ever been, and I do not care for how it makes me feel,* he admitted, now that it may be too late. *May be? Ha!* he mocked himself. *It would be a full certainty, you fool! You have blown it all! Not only for your own self but for her, as well.*

Mazar gazed lovingly and sadly back down to the peaceful-looking face of his Truemate. *What about her?* A humorless laugh tried to escape him, but he tamped it down not wanting to disturb her slumber. All anyone ever got was one Truemate. After they Bonded, they could never be permanently separated, not without losing their minds in earnest. At least, he had never known any who had survived the loss well, if at all.

He could only shake his head at himself and his ineptness. Before even knowing her, he had sentenced her to such a fate. For about the hundredth or so time this day, he wondered again, *What have I done, and why?*

Before he knew it darkness was quickly descending, as was the temperature. He quickly snapped out of his shocked, saddened state knowing if he did not get her to a better location, make a campfire, and find her some foods, she could fall ill...or worse.

Realizing he truly knew nothing about her, not even what she was, he decided none of that mattered for now and gently scooped her sleeping form into the strong embrace of his arms. Rising, he reveled in her softness, her scent; finally, something to bring a smile to his lips. *She is positively exquisite.* This would be his Truemate, if only there was a way to work out his other situation. He had to think, there had to be a way to make it work. *There simply has to be,* he vowed.

After walking smoothly—he would not awaken her if he could help it—for quite a distance, he finally came upon a decent sized clearing. Taking in all the conditions and the area as a whole, he quickly decided this would be a suitable location to make up a small camp. It took a few minutes and some careful balancing, but he managed to make a small pallet for her out of some large, soft tree leaves. Carefully as possible, he lowered her luscious form down onto the pallet.

Obviously she was simply worn out and exhausted. He sensed an overly strong inner-need for her to work. Too much. The thought profoundly unnerved him; any Truemate of his would not do such a thing. This he would demand she cease, and at the soonest! Venturing further into the subject, he tried to think of what kind of work she did. Since he had no idea of *where* she was from, or *what* she was, it was rather difficult to discern any type of work or activities in which she may partake. He scowled at the thought. He *should* know these things! He should *know* her! Or, at least some things about…*her.*

Knowing he would get no answers anytime soon, he went to make a campfire. In a short order, a great fire blazed in the clearing where Mazar simply sat and watched her sleeping form. There had been no more of her which, oddly enough, troubled him almost as much as her earlier words. He knew the answer to this conundrum; he simply loved the sweet sound of her voice. Even if it was only hushed ramblings in her slumber, it was still music to his ears, a balm to his soul. More calming than anything else had ever been.

Mazar had let her be, wanting her to slumber peacefully for a couple more hours. Once darkness had come, he noticed her making small movements when he added more wood to the campfire. He thought she would most likely awaken soon due to her actions, but he waited; no one ever wanted to be unnecessarily awakened, and there had been no reason to bother her.

Reclaiming his seat on a log across the campfire from her, he waited to see how long she would continue to slumber. As he continued to wait, a frisson of fear snaked through him; fear that she may not be as accepting of him, and that they would not be able to communicate effectively—recalling her ramblings from earlier—none of it had made any sense to him.

When she finally stirred and spoke aloud, just as he had feared, he did not understand any of what she said. While he tried to think of how to make their communications a bit easier, or even possible. When she sat up and saw him, she froze. Then he froze, at her beauty, the wild look in her lovely, bright-green eyes, which were exactly how he had imagined them. All of her features, along with her other considerable attributes, were lovely.

Perhaps this will go better than I had thought. He smiled.

When she suddenly began to ramble in those unfamiliar words, he did not care overmuch, he simply enjoyed the sound of her voice. Then he asked her if she was warm enough and if she required nourishment. Her only response was physical as she stared at him for a few long moments. It was as if she could not help herself, and to this, he allowed hope to rise inside of him.

Then, as he stood and crossed his muscled arms over his rippling chest, she tried to communicate with him in her unfamiliar language. *Perhaps this will be more difficult than I had considered,* he admitted to himself. Still, he could listen to her voice forever. It was smooth, strong—as was she—and far more feminine than one would expect, given her tough persona.

Once he had figured out her name was 'Iaxsss,' he liked the way it felt on his tongue. When he tried to get her to understand his own name, she had gone mad; running around the campfire yelling quite loudly, spitting strange words in his face, and poking her finger in his chest, *hard*. She was obviously distraught, but he only wanted to help her, to figure her out, and perhaps calm her down.

When she mentioned Yoren, however, a sick feeling bubbled up in the pit of his belly. *How would she know Yoren, and what does she care, anyway?* he worried. She was not from this Dragon Realm, which made him worry again over the reason for her presence. *Did it even matter?* he questioned himself. She was also a high-spirited female; Mazar had not had such fun in…he could not even recall. After he had loosed her soft, beautiful finger he had gone to the other side of the campfire to observe her glorious, fiery rage from a distance which obviously angered her even further. It could have also had something to do with the fact that he was grinning at her like a fool. He could not help himself.

All that changed when several things took place simultaneously; Mazar heard and sensed unfamiliar beings racing in their direction. From there, he could not have changed what happened whether he had wanted to or not.

Chapter Sixteen

Following the figure floating just in front of her, Gemma felt a shift in the air and heard the almost imperceptible sound of a voice; a decidedly *female* voice. Also hearing it, Skenyah pulled up next to Gemma where they halted their trek to discern what was happening. It only took a moment to realize the voice was Iax's, and she was highly agitated, to be sure. Gemma chuckled. "The furious voice we hear would be our Iax, in that direction." Gemma pointed up ahead and to their left. "I would say she must have found her male, or he found her. I am uncertain of the reason but I can determine for certain, she is not happy, not at all." She smirked.

Iax's ranting became louder and more crude as they made their way closer to her location, and Gemma almost felt sorry for the male. She knew from firsthand experience, it did not always take much to set her friend off. Who knew what the male had said or done? She couldn't quell her chuckling again, which earned her a scowl from Skenyah.

"What do you find so humorous, Gemma? I feel a terrible upset in Iax. How can you laugh at such a time?" Skenyah reprimanded, and then resumed her mission to find and aid Iax.

"If you knew *our* Iax, you would not be so quick to question me. Assuredly, you have no idea how sharp her tongue is, nor how quick her temper can flare. Are you hearing the words she is saying? Can you honestly tell me that you have knowledge of them?" she hedged, with a bright smile.

For Skenyah's sake, they halted once more so the female could hear precisely what her precious Iax was spewing.

Gemma had to tamp down the urge to laugh aloud so they would not be heard. She wanted their arrival to be a surprise so she shook her head instead, more amused than she had been in a long while. *I suppose I did not need to worry over Iax, after all. She always could take care of herself quite well, for the most part,* she admitted.

Skenyah turned her gaze back on Gemma, her expression puzzled. "I do admit, I know not what she is saying. I can understand some of her words, but not most of them. She sounds angry. Does she truly anger oft and easily?" she questioned.

Oh, if you only knew, Gemma mused, her smile widening. "Yes, I would say so. She does both of those things. She usually means well, so whatever the male said or did, he most likely had it coming. Iax is not completely unfair, or at least not always..." she trailed off, murmuring the last part under her breath. The more thought she gave to her friend, the more she realized she could be mistaken. At times, Iax's temper flared for little or no real reason at all. She wondered if it was possibly a trait of her lineage. She knew from Iax's stories, the parents who raised her were not that way, nor did they approve when she acted out in such a fashion. She frowned.

"What is it? You were glowing for a moment and now you frown. Did you recall or sense something else, regarding Iax?" They were on the move again and Skenyah was quicker than her. Gemma had to go faster than normal to keep up but it was not a problem, she could go as fast as any being, and she did.

"I will concede there are times when it does not take much for Iax's temper to flare. As for her words? You do not want to know what they are or what they mean. She has always spoken this way, always uses inappropriate language, and simply does not care if it offends. It is only one of the reasons I so care for her." She smiled. Even though she chastised her friend oft, it was still some of her fondest memories of time spent with Iax.

"Well, I can say I most certainly do not like the sounds of what you speak. It simply will not do! Whether she knows or likes it, she is Royalty, after all. As such, she will have to conform to our ways," Skenyah clipped out, obviously not thrilled at the aspect of Iax's ways.

You better get used to it Skenyah. Iax will not change for anyone, not even your fancy Royal family, Gemma quipped to herself, as a small snicker escaped her.

"I do wish you would cease poking humor over this, it is not acceptable. It is already clear that I will have much work to do regarding Iax; much tedious, hard work which she will most likely not even appreciate, if what you speak is true," Skenyah all but spat.

Even though the female's reaction to Iax did not surprise Gemma, she still felt her ire rise. She did not appreciate such harsh judgements being made upon Iax, before Skenyah had seen or met her. *This does not bode well. I do hope she gives Iax a chance. She is not a bad female simply because she is tough, unruly, and speaks as she does, in her own way,* she contemplated.

This meeting would not be fun for any of them, leastwise Iax. Gemma felt a bit sad while mulling it over. She only wanted good things for her friend, and she already knew Iax would never *conform* for anything or anyone. There was nothing to be done about it now, in any case. They would all have to wait and see how Iax received this news. Gemma did not envy any of their positions, not after seeing Skenyah's presumptuous reaction, and especially not after she got to know Iax. It would not go well for either of them. *Poor Iax,* she wished she could meet with her alone—before Skenyah found her—to warn her of what was to come. She sighed.

****

One minute, Iax was still staring at Mazar trying to figure out what to do with, and how to communicate with him. His hotness wasn't helping! *Seriously, how much is a girl supposed to endure? Gawk at him? Don't gawk at him?* Not as easy as one might think.

Suddenly, Mazar's head snapped to one side, then the other. His entire demeanor changed, as did his…*skin? Oh, shit! He's shifting!* She had only thought it was hard to look away from his glorious form before. *But this? No fucking way.* Every bit of his beautifully tanned skin took on a radiant affect, and then his entire form was encased in a glowing, bubble-like thing which made it impossible to look directly at, and clearly focus on him, during his transformation.

It all happened so fast, and a split-second later, there stood a massive, beautiful, defensive Dragon. "Holy shit!" Iax exclaimed rather loudly. She felt something…just barely, but it was enough to know he sensed a threat of some kind. She kind of did, too, but she also felt a peacefulness, and yep…Gemma. Funny, how she always knew when the woman was close, at least after they'd spent a little time together.

Knowing full-well that Gemma could undoubtedly hold her own, and only now remembering that they'd probably been apart for a few hours, she suddenly realized that Gemma must have come across someone else out here. *Probably someone looking for Mazar. Shit. This could get ugly.* She frowned. Of course, she always had Gemma's back, but why did Iax suddenly have an overwhelming urge to protect Mazar? *I gotta stop this shit, now!* She knew.

Mazar turned toward the dense woods from which their visitors approached, and Iax moved to stand beside his crouched, Dragon-form. She instinctively knew he would not harm her; with a shaky hand, she tentatively reached out to touch his side. The moment her hand came in contact with his thick, surprisingly soft scales, his enormous wings flapped, but not enough to move him. Then she felt a strong *zap!* They jumped as if they'd been electrocuted. Not painfully, but still. *What the hell?*

At least he's looking at me now. For this she was grateful.

He stood tall; the top of his head to the ground was at least forty or more feet, and every bit of him was covered in large, shiny scales. The dominate color was gold; a thick, brilliant swath outlined his full shape, and blended with the colorful interior design of his immense Dragon-form. Different hues of blues, greens, and even some purples. *Oh, my…holy gorgeousness.* His eyes were an intoxicating yet different mixture of the same colors; blues, greens, purples and golds, but unlike his body, the hypnotic coloring of his eyes swirled round and round, much like a vortex; a beautifully mesmerizing vortex. Even worse—or maybe better—than his Dragon-form, they beckoned and called to her to lean forward and let herself fall into them.

Snap out of it, Iax! You have to help the situation, not make it worse! she scolded herself.

She was thanking God for the extensive training she had for this exact scenario; recalling the Mr. Green Things, she knew she had to fight it and not allow anything to mesmerize her. It was an effort, but she tore her gaze away. She had to diffuse the situation before it got out of control.

Here goes. Slowly shaking her head, not wanting to startle or agitate his warrior fight-or-die senses, she made sure all of her movements were deliberate and slow as she spoke to him. "Hey, Big Guy. That's it, look at me. It's ooo–kaaay. Nooo fight." Feeling silly, she spoke to him as if he was a three-year old, using her hands, arms, as well as shaking and nodding her head, but he did appear to relax a little. She released a soft, relieved sigh.

"Good. Very good. Let's go back over here." She hiked a thumb over her shoulder and turned toward the clearing. Iax pointed while slowly making her way to the campfire. And what do ya know? He followed! *Yay! One for me!* She beamed with pride.

Nodding her head, she pointed to herself, then the ground, and then she sat down Indian-style. He warily eyed her for a moment, then settled his ginormous frame beside her. His thick, deadly-looking tail had been swishing back and forth at first, but it also seemed to calm down.

Taking a smaller branch from the wood pile he'd obviously gathered while she'd been on a snooze-fest, she slowly pulled off a smaller piece of the wood, and used it to draw in the dirt. She hoped he'd understand. "This is me, here." She pointed at herself after sketching a stick figure. Drawing another figure close to hers, she indicated the two. "This, Iax's friend."

She maintained steady eye contact, when she wasn't doing her best Leonardo da Vinci, and even tried to smile a little. She had experienced some shifters who got downright nasty in their 'other' form. Yet she felt oddly safe in his presence, and wanted to calm him so he would shift back, and not attack Gemma and whoever was with her.

Making a circle around the two stick-figures, she hugged herself then patted her heart. "Friend. Iax's friend." She pointed to the woods where he had sensed what he thought was a threat.

Mazar eyed the woods for a moment and softly snorted, releasing a tendril of smoke from his nostrils and a puff of fire from his mouth, and then he nodded. She was thrilled at the small measure of progress they were making.

"Iax go to her friend." She pointed toward the woods again. "Mazar, stay here." Patting the ground, she enunciated her words as she slowly got to her feet. He shifted his position a little, keeping an eye on her, and another on the woods. Just as was making her way across the clearing to call out to Gemma, she smelled, felt, and heard a blast of fire several yards to her left. Twirling around, she saw that his eyes were glowing and he was crouched back in a defensive stance. *Great. This isn't going at all well.*

Slowly raising her hands, palms facing outward, she instructed, "Mazar, no. Iax, okay. Stay." She pointed to him, and then the ground. He settled, but his eyes were still ablaze. *He's a little scary like this.* She shivered. Staying put seemed like the best plan, so she did. Keeping herself angled to watch him and the woods, she chanced a glance toward the woods. "Gemma? That you, babe? Looket, if so, ya gotta come in cool. Got it?" She was sweating and almost dizzy.

Suddenly, she felt her skin grow hot and tight. *What the fuck, now?* She was so sick of this shit! Always something since she'd arrived here. Her temper totally died away when she glanced down at herself; arms outstretched, she turned her hands over and her jaw dropped. She was…*glowing.* Just as Mazar did right before….

Everything happened so fast, she didn't know what to do as a piercing pain tore through every cell in her body, ripping through her muscles and shifting her bones. Fire burned a wide path from her head to her toes. Her mind went foggy and she thought she might faint.

"No! Iax!"

Reflexively, her head snapped over to the right toward the woods when she heard Gemma's voice calling out. She knew her friend was yelling—that thing she never did—and she was acting defensively for Iax.

Iax tried to call out in response to her friend, but no words came. She suddenly noticed how small everything around her was. *Very small. What? Oh. My. God.* Her brain was only half getting what was going on. Feeling some weird-ass Spidey-Senses, she was kind of glad for it, because that's when Gemma ran from the woods in her direction. And she was being followed by a glowing, shimmering, beautiful female being of some kind. One who immediately felt familiar to her.

Her senses kicked in, and she knew without even looking that Mazar was getting ready to fight them both. Not her, but Gemma and her new friend were about to be toast. Burnt toast. Iax swirled and almost fell—since she'd never been in *Dragon*-form before, which she didn't have time to contemplate just then—mid-turn as her tail smashed into a large tree. It broke down low near the ground, and knocked it over where it almost landed on Gemma's friend.

That's when things got weird.

The shimmering female with—*wings?*—was a glowing ball one-second, and in the next, she was a gigantic, breathtakingly-gorgeous Dragon. She was immediately airborne and heading straight for Mazar.

****

Gemma, still hot on the heels, or rather, the mist, vapor, or whatever it was, of Skenyah, kept up the pace without a problem. She knew they needed to make time and quickly reach Iax. Although she did not sense anything nefarious regarding Iax, the strong urge to be near her did something strange to her belly. A painful kind of strange.

She had fervently tried to get Skenyah to understand and realize that her idea of simply 'taking' Iax back to their Realm, would be a horrible plan. Iax would not do it, Gemma knew this as surely as she knew her own name.

They were nearing the edge of the woods coming upon a clearing, when she finally heard Iax calling out for her. The last part sent a streak of white-hot panic through her insides. Something was terribly wrong. The "Ya gotta come in cool. Got it?" portion of Iax's statement suddenly made Gemma fear not only for Iax, but for Skenyah and herself, as well. *What is happening?* Gemma puzzled.

Iax's voice was steady and strong, yet things simply did not feel right. She put on an extra burst of speed, passing Skenyah and not looking back. As she entered the clearing she saw two things, which she now knew to be the source of her fears and worry. First, she noticed a male fully-shifted into his Dragon-form who was breathing fire. A whole lot of fire. At her. Next, she noticed a second fully-shifted, beautiful Dragon, which was confusing because she knew without doubt, Iax was here. At least she had been only scant moments ago. *Where is the female now?* she worried.

That was when it hit her, and for only the second time in her many long years, she was truly afraid. For Iax, and herself. Suddenly, she realized the second shifter was Iax! *I would know that female anywhere, no matter her form. Holy shit!* She could not even think about the humor she normally would have over using those words of Iax's. It was simply the only thing her mind was willing to accept.

"No! Iax!" is all she got out just as she froze. She could not move, speak, and could only barely breathe. Her next memory was

Iax's Dragon-form; stunning, beautiful, and magnificent, along with Skenyah's Dragon-form, and the male's Dragon-form. They were all inflight, propelling themselves at dizzying speeds toward one another.

She wanted to do or say something, anything, but she was rooted in place. It almost felt as if she had been put under compulsion, but she knew better as that did not work on her. So, she figured in her hazy mind, this must be another of those emotions Iax has spoken of; shock. Once more, Gemma did not care much for it, nor for any of what was playing out before her very eyes.

****

Mazar knew the second he felt the change coming on, things were about to go badly. But when he felt a threat which could be aimed at his Truemate, there was no other choice, literally. When one felt an imminent threat toward their Truemate, they automatically shifted. It was a simple fact.

As he stood crouched and battle-ready, he jumped when he felt a *zap* travel through his large Dragon-form. Glancing over his shoulder, he saw Iaxsss also jumping back just as she had touched him. His inner-Dragon smiled, then frowned. *What just happened?* he puzzled.

He had felt a threat coming from the woods, quickly shifted, and now stood ready to kill for her, yet she seemed as if she did not welcome it, and this confused him. All warriors fought for their Weyr, moreover, for their Truemates. From her motions and sounds, he gathered that she wanted him to follow her, so he did. He would follow her anywhere. His inner-Dragon sighed.

Once she had seated herself upon the bare ground, he settled at her side as he took in her every move. When she started to make a plan in the dirt, he paid close attention, all the while keeping his senses open to whatever, or whoever, was in the woods quickly coming their way.

It took a few moments, but he was certain she was letting him know that whoever was approaching was friend, not foe. He felt a bit of relief. He did not *want* to battle, but he *would.* However, when she got up and walked toward the woods, his senses flared once more, and he could not stop the rush of flame from escaping his mouth. Even though she had communicated 'friend,' he felt something…else, another sense which did not feel quite so *friendly* to him.

All of a sudden, Iaxsss was a glowing, blinding ball of fire! She was…shifting! His heart hammered inside his chest. *She* is *a shifter!* Not of his own kind but a shifter, nonetheless. He could not have been more surprised or thrilled!

Her Dragon captivated his every sense, leaving him temporarily paralyzed. She was large, though not overly. Her form was long and lean, yet not dainty. Every inch of her was well-muscled, and her coloring matched the Dragon image burnt into his flesh. *Amazing.* She was thirty or so feet tall, her tail was long and sleek. Wings over her back in shades of turquoise and purple slowly flapped. Her main body color was a lighter purple, still rippling with the aftereffects of her change.

As she turned her head to glance in his direction, he practically swallowed his own huge tongue. Her eyes were glowing orbs of a strange blue-green shade, so faint they almost appeared translucent.

Just then, a female came rushing out of the woods and headed straight toward his Iaxsss, yelling words he did not know. It quickly brought him back to reality. *No!* he wanted to bellow, but could only spew fire and smoke. *Nobody nears my Truemate if I do not know them or their intentions!* If only he could speak, make them all understand, they could most likely end the battle before it began. But he could only communicate telepathically with other Dragons in this form. In other words, he could not communicate with the female charging toward his Truemate, who was most certainly not a Dragon.

Shooting him a fierce look, his Iaxsss made it clear that this was her friend. He was willing to allow the female passage, as he did not feel a threat from her. Then another female, no, not simply a female, but an Amethyst Faerie Dragon-shifter, also exited the woods, glowing and shimmering. Mazar went into attack mode; there nothing to do about it at this point.

The other shifter allowed the change to overtake her, and then flew straight at him. He had to act quickly; he did not want to harm any friend to Iaxsss, but this was kill-or-be-killed time. He launched himself into the air.

To his further shock and horror, Iaxsss launched herself up at the same time, resulting in a thunderous clap when the three shifters clashed midair with a brutal force. Instantly, he hissed at the Amethyst Faerie-shifter when they all collided, just before they all fell and landed in a heap upon the ground.

Hearing his Iaxsss' painful grunt stayed his killing impulse.

His Truemate lay on the ground unmoving for a few moments. It felt like an eternity, but soon she relaxed enough to turn her beautiful, bewildered gaze back and forth between himself and the other shifter.

Letting his guard down for a moment, he did not see or sense the female friend approach from the edge of the clearing, where she had stood in place while everything had happened so quickly.

"Oh, dear! Are you alright, Iax?" she spoke in his language; a warmth spread over him inside and out. She was unquestionably friend, and one who was deeply worried about his Truemate. This pleased him, knowing she would never harm his Iaxsss. The other female, however, the Dragon-shifter, was now pulling herself into a standing position, eyeing them all and their surroundings with something akin to wariness, shock, and…strong emotions. All of which were targeted at his Iaxsss.

Who is she, and what does she want? He was baffled by her.

She struck a protective stance, angling herself halfway between himself and Iaxsss, her eyes were all but shooting flames at him as if she could blast him with only her glare. She was protecting Iaxsss.

But from what? Or whom? I would never harm a silky hair on her head, or a scale on her captivating Dragon-form. After a few tense moments, and against his normal battle-sharp instincts, Mazar allowed himself to shift back into his male-form. He knew this was showing a great vulnerability, but he felt a strong need to let everyone know he was in no way a threat to his Iaxsss.

He shifted back, and allowed the fire to burn through his body as his muscles and bones retracted and reshaped. When the change was complete, he stood there wondering why they were all openly staring at him. It only took a moment to figure it out. "Oh! Apologies! I–I…" he trailed off, realizing he was standing there bare arsed! He had never been ashamed of his nude-form, but one of these females was now his own, and the other two should not see her male nude; this much he knew.

Fleeing into the woods in a blur, he found a few large leaves with which to cover himself. He quickly secured them around his lower-region using some of the thinner, softer branches. Certainly it would do, it had to. Grabbing a few more supplies to cover his Iaxsss when she changed back, he smiled at the feeling of doing such things for another. It made him feel valued. Useful. Important.

When he reentered the clearing, both shifters had changed back and the female friend was hovering over Iaxsss' bare form. He quickly realized her breaths were coming in ragged, heavy gasps, and she was having difficulties with the change. *Why would she have difficulties? She is a shifter, after all,* he worried. The dawning hit him as if it were a slap in the face; she had never shifted before, which was why he had not sensed it in her. This was her first time and it was brutal, far too fast, and she did not have any aid or training because she…was not aware, until now.

Heavy new emotions threatened to be his undoing. *What can I do? What should I do? For my Truemate, I will do anything, no exceptions, to see her well.* Mazar genuinely needed to know, so he humbled himself as he begged and beseeched his Goddess, *Meynix,* for help, for answers…for anything.

He was at her side in less than a second, and noticed one of her arms lying at an odd angle as she tried to hold it near her body. Mazar all but shoved her friend and the Faerie-shifter—who hissed at him—out of his way. Making quick work of covering her delicate female parts with the supplies he brought from the woods, he was confused and did not know what to think or do about his female's current state.

Speaking in the Universal Dragon language, he snapped at the Faerie-shifter, "Do *not* touch her! This is *your* doing! What has happened? Why is she in such a state?" he roared, furious that his female was ill.

The female friend spoke up, "First, I am Gemma. Next, she is not, or rather, *was* not a shifter. What I mean is, we were unaware of her lineage. She is…*was* not of the Dragon Dimension. She is a peacemaker, as well as a warrior from another world. She came here to retrieve an abducted, Weyr Chief's Truemate, who is also carrying. I only was made aware of her shifting ability moments ago, by her." Gemma turned to point at Skenyah. "This would be her aunt Skenyah. She speaks that Iax's mathair and fathair were felled in an attack when Iax was a new-youngling. Iax was then taken to another world at the insistence of her makers, just before they were slain, to keep her safe until she was to return near her twenty-fifth-year, which is now. Iax does not know any of her past, or did not, before now," she finished as Iaxsss was trying to move.

He could sense this Gemma's gratitude in seeing her friend's expression relaxed, no longer the pained one from moments ago. That she thought it best to wait and not allow Iaxsss to move yet, only softened him to her even more.

Gently rubbing her friend's arm with one hand, Gemma reached down and swept some hair off Iaxsss's sweating face. She looked almost stunned when the poor thing smiled up at her, reached up to cover Gemma's hand with her own, and then nuzzled her face into it.

****

"Gemma…I–I…" Iax didn't know what to say to anyone. She'd heard Gemma using that Dragon-speak on Mazar, and normally she wouldn't have understood any of it. But this time? For the same reasons still confusing the hell out of her, she understood every word that had passed between the two.

What she really wanted to hear was this supposed aunt of hers speak, she had a feeling she'd recognize the female-shifter's voice anywhere. If what this Skenyah had said to Gemma was in any way true? Well, she was at such a loss, she didn't know where to go or how to come back from the abyss her mind was teetering on.

My mathair and fathair? My aunt? What the fuck kinda suck-ass-jackrabbit-hole have I fallen into? Of all the weird, crazy, unexplainable shit she'd ever seen, heard, and been through, this totally took the cake. *Faerie Dragon-Shifter? Me? No way.* She felt so disconnected after that whole ripping and burning thing had taken over every inch of her body, and she knew she'd shifted into a… Dragon. *But, how?* If what Gemma just said was true, then her entire life had been a pack of lies. *How could it be? Why didn't Mama and Dad ever tell me? They had to have known, didn't they?* she numbly wondered.

"How?" is all she could croak out. *This can't be happening.* She felt Mazar's presence; a large, gentle hand rubbing small, comforting circles on her lower back. She had to admit it felt exceptionally relaxing, which was great 'cause she felt like puking. But it also felt weird 'cause, well, it was *Mazar*. Weird didn't even come close. She was still thankful for whatever he was doing, as it was taking away all the ick-feelings.

I'm supposed to hate him, aren't I? she questioned herself. *Furthermore, why is he acting so protective on my behalf? I thought he was...well, many things, and none of them good.* She didn't have the energy to think of the many things she either had, could, or wanted to call him. For some even more unfathomable reason, she didn't even want to, if that made any kind of sense. It sure as hell didn't to her.

Ah, there it is, and thank God! Her tongue; her armor, even if it was only in a mental state, at least she had it. If she could have peeled herself off the dirt-packed forest floor, she would have jumped up and did herself a happy-dance! But again, she was fading fast and feeling almost lethargic.

Not diggin' this emotional roller-coaster, she let herself know, then added, *Guess it's not the forest floor. I'm still in the same clearing I just awoke in. Wait. What? Just awoke? Seems like a couple hours have flown by.* In reality it couldn't have been more than just a few minutes, half an hour, tops. *Whoa, dizziness, feeling faint, ain't likin' none of it.* Like it or not, that was it, lights out for Iax again. Although she'd never admit such a weakness to anyone, she welcomed the darkness that threatened to swallow her whole. She also prayed and hoped that next time she'd *really* wake up, and all this Alice-in-Wonderland shit would be just a horrible, awful dream.

She must've hit her head harder than she'd thought when she fell, and of course her wondrous full-on-face-plant with the stupid damn tree. How could she have forgotten all that fun?

What else ya got, huh? Bring it on! Bring it on, whoever you are fucking with me and my life! What the hell did I ever do wrong? I'm no Saint, I get that, but am I that terrible? No, I'm not! I've always helped and done for others, just like my parents always taught me, she angrily protested to herself.

It was either fade away, or start making a list of reasons to be seriously pissed at trusty ole Mama and Dad, which she really didn't want to do...yet. Taking in a big, shaky breath, she let it out on a long sigh, and allowed the darkness to take her in only a matter of moments.

And amen for it.

It was probably best. At least this way, she wouldn't be awake or aware of what was about to happen next.

Chapter Seventeen

It did not take Gordell long to arrange for his journey. After delegating certain chores and various other crucial tasks to a few trusted souls, and making sure the warriors who had stayed behind were all on point to guard his holdings, he was ready to go get his Yoren and bring her home where she belonged.

Earlier, he had been pleased to learn the details from the male-young who had delivered his message. However, he was now only half pleased with a couple new bits of information; Darkan had led their warriors on an uneventful journey to the other Weyr territory; pleased. His First's meeting with the other Chief went relatively well; pleased again. Yoren had been found safe and unharmed; exceptionally pleased. But much to his dismay, Mazar was nowhere to be found; extremely displeased. Although in truth, this fact did not surprise Gordell. The male had to know things were not going to go well for him. He supposed he most likely would not want to be in the fool's shoes right now, either. But it was still no excuse for the coward simply taking off and hiding.

"Hide all you like, fool, I will find you, and you will not enjoy our meeting," he promised the slight breeze fluttering around him. His wicked-grin returned and spread across his lips. "Oh, but I will savor every single moment." He felt a sudden warmth as his grin bloomed in full.

His plan was to take to the air, make straight for the other territory, and find Mazar, himself. And when he did, may whichever Goddess the male prayed to, have mercy on his soul, because Gordell would have none.

Letting the warmth overtake his heavily muscled-form, he dropped his head back, both arms outstretched. Feeling the sun warm his face, he donned a heartfelt smile and allowed the change to tear through him. The shifting of bones, the ripping and tearing of muscles, the fire freely flowing from his head to his toes; it all felt good. Better than good. Airborne in only moments, the wind and sun showering over his Dragon-form felt like a welcome embrace. It had been such a long time since he had flown solo, and he would enjoy every moment.

Since his male-form was so large, his Dragon-form was massive, one of the biggest in the Realm. Gordell glided through the air and did a few dips and rolls, merely for the sake of fun and freedom. Not that he was forbidden from leisurely things, but this was one of the best, most freeing sensations one such as he could experience. He felt all of his muscles relax as he enjoyed himself and gave his Dragon free reign.

Before he realized how far he had quickly traveled, he was approaching his destination. Slowing his speed, he scanned as far as his Dragon-eyes could see as he let his other senses roam. *That is Yoren's scent. I am on the correct course; a fine start.* Excited, yet keeping his alarm and worry at bay, he began a slow, steady descent to land on a dense forest mountaintop, in the opposite direction of where he smelled his Truemate's scent.

This was about finding Mazar, *that bastard,* he fumed inside. Already certain his Yoren was safe, meant he had plenty of time. And since no one here was aware of his arrival, he would use this time wisely and to its fullest.

The sun was quickly slipping beyond the horizon as it shimmered in yellows, pinks, and purples, and left in its wake an otherworldly impression of a properly done painting. The inky-blackness that rapidly swallowed the beatific array of the sunset, mattered not. In both forms, especially his Dragon-form, all of his senses were highly acute; his vision and hearing were sharp and unmatched, as was his sense of smell—not always a pleasant thing—which aided in scenting and locating others without delay. He did not recognize the scent he was now picking up on, but something about it was unquestionably bothersome. It felt as if someone was in trouble, or possibly injured.

Gordell put on a burst of speed, and the only outward sign of his aggression was his thick, long, powerful tail swishing and trailing him from side to side. *There are females present, and they are alarmed? No!* he roared inside his head. He could tolerate many things, but a female being mistreated or harmed in any fashion, was not one of them. Mowing over treetops and smashing others in his path, he made a straight line to where he sensed the commotion at its strongest. He was more than lethal in this form. As for his mood? He almost feared for whomever dared to mishandle a female, when he got ahold of him. He instinctively knew 'it' was a him, and something untoward was happening at that moment.

Ahead several lengths, he spotted an opening of a clearing. There was a huge campfire ablaze, and a sense of dread hung thick in the air all around him. But that was not what caught his notice first; there were many abnormally bright flashes, as if there were several shifters taking on the change all at once. *Odd; it should not be so bright,* he contemplated. The mixture of scents registering in his flaring nostrils told him there were two or more species in the clearing. *How is this possible? As a Weyr Chief, I would have been notified if there were to be visitors to our Realm.*

Upon the occasion of outsiders visiting any Realm—which was not an overly common occurrence—all Chiefs were made aware, and with as much notice as possible. This made no sense at all to Gordell. His suspicion piqued, but he would get to the bottom of that later. For the now, he had work to do.

More so alarmed at the prospect of *who* was here and *why,* he slowed just before reaching the clearing; he did not wish to give away his presence just yet. He needed to discern what was happening *before* he burst into a scene, for which he may not be prepared.

Attempting to remain mindful of the noises his large form was making, he practiced caution as he quietly peered through a few trees where they had thinned out at the opening of the clearing. If Gordell had been in his male-form, his jaw would have dropped! He had been correct about several shifters, but not quite as accurate as he would have hoped. There were well over three-hundred warriors;

merely a handful had yet to shift, but from the looks of things, that would soon change.

Pulling in a few deep breaths, Gordell tried to come up with the best strategy. Though he was yet unaware, something was amiss, here. He neither spotted, nor sensed any females, and…. *Oh, no, Meynix, I am too late! No, I beseech you, my Goddess; if there were females here, and my late arrival allowed enough time for them to be killed….* He ceased his line of thought, for it was counterproductive. Additionally, had he not been in his Dragon-form, he surely would have retched at the ugly, heinous acts playing out in his mind's eye, into which he had to force their submission. He prayed he was wrong. *Certainly, no male of worth, formidable shifter, or any decent being of any type, would force his unwanted attentions on a female– would he?* There were so many shifters, the flaming knot in his gut felt as if it would ignite his insides right where he stood. *No, that cannot be the case!* He refused to believe that of any shifter from any Dragon Realm.

Edging as close as he dared, Gordell calmed himself for many reasons, and to avoid making unintentional movements. He needed to study the situation carefully before diving in headlong, and possibly causing many innocents to die, perhaps even himself. That would be his current luck; safely arrive here, and then be felled in a battle of which he had no knowledge. His Yoren would be taken home to birth and raise their youngling, without him there to help guide them…to live their lives without him. He snorted quietly as possible.

Sidled up to a large, ancient tree, which hid him well considering his abundant size, he could now make out a small commotion on the farthest edge of the clearing. There was a lone-female, who was not a shifter, and another female, fully-shifted. They were attempting to stay far away from the fray in the clearing surrounded by a dense copse of large trees. The shifter was apparently having difficulties, as if she could not draw air into her lungs. She was obviously very ill, and it deeply troubled him.

The other female, the non-shifter, hovered near the ill-shifter's side as she rubbed her hands over the her face and neck, murmuring words in a language he did not recognize. The females were not being bothered, nor did they seem to be frightened. The entirety of everything he was witnessing made no sense.

The warriors, almost all of whom were now shifted into their Dragon-forms, seemed to be split into two groups. That was when he felt like an absolute fool as the dawning rushed over him; many of them were his very own warriors! He had been so busy trying to locate and check on the females, he had not even recognized his own males! Their scents alone were a sure giveaway. With no reason to remain hidden, Gordell straightened to his fullest height, which made him taller than almost all the shifters he now faced. Then he marched into the middle of the chaotic clearing, and halted next to a blazing campfire.

It only took a moment for his males to realize his presence, and they immediately ceased what they were about, to turn and lower their large, Dragon-heads in fealty to their Chief. It was impossible to see expressions on a Dragon's face, but he could scent their roiling emotions. Immediately, he detected much confusion, anger, and even fear; not for themselves, he realized, but *of* him.

A piercing scream rent the air, stealing everyone's attention. All the shifters turned their heads as one to spot the ill female-shifter still lying on the ground. Her entire body shook with a violent force; a horribly visual account that something was definitely wrong. *But, what?* Having never seen the shifter or her friend before, he had no idea.

Just as Gordell turned to go to her, he glimpsed a large, thrashing form at the opposite edge of the clearing, whereby several of his warriors stood sentinel. Only then did he notice that the other shifters—the ones he did not know—held themselves back. It was as if they awaited something, and though unaware for what, Gordell did notice they were neither held captive, nor did they attempt to battle *or* aid his warriors.

Confusion wreaked havoc in his mind, and he shot his gaze all around trying to locate his First, Darkan. The male had to have known right away that Gordell would want to have words with him, now that they undoubtedly had all noticed his presence. Sure enough, Darkan came forward as he cut through a thick row of his fellow-warriors.

While in Dragon-form, they could not speak as they did in their male-form; but instead, they communicated mentally. Although, each Realm spoke a different language, all Weyr from the Dragon Dimension as a whole, could communicate with one another in the Universal Dragon language they learned as younglings. Some never needed the knowledge, but it was there in case they did, during times such as these.

Nodding his overlarge head, Darkan acknowledged Gordell mentally, "Chief." Gordell observed his First's overall demeanor, and when he noticed Darkan was short of breath, he was puzzled; such an odd circumstance for their kind. After a moment, Darkan continued, "We have him restrained. One of the most difficult males I have ever encountered, our Mazar. He is over there." He motioned with his head to flailing shifter, who still valiantly fought the *restraints* which were quickly being reduced to useless rubbish.

Gordell observed, and what he saw utterly surprised him. His warriors never had experienced any real resistance or trouble restraining another single-warrior, in either form. There must be far more to *Mazar* than any of them had initially guessed. Gordell's contempt for the male almost tamped down—somewhat—by an unexpected twinge of respect he suddenly felt for the other shifter's strength. Almost, as it was only a small twinge.

Wanting to get a better look at their captive, Gordell strode a few paces toward the visibly enraged male, as Darkan continued, "Chief, there is another matter here. We did not know, nor did Mazar, indeed, from what the female over there has told us, until only a while ago." He flicked his gaze in the direction of the two females.

Squinting—a habit of concentration—though in his Dragon-form no one would notice the small action, Gordell started when a new fully-shifted female, who was not from this Realm, stepped in front of the other two. *Who is she, what is she doing, and where is she from?* he puzzled for a long moment.

This was ridiculous; he was a Chief, and not one to be intimidated. Especially not by a lone female-shifter, even if she was much larger than any female-Dragon he had ever seen. There was more to her, and as he curiously studied the female, he noticed her form; she shimmered. It almost seemed as though she floated, rather than her feet being settled on the ground. Her eyes were of a color he had never seen on any Dragon-shifter, in any Realm.

His confusion mounted as he made his way to the females in slow, deliberate steps. He did not want to move aggressively and upset the new one, nor did he wish to further agitate the other one who was ill and struggling so. Stopping a few feet in front of the new female-shifter, he inclined his head as a subtle show of respect, at least for the moment. He needed to figure out what she was about.

She only glared at him. Not a particularly friendly one; this female.

Then she spoke and her words swirled, the sound of her voice threw itself in all directions. *What goes here?* he wondered a bit worried and equally curious.

"You will back away from us at once! This female is *not* to be touched by any of you!" she hissed. "If these are all your warriors, you must make them cease now, they are taking her life as we speak! Release her male *now,* before it is too late!" Her vivid turquoise-eyes flashed as lightning would strike in a stormy sky.

Gordell backed up a step; he was dumbfounded and even a bit intimidated by this female. She was a force to be reckoned with, which he respected, even if her behavior did unnerve him somewhat. Only then did her words finally reach his brain. *"They are taking her life as we speak! Release her male…"*

He swiftly turned and glared at Darkan, who had finally caught his breath as he stood awaiting Gordell's orders. The male knew something, but he had not yet conveyed anything to Gordell regarding the ill-shifter and *her male*.

"What does she speak of? If what she says is even partially true, why would you allow a female such suffering? I know not who *her male* is, but if you are holding him and it is making her ill, you must release him, now! Where is he? Speak to me!" he growled and almost winced as all the shifters present took a step back.

Darkan's emotions drastically changed from confusion and uncertainty, back to fear, Gordell realized, of himself, more so than moments ago. *As they should all fear me.* He was thoroughly baffled at this point and in need of answers. It would obviously be up to him to find solutions, which was as it should be. He only wished he was not so clueless as to the whole of what had happened here this day. Closing his eyes to will away his confusion and uncoil his rage, Gordell nodded to Darkan to allow his First to speak freely, and without fear of consequences.

His First lifted his large, Dragon chin. "We arrived earlier this day and met with Chief Zarckael Treuamarias. When he sent a warrior to retrieve Mazar from confinement, the male was not there, nor had he been." He sighed, resigned and worn out. "I was not going to wait for Zarckael to get results, so we left his holdings. As we walked through their village trying to track and locate your Yoren, she actually found us as she was leaving the home of two kind females, who had cared for her while she awaited rescue."

At the sound of another horrifying scream from the ill-female, the restrained male's thrashing efforts doubled. Gordell needed to put a stop to whatever misery was taking place. Then he felt the fool anew; *Mazar and the ill-female are the pair Darkan was trying to speak about.* A sense of dread heavily blanketed his entire being. "It would please me, Darkan, if you would get straight to the point. What goes here with the female and Mazar, who is about to free himself of your restraints?" If he was in his male-form, he would have pinched the bridge of his nose, rubbed his temples, and probably glared daggers at his First.

Darkan spun so quickly, his tail accidentally slammed into Gordell. Any other Dragon-shifter would have been sent flying and most likely sustained injuries. Luckily, Gordell's Dragon was larger, stronger, and tougher than most. More of why his Weyr loved and respected him; he was always reasonable, usually friendly, cared well for his Weyr, and was more than a little intimidating when need be. They most likely also had a mix of fear in them, too, for knowing he could take on anyone, and for his abilities to win to keep them all safe.

Except for his own Truemate. *Not the time, nor the place; she is safe,* he scolded himself.

"Apologies, Gordell! I–I…" Darkan stammered, his eyes wildly bouncing back and forth from the ill-female to the thrashing male. Darkan chose the thrashing male, clearly sensing a deep and mad desperation coming from him.

"Go. I will check on the female, and you have a care for, as you already know, Mazar is much stronger than he looks." Gordell was still surprised at this revelation. Turning once more to check on the ill-female, he saw that she had not moved an inch. Nor had the other female-shifter's fiercely protective stance altered at all. *Perfect,* he thought. *This is not going well.*

He could be diplomatic, it was required of him all the time; this would be no different. Of course not. "I mean no threat to your female. I only seek to aid her, if I may. What is the matter with her, and who are you all? The three of you females, that is." He waited in place.

After glaring daggers at him for a few moments, her wings— which wavered oddly in a *there,* yet *not* there translucent fashion— began twitching in agitation. She stayed where she was and straighten almost eye level to him as she spoke. "I am Skenyah, aunt to *my female,*" she growled the last words, emphasizing her discontent for him and most likely everyone and everything in the area.

"She is dying, you fool," she sneered. Even in their telepathic communications, it was full of malice. He almost shrunk back. *This is ridiculous!* he wanted so badly to say, but she went on, "Because she only found out a short time ago that she even *is* a shifter and as her first change took over, she was not at all aware of what was happening. Indeed, mid-shift, she launched herself up between myself and him." She flicked a rude nod of her immense Dragon-head in Mazar's direction, obviously not caring to hide her contempt of the male still being held captive, if only barely.

The male did not seem to be adept at making friends, of late. Gordell almost laughed but quashed the urge; she would hear and take it as a lack of respect. He wholly did not want to be even further entrenched on her bad side than he obviously already was.

"It was instinct; she did not realize what was happening until it was too late, and the change was upon her. She had not yet seen me, and must have sensed that I was a threat to her male. Her senses are exceedingly acute, as I *was* a threat to him. However, I do not wish her to perish, for we have awaited her homecoming to our, or rather, *her* Realm and her true birthland, for many years. Yet, instead of finding her in the world she had been sent to as a new-youngling, I found her here." Skenyah let out an exasperated sigh.

What is she babbling about? Gordell was getting further rather than closer to comprehending what was going on. "I do not understand what you are speaking of, none of this makes any sense. What world was she sent to, which Realm are you from, and why are any of you here in the Dragon Cove Realm?" he calmly asked, his thoughts mingling with suspicion.

"We are of the Amethyst Faerie Dragon Realm, under the guidance of our *Famista*." Skenyah nodded her head toward the ill-shifter, still on the ground. She was seemingly settling, if only by infinitesimal degrees, and he thought it was still a positive change.

"She is Iax Sarvias Eluhyax, Royalty from the original Amethyst lineage, and she will be our new Ruler as is her due by birthright. She was taken to another world to be kept safe, and return to our Realm upon her twenty-fifth age—which is upon her—as is clear for all to see. I was sent to retrieve and start preparing her, as well as to begin the training of her heritage. She is obviously already undergoing many of the new changes, through which I meant to aid her. I did not have time to help her with that, nor was I able to teach her how to hone any of her new skills yet. Her first shift was sudden, and her body did not understand what was happening. Since she is so new, her injuries will not heal as quickly as those of us who went into our shifting-state naturally." Her head went up another notch.

It was much to take in, but before Skenyah could continue, he needed some clarity on what he had already deduced. "You are saying that not only is your Iax and the thrashing male over there Truemates, but she only just discovered her shifter-lineage? And by discovered, you mean she found this all out *while* shifting for the first time? How...why...?" He felt a heavy sorrow for the female, Iax. *What a horrible and terrifying way to find out something so monumental.* What else could he say, or ask? It was clear that the pair had somehow Bonded, and Mazar being restrained was harming her. This could become fatal, as anyone with eyes could clearly see, they were fueling each other physically and emotionally. Everything became painfully obvious. Gordell sighed, long and deep.

Even though he had come here with full intentions of making certain Mazar suffered, he could not in good conscience go through with those plans. He did not see how the male could possibly suffer any more than he already was. Gordell felt genuine sorrow for him, too. Knowing what had to be done in no way made him feel vindicated, but for the most part, it would have to suffice. He knew he would be going out of his mind if he were in Mazar's place.

He turned to make his way over to where almost a dozen of his warriors attempted to hold Mazar down. The male was extremely strong; he could end up injuring himself and several of Gordell's warriors, if a cease was not ordered at once. Reaching the tangle of exhausted, struggling warriors, he growled low in his throat. It was enough to gain their attention, and they all craned their heads to glance his way. The thrashing Mazar stilled and glared up at Gordell. He looked crazed, blood smears covered most of his body, and his large wings looked to be in terrible shape. It was not a sight Gordell ever wanted to see again, especially since it involved a Mated pair.

Nearing Mazar, he kept his mental connection peaceful. He would order the male's release, but not until he was certain Mazar would not attack any of the warriors who had been restraining him. "Mazar, I am Gordell. I believe you are the male who abducted my Truemate?" he asked with no malice in his communications.

Mazar's emotions changed from outright rage, to sadness and shame. Gordell also sensed a large amount of regret for the male's actions. He waited patiently and as he began to think he would get no reply, the male finally spoke.

"Yes, I am Mazar. Yes, I took your Yoren, and I offer my deepest apologies. I know you have every right to take my life, but I would beg your forgiveness. I know I do not deserve it for what I have done is unforgivable, but as you can see, everything has changed. I finally found my own Truemate, unexpectedly and only hours ago. She needs me, and I need to be near her, or she will die. Can I at least go over and try to help soothe her, before you deal with me? She did nothing wrong and I cannot bear to watch her suffer so." He squeezed his eyes tightly shut, as guilt and shame twisted his expression.

Gordell stood there as Mazar's words rolled around in his mind. He already knew his answer, but he felt it was only fair to make the male sweat a bit more, at the very least. He had caused a significant amount of trouble by taking Yoren and their youngling.

A guttural and sickening sounding scream snapped Gordell back out of his head. This had already gone on far too long. "Release him, now. His female needs him, and he is correct; she has done nothing to warrant this suffering," he ordered.

All of his warriors eyed him with concern, and fairly so, worried that Mazar would try to attack them. "Mazar, the only condition I would place upon you is an absolute understanding that attacking any of my warriors will be your final act," he made it a statement, not a question or request.

Without hesitation, Mazar nodded his large head. "I will not touch or move on any of them. I seek only to comfort my female, and you can string me up and gut me if I do otherwise. This is the only reason I have fought to begin with; they stormed in here and attacked us, and I merely moved to protect my Truemate and the other females."

There was no indication that Mazar was lying, nor did Gordell believe he wanted to do anything other than what he had stated. With a nod, his warriors cut the restraints so Mazar could go to his female's side.

"Gratitude, Gordell. I do not deserve your kindness but you have my thanks, anyway. Also, I did not harm your Yoren. I can tell after only being around her for a short time, you have your hands full with that one. I mean no disrespect, but I would gladly see you take her home," the haggard, distraught male rasped out, his voice dry and scratchy. As Mazar stood and stretched in obvious pain, Gordell laughed. His Yoren had used her sharp tongue on the male, just as he had expected.

All the warriors, including the ones from Mazar's Weyr, cut a wide berth to allow the male to make his way over to the writhing female who did still not look at all well. He truly hoped Mazar's release and attentions would help aid in her recovery, and soon. *She should never have been put in such a position,* Gordell silently seethed, still displeased at all that had transpired here. Those thoughts made him ache to see and hold his Yoren. *Soon, she will be in your arms,* he reassured himself, as he watched Mazar go to his female. The male was moving rather slowly, he must have injured himself as he fought his restraints and Gordell's warriors. One of his wings dragged behind him in the dirt. Luckily for Dragon-shifters, their injuries healed quickly.

Overall, Gordell was proud of his males; when it came down to it, they did what they were sent to do. Even though the female's suffering had pained and made them feel uncomfortable, they had done their job well. *This would be cause for celebration,* he thought. Then he turned toward his warriors, not wanting to be intrusive by watching Mazar and his female during such a private moment.

"Let us be away from here, and take me to my Yoren. It has been far too long since I have seen her, and I will be delayed no longer. Clean up this mess and let us be gone," he ordered.

With a quick backwards glance at the Mated pair, he smiled inside as he noticed the female visibly relax the moment her male reached her. He watched Mazar change back into his male-form at an impressive speed. Normally, it took an injured and recently enraged shifter some time to shift back. He then leaned down and started speaking low, comforting words to his Iax, while her friend handed him some large leaves and thin, soft branches to cover himself. After doing so, he patiently tended his female until she was fully-shifted back into her female-form. The male was a patient one; a good trait, indeed.

The non-shifter female aided Mazar in blocking all view during the ill-shifter's change; not that anyone was watching, they all knew better. Gordell discretely watched the male's back, only to keep an eye on his movements in case he attempted to attack any of the warriors. Something he obviously had no desire to do. After covering his female's bare form with spare leaves and stems, Mazar scooped her up off the ground, and disappeared into the woods. *The pair is a strong, suitable match,* Gordell thought, as all of his anger and resentment toward Mazar vanished. *Who could have known the male would find his own Truemate, just after abducting Yoren?* Of all the things life threw at one, you never knew what the next day might bring.

After further communications with Darkan, Gordell was filled in on the reason for both Weyr being present. Darkan and their warriors had gone to locate and return Mazar to the other Chief. Upon entering the woods, they scented the Chief's warriors who, unbeknownst to them, had also been sent out for the same reason. Darkan had held-fast to his duty and right to personally deal with Mazar. The other warriors, though they were not happy about the events, merely stayed in hopes of keeping the peace.

The whole group had been assembled for not yet an hour when Gordell happened upon them. *Perfect timing,* he conceded, just before announcing it was time to be away from there, so he could find his Yoren.

Chapter Eighteen

Iax felt like she'd fought her way through a war, yet ironically, she also felt like she was floating on clouds; big, soft, fluffy clouds. She was warm and snugly wrapped in exceptionally soft blankets, and lying on an even softer surface. *Maybe a bed? Whatever, it feels fabulous.* She snuggled deeper.

It was strange to feel so good and so bad at the same time. *Where am I, and what's going on now?* she pondered as she peeled her sore, dry eyes open. If only it was that easy, but no such luck. When she tried to pull an arm out of the blankets to rub her eyes, alarm set in when she couldn't move at all. With a large amount of discomfort, and an even bigger amount of pissed off, she finally got her eyes to creak open just enough to get a peek at her surroundings. Surprisingly, she found that things could have been worse.

She was clearly lying on a bed; one of those stunningly beautiful four-poster-numbers made of wood. Sheets of sheer fabric hung in layers from the canopy, flowing down to curtain off her view past the bounds of the bed. With the exception of the side she faced, which was pulled open to allow her vision to roam a little. *Mind over matter?* Must be, 'cause her eyes were now wide open as they drank in the details of the room. It was one of those fancy *bedchambers* where everything was made of wood or stone. Spectacular.

She assumed that the door led out of the room, or rather, the *bedchamber*—that always cracked her up—which was straight ahead in her line of vision. Slowly and carefully, she turned onto her back to see more of the room. *Ouch, that sucked-ass. I can do this. I've done worse–right?* Damn straight she had, and most assuredly would again.

Squeezing her eyes tightly shut for a minute, she took a few deep breaths—which also hurt like a bitch—reopened them, rolled to one side to support herself, and slowly sat up. Very. Slowly. More deep breaths made things a bit more…tolerable. *Ugh! What the fuck happened this time? Never in my life has one trip brought me so much trouble. And pain.*

Every inch of her felt tight and sore, so she stretched her neck forward, backward, then from side to side, which resulted in many snaps, crackles, and pops; it felt great, and made her sound like a bowl of Rice Crispies. She re-closed her eyes, hung her head forward, and released a long, contented sigh.

Just then, the door opened with a small creak, and someone's footsteps softly fell on the stone floor. At the same time, her senses flared, invisible fingers reached throughout the room letting her know whoever was entering was familiar—but not—and they were approaching her.

Senses? This is new, she contemplated. *New, and totally fucking awesome!* Without looking, she strongly detected, from whoever was walking over to stand next to the bed, that it was a 'he,' and he was extremely worried about her. Agonizingly worried. *What the hell? Who is he, and why would he give two-shits about my well-being?* It was kinda sweet and all, but still didn't make any sense.

Iax let out a small yelp and slightly jerked as a large, gentle hand came to rest upon her left shoulder. It didn't hurt, but it startled her. Popping her eyes open, she swung her head over and up, and up, and...up, till her gaze finally met with his. *Hot-Dude,* the realization quickly rushed through her brain. But this wasn't just Hot-Dude, he was Mazar. *Shit!* Although she remembered him being unnaturally tall, now he appeared even more so. In fact, his extra large build fairly took up most of the room, as he tentatively looked down upon her.

His facial expression was more pained than any she had ever seen. A pair of tight, beige-colored, leather breeches was all he wore, which left the rest of him bare for her viewing pleasure. And what a pleasure the view was. His upper body and arms were riddled with barely raised markings; small pink spots and slashes in and upon his marred flesh. They looked to be cuts and scrapes that were almost healed. *What happened to him, and why?* He looked awful, yet wholly delicious, at the same time.

And his eyes...breathtaking, stunning, deep, emerald-green eyes were sad and bloodshot, but they somehow managed to make her heart rate speed up to an uncomfortably fast pace. To her further confusion, she could hear his strong, loud heartbeat, which matched hers. She didn't have the energy to question it.

Without removing his hand from her shoulder, he slowly sat down on the edge of the bed; he obviously did not want frighten or upset her. *Yeah, like that would scare me?* She laughed inside. *He doesn't know me at all; takes a lot more than that to simply worry me —never-even-mind—to scare me.* A little voice in her head interjected an amused, *Uh huh, keep saying that to yourself, Iax.*

Narrowing her gaze on his beautiful face, she didn't want him to think for even a second that he actually affected her, at least not in the he makes-my-blood-boil, and in a not-so-bad kind of way.

"What's going on, where am I, and what the fuck are *you* doing here?" she spat, and immediately felt guilty for treating him so brash. She frowned and looked down at the other large hand he had propped himself up with on the mattress, only scant inches from her leg. His eyes bore into hers, and it made her feel woozy, lightheaded, but not altogether unpleasant.

Suddenly, her heart started racing anew as a flood of strange memories assailed her throbbing-noggin. It would be less painful not to fight it, she quickly decided, as she closed her eyes and allowed the assault. Right away, she realized this was important, and that everything she was seeing had happened. To her.

Oh. My. God. I shifted. Into a–a Dragon. An unexpected, yet pleasant numbness enfolded her entire body, like a well-worn security blanket. Tears stung the backs of her closed eyes; too tired to fight it, Iax allowed them to seep through her closed lids as they overflowed and freely streamed down her face. *What. The. Fuck.* Not a question, she simply didn't know what else to say. Or do. Or feel.

She saw it all; everything that had happened at the clearing in the woods. Waking up to him. The introductions. Her, *'I'll kick your fucking ass,'* tantrum. *Him* shifting…to protect *her.* Gemma and… Iax's *aunt* showing up? Iax shifting. Iax passing out. Iax waking up to a war. And then a shit-load of other Dragons holding down and restraining Mazar, while she suffered pain such as should have been impossible.

There was a moment of blissful-nothingness, and then she recalled an enormous Dragon—one bigger than the already massive and quite impressive Mazar—who had made an appearance, just before he had began to call all the shots.

Gemma remained a constant at her side as she tended and soothed to make her feel better. The internal fire had felt like it would consume her. It had all started, or at least amplified, when those Dragons were restraining Mazar. Her instincts had kicked into protection-mode as an inexplicable urge to assist him, filled her entire being. That's when the change suddenly overtook her at lightning speed, but weak as she still was from the most recent of her two changes—which had also been forced and too fast—Iax had been unable to do anything. Now, she experienced the pain again as she had writhed and felt like she was being cooked from the inside out.

The longer he thrashed and fought, the worse her pain became, until she could barely draw air into her dry, scorching lungs. Her body was stuck between her human-form, or rather, her *female-*form, and her Dragon-form. It seemed like the agony had gone on for several lifetimes, and then it suddenly stopped, as if someone had flipped an off switch. She had still been in pain, but mostly a residual type.

Mazar was there at her side, and had somehow coaxed her into changing back into her female-form. She felt him feather soft kisses on her head and face, and run gentle, caring hands over her arms, legs, and back, and whispered soothing words to comfort her, in ways she knew, only he could. *Huh? Still not making much sense here.*

Gemma had backed up to allow him room for his ministrations. The way he gently caressed and touched her flaming, aching body felt like a heavenly shot of morphine. *Oh my, that was better than anything,* Iax relived the moment.

He stood after sensing that the worst of her pains had subsided, and stretched his taut muscles. After only a moment, his eyes never leaving hers, he slowly leaned down and carefully scooped her up off the ground. The moment he pulled her body against his, she sensed and literally felt the immense pain he was in, but she instinctively knew he would never allow that to get in his way. He held and cradled her body so close to his own, and she felt his strength that almost made her want to weep at the tenderness he handled her with. He held her as if she was merely the weight of a bag of feathers—a priceless, precious, his-life-depended-upon-it, bag of feathers—just before he carried her away.

Raw emotions regarding her; fear, guilt and—*love? Yikes!*—definitely love, oozed out of his every pore. Oh, and there was that whole mating thing. *Wait, what the...?* She could say, "Oh, sorry, forgot about that," because she honestly had forgotten everything, but she also knew that wouldn't fly.

And, her aunt *Sken...* something, she was a trip-and-a-half. Iax remembered small snippets of her aunt guarding her like a Pit-fucking-bull. On steroids. With rabies. Talk about intense! That one could kick some ass, Iax knew without a doubt. *Guess it explains some of my shit, if I am related to her,* she considered. Still, it was a shit-load to take in, let alone believe.

She felt Mazar slowly remove the warm, comforting weight of his hand from her shoulder, and immediately missed it. The second physical contact was broken, the memories stopped altogether, just dead ended. Iax swung her gaze to him again, more confused by all the shit being thrown at her, just as another vague memory floated through her brain; they could communicate since she was now a...*shifter.* That was too fucking weird to even think about, but she knew it was a fact; no use in denying it now.

Frantically trying to come up with what she wanted to say or ask, he spoke before she could. "My beautiful Iaxsss, how do you feel after your slumber?"

Oh, his voice...so deep and smooth. If she'da been standing, her knees would've gone weak.

A beyond sexy half-smile hitched up one side of his lips; such delectable, soft-looking lips. Although she could tell it was a forced smile, it didn't matter. She couldn't *not* stare at them, nor could her brain stop throwing out all kinds of tasty attributes regarding them; *luscious, edible, soft, warm, wet, pliant, mine...* mine? *Oh!* That snapped her back into reality. She tore her gaze away from his lips—from *him.*

There was no way she could concentrate while staring at him, or more like gawking and drooling. *Ugh, Lord, please just kill me now,* she prayed, but only halfheartedly. Already, Iax knew he was Kryptonite to her Superman. She thought again about maybe correcting him to say her name right, but she couldn't bring herself to do that. It sounded way too sexy rolling off his tongue. *Oh, my. His tongue. Knock it off! This is sooo not the time. Fine, but if not now, then when?* she argued with herself.

She had a fleeting feeling this should be a little bit awkward, but it wasn't. Not at all. It felt like they could sit and enjoy a companionable silence for long amounts of time, and neither would ever feel anything but safe and comfortable, like they were *home.* No matter where they physically were, *he felt like home.* Her face flushed and she had to look away.

As she turned to gaze to her right, at the last second she barely caught it when both corners of his mouth hitched up into a real, full smile. *Ugh. No way.* Without further pause, she forced her stubborn head to follow through with the original 'look away' plan, so she could stare at the wall through the layer of sheer fabric that hung from the canopy. The canopy covering the enormous bed they were *both* sitting on. *Together.* At the *same* time. *This is too much!*

She jumped just a tad at the sound of his deep, smooth voice. It was that Dragon-speak, which she vaguely recalled understanding before. Weird and cool, because now that she was one of them, it came through loud and clear. And deep. And rumbling. And sexy. *And knock it the fuck off, Iax! Get your shit together! Jeesh, you act like you've never had feelings for, or been so near a hot dude.* She frowned. *Maybe that's 'cause you haven't.* She'd never experienced any of these feelings, not even once. *Chemistry. Butterflies in my belly. Shit.* She sighed.

Fucking chemistry *and* fucking butterflies. *Who-da-thunk-it?* Surely not her. All she'd ever known on those subjects, at least in the metaphorical sense, was that they weren't for her. Her friends? Absolutely. Her? That would be a whopping nega-fucking-tory. She didn't want, nor did she need this shit. *Did she?*

"Iaxsss, do not fear me for I would never harm you, nor would I allow another to do such. I am only here to be certain that you are well. Which, by your actions and ability to move, I see that you must be. Feeling well, I mean. Do you require anything? Nourishment, drink? Anything you desire, I will see it done. Anything."

She couldn't think. Embarrassed beyond reason, she knew her face flushed at least ten shades of the deepest red. *What is it with him and me? Okay, stop stalling and at least say something! He's here, he's friendly, he's...sexy as hell,* she tried to bolster herself. Iax cleared her throat; she could do this—more like she *had* to—of which she was well aware. "I–I–I..." she stammered like an idiot. *Bitch, please! Are you fucking kidding me? He's just a dude. One single very hot dude.* She moaned out loud, and let her head hang forward again. As she was closing her eyes, she caught a quick glimpse of the smug expression he now wore, and man-oh-man, did he wear it well. But wait—she was supposed to hate him—or at least be seriously pissed at him. *I can do pissed, no problem.*

Her mind made up, *It just figures,* she thought. *I can do the math; a hot dude always equalled arrogant, which always equalled asshole.* She shook her head, and gladly noticed it didn't hurt to do so, now. Finally, good news.

"All right, it is clear to see that speaking to me pains you, in one way or another. What about this; I will explain a few *issues* to you, and then if you have any questions or concerns, it is my wish that you be at ease to simply ask. Or if you prefer, you can express yourself in any manner with which you are most comfortable," his last few words were equivalent to a Lion's purr. A large, strong, *very hungry* Lion. And, not for food.

Dear Lord, please help me out here. I have no clue what's happening, what to say, or do, or...or, anything. Please? Extra please? she silently prayed, and meant every word of her plea. Her head remained rested in its forward slump, eyes still closed, the only response was her small, almost imperceptible nod.

"Much gratitude, my Iaxsss—now that you are more aware of what took place upon our first meeting—all for which I offer you my deepest apologies. You never should have witnessed that, nor should you have experienced such suffering. I now know who you are and why you are here, and again, I offer apologies from the depths of my soul. I felt that I would perhaps go mad—or already had—but I knew not what to do. Taking Yoren the way I did...was wrong. I am aware of that, and I will forever regret my selfish actions," he finished, and she heard him breathe deeply for a moment.

He certainly *sounded* sincere. *This is a decent start–right? Wait, a 'start' to what? Cool your jets girlfriend, you're only hearing him out. That's it. That's all.* She gave him stiff nod.

"Gratitude, again, my Iaxsss. I do enjoy how your name rolls off my tongue and falls from my lips. Even though your friend has told me it is simply 'Iax,' I cannot help myself and shall forever address you as *my Iaxsss.* You must now know we are Truemates– yes?"

Iax shivered at his words, his voice, and the tone it held. Before she could reply, he went on. She was pretty sure that was his plan; keep speaking so she couldn't. She smiled inside; he honestly didn't know her at all 'cause, when Iax *wanted* to speak, Iax *would* speak. Lucky for him, she was willing to be patient just this once and hear him out.

"No matter, yet. Understand that I am willing to give you all the time you require to adjust these…changes, the differences in our worlds, and in our upbringings. I cannot imagine how you must be feeling, what thoughts must be filling your beautiful head, at present."

Oh, my. Another shiver ripped through her body. If her eyes were open, she knew they'd be rolling back inside of her head. At this rate, she'd have a full-on orgasm just listening to his smooth, liquid-sexy voice. It was so deep, perfect, and absolutely seductive. She suppressed another humiliating moan, but couldn't stop the squirm her traitorous body did, which he mistook as a sign of physical pain. Not that she felt much of that anymore, unless feeling like she would explode any second now, could be considered painful. Truth tell, the ache deep down in her lower region that heated, throbbed, and spread out to infuse every nerve in its path, truly *was* becoming painful.

As a result of his confusion, he quickly got to his feet, was across the room, and then back in a blur with a pewter-like mug of something for her to drink. His movements caused her eyes to flitter open, as they tracked his form. Gazing up at him, Iax didn't even wait for him to offer her the drink. Her mouth had long since dried up like a shriveled prune, anything would be better than what it felt and tasted like now.

"Thank you," she offered, quickly reaching for the mug. To her surprise he held-fast and didn't allow her to take it from his grasp. Instead, in another too-smooth-movement, he sank back down onto the edge of the bed, and then carefully scooted his glorious, heavily muscled form closer to where she sat, in the middle of the bed. Her breath caught in her throat, and she thought it plausible that she could truly drop dead. From everything drying up; from his closeness; from his scent, which was an enticing mixture of just-sawed wood, freshly cut grass after sunshine had warmed it, and of course, man. Unadulterated, one-hundred-percent, pure, hot man.

Iax felt her chapped lips open a mere slit, and she couldn't stop gawking again. He was a sex magnet. *Get a hold of yourself, girlfriend.* She *needed* that drink. "Please, I'm so thirsty. If I don't drink something soon, I'll probably pass out again. Please?" she almost begged.

He smiled, and perfectly straight pearly whites gleamed only inches away from her inflamed face. "Ah, then a drink you shall have. Allow me, my Iaxsss." She felt her head nodding without her permission, and there was no way to fight it. She had no control whatsoever over any of herself anymore. Did she want to? Did she even care? Oddly, she couldn't make herself worry about any of that.

His eyes trained on hers, he slowly brought the mug to her and seductively pressed it to her lips, then he tilted it back just enough for the cool, refreshing, sweet liquid to trickle into her sandpaper-like mouth. She audibly moaned again as it instantly relieved her mouth of its scratchy, dry heat.

Between him and the drink, she couldn't think straight. She closed her eyes and allowed him to pour a slow and steady stream of the life-giving stuff through her parted lips. After a moment she lifted a hand in a gesture for him to stop, and felt the mug move away. She sharply inhaled when something warm and soft touched her lower lip, and then slowly moved down her chin.

Eyes only open half-mast, she couldn't make herself pull back from Mazar as he stared straight into her eyes. They sparkled brightly and intoxicatingly as he licked what she assumed was a drip of the drink, from her lower lip and chin. *Oh, my.* Both of their breaths were coming in short, hot gasps, and one of his large hands moved to gently cradle the back of her head as he supported and coaxed her to allow his attentions. Warm, supple lips gently feathered over hers, apparently done mopping the liquid from her chin.

It made her nervous and she shivered all over, Iax was unable to stop herself from melting into him and his delectable kisses. *This is amazing.* He was amazing, and she never, ever wanted him to stop. An urge ripped through her from head to toe, with a force she had never experienced. Moving with far less grace and careful deliberation than him, and acutely aware that he had just bathed, Iax threw her arms around his neck, greedily grabbing handfuls of his thick, damp, golden hair. Her fingers ran through the silky masses which were softer than she expected, and it turned her on even more.

Suddenly, she was climbing all over him, straddling his sitting form, writhing and yearning to get as close to him as possible. Not that she believed it was possible; to get close enough to him. She wanted—*needed*—to climb inside of him, to snuggle down and stay there forever. Tongues collided, tangling and dancing around one another, as flames of the hottest passion stirred in Iax's entire body. They were sweating, running their hands over each other's back, through each other's hair, and anywhere else they could touch the other. Neither could get enough, as their hearts beat in perfect time.

Although it was a massive effort, Iax pulled back for a moment; she *had* to gaze into his emerald-green eyes, she needed look deep into them because never, anywhere, had she seen any so mesmerizing and hypnotic. He cocked his head to the side as if he'd read her mind, as if he knew she needed more than anything, to check out his killer-eyes. He gave her the moment, then flashed her another of his million-dollar smiles. They're mutual heat was such that it felt like the air surrounding them sizzled.

In quick, ragged breaths, she finally felt the need to 'express' herself, just like he had asked her to. "Off. Clothes. Both—" she abruptly stopped after glancing down, only to realize she was already naked. Shrugging a shoulder, she smiled wide. Always proud of her body, she felt giddy inside that she was already undressed.

Now, if only he would hurry up and get with the program, then everything would be perfect–right? Of course it would.

His smile faded a tad, and she watched tension work its way into his broad shoulders. *Oh no. What now? I thought he wanted this?* Straight faced and serious, she narrowed her gaze on his; whether he liked it or not, she would demand that he tell her what the hell the deal was. "You can't tell me you don't want this! I know you do! So, I make the moves, and suddenly you're done? I'm not hot enough for you? Fine, then fuck off! How 'bout that," she spat at him. Still shocked that everything she said came out in Dragon-speak.

Mazar's brows furrowed in momentary confusion, his expression no longer the relaxed, elated one it had just been. "What do you speak of? Of course, I want you. Why would you think such a foolish thing?" he asked, too quietly.

What the...? Foolish? "Did you just call me *foolish?* You fucking kidding me right now? Ugh! Why–why did I even bother? Nobody's ever stuck around, tried to get to know me, or even cared about my feelings. Why the hell would I expect anything different from *you?*" she sneered, quickly moving to get off the bed. She didn't want to be anywhere near him now, which made her sad on top angry. *Men! All assholes!* she fumed to herself.

Before she made it an inch, strong arms firmly and carefully encircled her waist, and pulled her back against his front. Out of habitual instinct, she almost fought, but didn't. She couldn't. She sighed and let her chin drop back down onto her chest. His soft, hot tongue touched the back of her bare neck, where her hair had all flung to one side when she tried to get up. Oh, and did he take advantage of that opportunity...when she heard a low growl rumble through him, and then felt it seep into her back. She couldn't and didn't even try to stop him, though, she probably should.

"I will always want you, my Iaxsss. I will always be here for you, in every way, for anything you may ever need. You must relax, my love. I was not disregarding your feelings, I was but momentarily stunned at you, your brazen, your beauty, simply at you. All of you. And no, before you ask, I do not think you being 'brazen' is bad. Indeed, I rather enjoy it." He licked and rained kisses down her neck, warming her from the outside in.

Iax leaned back and molded her naked-self against Mazar's hot, sleek, muscular torso. That's when she realized his beautiful, smooth skin was bare, at least his upper body, and she felt the fool anew. Of course it was bare, he'd entered the room wearing only those sexy leather pants. His build—honed over God only knew how long—was absolute masculine perfection. That's when a funny thought struck her. Well, maybe not *funny-ha-ha*. But, for the first time as far as her away jobs, and the second time since he had entered her room, she felt utterly and without a doubt, safe. *Right here. Right now. With him.*

She'd always felt safe and loved with her parents, or rather, those people who had raised her, whom she had already forgiven. She knew that whatever had happened, was done out of love and in her own best interest. Iax also knew they'd treated her far better than she deserved at times, even when she had messed up major. They were always there for her in every way, no matter what.

Quickly and mercilessly being brought out of her own head —still baffled at the speed and accuracy of his movements— suddenly, she found herself lying on her back, right where she'd started out, alone in this room, on this huge, comfy bed, only moments ago. She glanced up, and her breath caught in her throat again just looking at him. Those sparkling, emerald-green eyes bore down into hers, into her very soul. He was a beautiful man...er, *male.* She supposed she ought to get used to saying males and females, not men and women. It would be difficult, but she'd do it, she had to.

Reining in her wandering thoughts, she didn't think most males would appreciate being called beautiful. But how does one deny or fight the truth? She was in awe of every single thing about her male. "You are beautiful, Mazar. I mean it. Gorgeous, indescribable, just…I don't even know how else to say it other than, you are all that is perfect." It was a bit embarrassing to go on this way to a dude…er, *male,* but she felt it was something she'd be doing often in their life together. *Why not start now?* She already noticed herself softening, at least around him. It went against her very grain, but for him, with him, anything to do with him, it felt more natural than anything before.

His smile spoke volumes; he didn't appear to agree, in fact, he looked like he disagreed, but would not argue her opinion. It wasn't conceit, he only wanted to make her happy. Even if it meant letting her have her way—at least in smaller matters—she knew he would. *Hot and sensitive–how did I get so lucky?* She smiled back.

In a torturously slow descent to take her mouth, Mazar veered off at the last second, and with a gleam in his eyes, began his attentions on her right ear. He then moved across her face, paused to kiss her cheek, her nose, her other cheek, and then he finally landed a deep, scorching-hot kiss on her lips. They savored and drank from each other's mouths, and then he pulled back. She let out a frustrated moan the moment his lips left hers, she instantly missed their silky heat. Then she blissfully sighed as he renewed his attentions and made his way down from her chin to her neck, then even further down her throat.

By the smells wafting through her senses, all of which became more sensitive by the minute, from her own hair and skin, Iax realized she must have been bathed while she was unconscious— by Gemma—she fervently hoped. She wanted Mazar to be enticed by her scent, and judging his current reactions, she supposed he was. His heated gaze gave her the impression he thought of her as edible. She shivered again, hoping she was right, hoping he would find every inch of her better and softer than the one before.

Still working on her throat, he took his time to lick and sprinkle soft kisses on her overheated flesh. He paused for a moment to lift his head and smile at her, and then let out a deep groan when she thrust her body upward, melding their bare flesh together. Only then did she realize that he had nothing on, and oh my God, he was glorious. All golden and glowing, whether it was his hair, his skin, or even his eyes, all of him glowed in an enrapturing aura. It wasn't the same glow they took on while shifting; no, this was wholly different and supremely sexy. He was an overlarge male and every inch of him was heavily-muscled, but he made sure he didn't crush, or in any way make her uncomfortable, under his marvelous weight. It was a matter of balance inside and out. They struggled to keep themselves under the slightest modicum of control, though both of them wondered; *Why?* Neither wanted to harm the other, they need not be overly careful because they were made for one another.

Iax could sense and see it in his expression; Mazar was entirely pleased—as was she, though it was kinda embarrassing—with the way she squirmed, gasped, massaged, and carefully pulled his hair, as he took her over the precipice a couple times first with his mouth, then with his deft fingers. Both of their desires piqued, there was no way to slow down their imminent lovemaking; playtime was over, they were more than ready.

Looking into the gorgeous depths of his eyes, she had to ask, as it wouldn't be at all responsible if she didn't, "What do you use around here for protection, ya know, like, so no too-early-itty-bitties happen?" As she felt the slick, large, throbbing head of his length settle at the entrance of her core, she was tempted to forego good sense. *But, then what?*

Everything was happening so fast, too fast, and the passion was such, Iax hadn't even thought about it until now, as she briefly recalled all that 'butterfly and chemistry' bullshit. And where was she now? In bed with her *Truemate* fixin' to get it on. *Shit, he's enormous! This is really, really gonna hurt. Should I tell him? Should we maybe stop? Oh, Lord...what to do?* She couldn't concentrate or think clearly.

Suddenly, it didn't matter anymore. Eyes closed, Mazar pulled back and in one, smooth, strong forward-thrust, he was through. Her barrier was breached. At once, she almost cried out as it burned and pinched like a mother-fucker. *Shit!* She tensed, squeezed her eyes tightly shut, and held still for several long moments trying to control her breathing. The pain subsided faster than she expected, for which she was grateful.

When she finally gazed into his eyes, her breath caught and every bit of fear, worry, or pain she'd been teetering on vanished. But his expression was pained, his neck muscles were strained like they might explode. *What's happening to him?* she wondered, *Isn't it only supposed to hurt for the girl?* 'Cause, he wasn't looking so good. Well, of course he was still hot—hotter, truthfully—but something wasn't right. "Are you...okay, Mazar? Y–you look pained. What can I do?" she stammered, nervously chewing on her lower lip.

He graced her with the most tender of smiles, "You, my love, worry that I am pained?" his voice shook with a violent force.

Then it hit her. *He's waiting for me. He knows.* The thought made her insides go all gushy and melted her heart. He was being a gentleman, giving her body time to get used to his considerable size. "My silly male. I'm fine, really. And if you don't get to movin' soon, I'm gonna have to take over and make this happen myself. Sooo, what say?" Beaming her best smile, she playfully swatted one of his delectable ass-cheeks. *Was that my voice? I've never sounded so...so strange, I hope it's not a bad thing,* she worried, but only briefly.

Apparently, it was all the encouragement Mazar needed, because he most definitely moved, and in all the best ways; slowly at first, deliberate and careful. Being with Mazar was pure ecstasy, something she could get used to. Iax had never thought about it one way or another whether she'd be a 'screamer,' but when she caught herself doing just that, she quickly stopped. Feeling a flush scald her entire body, she squeaked in embarrassment. He only smiled down on her.

Once she started softly scratching and sinking her shorter-style fingernails into his shoulders, his back, and then his ass, he moaned, and she echoed the sound. *Fucking butterflies* and *fucking chemistry; now I get it, and it's totally amazing!* were Iax's last coherent thoughts.

Chapter Nineteen

Yoren was content simply sitting and visiting with her new friends. She was still flummoxed at why she felt such a strong, strange connection with the two females. They were comfortable to be around, kinder than most, and she could have easily spent days upon days in their company. Toralynn and her female-young, Jolsynn, had an air about them that put her at ease. She had always gotten along well with most anyone, but this was different in ways she did not understand. The more time she spent with them, the less she let her concern bother her. It truly was not even concern, more simple curiosity.

She had finally taken a rest, after convincing an overly stubborn and still angered Darkan she would be well, while he went to locate the mysteriously missing Mazar. She smiled—Darkan—Gordell could not have chosen a better First. When the male was dead set on something, there was not anything, nor anyone, who could persuade him otherwise. An admirable trait, she conceded.

Gordell had always tried to protect her delicate sensibilities, as he named them. Still, she had heard parts of rumors here and there, and plenty of details regarding some of the battles and the serious aspects of her Truemate's duties, all of which only confirmed what she already knew; he and his warriors were victorious, without fail.

Gordell, her Truemate. She sighed. *Where is he now, and what would he busy himself with while I am away?* Darkan had given Yoren a full account that not only he, but all of their warriors had wholeheartedly agreed it best for Gordell to remain at their home. His presence would only make matters worse here. Although she agreed, to a point, she also missed him more than she ever thought possible. Sitting and partaking in idle chat with the two females, Yoren could not cease thinking of him; mere thoughts cascaded into fantasies, and Yoren thoroughly loved to fantasize about her male.

This particular fantasy was one of her favorites, from real experience. When Gordell came home in the eve, he was always filthy. Yoren took immense pleasure in preparing him a hot, soothing bath in their large bathing pool, moreover, she relished in cleaning his entire body.

She would slowly, meticulously remove all of his practice gear he wore when he and his warriors would train. Each piece would fall to the floor one at a time with a heavy *thud*. Once his mouthwatering, bronzed-form was bare for her eyes alone, she would take one of his large hands into one of hers and lead him to the pool in their bathing chamber.

His long, muscular legs would step over the side of the bathing pool, which would cause his every muscle to ripple and bunch. It always made her mouth go dry. After he was settled, she would get behind him outside of the pool to wash his thick, soft, raven-black hair. Lathering the soap through his long locks, she would take extra time to massage his scalp, which made her own fingers tingle. Letting his head fall back to rest on the edge of the pool, he would growl low in his throat from satisfaction. He always told her those massages soothed the pain he would have in his head after a long, difficult day.

As she rinsed the soap from his hair, he would lean forward so she would not miss any, and so she could begin her ministrations on his neck, shoulders, and then down his back. Oh, how she loved his back; large muscles, soft, bronzed-skin, all of which was such a temptation. She would have to be patient and finish bathing him before she could indulge in any of her flaming desires.

When she finished bathing his back, chest, and stomach, she would skip the middle to clean his legs. Always fascinated at the dark hairs flowing and swaying in the water, she spent a few extra moments rubbing out his taut muscles there, too. Leaning over to rub his marvelous legs, she would act as if she did not notice his hands deftly working the ties on the back of her dress. She would smile.

"Are you quite finished, Yoren?" he would ask in his low, sexy voice.

Batting her long, dark eyelashes, she would give him a hungry grin. "Yes, my love. I believe you are as clean as you will ever be. Why do you ask?" She truly enjoyed the flirty banter they shared.

"I have no real reason…only this!" In liquid fast movements, he would have her dress off and her naked form planted firmly in his lap, straddling his narrow hips. They would smile enticingly at each other, just before the frenzy began.

At the worst possible moment a loud, sharp knock came at the front door. *Ugh! We were getting to the best part,* she complained to herself with a pouty expression.

Turning around in her chair, she watched Toralynn stroll across the small space to answer the door. At once, Yoren was up and at her side, and there he was! Her Gordell! Yoren instantly blushed at the timing of her wonton fantasizing. Leaping up into his strong arms, she practically bowled him over. "You finally came for me! Oh, I missed you so!" she panted, reigning desperate kisses all over his face and neck. She melted at the perfection and familiarity of his arms pulling her tightly up against his solid chest, as he let out a low chuckle.

"Yes, my Yoren, it is I. Are you well? Let me see all of you. Stand back you little troublemaker, I need to check you for myself." His reprimand belied by the twinkle in his eyes.

Too bad they had an audience, she would have gladly stripped and allowed him to check every inch of her bare form. Alas, she had to accept their situation and let him turn and twist her every-which-way to ensure himself that she was, indeed, well. More so now than she had been for a long while.

Gordell's deep-blue eyes darkened as he narrowed his gaze on the cloth strips still tied around her wrists. "Darkan tells me that you injured yourself? Astonishing, I must say, that said injuries happen to be where one would have been tied up, if one had been abducted." He raised one, dark, challenging brow.

Her cheeks flamed, and she shot Darkan—standing only inches behind her Truemate—a quick, subtle 'I will get you later' glare. In the next second, she peered innocently through her long lashes up into Gordell's sharp, all-knowing gaze and smiled. "Yes, I did. You know how I can be such a bumble klutz. Why is that so difficult for everyone to believe?" She giggled, knowing it sounded like the lie it was. She hated lying to her Truemate, but she merely wished for all the male blustering to cease.

With an exaggerated squint, his narrowed gaze on her deepened. "I suppose, besides being a troublemaker, you are also a bumble klutz. You truly must watch yourself better, you have not been doing a very commendable job of late." He gave her a forced smile, guilt written all over his face.

This is not how I wanted our reunion to go. Needing to quickly change the subject, she kept one of his hands in hers and turned to her new friends. "I would like for you to meet my saviors; the beautiful Toralynn, and her lovely female-young, Jolsynn. They are wonderful and we are indebted to them." She smiled as she swept an elegant arm through the air, bringing his notice to the females.

"You are correct, my love," he quietly acknowledged his wayward-Truemate with a smile. "It is a pleasure to make your acquaintance, beautiful Toralynn and lovely Jolsynn. Our little bumbling troublemaker is correct, and I would offer you a token of our gratitude. I cannot offer thanks enough for caring and keeping Yoren well, here in your home." He bowed to the females.

They both blushed furiously while they attempted to execute awkward curtsies, fumbled with their full skirts, and tried not to trip over one another. Yoren giggled, knowing just how they felt at the sight of her handsome, sexy, and ofttimes intimidating Truemate."You are more than welcome, your Chief–ly, um, your—" Speechless, Toralynn gave up.

Gordell sighed and stepped up to the silly females. "Gordell. To you two, it is simply Gordell. Now, I insist that you accept this." He reached into a pouch that dangled from the hip of his breeches. Yoren almost could not wait to be away from everyone, she had missed him far more than she had even realized.

He extended a hand that held a smaller leather pouch, filled with more than enough coin to get the kind shifters through a few harsh seasons. As he reached out with his other hand to clasp one of Toralynn's more dainty ones, he deposited the pouch into her palm. After he sent up a prayer of gratitude to *Meynix,* for the females, and for getting a safe and healthy Yoren back, he closed her hand that held his offering, and then smoothly released her and took a large step back.

Next to his Yoren—who smelled positively sublime—Gordell stood and heaved a self-pitying sigh. If he had to wait much longer to be alone with her, it would be far too much to expect from him. *Such a waste of precious time,* he fleetingly thought. If it was up to him, and had it not been for a full audience and all eyes resting upon them, they would both away from here and secured somewhere private this instant. *Soon, my love. Very soon, it will be only the two of us,* he vowed.

He remained lost in his own head for a moment, and returned just when Yoren firmly embraced the females. Bittersweet feelings were clearly etched in her exquisite features, as loving smiles were passed all 'round. "Many thanks again. You are wonderful females, and I cannot fully express my gratitude for your selfless caring. You will always be welcome to our territory, and I do mean to stay in touch with you both. I hope that will not be a problem?" Tears streamed down her face. Yoren had a more difficult time than she had expected, saying goodbye to her new friends. She blamed it all on her carrying state.

Toralynn shot her wide, nervous look at Gordell; she did not know how to react to the overlarge and wholly intimidating male, but she gave it her best try, anyway. "My thanks, Gordell. And though this is unnecessary, it will be most helpful to us." She tried to smile. "If only my Truemate was home, I know it would have pleased him to meet you," she finished with a small nod.

Far more relaxed, she turned her attention to address Yoren. "As for you, Yoren, you are most welcome. It was an honor to take you in and care for you. Staying in touch sounds wonderful, and I think visiting shall be lovely. Many thanks for your kindness," she replied on a small sob.

"Yes, we shall visit, and I almost cannot wait! I have never traveled away from our territory, and I have heard your own is quite beautiful. And you are more than welcome. We were pleased to have you, although it would have been better under different circumstances. Yet, we still very much enjoyed our time with you, and we shall treasure it always. I also offer you my thanks," Jolsynn smiled wide, her exuberance and excitement was palpable. She pulled Yoren into an almost painful, crushing embrace, but Yoren did not pull back or complain. This was an exceptionally strong female inside and out, and Yoren still knew deep down that she would do extraordinary things in her lifetimes. Many long lifetimes—Yoren was positive—awaited young Jolsynn.

****

After the slobbery, teary-eyed, goodbye display he had just witnessed, Gordell thanked any Goddesses who would listen, for the stench of his current filthy state; a reminder of his fierce warriors, and the deep appreciation he held for them. He longed to be away from all females, except his own, of course. He also felt a deep need to be near as many ruthless, dirty, spitting males as he could find, preferably rolling in a deep, nasty patch of muck.

Females truly are insane. Their blather is such that a male could take his own life without a second thought. He shuddered at the memory. Still, he was thrilled to have his Yoren by his side, tied to his belt, just as he had earlier vowed. She was not overjoyed with his new way of doing things, but it mattered little to him. He meant it when he had vowed she would not leave his side or sight, ever again.

As they moved along at a brisk pace, Yoren easily kept up with her long-legged strides, which matched his in perfect synchronicity. They marched onward to Chief Zarckael Treuamarias' holdings; the short walk that it was. They were granted entrance, seated, and in a matter of minutes, they had been served foods and drinks.

Worry etched Gordell's handsome features as he watched his Truemate shovel the wonderfully prepared foods into her mouth, as if she had not eaten in days. "You are absolutely famished, my love. Did your new friends not feed you?" His brows furrowed.

With one hand raised—signaling him to wait—she chewed and swallowed her current mouthful, and then answered him, "Yes, of course they did, love. In case it has slipped your notice, I am carrying and require far more nourishment than ever. It is not something I can change, it simply is," she finished, making quick work of another mouthful of the foods she was so deeply immersed in.

Gordell chuckled and shook his head in amusement at Yoren, simply being Yoren. Then he vigorously dug into his own trencher; laden with all manner of roasted foods and fresh bread made him curious to taste everything, and see why she loved it so much. With the first bite, he knew. Some of the drinks were also better than theirs back home, and he felt a deep need to know which ingredients had been used for the feast.

Yoren had earlier explained that she planned to get Toralynn's strain-mix, since her first taste of the delicious drink. Gordell was not surprised when she had done just that, before they left the humble home of the two worthy females. Gordell was now appreciative, and pleased by what she had done. Although his own territory—home to Weyr Rhaumonesthius—had much more sightly lands, as well as wide varieties of anything needed to make the best of everything, this was still some of the best foods and drinks he had ever consumed.

Other than one river and three mountain ranges, two of which were a great distance from the main village, much of the area around Weyr Treuamarias' main village was all but barren. He did not know what their supplies were, nor where they came from, but he would find out. It was too dreadful to imagine these flavors never gracing his taste buds again.

They had been seated and eating as ravenously as starved animals for several minutes, before Chief Zarckael Treuamarias made his appearance. Since the male had no forward knowledge of Gordell's arrival, as well as the return of his own warriors and Yoren, Gordell was humbled and thankful for such a warm, kind reception by the servants who had tended them.

Gordell stood to his fullest height and approached Zarckael, with his right arm extended to greet the male in the respected way of all warriors. Zarckael's eyes shone bright, and even though he had to look up to meet Gordell's equally shining gaze, instant respect was felt on both sides. After the normal small talk and some introductions, everyone reclaimed their seats at the long tables in the Great Hall.

Gordell's impression that Zarckael was a gracious, generous Chief, was confirmed when the extremely hospitable and worthy male extended an invitation for Yoren, Gordell, and his warriors to slumber here this eve. Everyone was worn out—evidenced by their haggard expressions and lack of conversation—from this day's events, combined with the guilt written all over Zarckael's face, told Gordell that the formidable male could do no less. Gordell kindly accepted the Chief's invitation.

Mere moments later, Torkquin, Zarckael's First, strolled in with an air of a recently satisfied male. Zarckael laughed as his First claimed the seat to his right. A moment later, a flustered and somewhat disheveled female-young entered the Hall from the same direction Torkquin had. She noticed the Chiefs openly gazing upon her state; that they likely knew what she had done, gave her a mortified expression, the Chiefs noticed, which made her flush a deep crimson. Without further thought, she turned on one heel, and quickly fled to the kitchens. Unless Gordell was mistaken, this particular female was none other than Jolsynn, the healer's young.

Comfortably seated at Zarckael's left, Gordell nodded in acknowledgement to Torkquin, and a humorous grin gave away the male's secrets. Gordell quirked a questioning brow at Zarckael, then his First, and they all shook their heads and laughed aloud. It took only a moment for them to sober themselves back to a state where they could have serious discussions.

To his left, Gordell caught the expression on his lovely little troublemaker's face. She also thought it humorous, but as his Truemate she was unwilling to publicly shame him by making a scene, proven by her clamping down on the urge to join the males in their moment of revelry. Gordell leaned over and gently nuzzled his warm, soft lips to her right ear. "You, my love, are a troublemaker. You know this–yes? Ah, but no worries. I will not beat you for your insolence in this matter. I offer my thanks for biting your sharp tongue, for which I will show my gratitude the moment we are alone. That shall be your *punishment*." he whispered the tease, and ran his hot tongue around her outer ear. He relished the shiver he felt run through her, and growled low as he kissed her ear, before straightening in his seat. The painful bulge in his breeches made him squirm to find a comfortable position. *This eve we shall make up for lost time,* he made another vow.

"I would offer sincere apologies to you, Gordell, regarding Mazar's actions. Of all my warriors, I never would have guessed that he would do such a thing. To that end, I offer more thanks for your generous act of kindness. Leaving Mazar to Bond with his newly found Truemate, was far more than anyone else in your position would have done." He sighed. "I was certain he would not live to see another day, for which I must admit I felt a heavy sadness. Mazar has always been extremely loyal and trustworthy. He must have been truly going mad to…well, you already know. I am still beyond baffled to learn that he found his Truemate, and that it happened only a short time before your warriors descended upon him, is beyond my comprehension." Zarckael shook his head, confusion and relief clearly marking his expression.

"I believe one would have to have be there, to fully understand what took place. Your Mazar is quite the formidable warrior and male, to be sure. After witnessing him and his Truemate's suffering, I could no longer harbor ill feelings toward him. He had already been tortured enough simply by having to witness, yet be unable to aid her. I do not know how I would have handled what he did. And, I would like to believe most males would have done the same as I," Gordell finished, stabbing more food onto his fork.

"So I have been told, and I offer more apologies for the female's suffering. Apparently, it was difficult for all our warriors to discern the proper way to handle the delicate situation. I am grateful you arrived when you did. Who knows what would have happened, and how much more she could have endured? For now, they rest together in one of my upper bedchambers, herein. After seeing the pair, I can only imagine what you witnessed. They will be left alone to heal for a couple days, and then we shall host their Mating Ritual. You and your lot are also welcome to stay for that, if you wish. It will last…what am I thinking?" He laughed at himself. "You are also a Chief, of course, you already know how long Mating Rituals last. In any case, you all are welcome to stay. Once it is finished, though, Mazar will need to make a decision." Zarckael finished.

"It was rough to witness both of them in such a state. I agree, the timing was unbelievable, but I could not dispute the truth of what happened right before my eyes. Although, I did want to kill your male with my bare hands, but once I was assured of Yoren's safety, I could not in good conscience, further harm him. Be glad you missed it, as I do not wish to behold that sight ever again." He drained the rest of his fire-brew, and slammed the wooden mug down on the wooden table hard enough to draw everyone's attention.

Tall and proud, Gordell rose from his seat and announced, "Our thanks to Chief Zarckael, for his gracious invitation that we stay here for the Mating Ritual. We shall stay and enjoy the next few days, as I believe we could all use a bit of entertainment, and an extended break. Now, I know not about the rest of you, but I am full, tired, in need of a bath, and will not be delayed another moment to spend time alone with my little troublemaking Truemate." He winked at Yoren, who blushed a deep red.

Turning to Zarckael, he bowed, reached back and grasped Yoren's hand in one of his, and the two of them left the Great Hall, with far too much energy to be as tired as Gordell had just proclaimed. All of his warriors smiled, a few snickered, and many clapped their meaty hands, including Zarckael. As he observed the scene unfolding in front of him, Gordell and his Truemate, the male's warriors, the openness with which they all cared for the pair; it was obvious how much they were in love. He smiled and was grateful for the way things had turned out.

Chapter Twenty

Gemma had seen many things in her overlong life, but watching her friend suffer as she had in the clearing, shook her to her core. She had always suspected there was something different about Iax, something even Iax, herself, was unaware of. But this...this was unbelievable. And though she no longer had any reason to doubt Skenyah, it still troubled her. Knowing what lay in Iax's future increasingly worried and frightened her, as she pondered over what Skenyah had revealed, regarding Iax's lineage.

The Amethyst Faerie Dragon Realm. All the inhabitants were widely known for how fiercely they fought to protect themselves, and their ability to reign supreme, as they had stood leagues ahead of all the other Dragon Realms combined. Yet, it was still unknown whether the Dragon Cove Realm, or the Amethyst Faerie Dragon Realm, had been formed first. In any case, it was also widespread knowledge that the latter had suffered many harsh attacks.

Additionally, it was well-known that they had some of the best lands in the entire Dragon Dimension. Stories had been told since before Gemma's birth, of their soil that produced the largest and best foods, as well as the strongest and most potent healing herbs, and more. The Amethyst mining, for which the Realm was named, was very impressive, too. There had, indeed, been reports that single stones the size of Gordell's Dragon-form, had been mined from the darkest depths of the Realm.

The battle Skenyah had recited to Gemma upon their first meeting, was the closest the Realm had ever come to being overthrown. It would have been the end of their lineage; stripped and ruined by those merely in it for the taking and the monetary gain. The intruders did not care for the lands, only the stones that could only be found there—unaware that the Realm's precious and rare soil was key to the stones existence—which held unimaginable healing properties, that is, as long as one knew how to use them. They were also considered invaluable.

Knowing the full story as she now did, Gemma was saddened that the awful intruders had killed Iax's birthparents. She was likewise thankful that the murderers had been killed in their despicable attempt to overtake and destroy the beautiful Realm.

She had been there with Iax on one journey, and though they had only been there for one night, Iax had impressively excelled. She had located and eliminated a much smaller scaled attempt at invasion, and in short order. Gemma supposed it all made perfect sense now, that Iax's abilities had grown tenfold while they had been there. Her birthright; her homelands had called to her, spoken to her very essence, as they had guided and assisted her while she fought to set things right.

She was happy for Iax, now that her friend no longer suffered as she did earlier. It had been horrible, and Gemma almost had not known how to aid her. Gemma had tried to calm and soothe her friend, but all the while she had been afraid Iax would perish. That was not something Gemma could allow. She had almost broken all the rules, and was now thankful she had not needed to resort to such desperate measures.

As much as she had resolved herself to dislike Mazar, she could not help but change her opinion of him, once she finally figured out who the male was. Especially, not after seeing how deeply he cared for Iax, and how well he treated her. His love for her seemed to be the truest and purest in nature.

She had only witnessed a handful of males in the state of upset Mazar had been, in her entire life. It was most certainly not something she ever cared to see again.

After Mazar had carried Iax away from the clearing, Gemma and Skenyah had remained to help with the cleanup. When a battle took place—unless it was unsafe to do so—the victors would stay and banish any evidence of the fight. It was best for the lands, and so it was done. Luckily, there were many of them once all the shifters had changed back into their male-forms, so it had not taken overlong. It was unheard of for both sides to aid each other, as there usually was only one side left standing. They chore had been performed in a quick, efficient silence.

Upon completion, they had all been led back to Chief Zarckael Treuamarias' holdings, where they were offered baths, foods, drinks, and a place to sleep for the night. Gemma was overwhelmed and surprised at how generous this Chief was, considering all that had happened.

Now, lying in a clean, comfortable bed in a clean, warm bedchamber, she could not turn off the thoughts and memories that bombarded her mind without cease. She imagined they would plague her for some time to come. It also saddened her that Iax would be forced to make a choice. She knew if Iax truly had choices, there would be three. One: Stay here with Mazar. Two: Go to her birthplace, the Amethyst Faerie Dragon Realm. Three: Return to her own world, her Earth. Alas, number two was inevitable, and not a choice at all.

Gemma felt a strong sense of disconnect, as she realize her and Iax's time as bestest friends was all but at an end. The thought made her eyes leak onto her pillow, because she never wanted their friendship to end. Iax was the only real friend she had ever had, and she simply could not imagine not getting to work with her again, not getting to see her, no more laughing with or at her…nothing. A soggy laugh escaped her at some of their past adventures. Gemma turned over her tear-soaked pillow, and settled her weary head on the dry side.

If only that was the whole of what weighed so heavily upon her mind. Squeezing her eyes tightly shut, she begged for sleep to claim her. The knowledge of what tomorrow would bring was heartbreaking, at least for her. But there was nothing to be done about it now, and she needed a full night's sleep to face the rest of her life. In her own world. Alone.

****

Skenyah had to admit, she felt a large amount of respect and gratitude for the female, Gemma. She had easily located Iax in her time of need, as well as cared for her as if she were kin. It brought an idea to mind, one which may help them all. She could offer the female the opportunity to travel to the Amethyst Faerie Dragon Realm, and assign her as Iax's First Guardian. Certainly a highly esteemed position. *Surely it would be advantageous for all involved?* She smiled, quite pleased with herself.

She did not know Gemma's origins, but she had a strong sense that wherever she was from, she did not relish the thought of returning. She also knew, as she had from the start, that Gemma and Iax were extremely close. As Iax's First Guardian, the two would always be together, day and eve. It would be perfect for them both.

Of course, this idea would be propitious for Skenyah, as well. She needed someone like Gemma who could assist her in all-things-Iax. The female obviously knew much of Iax's ways, therefore, she would be of knowledge to help make the transformation far easier, smoother, and more comfortable for them all.

Having eaten her fill, and bathing overlong to rid herself of the disgusting, charred odors of battle, Skenyah was grateful to be in a warm, clean bedchamber readying for her slumber this eve. She knew she felt drained on the short journey to this village, but she had not realized just how tired she was, until she spied the large bed that beckoned her to nestle into its depths under the warm, soft covers.

As she lay considering this day's events, she had to admit her niece, Iax, was formidable and one to be reckoned with. A force of her own nature in any of the Dragon Realms, by her blood, her strong lineage, and her birthright. Skenyah's sastair, Eluhyax, and her Truemate Sarviar, would be overly proud, and rightly so, of their female-young.

Now she wondered what everyone could expect once Iax finally returned to her birthland? This was the biggest question, and only *Famista* knew. She proudly smiled in appreciation, and instinctively knew Iax would be the best leader for their ofttimes troubled Realm.

Attempting to seek a more comfortable position, she was surprised at the minor aches she had never before felt. Suddenly Skenyah recalled her change and what she had not noticed at the time; mid-shift, she simultaneously called forth her solid form, because it would have been impossible to shift without a tangible body. Something she had done in training, yet never in a real life situation. It had been painful and everything happened so quickly, in the blink of an eye.

All she had time to do was call upon her corporeal-self, yet only halfway into that change, her Dragon had taken over. Her smaller wings had disappeared, since she did not need them in her solid state, giving way for her much larger and stronger Dragon wings. Although after she had fully changed, she had felt in her movements and heard in her voice, that some of the astral affects still clung to her. When the Dragon-shifter—Gordell, she thought was his name—had shown up in the clearing, he was obviously confused by her appearance. Who would not be? She must have looked the strangest kind of strange. That had not bothered her as much, though, as the dual sensations during her change; it had felt as if she would be torn apart from the inside out. Thank *Famista*, she had not.

In the magnificent bed, her muscles still pained her as she lie trying to sleep. *Only for a short time,* she reassured herself. Her injuries would sooth and heal themselves before sunrise, so she could handle it, for now.

****

That eve, all within the keep of Chief Zarckael Treuamarias would be well, as they enjoyed a much needed, long-overdue, comfortable slumber.

All except for one Mated pair; Mazar and Iax, who had wholeheartedly agreed that sleep was far too overrated. Furthermore, they had decided there were much better things to do with their time; ideas turned to goals, several experiments yet to test.

Iax was more than grateful now that Chief Zarckael had called upon his best healer, Toralynn, to help with her injuries. Though Iax had never actually seen the woman, she'd been given a full account of what the healer had done to help her and Mazar. Toralynn had mixed up a poultice to apply to their scrapes and bruises. It had worked wonders on the mere flesh wounds, and in record time. Toralynn had also concocted an elixir of some kind, that helped with their internal aches and pains, even though Mazar didn't suffer quite as much as Iax.

That wasn't really fair, she'd thought, but he had also promised her that in time, she would also enjoy the benefits of their almost instant healing times. Since Mazar's answers could be a bit cryptic, she had been thrilled to discuss in detail with the healer, how it all worked. In her case—the way she had shifted and not even known she could—her fast healings were still guaranteed, but would be gradual. To a point, her body always had healed quickly, so it would obviously be more prevalent now. Something no one would ever hear her complaint about; she saw it as yet another bonus, one she was grateful for. It had only taken a couple days of the healer's ministrations, and Mazar's extra tender loving care, before Iax finally felt pretty solid. In fact, she felt better than she had in a long while.

Putting away thoughts of the healer and her recuperation time, she reveled in the now, and the male who held her with such care. Being with Mazar like this were the best times in her life, and nothing short of ecstasy. Incomprehensible results of their love making ensued over and over, until the inky darkness finally claimed their sweaty, exhausted forms again this night.

Mazar and Iax accepted the slumber with satisfied smiles on their faces, as they curled up spoon style, her back to his front. Nothing had, nor ever could, come close to the deep, intense love they felt for one another. And though they had only spent a short time in each other's lives, it seemed as if they had already known each other forever.

****

Two sunrises later, all who had slept within Chief Zarckael's holdings slowly began to stir. Having so many guests kept the servants more than busy. Breaking everyone's fast two morns in a row, was a much larger affair than Weyr Treuamarias had hosted in longer than most of them could recall.

It was a peaceful gathering, a celebratory one, and moods were indeed high as most everyone's spirits soared; everyone except for Gemma. She had yet to enjoy a peaceful slumber she hoped for and needed, to revive herself and get through this day. She could not recall feeling so down and lonely, and the expectation of having to return home soon was dreadful. Doom and despair thoroughly consumed her.

Thoughts of her overbearing brother and his unnecessarily harsh manner of Ruling, sent a shiver racing down her spine. She had yet to understand what made him feel the need to be so mean and unrelenting to their people, whom had always been loyal and even caring to him, despite his heavy-handedness.

A sharp knock at her door brought her out of her musings. "Enter," she called out. The large, heavy door creaked open to reveal a radiant Iax, whose smile was wider than Gemma had ever seen.

"Good morning, Gemma," Iax offered. "How are you? Did you sleep well?" The female's movements flowed, languid and smooth. Gemma could not help but smile back at her friend. Even though she was sad, she was also truly happy for Iax, who was obviously very much in love with her newfound Truemate.

The whole scenario was so unexpected, Gemma was still unsure of how she should feel, or how to interact with Iax about it. "You are positively aglow this morn, Iax. I take it you slept well? Or, well…you know what I mean," she whispered the last part, as she blushed and was a bit embarrassed. She knew what Mated pairs did, but not how to approach the intimate details of such a union, and one so new.

"Awe, you blushing girlfriend?" Iax gave a heartfelt laugh at the situation. She always knew how to take the awkwardness out of things. But Iax was correct; Gemma was blushing, which cause her to laugh at herself. Another thing Iax had showed her how to do.

"Yes," Gemma answered. "I suppose I am. You seem so… happy, and I am pleased for you, Iax," she ended on a small sob. Iax was there immediately pulling her into a fierce hug.

"Don't be sad, I know you're happy for me. I also know you've been sad since I arrived here, I'm just not sure why. What's going on…what's making you so miserable? If it's a person, I can go kick their ass for you, if you'd like?" They both laughed.

"Ah, Iax, you truly are my bestest. I do not know what to think or how to deal with this new situation of yours. What are you going to do, where will you go, and when?" Pulling back, hands still clasped, Gemma gave her a forced smile. She didn't realize until Iax wiped her cheeks with her thumbs, that her traitorous eyes were leaking. Again.

"Bestest." Iax nodded, she didn't have the heart to make any corrections at the moment. And even though it could have been funny, she knew Gemma didn't need humor right now, she needed reassurance. A friend. Her bestie. Her *bestest*. She smiled and tears blurred her own vision as she continued, "Yes, bestest. The bestest-bestest I've ever had. Now, as for what I'm gonna do…not quite sure yet. Apparently, my new auntie has *big* plans for me, but that's all I've heard. You know what the hell she's talking about? I sure as shit don't, and you know how much I love peeps sticking their noses into my biz." She made a funny face that made Gemma giggle. "So, what say, got any info for me?" she asked, and then took a seat.

Waiting for Gemma to get it together and maybe divulge some relevant info, Iax took in the finer details of the bedchamber Gemma had been using. It was medium sized and sparsely furnished, and along one whole wall stood a gigantic fireplace with wood piled high at either end.

Just like the chamber she and Mazar had spent last night in— it was her turn to blush—the bed was another of those four-poster-doodads, obviously well-made and handcrafted. There were also matching night stands flanking the beautiful beast. The table and chairs where she sat, also matched. Under an alcove of windows, a bench seat ran the full length of the far wall with a fluffy, bright-blue padded cover.

The floors were made from some kind of stone, maybe sandstone or some such shit. She wasn't an authority on what-was-what in the way of building materials. She was, however, drawn to the finer details if they sparkled or were in some way blinged-out. She also knew what did or didn't look awesome, and lucky for whoever built this place, the whole thing was incredibly impressive. All-in-all, cool digs.

She could handle living in such luxury; it wasn't like her places weren't blinged-out, but they had all the normal shit such as running water, indoor plumbing, easy access to any kind of food one would ever want. The food here wasn't bad, just different. Iax loved to cook, but hardly found the time to do so. Maybe she could show Mazar some of her favorite dishes from home.

It would also be helpful to have some kind of power source. "Shit!" Iax accidentally shouted, a little louder than necessary.

Gemma's head snapped to where Iax sat, worry etched small lines into her beautiful face. "What is it, Iax?" Gemma's worrisome gaze darted all around them. When Iax did not answer, she went over and softly shook her shoulder to capture the female's attention. "Iax, are you well? What has upset you?" she implored.

Embarrassed over her little outburst, Iax laughed at herself and patted Gemma's hand still resting on her shoulder. "Oh, it's silly. I was just trying to imagine me...*me*, living like this." She opened both arms wide to include the whole room, "There's no electricity here. How the hell am I supposed to live without my stuff? I got my, well, you don't have them so you don't know, but trust me, I have *tons* of cool gadgets and toys. But they don't work without electricity." She shook her head in part humor and part dismay. Mostly dismay.

She suddenly piped up as an idea hit her. "I wanna bring a few of my toys. There's nothing wrong with that–right? No one here understands them or me, and I get it, but I've always had them. They're fun, smart, and help me figure things out. I *need* my gadgets, so maybe I can bring enough batteries, and if I'm careful they'll last a long time!" She smiled at her brainstorming talents. "Mazar doesn't know what any of it is, but I've explained much of it to you. So even if you've never seen it, you kinda get what I'm saying–right?" Her expression beseeched Gemma to show some kind of understanding. She genuinely needed it right now.

Always the voice of reason, Gemma comfortingly squeezed Iax's hand, gave her a bright, forced smile, and then nodded her head. "You will be fine, Iax. Not to worry. You are smart and will figure it out. Also, you will be extremely busy. I doubt you will even have time to miss your toys, or whatever they are—" She flinched, startled at being abruptly cut off by Iax's new tirade.

"Shit!" Iax exclaimed as another horrifying thought trailed through her brain. "Those things don't even work here! What– how'm I supposed to do anything? I'm not even *me*—" she slapped her chest hard for emphasis, "—without my toys. It's who I am! Shit!" Shooting up out of her chair, she had to pace and think. Her expression fell and she felt deflated. "Don't know what I'm trippin' about." She shrugged a shoulder. "I'll never be able to use any of it again, anyway," she quietly murmured.

Iax wasn't familiar with all-things-Truemates—or what-the-fuck-ever it was called—but she did know that once they Bonded, they couldn't really be apart, at least not for long. She still had stuff to deal with such as family, like it or not. Speaking of, family, to her anyway, was back on Planet Earth, not here. *Shit. Shit. Shit.* Panic tried to settle in. It wasn't like she didn't have a job, a home, or rather, two homes, along with all her friends, coworkers, a boss. *Just fucking fabulous.* More like a gonna-be-real-pissed-off boss.

It was all too much at one time. Iax could do stress a thousand different ways, sideways even, but this was stretching her ingrained knowledge and experience of even the O.W.O. Unit's 'norm' in a big, twisted way. There was no getting around it; she had to go back, even if only to say her goodbyes, gather some of her stuff, and wrap up loose ends. *But, how will it work? I guess if they can have me show up somewhere, like here, fully dressed with a full pack strapped on my back, there has to be a way for me to bring some of my shit to the other Realm, too—right? Sure, there has to be.* Still, the more thought she gave it, the more she dreaded the move. It wasn't going to be your ordinary, everyday kind of move.

"Gemma, I have a lot of stuff, ya know? Like, just regular household stuff, and I don't wanna leave it all behind. What the hell am I supposed to do with it all? You think the 'powers-that-be' will allow, or maybe even help me bring some of it back? That's another thing—when are we leaving? I don't even know how long we're staying here before going to Auntie's Realm." Reclaiming her seat, she buried her face in her hands, elbows on her knees, and shook her aching head. She hadn't given her new future any real consideration. It was all piling up in her head so fast, and she didn't know what to do. *This is what happens when one's been too busy being selfish,* she admonished herself.

Resting her hand on Iax's upper back, Gemma could feel the female's panic, but all she could do was be supportive and try to comfort her friend. She did not have the answers Iax was in search of, but she did understand the feeling of being wholly overwhelmed. *And, it sucks,* she thought. A slight giggle escaped her over one of Iax's much used quips.

Peering up through her intertwined fingers, Iax glanced at a different Gemma than she'd ever seen. This one was not at all sure of herself, nor would she have the answers Iax so desperately needed right now. But she had giggled, and Iax wanted to know why. Maybe it would make her laugh, too. "What–what's so funny?" she asked.

Shaking her head in amusement, Gemma smiled a real smile as she answered, "You, Iax. You, are what is so funny. I will always cherish the humorous words you have taught me. I was simply thinking on your situation, and my own. The only sure thing I came up with was that it sucks, as you enjoy saying," voicing it aloud made Gemma laugh harder, and Iax joined her.

Getting to her feet, Iax hugged Gemma. In no time she was on a roll, saying all kinds of her funny words and quips. The two giggled, reciting Iax's humorous aphorisms and metaphors until they both lie on the bed, tired, leaky eyes, and all. What made it all the better was their laughter; it was the real, feel-it-in-your-toes kind of fun. They heaved long, relieved sighs.

Just then, another knock came on the heavy wooden door. They both jumped off the bed, not embarrassed, but not really knowing anyone here, neither of them wanted anyone to get the wrong idea of them being on the bed *together.*

A timid servant-looking girl stood on the other side of the door when Iax pulled it open. Luckily for them, their much needed laugh session had calmed their nerves, and left them all smiles and bright eyes.

"Can I help you?" Iax asked the girl. She was shorter than the norm for these shifters, and her coloring was off. Iax had noticed that even most of the females were all at least her six-feet in height, or more, with bronzed-skin. Their hair colors ranged from blonde to a light brown. And they had either green, blue, or hazel eyes. But not this one; she was more petite, her long—as in, hanging past her ass —shiny locks were a deep shade of purple. *Plum, maybe?* Iax pondered. Her eyes were an incredible shade of lavender.

Gemma's violet-eyes were gorgeous, without a doubt. But this? Fuckin' A, they were hard to look away from. Her pert, regal nose was small and straight, her bone structure thin and dainty. Finely arched brows stood out on the girl's fey-like face, and accentuated those crazy-cool eyes which, the more Iax stared at, the more she realized, they weren't just a weird lavender color, but also a light shade of aqua; the mixture mingled and swirled.

What the fuck? Iax practically blurted out. Instead, she quickly and clumsily backed up, almost knocking Gemma over. She didn't feel threatened by the girl, but something unnerved her, which was saying something; it took a lot to unnerve Iax. "Who are you, and what do you want?" Iax finally managed, still waiting for a response.

Gemma's strong hands steadied Iax as she gripped her upper arms. They stood and waited for the strange girl to reply. When she did, Iax felt Gemma's grip tighten almost painfully. Iax then realized, Gemma knew this girl. *Great. What now?* she worried.

"Leua-Menarius-Gemmall-Naustaurial-Hannah." The girl bowed low. "You are summoned. King Mallorious-Givonea-Andoral-Naustaurial-Hannah, Ruler of Annistal, demands your return at once," she spoke without looking at Gemma, her voice was monotone, cold as ice, and her head remained bowed.

"Weirdness," Iax chirped. Then, confused as hell, added, "The who says what? And, what the fuck was all that other…stuff?" Iax asked, eyeing Gemma who had gone alarmingly pale. *This doesn't feel right.* She was certain. *Something's off, and I'll be damned if I'ma let anyone upset or harm a hair on Gemma's head.*

Just then, Gemma shook her head, almost as if she thought she could physically shake off whatever was going on between herself and the rather frigid bitch still standing outside the door, head still dutifully bowed, hands clasped in front of her. This girl was definitely well-schooled in dutiful submission. The thought almost made Iax feel a tinge of sympathy for her station. Almost.

That whole shaking-her-head thing was odd for Gemma to do. Iax's brows shot up in confusion, and her friend cleared her throat. "I believe this is what you would call a fluster-cuck, yes?" She tried a little too hard to beam a fake smile at Iax, confident at finally getting one of her saying correct. Her smile didn't meet her still leaking eyes. Tears shimmered in their depths, it all made Iax's heart break and her fury mount.

"Looket, chicka, I don't know you or who the hell this King Mallo-Givo-Anal-Fucking whatever is, but you can tell him that if he wants to see Gemma so badly, he can come here and—" she abruptly shut it, when she saw the barely-there shake of Gemma's head, as if she was afraid or something. Not much infuriated Iax more than feeling helpless, which was exactly how she felt just then. "What is it, Gemma? Who 'demands' your return…" she trailed off, suddenly realizing what was doin'. "That's your bro–right? Why's he sending her for you? Why right this minute?" Trying to keep her voice down and restrain her temper, she now understood why the girl acted the way she did; she had to, probably had since she'd been able to walk and talk. This was worse than she'd thought a minute ago. *How sad and utterly wrong!* she seethed.

She remembered bits and pieces of stuff Gemma had told her in the past about her asshole-of-a-brother. Apparently, after their parents both passed away, Dickhead—as Iax had nicknamed him— became their Ruler. He also enjoyed the drink-and-dunk; getting shit-faced and then screwing any female within the vicinity, none of whom were allowed to turn him down. Ever. He also liked it rough, according to Gemma's accounts of some of his conquests. Everyone feared him, and rightfully so. *Shit.*

"Yes, that would be my brother, our King and Ruler. He must be aware that I am no longer needed here, and would have me return home." Gemma lowered her head, fighting a full-on bawling episode. If Iax knew where to go and how to get there, she'd go right now and beat the living shit out of Dickhead. But, she also knew that whatever their King wanted, he got, including Gemma's compliance whenever he felt the need to assert his authority.

Iax ground her teeth in an attempt to keep her trap shut, knowing it wouldn't do anyone any good for her to go off on some tirade the girl wouldn't even understand. As it was, the poor thing was already shaking. *Because I'm too abrasive.* Iax realized, feeling like a total heel. *Great job, fuck-head. Now what…slap the girl around? Shake her up even more? Of course not, even I have* some *common sense.* She sighed.

Then a crazy-cool idea hit her. *Oh, yeah, this'll be wicked fun. Wait'll the little assbag gets a load of what'll be coming his way, he'll wish he'da never been born. Silly little man, din'tcher mama teach you to never fuck with a female-warrior? No? Yes? Dun'no?* Although she was still about a dozen different kinds of pissed off, she wanted to laugh, but somehow managed to hold it in; she grinned instead. *Little-prick-mother-fucker, you ain't never gonna see this coming.*

Chapter Twenty-one

It took some doin' to get them downstairs to eat, but Iax finally convinced Gemma and the messenger girl—whose name she couldn't even pronounce so she'd resorted to calling her 'Itty-Bitty' which didn't seem to bother her—that no one would die if they joined everyone and at least got some food in their bellies. Overtly observing Itty-Bitty, Iax noticed not much at all seemed to bother the girl. She supposed living a life of servitude under a Ruler like Dickhead, would probably do that to a girl.

Everyone had gathered and were laughing, visiting, eating, and having fun down in the opulent Great Hall of their host, Chief Zarckael. The spread was spectacular; any manner of roasted meats, vegetables, and fruits—all of which seemed exotic to Iax—as well as several nameless succulent treats, graced long-tables. Not to be left out, another long table was equally laden with a vast array of freshly baked breads, a variety of honeys and butters; it just went on and on. The drinks alone were definitely 'write home about' worthy, as they tickled and flirted with one's taste buds, some almost peaking to orgasmic levels. Iax wanted to the recipes for everything here, take them home, whip them up and—she was certain—she would make a killing.

Boisterous laughter erupted from several males, and Iax was sure, a few females, too, from the far end of the table at which they sat, up by the Chief's dais. Leaning over her plate, Iax tried to get a visual on what was doin' to cause such revelry. She immediately noticed Yoren, whom she yet to meet, the beautiful female was laughing so hard, tears streamed down her flawless face, as she tried to speak at the same time.

Though her own new abilities were amazing, Iax hadn't yet completely honed them. Her hearing was difficult to deal with; it was like a volume thing, and she had to concentrate hard and manage the noise levels all around her, but she wasn't there quite yet. Knowing Gemma had supersonic hearing, she asked her what

Yoren was saying; the female's refusal to answer Iax made her laugh harder than she had in recent memory. It must've been really bad. Or just that good.

"She is much like you, Iax, her mouth is a seller, too. You two are the only females I have ever come across who speak such filth," punctuating her final word with a smug smile, Iax had to laugh at her friend. Times like these were the best; laughing, relaxing, and just unwinding for a bit. She would hold tight to these moments, knowing all-too-well how fast things were about to change, yet not even remotely sure how those changes would turn out. The thought was sobering, and threatened to quash her great mood. She breathed deeply, then released a long, satisfied sigh. *Iax don't give up that easily.*

"So, our mouths are sellers? Hmm, guess there're worse things." Gemma's expression made her laugh again, and when the female grunted, Iax laugh so hard, she snorted. "Oh...you're killin' me here. It's 'a mouth like a *sailor,*' love." Still laughing and wiping tears from her eyes, she started hiccuping which had her shaking her head. What a mess she was now, but it was a fun, all-good kind of mess.

Iax decided she'd *try* to be better about her mouthiness, and maybe even *discourage* rather than *encourage* Gemma from following her lead in that department. Gemma was proper and well-spoken, she certainly didn't need to prove herself to Iax by word or deed. The female had already accomplished that many times over. Iax respected Gemma more than anyone she'd ever known, aside, of course, from her family.

That thought killed her laughter.

Iax neither wanted, nor did she need to *go there* right now; what she *did* need, was to keep her mind on the move. That would definitely be her best plan, at the moment. She turned to face Gemma as she spoke, "Hey, chicka, I have too much on my mind, but I can't and don't even want to deal with it just yet. Think I'll go pay my male a visit, surely that'll help keep all the bullshit in my mind, at bay for a while." With a smirk and a wink, she got up from the bench seat, and scanned the room until her gaze found his. Shoulders back and chin up, she marched over to her delectable Truemate. Still sore in places she didn't know she had, she smiled 'cause it was an all-good kind of sore.

****

Mazar was more than humbled and pleased beyond measure at how forgiving his Weyr brethren had been over his stupid stunt; abducting Yoren and bringing them along under false pretenses to ensure their aid.

Last eve was the best in his life, the incredible lovemaking with his Iax was more than he had ever prayed for, and he had prayed for much. What they shared had been mind-blowing; an unfathomable stretching of their new, intense emotions, and beyond imagination. No wonder when one found their Truemate, not much of them was seen for quite some time. If he and Iax did not have to be here now, they would not.

After his Chief had forgiven and put him and his Truemate up in one of his grand upper bedchambers for the last two eves, he could do no less than indulge him. Now, he would make an appearance to everyone, who was being so supportive of his new union.

Today, plans were in the works for their formal Mating Ritual; the first half of the Joining Ceremony. In keeping with the ancient ways, the entire Ritual would last a period of one week and one day. Each day after the first day, he and Iax will be required to perform a different task or competition, to prove their loyalty to each other and his Weyr. On the eighth and final day, the second half of the Joining Ceremony would take place; it was believed that once their Mating Ritual was finalized, on the eighth day, it brought them full circle and sealed the week spent enduring the physical elements to cement their Bond.

They would participate in various ritualistic events performed in the same manner of their Weyr ancients and the same ways, to ensure their Bond would be unbreakable. And *Meynix* will it, this would allow them to spend the remainder of their overlong lives together. He felt it was a bit unfair to her, as she was not of this Weyr. However, he was also aware that they would be required to have a similar Ritual in her Realm, to which he had already decided, they would begin their journey the day after this Mating Ritual was completed.

There was no question as to where they would reside, especially since she would become Ruler of the Amethyst Faerie Dragon Realm. He was one of the head warriors here, but he was also replaceable. She, on the other hand, was not, as it was her birthright and not something she could get out of. Even if she did not welcome it, the position was hers. Period.

She had expressed her desire to travel back to her own world first. Apparently, she had acquired many personal items in her short life, and wanted to bring some items forth to her new home. It was understandable, he had agreed. Though he was still unsure of how she planned to transport her items, he would aid her in any way possible.

As he sat eating and visiting with his Chief and Chief Gordell, he was unable to tear his gaze from his Iax. She was mesmerizing in everything she did, from the way she laughed, to the way she flung her long, shiny tresses over a shoulder every few minutes, to the radiance of her entire form. He was a lucky male.

After a strange commotion took place between Yoren and a few of his fellow-warriors, he noticed a tension in Iax and her friend, Gemma. He was just about to go to her and Iax, but apparently they had already smoothed everything over. *Good,* he thought. *I did not want to interfere, anyway.*

And now he was more than glad he had not gone, as he sat and watched her make her way to him. Lost in her sleek, sexy curves, her hungry, saucy smile, and the determined expression on her glowing face—which he was proud to know he had put there—as she stalked toward him. He growled low in his chest, garnering knowing smiles from the males all around him. Not that he was embarrassed, never would anything involving her shame him. He could not help his physical reactions to her.

Smiling back at her, he felt his breeches tighten as his groin swelled an almost unbearable amount. Again, he did not mind, as it was because *of* and *for* her. Recalling the eve before last, the first they had shared, she had greedily accepted everything he had to offer. Discovering she had never before been breached, no other male had ever tasted her most private secrets, made their coupling all the sweeter. Pride swept through him like a raging fire at the memory.

She must have guessed his thoughts, as she licked her lips and her eyes twinkled in a luring, inviting fashion the closer she got to him. Situating her lithe form on his lap, his breath caught in his throat and threatened to cut off his airway, and he shifted to relieve some of the pressure in his still-tender-nether-region; a tenderness he would happily suffer every day for the rest of their lives together.

"Hey, babe. How's it hangin'?" she whispered seductively into his ear. Whether she knew it or not, he could not tell, but every shifter within a fifty-pace radius could hear her words no matter how quiet her whispers. He cared not. Her strange words were nothing he understood, but he found them humorous and sometimes enticing. Her voice alone could arouse him if she was happy or mad.

He smiled and turned to face her, and her arms possessively draped around his neck made him ache to be alone with her again. It was unusual for a Mated-pair to show this much public affection, but she was not a *usual* female. He knew that within moments of her waking fireside, upon their first meeting.

His answer was a whisper in her adorable little ear, "I am unsure of what 'hangin' means, though I can assure you, *all* of me is well. *Quite well.* What of yourself, my Iaxsss?" he drew out her name. He loved the sexiness of the sound and what it did to her; the way her eyes dilated, and the heat that radiated from her flesh, every time he did. In turn, his own flesh heated, tightened, almost too much for comfort. Almost.

Someone cleared their throat overloud, and he promptly minded himself; they should be more cautious as they were on display in front of most of his Weyr, and much of Gordell's. Speaking of him, he saw the Chief roll his eyes at them, his own arm possessively wrapped around his Truemate's shoulder. The male smiled and winked at him.

He had to admit, Gordell's absolution and forgiveness over his horrible sins were more humbling than anything in his life. As he had thought once before, the male was a worthy one. And, though there was no excuse for his own actions, he began to think maybe his stunt had happened for a higher purpose. The two Chiefs seemed to be getting on astonishingly well, more comfortably than he would have ever expected. Ashamed as he was, he started to feel the load ease from his shoulders regarding the whole abduction incident. The Mated-pair acted as if nothing of consequence had ever happened. Mazar was relieved at the sight of them, obviously much in love. Since he now understood those feelings, he returned Gordell's smile in earnest.

****

Skenyah had to admit, witnessing all these beings in such a relaxed, seemingly familiar setting was rather soothing to her. Not that her Weyr never relaxed or showed affection, but this bunch was so open and different in many positive ways.

Cautiously observing Iax and Gemma interacting, she felt confident her plan was best for all involved. How could either of them naysay her solution to their current predicament? With her superb hearing, she had overheard Iax's proclamation of not letting Gemma leave until she decided for it to be, thus, her plan would work out even better. She would need a bit of time to persuade them both to journey back to her Realm, and it would be easier if they had some time to mull it over.

Her kin back home would be pleased with this Gemma. The female was much more proper than Iax, yet she was also obviously a strong female-warrior; something they could always use more of. This line of thought made Skenyah momentarily sad. Even after many long years, she still missed and grieved the loss of Eluhyax, her sistair and mathair to Iax. Stiffening her spine, she filed her emotions away; this was neither the time nor the place for such things. At present, she needed to separate Iax from her friend, and approach them one at a time.

Famista must be with her, because just then, she noticed Iax moving swiftly away from where she had been seated next to Gemma. She smiled. "Perfect, Iax, absolutely perfect. My thanks," she quietly murmured to herself.

Quickly making her way over to claim Iax's seat, she hoped to have words with Gemma and persuade the female to agree with her excellent idea.

"Gemma, how are you this morn?" she asked smiling, as she gracefully slid into the empty spot on the bench next to the female.

With a forced smile, Gemma seemed sad, but she kindly replied, "I am well, thank you, Skenyah. How are you this morn?"

"Very well, and I slept comfortably. How was your slumber?" She never was adept at small talk, but for this purpose she would make the effort.

"I…yes, I slept well, too. You look to have something heavy on your mind. Please, speak openly." Gemma felt an oddness about the female. Direct speaking was her way, nobody got anywhere by soft-stepping with one another. Raising a surprised brow, Skenyah let out a small laugh. Having only heard serious words from her until now, it was a rather lovely and unexpected sound. Gemma smile was real this time.

"Ah, one who gets straight to the heart of the matter. Good then, because I have a proposition for you. It is obvious you do not wish to return to your own home. I know not, nor do I have the time for concern over your reasons, but I do believe my offer will be propitious for us both. As for Iax, it assuredly will serve greatly in her transition to life in our Realm."

Narrowing her gaze on Skenyah, Gemma felt the female's pretentious attitude like a striking blow. Whatever her 'offer' was, made goosebumps prickle up along every inch of her skin. She sensed the female's feelings, and strangely, Skenyah truly felt her proposition was best for all involved. Yet Gemma also sensed a greedy and somewhat malevolent air about this whole situation. Not wanting to offend, she nodded her head for the female to continue.

"It is impossible not to notice the connection between you and Iax. That, coupled with your aversion to return home has given me a wonderful idea. How would you feel about journeying to our Realm, when I take Iax there? You could be her First Guardian, and ironically, as she just mentioned, her Formal Advisor." Tapping her fingertips on the tabletop, she gave Gemma a pointed, patient look.

Not return home after my brother has already demanded it of me? Is this female berries? Gemma was shocked at the offer, and more so at her own willingness to even consider it. Her mind was such a melding pot of emotions right now, she was not altogether certain she should be giving any real thought to such an important issue. *Wait, berries?* She almost laughed aloud. *Maybe it should have been nuts?* Shaking her head at her wayward thoughts, Gemma sobered her expression. "All due respect, it would be selfish of me to contemplate such an offer at this time. Though I do appreciate it, if you can give me time for proper consideration, I would feel much better about the whole affair," she replied. Skenyah's eyes lit up and sparkled like gems. Her confidence was disconcerting.

"Of course, please, take all the time you require. It is quite a weighty decision, and I would fear for such to be made in haste. Repercussions could be damning. By your brathair, I mean. Also, if you do not mind, I prefer to discuss this matter with Iax, myself," she stated rather than asked, her voice was a sleek purr.

"Absolutely. And you have my thanks, as I am certain Iax would prefer the same. I will let you know when I have reached a decision. Until then, good day." Gemma rose as she nodded, needing to quickly escape the female's company. Simply sitting so close to her had become alarmingly uncomfortable. Returning a nod, Skenyah's smile was lethal. Scary, even.

Chapter Twenty-two

It hadn't escaped Iax when her auntie made a beeline to Gemma, after she'd moved to join Mazar. Though she was totally in the moment flirting back and forth with him, she also kept a third-eye on the two females. Something about the way their postures kept changing, gave her pause. *What the hell is she up to?* she wondered.

Seated in Mazar's lap with his mouth close to her sensitive ear, Iax continued to study the two females. She had an unpleasant feeling about whatever Auntie was up to, and she was positive the female was up to something.

Deep, hot, and all sexy-like, Mazar's low voice rumbled in her ear, "Why do you pay so much notice to your friend and your aunt? Is something amiss, perhaps? I am willing to do anything you may need. You know this–yes?"

Ahhh...the last part was another of his purring caresses. Shaking her head to clear her thoughts, she knew she had to figure out what was doin' over there. She turned to face him, arms still around his neck, and whispered back, "I don't know what, exactly. I just have a feeling the bitc—" She cleared her throat. "Auntie is up to something. And I'm pretty sure whatever her intentions, they'll most likely have fuc–um...flicked up consequences for Gemma. Maybe even me, too. Guess I should go see to things, myself." Placing a quick wet-one on his mouth, they both laughed at the *popping* sound when she pulled away.

Mazar held firm and said, "I know not her intentions, nor this *flicked up* thing of which you speak, but again, I am here for you and your friend, my lovely Iaxsss. Never forget it." After one more maddening, dizzying kiss, Iax lingered for a moment and attempted to get her body back under control. This whole 'Truemate' thing; serious biz, no doubt.

With a full body shiver, a clearing of her throat, and a fiercely determined expression on her face, she turned to walk away.

For real, this time. Not that she wanted to, 'cause she'd gladly much rather stay on her Hot Dude's lap—the endearment always made her smile—sitting, lying, just touching any part of him. *Stop it! You seriously are a freakin' hoe-bag! Get it together!* she chastised herself. Anything was preferable to intervening in something she had yet to glean any info on.

Chin up, shoulders back, battle-face on, Iax marched back over to where Gemma and Auntie were seated. As she turned to go, Iax wore the most wicked-lusty smile on her face, which she happened to notice, was not lost on Mazar. Just before she made it, Gemma gracefully extricated herself from the bench at the long table, preparing to leave. Iax tossed a narrowed gaze over to Auntie, who was practically glowing as she smiled at Iax. A beautiful smile and all, but kinda scary at the same time. She shivered, then straightened her spine. *Sneaky bitch,* was all that came to mind.

Iax saw Gemma notice her, and walked the few steps to close the gap between them. Without a word or touch, Gemma motioned with her violet-eyes—red-rimmed and full of worry—over toward the long wall boasting several hulking, side-by-side fireplaces, most of which were brightly burning, and happily crackling away. Heating a room this large, she supposed, would require much firepower. As hot as the days were, the nights were equally crisp.

Two beautiful hand-carved chairs and a small table were situated in front of each fireplace, so they claimed a set. The chairs sat on an angle; half-facing the fireplace, and half-facing the small table. The arrangement easily allowed the occupants to visit and watch the cheery, blazing fire, without having to turn in their seats.

Checking out Gemma's features, trying to get a take on her friend's obviously not-quite-right emotional state—another of her funky new tricks; sensing other's feelings—Iax picked up on an obscene amount of pissed-off, and an even bigger amount of worried. *What. The. Fuck.* she wondered. It's not hard to unnerve Gemma, but whatever was doin' with her went beyond that, which made her worry even more for her friend. Never one to beat around the bush, she leaned in, clasped both of Gemma's soft hands in her own, and gave them a comforting squeeze. "What the flip is that batty witch up to now, and why're you so freaked out?" She waited with a concerned expression.

After watching the fire for a few long moments, and some self-bolstering, deep breaths, Gemma finally glanced at Iax. "I–I…" she stumbled over her words. Iax gave her a kind and confident smile. "I should not be discussing this with you. Not yet, anyway. I promised her that she could speak with you first, before you and I discussed…*things.*" She darted a nervous gaze all around.

Confusion and suspicion furrowed Iax's brows, her gaze took in as much of the room as possible but there we're so many people, or shifters…or *whatevers. Where the hell is Auntie?* seemed to be the question. *Nowhere in sight,* was the disconcerting answer.

"Look, girlfriend, I'm all about respecting your privacy, but something's eating at you. As my bestest, I cannot and will not sit idly by and watch you suffer. What the hell did that crazy-loon say to get you so worked up? And yes, I promise not to say anything to her. If or when she comes to me, I'll act like I have no clue. Deal?" She attempted a humorous smile to lighten Gemma's mood. It would be easier to get info out of her if she was more calm.

More nervous searching with her knockout, awesome eyes, a few more deep breaths, and Gemma sighed. A long, extremely over-exaggerated one. This already wasn't going well. Gemma, who never needed to steel herself, apparently felt the need to do so now, and Iax left her to it. "I will explain what I can, as best I can. And, I will hold you to your promise, Iax. You must never let her know we spoke about any of…*this.*" She absently waved a hand in the air, and raised an expectant brow at Iax.

I honestly hate this shit, Iax admitted to herself, giving her friend a stiff head nod. *Gemma didn't do anything wrong, and never has. She's always too busy saving my ass, being my friend, and helping me. Now, lovely Auntie shows up and rattles Gemma's cage like this? I. Think. Not. Dammit all!*

Gemma's hushed words brought her back to the present. "She has extended to me an offer. Quite a nice proposal, truly, but I am uncertain if I will be able to accept. She may be tugging my rope, I do not yet know. Although I would love nothing more, I..." she trailed off, and her beautiful eyes filled with tears.

Iax was too pissed to laugh or correct her friend, so she patiently waited as Gemma reaffirmed her resolve to finish reciting Auntie's offer. *Ugh! I know I'm new to this...shifter-shit, and I know Auntie's been one for, well, for who even knows how long. But still, if I could get my hands on her right now, I'd kick her fucking ass! How dare she fuck with my BFF? How. Fucking. Dare. She,* Iax silently fumed while she considered throwing her vow of cleaning up her foul mouth to the four winds. Pulling in a few long, deep breaths calmed her a little. She had, after all, made a commitment that she would *attempt* to curb her tongue, at least out loud, and for sure around Gemma. The poor woman was already frazzled, she didn't need to be subjected to Iax's foul-mouth or temper.

Iax still hadn't shared her light-bulb-idea with Gemma, and figured now may be as good a time as any, at least for some of it. She knew her friend wouldn't like it, or rather, she assumed. But who knew? Gemma had been full of surprises this time around. Iax pulled in another deep breath, let it out, and jumped in.

"Knowing her, you're probably right about her 'tugging your rope,' or as some would say, 'yanking your chain,' or whichever." Iax smiled. "Okay, remember when I told you upstairs not to worry about anything? Well, I have a plan, or an idea, anyway. To be honest, I also considered inviting you to go with us, but I didn't think it was a viable option. Being able to stay in touch would mean everything to me, but I can't think of a way to make it happen." She heaved a pitiful sigh, hoping her guise would work.

"Then I thought harder, and guess what I came up with?" Not giving her friend time to speak, Iax rushed on, "How better to make it happen than for me to plead, beg, grovel, or whatever else it takes to get you to go?" she finished with a smug yet hopeful smile, and a twinkle in her eyes. Against all odds, she hoped her little ploy would work, knowing Gemma's desire to stay in touch, too, and how easy it may be to change her friend's mind.

Gemma nodded.

"Well, obviously your people, or at least some of you, can travel anywhere and anytime–right?" Gemma nodded again. "Great. Well, I was kinda thinkin' maybe if you came with us to the other Realm, my soon-to-be home, and if you were my First, so to speak, even Dickhead would have major difficulties getting at you with all the other shifters there. Hell, even here, too, if he was of a mind to come after you now." She raised an expectant brow.

Gemma's eyes widened as her body stiffened. "Iax, that is the same as Skenyah's offer; for me to journey with you all and be your First. And though I rather like hearing the invitation from you, I still do not understand how you knew." She shook her head at Iax and tried to even out her breathing, but it didn't work.

Iax knew there was more to come—worse to come—and she was right; as much as Iax loved being right, she didn't in this particular instance.

"You have no idea what kind of war this will invoke, Iax! I do not wish to place you and your Weyr, or anyone else, in the middle of my own battles. I can handle my brother, just as I have my whole life. He is a tyrant, but he will not truly harm me…" she left off, unable to meet Iax's gaze.

"Yeah, tell someone who might believe it, girlfriend, 'cause I for one, do not. You forget that you've already filled me in on some of bro's little 'torture games'—your own words—so spare me, would ya?" Patting her friend's hand, she smiled. "Looket, s'all good. Just think about it, and look at it like this: I have a lot to do when I go home, well, what I *thought* was my home, and I'll need help. I'll need *you*. I have to deal with my family, my work, my friends, and my stuff. I have two places of residence and I'ma have to figure out something to do with them. *Shit!* I hadn't even thought about that." She squeezed her eyes tightly shut, and tried to stave off the ensuing headache.

"Iax, you must calm yourself, and I will consider your offer. Just remember, I do not enjoy putting anyone in harm's way, especially those whom I care about. To be quite honest, you are my closest person, my bestest. And who knows? Perhaps I will be able to accompany you to the world where you grew up. It sounds like a bashed!" Gemma excitedly exclaimed.

Eyes snapping open, Iax burst out laughing. "A bashed? Oh thanks, I needed that. I do love ya, I hope you know. And it would be a *blast,* but I can dig." She smiled and shook her head in amusement. "I need some fresh air, so I think I'll go grab my male and see what's doin' 'round here. You cool, for now?" she asked.

Gemma smiled back, then leaned over and tightly hugged Iax. "Yes, I am cool. Now, go. Enjoy your fresh air, and your *male.*" She giggled.

****

"Tell me how your discussions went," Mazar encouraged as he trailed soft, warm kisses down the side of Iax's neck.

Letting her head fall back to give him full access, she laughed, sighed, and then finally spoke, "As I thought, Auntie is full of surprises. She 'proposed' that Gemma to go to the other Realm with us. I admit, it would be hella-cool to have her around, but maybe not so much at the risk of causing a war with her brother." Wanting to ease into the details of her brainiac plan, she lingered a few moments, enjoying the beautiful day, moreover, the beautiful male paying homage to her neck.

"I see. I suppose your aunt offered Gemma a high position? Such would be her way, unless I have read her wrong—which is doubtful—I am generally quite insightful about these things. Other than this war you speak of, and wanting Gemma around, how do you think such an offer would benefit your aunt? Obviously she must have an agenda, any fool could see that is simply her way." His luscious lips feathered kisses over her collarbone. She shivered, and he chuckled low in his throat.

"Not that I'm complaining, but how do you expect me to concentrate while you're doing that?" Iax groaned in anticipation of him *not* stopping as he chuckled again. "And quit laughing at me, it's distracting. Even more so than what you're doing." She held him close to her heart and smiled against the top of his head, while she ran her fingers through his long, soft, golden hair.

"But, I thought you enjoyed my ministrations? I am happy to oblige for as long as you wish, my love."

All she could do was nod. He felt the movement on top of his head, and she felt his smile against her chest. *Ah, if only we could do this all day, every day, life would be perfection at its finest,* they thought in unison. Neither truly realized just how much of them, as a whole—not only a few mere thoughts and the beating of their hearts —were and would forever be as one.

He continued to work his magic on her with those amazing, full lips of his, pulling the front of her shirt down a little bit with his teeth.

"I enjoy *you.* It's that simple and that difficult. Everything about you is, simply put, enjoyment for me. But we do need to have a chat, you and I. In order for that to happen, we're gonna have to put a little space between us. And before you protest, no, I don't wanna stop, either, but this is extremely crucial. It's about Gemma, remember? I don't have anyone else to talk to like this, so you're it," she finished with a bright smile.

They begrudgingly released each other and stood mere inches apart. The small separation was an effort, but as she'd already pointed out this was important, and had to be done. His expression turned sour, and she giggled.

"Thank you. We can always pick up where we left off, but we'll have to wait till we're done talking. I have to wait, too, ya know. Don't feel like the Lone Ranger, Tonto, in you're suffering."

She gave him an impish smile. He rewarded her with his full attention and one of his sexiest grins. Her knees almost buckled. *How are we ever supposed to get anything accomplished when our hormones are doing all of our thinking?* she grumbled inside.

"Should I ask who this 'Lone Ranger Tonto' is? And what is it that you would like to discuss, my love?" He graced her with a wicked smile that melted her insides and continued, "I hope it is of grave import, or I may have to punish you."

Iax gasped, *he knows exactly what he's doing to me! Does he even care? I doubt it. So not fair!* She tried, and failed miserably to give him a scolding glare. The results? He laughed low and deep, and then winked at her! *Oh! This male is insufferable! Back to biz, Iax. Enough's enuff, already!* she scolded her hormones and frustrations, as she thought ignoring him would be her best option.

"Oh, it's just a saying. Some Pop Culture from my world, no biggie. And, thanks, but knock it off," she admonished as he reached out to hold her arms. He slowly moved back, maintaining his hot smile. *Fine, two can play at this game.* She grinned. "Okay, so we know Auntie's plan, and I kinda got a vibe on how Gemma feels. I think if it weren't for her Dickhead of a bro, she'd be on board for sure. You see, Dickhead is rather stubborn and she's afraid if she defies him, it'll start a war. She's probably right, too. But, who knows if it'll be here, or in the other Realm? Either way, I think between your Weyr, possibly even Gordell's, and for sure Auntie's... er, I guess *mine,* we can handle whatever shit he tries to throw our way. What say–you down, at least for the discussion?"

He crossed his muscled arms over his to die for chest, his *bare* chest. She shivered, and he smiled. "I know nothing of this 'Dickhead,' nor this 'bro' of which you speak. Think you could explain those, first?" He raised an expectant brow. She laughed.

"Oh, yeah. Gemma's told me some of the fucked up shi...er, messed up stuff he's pulled, and how he treats his own people so badly, even his own sister. So I, with my wicked-awesome, confounding vocabulary, gave him the nickname of Dickhead. And bro is just short for brother. See?" She was still amazed at how easy communication had become after shifting. It fascinated and impressed her how it all came out in Dragon-speak. Whatever she wanted to say automatically seemed to translate itself so the Dragons understood her, and vise-versa. Although none of them quite got her slang or profanity, she still enjoyed wielding her words.

Nodding his head, he urged her to continue. She went on to explain the whole of her and Gemma's history, how she wouldn't even be standing there now had it not been for Gemma saving her ass so many times, and on and on. She also explained her brilliant plan, the one she was certain would allow Gemma to make the monumental move with them, and stay indefinitely. Mazar, she had to admit, was the most patient male she'd ever met. He simply stood there, taking in every word Iax said. He paid close attention, asking questions throughout, interjecting a few of his own brilliant insights along the way. With their discussion—'Plan Brainiac,' they'd both dubbed it—finished, they could get back to other, more personal matters.

****

Lifetimes of patience made it easy for Skenyah to bide her time and study, calculate, and take in every detail she could regarding Iax and Gemma. She had not planned to include Mazar in her observations, yet she found herself watching him, as well. He was a worthy male, his love for Iax seemed to be pure, and the openness for which the pair showed each other affection, warmed even her heart.

Since she had lost her own Truemate during the same battle in which Iax's birthparents were felled, Skenyah had stewed in her loneliness season after dark season. Unfortunately, shifters only had one Truemate, and the knowledge that she would be alone until death, ofttimes bothered her on the worst and scariest levels. Her heart had turned cold and hard the moment she lost her only love. Most shifters either went mad or took their own lives after such a loss, but she was determined to see Iax back and in her rightful position in the Amethyst Faerie Dragon Realm.

She felt her loss deeply, and at times, almost followed through with ending her misery. But the vows spoken between her and Eluhyax, her sistair, on that fatal day were so ingrained into her body, mind, and soul. She would see those plans carried out, no matter the hardships, heartaches, and consequences.

There was no jealousy in her regarding Iax and Mazar's love, yet she did envy the pair. Certainly, Skenyah supposed, Iax was happy and in love, but she clearly did not fully comprehend how truly blessed she was. From what little information she had gotten out of Gemma, and that which *Famista* had gifted her with about Iax's beloved Earth, she had figured out that where her niece had been raised, males and females copulated merely for the sake of enjoyment.

That is something that simply was not done in the Dragon Dimension, at least not by the females. She could not wrap her brain around such brazen wantonness, and was overjoyed when Gemma had hinted that Iax had never given herself to another male before Mazar. She could only pray it was true, as the act was too precious to fling about so freely.

Iax did not seem to be interested in them creating a relationship, which saddened her. Even if it was not pure, they were still blood and their shared lineage was one of the most notable in all of the Dragon Dimension. She had gone through much to ensure Iax's safety and to track her down. All she truly wished for was a kin relationship with her fiery-niece, but Iax did not return the sentiment. Skenyah was not one to openly show her affections, but she was considering allowing herself to do so perhaps a bit, if it meant getting closer to this extraordinary female-young; daughter to her sistair.

After a few deep breaths, she cleared her mind of such thoughts and emotions. Presently, there were other issues to deal with, such as speaking with Iax about her offer to Gemma. It had not escaped her notice that Iax was already aware of the conversation she and Gemma had, but it did give her a better feel of how loyal Gemma was to Iax. It had only been a test when she told Gemma she wanted to speak with Iax, herself. She had hoped the female would go to Iax, which she had immediately done.

That only tightened Skenyah's resolve to persuade Gemma to join them on their journey to the Amethyst Faerie Dragon Realm. She missed her home, and could not wait to return and bring with her Iax, Mazar, and hopefully Gemma. It would be cause for the entire Realm to have a grand celebration. None of the threesome yet knew, but they would play the largest role in the restoration of their Realm to its former glory, and to secure and reshape their way of life.

Much of their Weyr had withdrawn themselves after being attacked so many times, which left their army to dwindle down to a pathetic number of warriors. Even though theirs was a matriarchal Realm, she had already decided that Mazar would be quite an asset, as of course, would Iax and Gemma. Seeing to her Weyr and their safety was her primary goal, and strengthening their defenses was of the utmost import whether Iax relished the idea or not. It was not up for debate or discussion; if only she could get Iax to fully comprehend their dire situation, certainly she would be open to Skenyah's plans, or more precisely, open to Skenyah, herself. She was not the harsh, ruthless female many seemed to think her, she was simply focused. Who else would save her Weyr, if not her? Skenyah sighed. *This will take time. Much time.*

Chapter Twenty-three

Rising early the next morning, Iax was kind of peeved, yet excited at the same time to finally be getting on with the whole 'Mating Ritual' stuff all Weyr Truemates go through when the time comes. On shaky legs, butterflies hijacking her stomach, and all that great shit, Iax truly was grateful to be getting things underway and stop feeling so nervous; another thing *Iax don't do.*

Who knew she, of all people, would ever find herself in such a scenario? *Certainly not me,* she grumbled inside. Still not too happy at the aspect of having others do everything such as bathing her; extremely awkward. The hands-on dressing her; even more awkward. And then diving straight into the whole hair and makeup scene; it was enough to make Iax run screaming in the other direction!

She'd never been real big on embellishments, and though she'd do anything for and to be with Mazar, she wasn't super thrilled about this part. As it was, she'd never get how or why so many of these females did all this shit every day of their overlong lives. A strangled, exasperated sound came from her throat. At least she was only expected to do it today, and again on the final day of their Mating Ritual. Ultimately, this meant everything to Mazar, and she would never mess up something so fundamental, so near and dear to his heart. And, to think they'd have to do this all again once they got to her Realm? Maybe not the same exact Ritual, but close, according to Auntie Skenyah.

After spending an unforgettable afternoon with her Truemate yesterday, not to mention those few hours they snuck in last night, Iax had finally spent some quality time with Auntie this morning. Shocked as she was, she actually enjoyed their visit, and even felt like they'd formed a bit of a bond. Stranger things had happened– right?

Sitting before a large dresser-buffet thing with three mirrors, she was trying to ignore what was being done to her person. But the multiple mirrors made that rather impossible, and as she studied the handiwork of the maiden-chicks who'd been gussying her up for hours, she had to smile. *Damn, they do excellent work. You are one hot-hot bitch.* She winked at her reflection. Amazed again at just how resourceful these peeps were, she couldn't help making kissy-faces at herself a few times. Whatever they used for makeup was impressive, and looked far better than anything she'd ever used back home. It apparently lasted much longer, too.

Everything was more like a stain-type of product, and it all was natural. Iax had asked and found out that everything was made from either berries, different kinds of soils, plants, even coal, and in some cases, all of the above. The first and last weren't a real surprise; she'd always known that women had used berries on their lips and cheeks, and coal around their eyes, way back in the day. Her modern-day cosmetics such as mascaras, concealers, lipsticks, blushers, eye shadows, eye liners, other various cosmetic pencils, powders, and more; the totality of which had always cost a small fortune back home. But not here where all their stuff was better for one's skin and the environment. There were no possible allergens, there was always a plentiful supply—no worries of running out—and being free was just another bonus.

Her and Mazar would be expected to procreate, like yesterday, if she had correctly heard all the shit everyone had no-so-quietly whispered about her and Mazar, and right near her ears. They all thought Iax's differences—her Royal lineage being the biggest—would enable her to start 'birthing younglings' soon. The excessive anointing they continually bestowed upon her were supposedly fertility blessings to aid in her. She wasn't sure she needed help in that area. But what did she know? Besides, a girl could never have too many fertility blessings–right?

The handful of females buzzing around applying her makeup, fixing her hair, fussing over her dress, and on and on; their pampering wasn't the worst thing she'd ever endured, just different. She wasn't used to being showered with this kind of attention, and the way they were laying it on so thick made her fidget. It also made her feel welcomed, and even somewhat respected.

She almost felt guilty for not wanting to make babies, just yet. She was still young and if all she'd heard was fact, they had several lifetimes to get the baby-train moving. Besides, doesn't practice make perfect? Iax was all-in for loads and loads of practice.

"Oh Iax, look at you! You are always beautiful, yet at this moment you are far beyond that. I cannot pull forth from my mind the proper words to describe you," Gemma beamed. She smiled and her eyes brightly twinkled like stars.

Coming back out of her head, Iax returned the smile with a nervous one of her own. "Thanks, bestest. I feel so different. Maybe 'cause I never wear makeup or dresses. But yeah, thanks. Hey, you be looking like all-that, too! Let's see, do me a lil' spin, please?" She giggled and twirled her finger around in the air.

Gemma blushed but obliged. "You are full-silly this day, Iax. And thank you. I feel and look different, too. I do not normally dress so, but for you I would do this anytime." She spun in two circles, as her full skirts flowed and fanned out away from her. Gemma wore bit of makeup, but not much as she didn't need it. Still, it made her shine, and she looked even younger with a blush kissing her high cheekbones. The female was radiant.

"Alright, no more dallying. It is time. We must bite this popping-stand and go downstairs where everyone awaits you. And Iax, please, do not fidget. You are flawless and absolutely perfect." Gemma gently took Iax's hands into her own, they both giggled and softly jumped up and down like female-young for a moment. The sudden dawning that they'd mess up Iax's kick-ass hairdo ceased their jumping. Right then, Iax realized what her bestest just said, *'Bite this popping-stand'?* She shook her head and chuckled in amusement; she would miss Gemma. If only she could talk her bestest into going with them to their new home when the time came. *Ugh. Wrong time, definitely wrong place, chicka,* she warned herself before she could get upset and sad over that.

Iax's hair went down to her ass; in other words, she had *lots* of very thick hair. The maiden-chicks didn't seem to mind, though, as they spent hours using short, medieval iron-bars—which, Iax was sure, could double as torture devices—to make loose curls all over her head. They had several of the implements and as they took one out of the bucket of raging hot coals, more would go in. Talk about hot, even as careful as the maidens were, she'd still felt the heat a bit closer to her skin than she would've liked!

Conair ain't got nothin' on these badass curling irons. Literally, foot-long pieces of iron which, after soaking in hot coals, would curl anything.

She wasn't sure what the goop was they'd used on each chunk of her hair to keep it molded how they wanted it, but it smelled fantastic and kind of fruity. By the time they finished, most of her locks were loosely piled high on top of her head, some hung down to frame her face, as the rest loosely flowed in a cascade down her back; like something you'd see in a glamour magazine. Seriously, these chicks rocked the hair and makeup routine. She'd never been this fancied-up, and she even liked it. For now.

"Okay, I think I'm as ready as I'll ever be. Where's my flower bouquet? Oh, of course, right where I left it!" Iax nervously giggled and snatched up her bouquet off the dresser. Turning back to survey the room, all four maidens, Gemma, and even Auntie bore wide, beatific smiles, their faces were shiny and gleeful.

You can do this, Iax. Breathe. In. Out. In. Out. Ah, that's it. You can and will do this, she reaffirmed herself.

Her dress was a breathtaking mixture of lavender and aqua, her favorite colors. Who knew? She wasn't sure how the dressmaker found out, but she was happy for it. Adorned with what looked like baby-pearl buttons every couple inches from the center of the low-cut bodice—which showed a whole lotta cleavage—to just below her belly button, it was handmade from their finest silk-like fabrics. It was so low-cut in back, she felt a small breeze kiss the top of her ass, which made her giggle again. And though the train was long and appeared to be thick and heavy, it was much lighter than Iax had expected. The four maidens easily and deftly held the yards of silkiness trailing out behind her as she led everyone from the bedchamber, to begin their trek down the three-flight stairwell.

Gemma hung on her right side, and Auntie on her left. Both females seemed happy for her, but she somehow knew Skenyah could lie her ass off and never even bat a lash. Gemma, on the other hand, detested lies; a respectable character to possess, yet Iax felt that her friend was, at the very least, fronting and not wanting anything to mess up this day. She still felt a heavy sadness in her friend, but it would have to wait, at least for a little while.

Approaching the top of the stairwell, she contemplated the three-fights they had to descend. *Ugh, this is gonna take forever,* Iax grumbled to herself. *By the time we finally get down there, I'll need a nap. Everyone will, if they're not already asleep.* Shaking her head to clear those ridiculous thoughts, she threw back her shoulders, lifted her chin, smiled like she meant it—even though she'd never admit it, she really did—and down they went.

This was the first-day of their Mating Ritual; the first half of their Joining Ceremony. Her and Mazar would essentially be getting hitched like people did in most places. Everyone got all dolled and duded-up, someone said the right words, blah, blah, blah, they'd exchange tokens of their everlasting love, kissy-kissy, and voila! They'd be married. Then, let the party begin.

Being a big music lover, Iax wished she had some now. At the moment, she was hearing another favored tune—which was, ironically, about music—playing through her somewhat muddled head. A woman going to a club, spotting a hottie, doing some dirty dancing, and a few smooth moves later, they're off for a private time. The upbeat song helped to calm her. Unfortunately, her inner-pop-rock-singer was silenced as Gemma gently squeezed her arm, bringing her back out of her head. Although she would much rather have remained there, in her head and singing one of her favorite songs, she knew she had no choice. "Ahhh," she released a long, audible sigh.

"If you do not have a care for the placement of your feet, Iax, you may accidentally fall down these stairs. Please pay attention, as many await you and the events of this day. Apparently, excluding recent events of which we shall not name, Mazar's fellow-Weyr members still respect him and are happy for you both. I think they may be somewhat put out if you land in a heap at the bottom of this ridiculously long stairwell. Do you not?" She winked at Iax, and they both smiled.

On the second level of stairs, she couldn't help but appreciate the music she heard coming from where everyone patiently stood awaiting her. Sounds of soft wind instruments tunneled up to the rafters and bounced off the walls, relaxing her frazzled nerves.

After a few deep, cleansing breaths, she smiled again. *One. More. Level. To. Go.* She was grateful for not having to wear high heels. Beside the fact that she stood six-feet-tall in her bare feet, they didn't have heels here, anyway; one more mark in their favor. Still, going slowly so her dress didn't meet with any mishaps descending the stairs, her 'slippers,' as they were called, pinched her toes and rubbed against the backs of her ankles. *They'll leave marks.* She was positive.

Quit your grumbling and bitching, Iax. This is one of the most monumental days of your life, so knock off the fucking pity-party. She burst into laughter recalling Gemma's 'potty-party,' and garnered stern looks from all the females around her. "Soo–ryy," she stretched the word out. But she *wasn't* sorry, 'cause it *was* funny.

As they finally rounded the stairwell that led to the main level, she breathed a sigh of relief. All humor was lost the moment her gaze found him. *Her Mazar.* The tenderness that shone in the depths of his emerald-green eyes, took her breath away. *Oh. My. God. He's beautiful. Even more so than me, and I'm the girl here.* Tamping down the urge to giggle like an idiot, she plastered a goofy smile on her face that made her cheekbones ache. She didn't care, this was unbelievable. *He* was unbelievable. Worth any amount of discomfort.

****

Difficult as it was to believe, Mazar stood with his own Chief to his right, and Chief Gordell to his left. Who could have ever imagined Chief Gordell standing in on his Joining Ceremony? Not him, to be sure. Proud and honored as he was that the male had even offered to do so, it humbled him beyond compare. He still did not quite understand where all the kindness was coming from.

While the Chiefs had taken to ribbing him and each other, and he joined in their fun. Suddenly, when they were all laughing and most of the guests were quietly visiting, the entire room fell silent. As he glanced away from the males, Mazar could have been knocked over by a mere feather, when his gaze found her. *His Iax.*

Her silky, spun-gold tresses were looped and partially piled atop her beautiful head, soft wisps hung loose around her face, and the rest softly fell down her back. The tiny white and purple flowers weaved into her locks were a sweet touch, and though he preferred her in a natural state, the small bit of face paint made her features more predominant; her eyes stood out like never before. The dress she wore hugged her lean yet solid form, and drew all eyes to her sexy curves. Mazar growled low in his throat.

"Hear, now. They only admire what they can never have, friend. Let it go," his Chief whispered from his right. He was correct, but Mazar still did not want other males ogling his female in such a disrespectful and open manner. Likewise, how could he blame them when she looked this way? He relaxed his shoulders, the tension was becoming too much to bear.

This was their first-day of being a Mated pair, and he would not allow anyone nor anything to dampen it at all. After learning only a small amount of what his Truemate had already been through in her short life, she deserved this day to be perfect. And he would do anything to ensure she got it. Anything.

Their eyes locked, smiles widened, and cheeks reddened. She must be recalling the same events as he from the never-enough short hours they had spent together last eve. They were not allowed to spend the whole eve together, so they had made each moment count. And now, he could not wait for this eve. No one would ever be able to put such ridiculous constraints on them again. Well, at least not once the entire Mating Ritual was completed by week's end. This one night was theirs, but for the duration of the Ritual, they were prohibited from sharing a bed or even a bedchamber. *We shall see about that,* he mused.

Her bright-green eyes sparkled, and made him squirm where he stood. Those eyes held all the love he had ever desired, and far more than he deserved. But, who was he to question fate, the Goddesses, or whomever? He would have and hold his Iax for as long as *Meynix* saw fit to bless and allow him to draw breath.

Her delectable, natural, berry-shaded lips were perhaps a shade deeper in color than normal, as they sparkled in the soft glow from hundreds of candles that had been placed all around the Great Hall. Glad he did not have to help with that task, he much appreciated the affect the flames made upon every inch of her. Their smiles never faded as she made her way to stand in front of him. They both quietly sighed in mutual contentment.

"Hey," she acknowledged him with a vixen smile and a wink.

In turn, he could not help himself and returned, "Hey, to you, too, my Iaxsss," his deep voice reverberated throughout his overheated, sensitive body. He truly hoped this would be done soon, as they stood and gazed into each other's eyes lost in new affections and emotions. After a few long moments of staring at each other, they both blushed when Chief Zarckael cleared his throat.

He was presiding and conducting this half of their Joining Ceremony, the legally binding portion where the entire Weyr would witness their joining. Then, Skenyah would preside over the eighth and final day that would Bond them together for all time. Mazar and

Iax felt only this day should be necessary, but they didn't want to rebuff tradition, and especially not one as old as time, itself.

"Are we ready to proceed?" Chief Zarckael asked. "I can give you more time, although I would think it rude to have everyone stand and wait for the pair of you to visit, as you leisurely and freely display your love." One side of his lips hooked up into a half-smile.

Sobering, both wanting this to be over and done so they could get on with more satisfying pursuits, they turned to face each other and gave the Chief their sides. "Yes, we are ready," they proclaimed in unison. "Git 'r dun, El Chief-e-o," Iax had to throw in. Everyone shook their heads as several in the crowd even chuckled, including both Chiefs.

"Yes, I will git...er, proceed." Chief Zarckael's brows scrunched together, obviously wanting to be in on the humor, but not quite sure how to do so in Iax's way of speech. He had nothing, so he began the Joining Ceremony and beseeched their respective Goddesses to bless their union and bind the words he spoke.

It seemed to last for a long time, but in reality it had only taken a few minutes. Finally, they had both spoken their own vows —far different from any vows she'd ever heard on Earth, though nonetheless heartfelt and meaningful—then topped it all off with a long, steamy kiss that made all the witnesses cheer, clap, and verbalize their felicitations rather loudly.

With this part of the first half of their Joining Ceremony portion—opposite the vow exchanging where time seemed to have slowed—now behind them, everyone was dancing, drinking, eating, and being merry in general. Iax sat at the edge of the Hall on a bench that had been relocated near one of the massive fireplaces. With Gemma at her side, they studied other female fashions, different styles of dance, and anything else females normally checked out at functions like this. Rapt attention, eyes wide, and smiles bright, they were both shocked at the sheer amount of drinking in which some of the females partook. Some sat and daintily sipped their drinks, while others stood and guzzled something obviously much stronger as they reveled with the big, tough males.

"I can't believe I'm married. *Me!* The one who always said, 'No, I'll never do something so stupid,' but looket! Married! Me!" Iax huffed. The smile twitching at the edges of her lips starkly contrasted her attempt to pretend this was a dreadful thing.

"Yes, I am surprised yet pleased that you are *Mated,*" Gemma corrected. "I did not, mind you by your own words, believe you ever would be. You simply never showed much if any interest in settling down. Long term, I mean," Gemma replied with a gleam in her violet-eyes.

A couple of females who'd been heavily enjoying the sauce, chose that particular moment to float and twirl past them. "How much you wanna bet they crash and burn?" Iax wagered, yelling over the lively din.

"Crash and what?" Gemma asked, raising her own voice as the noise levels had increased to a deafening degree.

"Burn," Iax yelled into her friend's ear. "They're gonna fall. Crash. Kaput."

Giggling, Gemma could only nod her head in agreement with Iax's prediction. Right on cue, the two soused females spun out of control as they barreled into a high table laden with various drinks. The whole room exploded into laughter, but the two females didn't budge. Once everyone realized they remained where they had landed in a tangled heap, their mirth quickly died down.

"Oh, I do hope they are not harmed," Gemma whispered. Even the music stopped as several females rushed to check on the drunken-twosome.

Shaking her head and still smiling, Iax couldn't help it. She'd seen such displays back home at parties and such. She was sure they were fine, but she couldn't speak to how they'd probably feel in the morning. *Oh, well...their own damn fault.* She sighed. "They're fine, just drunk. They'll have hangovers in the morning, then they'll be back to normal in no time. What's that shit everyone's drinking, anyway?" She'd noticed large, earthen jugs being passed around, and had to laugh at the sight of the burly warriors as they shook and shivered after taking long, deep pulls from the jugs, and multiple times each. Still, they all continued to partake.

"Ah, it is their fire-brew, which is said to—"

Iax cut her off, not to be intentionally rude, but she had this one, "Lemme guess; it'll put hair on their chests," she frankly stated, already knowing it as fact. Gemma nodded. "We have stuff back home that only few dare to drink. Nasty shit, if ya ask me. Then again, it's only one more reason I don't drink," Iax supplied, part in humor and part exasperation.

Iax had seen up-close-and-personal what alcohol did to people. Unable to do anything more than observe some of her closest friends as they suffered the consequences alcohol caused, she could only stand by feeling helpless and lost. A couple more emotions *Iax don't do well.*

"Are you all right, Iax? You seem far off. Are you in need of anything?" Gemma's comforting voice broke into her begrudging thoughts, and it made her feel even worse.

Time to suck it up, bitch. Stop trippin' and go find your male. Now. "I'm good. I just really, really loathe drinking. If you can hold your booze, fine, but it's been my experience more often than not, that most can't. So yeah, and that's all. Think I'll go find Mazar 'cause he owes me some dancing." She winked at Gemma, drew up handfuls of her dress as she rose, turned on her slippered-heel, and left in search of her male.

Iax had been correct from the beginning; "Sometimes when you unburden yourself, you feel much better," she had once advised Gemma, and it was true. *Iax, it is nice to finally see you do what you always tell others, and I hope it helped.* Gemma thoughtfully smiled. *If only you would unburden yourself more often, I believe it would provide you some of the help you need, just as it has for me.* She hoped and prayed her friend would see this for herself soon, before it was too late. Gemma had been a mess, but she had also noticed Iax's differences, and not only the ones pertaining to her new lineage. The female was still far too reckless and careless for Gemma's liking, so hoping and praying would have to be enough.

Chapter Twenty-four

Day two of the Mating Ritual would be a long day, Iax had already decided. For whatever reason, after the first half of the Joining Ceremony, Dragon-shifters used the next seven days of the Ritual for the couple to compete in physical tasks. *Why? Who the fuck knew,* Iax mused. *Am I looking forward to any of it? Maybe. Possibly. Just a teensy-weensy-bit.*

"Are you prepared for this day, my love?" Nuzzling her ear, Mazar stood behind Iax, every inch of his front nestled snugly against her back. She groaned, recalling the bliss they'd shared last night, and glad they had taken a walk to get away from everyone for a little while before today's competitions began.

"I think the better question is, are *you* prepared, my love? 'Cause I'm a vicious competitor and I fully intend to kick your hot-ass." Leaning her head to one side, she gave him full access to her neck. The dude did extraordinary things with that tongue of his. *Ah. This may not be as easy as I thought. Ooh, great ploy.* She grinned.

Just before he could answer her, she took off at a flat run. "Good plan, but you'll have to get up a lot earlier in the mornings to fool this chicka!" she yelled over her shoulder, giggling as she reveled in her new supersonic speed. Racing through the trees in a blur, she knew he was chasing her; that was her plan, after all.

"I never lose in any competition, my love. You would be wise to remember that!" he yelled back from somewhere behind her.

With a sudden *oomph*, she found herself rolling in a ball, yet no part of her body came into contact with the ground. Of course, he was faster than her, he'd had plenty of practice, but she had not.

Tightly holding her body against his, Mazar kept her in a protective shell as they rolled across the ground in a blur. Her gasping and still giggling until they came to a stop on the forest floor, made his heart sing. "I believe this means I win this round, my love." He deeply kissed her. She didn't protest one bit.

"Okay, I won't say I lost but I won't say you won, either. Fair? I mean, you've been able to move at rocket-speeds all your life, but I just started. So yep, I call that fair." Smiling and resting their foreheads together, they heard the blast of the village horn, the signal of start time for the games.

"Have you any questions on what we are to do?" he quietly asked her. Neither of them wanted to do any of it to begin with.

"Nah. I know it's to prove how much we trust each other and our endurance, guess they wanna make sure we're compatible in every way. I don't see how that's any of their biz, but we don't seem to have a choice. I suppose we'd better scoot-to-it." She jumped up and reached down to help him stand. Not that he needed assistance, she just genuinely loved to touch him.

****

"So, Zarckael, what will you have the pair do this day?" Gordell asked with a smirk. He knew what his own Weyr did while celebrating a Mating, but every Weyr had their own set of games. The games were simply meant to see the pair prove their trustworthiness, compatibility, and endurance to each other; the most essential components in a Mating, which also served to strengthen their Bond. Without those integral assurances, a pair would not last, and finding a second Truemate was unheard of. The Mating Ritual games always helped them realize they must be able to rely on one another at all times.

"First, one will have to outdo the other while hunting. They are required to track, take down, and field-dress as many *On'Laque*, the beastly animals in the forest, as they can. Their time limit is sunset; they need to be mindful of when the sun will set, cease all actions, leave their finds where they felled and dressed them, then return here to my holdings before the sun slips fully below the horizon. My males will then go out to retrieve both of their finds, bring them back here, and then we will all wait for the tally. Then, the foods will be cooked and eaten throughout their Mating Ritual.

"As the tally is calculated, they will be questioned separately in order to discover their thought process, and discuss their own techniques. Whatever their findings, as far as who gets more, is not the true issue, though it will determine the day's victor. More so, it is their ability to believe in each other, to trust that no matter the situation, one can and will be able to provide for the other. If they happen to be in a survival scenario at some point, which is highly likely from what I have gathered about the Realm they will be relocating to, they both need to have the knowhow and abilities to care for the other should serious harm befall either of them.

"That is the real test of this day. Of them all, this should prove to be the most difficult, yet one of the most important. They will not come to see this until the day is complete, when the results will show if one is truly worthy of the other. I have no doubts the pair was meant to be, any fool could gaze upon them and see how much affection they feel toward each other. This is a strengthening exercise in their love and commitment for one another. But, you already know all of this," Chief Zarckael finished with a mischievous gleam in his eyes.

"You seem to find much joy in other's suffering. Has this always been your way, or is there more to it? Perhaps, due in part to Mazar's actions regarding my Yoren? We are whole and well, and according to my Yoren, even our youngling seems to be thriving on all the excitement here. But then, how can it not? We are all excited to see the outcome of this Mating Ritual, and of course, to welcome our youngling into our Realm," Gordell retorted, an amused smile on his lips.

"And yes, before you ask, Yoren and I have fully absolved your male for his transgressions as whatever happened no longer matters. There is no deeper, more heartfelt forgiveness than absolution; it is fully encompassing and for all time. It was not difficult after what I saw in that clearing upon my arrival. Now, I do not wish to speak further on this matter. Other than if Mazar, himself, feels the need to approach and have words with me, I'm putting an end to this, once and for all."

It felt as if a giant weight had been lifted from his shoulders by merely speaking those words aloud. He no longer harbored ill-will toward Mazar, and most certainly not against his female, Iax, who was a force to be reckoned with. Gordell felt he would thoroughly enjoy these games alongside his Yoren, who was increasingly rounding-out with their youngling. Neither of them could wait to bring their new life into the Realm. Excited would be an indescribable understatement, in terms of how they felt about their coming youngling.

****

Making it back down to Chief Zarckael's holdings literally only took minutes. *Damn, I'm lovin' this speedy-go-racer shit!* Iax quipped inside. She had always been a major fan of speed, so yeah, this was amazing in a variety of ways.

Standing before the Chiefs, expressions rather guarded, Iax felt a tad nervous but she wasn't sure why. She wasn't afraid of anyone or anything, although she had a gut feeling this day would undoubtedly push her limits. *As for Mazar?* Probably not so much since he knows everyone here, has been present for these Ritual things more than a few times, and knows the area far better than her. *Whateve,* she'd get it figured out. *No real worries. Yeah, keep telling yourself that, chicka. It helps every time–right?* Right. Just then, a female came running out of the Chief's holdings burdened with a mass of what looked to be clothing and other supplies. Eyeing the female for a moment, Iax turned her attention back to Chief Zarckael. Narrowing her gaze on his immense form, she couldn't help but wonder what the hell he had planned for them.

Mazar hadn't been any real help; according to him none of the Weyr members knew exactly what went on during each new competition, as they weren't allowed to go with the couple. Made sense and all, but still, someone along the way must have told others about their experiences, you'd think. Then again, from what she'd heard, the competitions were always different depending on how creative the Chief was, and of course, his mood.

She inhaled a few long breaths, which didn't help because each time all she tasted was Mazar. He would be her failing, she knew. Giving herself a couple firm mental slaps helped a little. *Stop thinking about him, or you're gonna fuck everything up for both of you,* she scolded herself. *Buck-up, you can do this.*

"Here are a few necessary items to aid you both in this portion of the Mating Ritual. You may not see their usefulness now, but you will later. I am told you have both been instructed on what this phase entails, and the requirements for you to be successful. If you have any questions, now would be the time to voice them. I want you to be victorious and begin with all the information you need," Mazar's Chief declared.

Reaching down, Mazar entwined their fingers and gave her hand a gentle squeeze—which she loved—but he was seriously rattling her cage. Against her better senses, she squeezed back and quickly released his hand, then scooted over a couple feet to put some space between them. She couldn't think at all, let alone clearly, while they were in such proximity. It dawned on her then that he probably kept doing those things just to distract her. Shaking her head, she gave him a reprimanding glare while fighting a smile. Then the ass winked at her! He was bound and determined to keep her off kilter; he was apparently unaware that two could play at his game. Licking her lips ever so slowly, she winked back. His face lost all flirty expression, and his eyes narrowed to read her like an open book. She innocently smiled.

"I do not recall ever dealing with a pair such as the two of you." Chief Zarckael laughed. "If you are ready, we will get you both prepared to begin your competition. Only if you do not mind, of course, since you both seem mighty busy. Though, that level of concentration will serve you well, as long as it is not misplaced." He winked at them.

Mazar's deep, sexy voice rumbled next to her. "We are ready, Chief Zarckael. Forgive my Truemate; she is merely attempting to addle my wits. I believe she thinks to ply me with her wiles as a constant distraction, which is clearly her way. Can you not see this for yourself?" he finished. Turning to look her in the eyes, he almost couldn't quell the urge to laugh aloud at the fire he knew ignited in her veins by his blatant slight.

That was decidedly low and unfair, and it was easy to see that he was having way too much fun. This was a no-holds-barred competition so, she supposed, he needed to use everything at his disposal to attain a win. *Good luck buddy, you'll need it.* She thought, glaring red-hot daggers at him. He winked his left eye at her, the one only she could see. Her body was vibrating with frustration, but only for a moment. She immediately schooled her features, took a few deep breaths, and was back in control. *I hope he can play the way I do. I'ma enjoy every minute of this.* She smiled inside.

****

"Which direction will you choose?" Mazar asked Iax. This part was up to them, as long as they stuck to the rules of play, they got to choose who went in which direction to begin this phase.

After being given various supplies and garments in case the weather turned, or they needed to change their clothing, Mazar had quickly folded his items and used the final and largest piece to wrap the rest, along with his few mandatory supplies, into an easy to carry bundle. He should have known, given her extensive training and background experience, Iax would excel even in their preparations.

She had some sort of already-made 'pack,' as she had called it. Familiar as she was with it, she apparently used the item aplenty. Rather than folding her clothing items, she rolled them up tightly, and quite fast. Her way took far less room than his and he felt a bit foolish at her 'one-upping' him—another of her word usages—on such a basic task.

Politely, Iax had declined the supplies offered to her, as she already had everything she felt she would need. Her pack had to be one of her most valuable assets, apart from her body and feminine wiles, he mused. Stopping himself from going down that damning track, he would keep his thoughts under control. She would not best him by means of her body, experience, or intelligence. He was always impressed by her, nothing new there, but he would not allow that, or *her* to affect him or his decisions in any way.

After much thought, she had scanned the path to their right, then their left. "Yeah, um, I believe I'll be goin' that a'way." She pointed her chin to the left. It was literally the path less traveled, she explained, and then added how she'd always been the type to stand and work alone. Things got done better that way and if mistakes were made, they were hers to fix and learn from. Never one to follow the herd, she had a gut feeling the least used path would be the correct one to take. He could not argue her logic.

Finally packing the last of her supplies, she inserted her 'flexible canteens'—about which everyone had been so curious, their rendezvous had been delayed for almost an hour as several shifters checked out the units—into her pack. He could almost see her brain racing while she had tried to sort out all the variables to get everything done correctly. She hated to lose, which was obvious, and didn't if she could help it. "Another thing *Iax don't do,*" Gemma had warned him.

"You have a strange method of thought, I will concede as much. I do hope you know, I have full faith in your abilities, my love. I wish to see you be the victor, but I do not play games lightly as such has been ingrained into me since birth. Apologies in advance for any actions which may not be as 'gentlemanly' as I would prefer. Well-wishes, and may the best male win!" Laughing like a child, he grabbed his bundle of supplies off the ground and was gone in a flash.

That's so cheating. Oh well. I know what I'm capable of. I can and will win this round. He may have intimate knowledge of the area, but she'd been to so many different places, Dimensions, Realms and such, she had the benefit of knowing to expect the unexpected, and it had proven useful many a time. "Watch out, hot-stuff, I ain't going down easy," she whispered into the light breeze, laughing and feeling practically giddy. Strapping her pack on her back, she took off at a dead run still totally diggin' on her new speed-factor. *Hells, yeah! This'll be wicked fun!* Giggling, she raced up her path, amazed at how silent her movements were. She supposed going so fast, her feet probably didn't even touch the ground. *Another bonus for me!* She squealed in excitement.

Iax had been working on honing her new powers—as she called them—such as extra-sensitive hearing, sight, touch, smell, and strangely enough, even taste. Now all five of the regular, built-in 'human' senses were amplified in triplicate, at least. All her senses were beyond intense and would allow her to win this thing, she was certain. Even if Mazar was born here and had lived this way for "lifetimes," as he'd proclaimed. She was still confident—always had been—and in awe of her new superpowers, all of which bolstered and strengthened her resolve.

They were searching for an animal comparable to a cross between the deer and elk from back home…er, on Earth. *What're they called?* she pondered. *Oh, yeah, On'laque.*

She heard twigs breaking about one-hundred-feet to her left. Being super-stealthy-like, she slowed her roll till she was standing statue-still. Scenting the air, honing in with her badass new hearing, she deduced the noise was an *On'laque. Jack-fucking-pot, bitch!* She celebrated with herself.

Putting her newfound stealth to the test, Iax wound through the thick, dense forest area and snuck up on her prey. She'd never hunted animals nor was she opposed to it, but this whole thing was still new to her, and she found herself loving every minute of it. So far.

Getting cocky was most assuredly the worst enemy of a hunter trying to outsmart their prey, so she still needed to keep her wits about her. This was the animals' turf, and nature was unpredictable for a reason. If she didn't have all her new abilities, there was positively no way she would even attempt this. Animals were smart, their environment was their own camouflage, and they knew everything about their home and surroundings. *Breathe, just breathe and relax. You're doing terrific, chicka,* she supported her inner-self.

The way she'd packed her stuff, all she had to do was reach back over her right shoulder to grab an arrow, then down on the left side of her pants to unhook her bow. She was the one with the mad-skillz when it came to weapons, remember?

In mere seconds she was focused, locked, and loaded, but the *On'laque*—which looked surprisingly like an Elk from back home— hadn't even noticed her. *Wow! Either I'm just that damn good, or Mr. Gonna-Be-Dinner isn't too bright,* she thought, forcing herself to not laugh out loud.

Pulling her bowstring back, Mr. Gonna-Be-Dinner lined up in her sights, she stuck with the way she'd always handled any weapon; she closed her eyes, let her head fall back just a tad, and quietly released a long sigh. Fully relaxed, she allowed nature's peacefulness to fill her, and loosed her arrow. Eyes still closed and waiting to hear the telltale *thunk*, she smiled when the sound quietly echoed back to her.

Reattaching the bow to her pants, she sped over to the fallen animal, and immediately felt a twinge of remorse for killing the poor thing. It hadn't done anything to anyone, but she also knew this was the kind of food that kept the shifters, including her Mazar, alive and healthy. As she eyed the thing, her unease palpable, she remembered they had a time limit; no time to fuck around. *Guess it's go-time. Step-up, bitch, and git 'r dun.* She grimaced.

Iax jumped in with both feet, both hands, both everything, and holy shit, this was *not* fun. Thankfully, Chief Gordell had given her detailed instructions on the whole field-dressing process. With no other choice, she pulled her long, serrated knife from its sheath on her right hip and did exactly what he'd told her, all in the space of about twenty-ish minutes.

Cutting its belly from stem to sternum, she was surprised at the heat and the nasty stench emanating from the body, when she reached inside. Next move was to crack the ribs open, then cut and split the pelvis to give herself more room to work inside. Then she cut the esophagus, detached the poor thing's head, and removed all four legs at the elbow joints.

After that disgusting bout of fun, there was plenty of room to get inside and pull out all its innards. Gordell said that they typically left it all on the ground, or tossed into the trees and bushes for other animals to enjoy. *The circle of life, natural selection; either way it was still a nasty fucking mess.* She groaned inwardly.

Lying on its left side, she began skinning the once-beautiful *On'laque* at the upper portion of the body. She got a tight hold on the hide at the back of its headless-neck, and—mostly due to her newfound strength—was able to carefully strip it away from the body. She had to use her knife in a few difficult areas but before she knew it, she was flopping it onto its right side to repeat what she had just done.

Apparently, the skinning aided the meat to cool faster, which preserved it for a longer period of time, until Chief Zarckael's males could locate and retrieve them. Gordell had explained how they would normally hang the *On'laque* in a tree to keep them off the ground and further help the meat cool. The other reasons for keeping them off the ground were to keep them from the dirt and such, as well as to keep them up so other animals couldn't get ahold of them and start snacking on the meat while you were away.

Thankful again for her new strength, she chose the perfect tree, which ironically, happened to have a couple strong, short limbs that appeared plenty sturdy to bear the weight of the animal. She hoisted and hung its ass-up in the tree.

Fighting the urge to puke, she tamped it down and spread the hide out over a large rock, figuring they'd use every bit of this poor guy. Knowing this would feed Mazar's Weyr members, and they'd put the hide to beneficial use, too, she shook it off and moved on to find her next poor, innocent animal to kill.

Once this day is done, I never wanna do this again for any reason. She shivered at the stinky, sticky, sick mess. There was so much blood, and the poor thing's innards had been lying on the ground all around her in big, bloody, heaping piles, before she flung them away into the bushes as Gordell had instructed. The odor made her want to vomit; a definite downside to her new acute sense of smell. *Guess everything has its pros and cons.*

She decided to check the position of the sun after repeating the nasty killing process several times, and calculated that she had roughly another hour, maybe more. At this point, she'd already done over a dozen *On'laque*. The field-dressing part had become easier with each one, but she still had not enjoyed it at all. She was covered in blood from the top of her head to the tips of her booted feet, as it were. She was also hot and smelly because the blood had coagulated and become sticky; it was almost too much even for her.

Good thing she never had any aversions to blood, but after this, she may have to rethink her outlook on the subject. There was so much, and the smells combined with the sticky, nasty textures, she wasn't sure she'd ever get it all washed off of her body and out of her long, thick hair. She'd even had Gemma braid her mane, but with all the action she'd seen today, half of it had come loose and was hanging down around her face, sticking to the blood there and on her upper body. "Ugh! Calgon, take me away! That would be a dream come true, if it was even possible," she said out loud.

Deep in her thoughts, she hadn't heard anyone approach. When large hands covered her eyes from behind, she was so startled she spun into action. One moment she was standing there talking to herself, the next, she had him on his back pinned to the ground before she realized her assailant was Mazar. Who, though surprise was etched all over his too-gorgeous face, was smiling up at her like a naughty schoolboy. Truth tell, he looked more like an irresistible rogue. She returned his smile, dropping to lay fully over the top of his rockin' bod. He felt better than anything. Ever. She never wanted to move. Too bad he had to speak and ruin the moment.

"Ah, my love." Wrapping his powerfully strong arms around her and rubbing his hands up and down her back, he made a strangled noise deep in his throat. She pulled her head back just enough to look at him, and noticed his attempt to smile failed miserably as he scrunched up his nose. He was repulsed by her smell, probably by everything about her, yet by the sparkle in his eyes and his sexy half-smile, maybe nothing had been ruined, after all.

Still, she felt inclined to ramble, "I'm sorry. I know I'm a mess." Her worn out muscles groaned in protest as she wrenched herself up to stand next to him. "Either you lost big-time, or you're kick-ass at hunting. That's not fair, I hope you know." He didn't reply, but just lay there smiling his sexy smile and looking all hot as always. *Not fair.* She frowned.

"Rest assured, I do not lose. You obviously did…something, from your appearance, but I am still confident in the number of my finds. We are not allowed to discuss the particulars, so let us be away from here. The sun is about to set and I hunger." The twinkling in his emerald-green eyes melted her insides and her resolve.

"I thought we still had a while before the sun went down. Aren't we supposed to stay out here till then?" She glanced back up to notice the sun had clearly dropped faster than she had expected. *Man, chicka, your calculations were way off. You must be tired,* she admitted to herself. *And, he 'hungers' now? No way—I can't believe I'm even thinking this—would I be able to do anything right now. Not sure if I can stay awake long enough to bathe,* another humiliating admission.

Instantly, he was up and at her side. "My love, you do not look well. I mean only to say, you look rather ill and tired. We are to be back at the Chief's holdings by sundown." He gave her a quick peck on the lips, scooped her up in his solid arms, and then they were zooming through the forest at lightning speed.

Resting her weary, filthy head against the soothing sound of his beating heart—which matched her own—the radiant warmth of his intense love fully and unconditionally enveloped her.

Chapter Twenty-five

Days three, four, and five passed Iax and Mazar by in a dizzying blur. After exerting so much energy during the daytime while competing, not to mention—though no one else knew—their extracurricular activities at night, they were both beyond exhausted. The flurry of speed in which they both performed and maneuvered their tasks was highly impressive, even to them.

Any Weyr members who had neared the pair admired their fierce determination; the raw drive they possessed, and whatever else it was that kept them going, when they could have easily given up and slept for several days in a row. Even both Chiefs were evidently pleased by their conviction and the stamina that pushed them.

There had been whispers of ending the Mating Ritual early because, as it were, the pair had gone above and beyond all limits and expectations of everyone, but they would not have that. Two more days; simply two more days before they could both be victorious, and their Ritual would conclude, just as every Mated pair who went before them. They expected no less from themselves.

And there was still the matter of finalizing their plans, then putting word into action. They would have to first figure out how to journey back to Iax's Earth. 'They,' included Iax, Mazar, Skenyah, and even Gemma had conceded and eagerly agreed to attempt the trip with them. She had always hoped to visit Iax's home, or rather, where she had believed her home to be, and could not have been more excited had she tried.

Somehow, the foursome would attempt to procure at least some of Iax's belongings and bring them back when they returned. Most likely they'd go from Earth directly to their new home in the Amethyst Faerie Dragon Realm. Skeptical as Iax still was about Auntie's plans, she still looked forward to returning to the Realm she'd been to once before. *Twice,* she amended.

No wonder everything was so different when her and Gemma had been there. She'd felt ten-feet-tall and bulletproof, as they say. Everything she did just...worked. She felt in-tune with the very air around her as if she were a part of the place. Apparently she was, is, and always will be.

The biggest downside to this whole thing would be the long sit-down with the mama and dad who had raised her. After all these days, not to mention being so busy, she had cooled down and couldn't, in good conscience, hold on to those hurt feelings she had upon first learning of her true lineage. But, she would let them know they could have told her and she wouldn't have loved them any less. Probably more, if that was even possible. They obviously loved her far more than she'd ever realized, too.

Now, the need for them to relocate so often all made sense; she thought maybe they had been afraid of discovery either by one of her own, or even scarier, one of those of 'mad-scientist' wing-nut groups. *Those crazy-fucks would've surely gotten off on testing every inch of me.* She shivered and almost needed to puke. *What would they have found?* She didn't know, but she did know it wouldn't have been a party for her. So yeah, plan 'Harshin' on the Folks' was an abort-mission now and always. If they loved her that much, enough to inconvenience themselves so often and in such significant ways for her safety, she could do no less than respect them even more. Accepting it and loving them all the more still didn't seem even close adequate.

How would they take the news that she had no choice but to move? And not only move, but permanently relocate to an entirely different Dimension? Probably not well, especially not her mama. Elise Conifurr was the most compassionate, easy going, nonjudgmental person in the world. Period. More beautiful than anyone, even those 'perfect' things you see on TV and in rag-mags. Her mama was a natural beauty inside and out, and being loved by her was one of the purest blessings one could ever wish for.

Then there was jolly old David Conifurr, or as Iax referred to him, Dad. He had worked for the C.I.A. since he was twenty or so years old, according to what she'd been told as her mama and dad never went into details related to his work. But when she'd been hired and then found out the man she'd always considered an uncle was to be her boss, she had demanded a few answers. Well, she hadn't gotten very far, other than to find out her dad's position had more to do with landing her job than anyone was willing to discuss. So she had left it alone.

"Sometimes less is more, yeah? Everything in due time but for now, the less you know the better off you'll be, kiddo," Fred had advised on her first day of work. He was brilliant and almost always right, and so far he had, been regarding that sage little piece of advice.

All-in-all, her folks were salt of the earth kind of people. So were Fred and his quiet little mouse-of-a-wife, Dana. She never spoke much but when she did, people listened. She'd always doted over Iax, giving her fun girly gifts for birthdays, Christmases and such. Even after her and Fred had two kids of their own; a son named Garreth David Travett—who'da imagined?—and a daughter named May Elise Travett—seriously, idolize much?—both of whom were always polite, well-behaved, and just pleasant to be around. To be fair, May was the name of Dana's mother, and Garreth was the name of Fred's dad, so she guessed it wasn't too weird, but still.

Dana always dressed in sharp, dark dress-suits, hair up in a tight bun, and those thick-rimmed glasses that always took up half of her plain yet still pretty face. Apparently, her and Fred had been hired by the C.I.A. the same year. After a few awkward run-ins at work and some prodding by Iax's dad, Fred had finally asked her out. She had said yes, and the rest, as they say, was history. *Wonderful people who all must have known about me; who were more than willing to do anything they could to keep me safe,* she sternly reminded herself.

Iax knew her folks had tried unsuccessfully for years to have children before she was born, and were getting into their middle years when they had her. Iax remembered, as her mama never went into details, but her 'hidden' pain wasn't all that well hidden when the subject came up here and there of all the miscarriages she had suffered before Iax's arrival. She would come across one of those 'I just adopted a baby' TV shows, or whatever, and her mama would smile, and then just disappear. Iax was certain on more than one occasion that she'd heard her quietly sobbing in another room. But it was off limits, better left alone. They'd 'had' her and never seemed remorseful, so she never went there.

Realizing she was only depressing herself, Iax snapped back to the present; her current predicament and the big move, moreover, the big sit-down with Mama and Dad. At least they were familiar with the unfamiliar as far as all the various Dimensions and such. That would be a tremendous help; explaining such a thing would be impossible to anyone not in-the-know. They knew how it all worked, how each Dimension was essentially a different cell in the galaxy. Within each Dimension were all the various Realms and Alternate Planes. Moving to another of those, anywhere other than somewhere on Earth? They'll understand what she's about, but it still wasn't going to be easy for them to accept. Blood of their blood or no, as the case now was, she was still their only child, the one they'd loved and raised and protected every day of her life.

How did I become such a lucky-duck? Seriously, how many peeps have folks like mine? And who can say they're from another world? No one who she was aware of. And then dealing with her friends? *Shit, this will undoubtedly suck-ass.* It'll be just like growing up and how mama said the same thing every time they moved. "It'll be wonderful, baby girl. You're so sweet, smart, and pretty, you'll easily make new friends. It'll be fine, you'll see." *Right.* It had never been so easy, but she'd never had the heart to tell Mama how hard the transitions always were. Kids are straight-up mean and rude; always have been and probably always will be.

Besides, she was done with that, and she'd not only survived but thrived and excelled at everything. It had all worked out, just not in the same way Mama had always assumed. *And, now you're gonna stop thinking about Mama, Dad, Uncle Fred, Auntie Dana, anyone you forgot, and everything else. Focus, you only have two more days to go!* She dramatically sighed.

****

Mazar was pleased with the results of their competitions thus far. His Iax had done remarkably well each day. She had bested him by one catch on day-two, when they had to hunt separately. When he had finally found her at the end of the day, covered in blood as she was, he had a feeling she was the victor. He did not mind admitting to her or anyone else how extremely proud of her he had been. Not many females could have done what she did.

Day three, they had been blindfolded. Both Chiefs had changed into their Dragon forms, flown them to separate, secret drop locations, and then left them to find their way back to Chief Zarckael's holdings. Before their departure, she had gone on and on about a G.P.S. thing, he thought she had called it. Some kind of tracking device from her Earth she wished she had access to. Although she had made a valiant effort to get him to understand the device, he never was able to grasp the concept.

Here, everyone knew to simply let nature be your guide; the sun, anything that stood out such as a particular mountain, river, the direction of the wind, the change in natural growth on the ground, and on and on. He had never gotten lost in his life, nor had he ever used one of Iax's G.P.S. devices, either. Certain he would win this competition, Mazar had taken his time, simply enjoying the outdoors. He had always loved nature, being one with everything around him.

Little did he know, his sweet, delicious Iax played a game of her own. His female was crafty, something he would do well to remember. She had later explained to him, after winning the day's competition yet again, that she had what she liked to call a 'built-in' G.P.S. of sorts. She used all the natural resources, as had he, but she was also used to tracking in unfamiliar places for a living. After finding herself lost once, she had vowed never to be in that position again. Apparently, so far she had not.

Day four, they had to navigate separate obstacle courses organized deep within the woods. She almost did it again, but his resolve was absolute. He did not mind her winning sometimes, but he wanted to have at least a couple of his own victories. So he finally won, then almost felt guilty for it. She told him that she was proud and happy he won, yet he could see it in her eyes, she truly hated losing. Still, she succumbed to his love-play every eve. Their private time spent together was more than he had ever hoped for with a Truemate.

Day five, they both believed was set up more for basic sport. 'Fun,' she had called it. The maidens and both Chiefs had gone through every bit of the holdings, which was overlarge to begin with, placing items in strange, hidden places. His Iax had called it a 'scavenger hunt.' They were to find every item, just as the other days, before the sun would set, and see who bested whom. The items were small and large, all pieces of various weaponry, things one would need to survive in battle and in the wild. After finding each piece, they were to assemble whatever the item was as a whole, place their cache where the other would not find it, then in the end, both Chiefs would check over each of their stores and deem a winner by whom had collected and properly assembled the most items.

Iax had easily won that competition. He was baffled at her intellect, even though he knew how smart she was, for her to have so much knowledge of things she should not was particularly impressive, indeed. She was simply smaller, more lithe, and quicker than his bulky frame, enabling her to get into smaller alcove areas, niches, and the like to retrieve the most minute of pieces. She would find as much as her arms would hold, and then take it all to her private cache. When she was positive she had everything she needed, she assembled everything to perfection.

Mazar had served his Chief for so long, he was positive he would be the victor of this competition as he knew the holdings inside and out. He may have been a bit cocksure, as well. Thus far, she had only been in the two bedchambers they had used, and the Hall where everyone enjoyed eats and drinks. How she had puzzled out the entire scope of the enormous holdings confounded him, to say the least.

Shaking his head to free his mind of those thoughts, she was well-adept at addling his brain whether she was near him or not. As for now, they both needed nourishment, baths, and much sleep so they could awaken in the morn and learn what the next day's Ritual would bring. Mazar wished to be victorious at least one more time, yet he was heavily leaning toward letting her win. Again. Anything to see that dazzling, brilliant smile upon her face, which always melted his hardened-warrior's heart.

Day six, they were to find materials and construct a shelter in separate locations in the wild. Both of them had been challenged when the weather had turned. Heavy rains had poured down, pelting them without cease, and the temperatures had plummeted close to freezing. He had been worried sick over her well-being, even though deep down he knew she was well able to care for herself. And, at this point, he was convinced without doubt that she could do the same for them both if need be. Still, he had prayed to *Meynix* for her safety and comfort. The sometimes harsh, unforgiving weather of this place was nothing for him, but he did not know what kind of weather she was used to.

Relief had never been more sweet than when he had returned to the Chief's holdings, and not only was she there, she was eating, drinking, and lively laughing with her friend, Gemma. At the time, his brows furrowed, his gaze narrowed on her sitting so peacefully in the Hall enjoying herself and their conversation. *How has she bested me once more?* he had asked himself. By now, he was beginning to feel like a true failure. Of course, he knew he would be able to care for her if ever he needed to in an emergency, it was who he was; a survivor. But, for her to continually best him? He was appearing the complete fool in front of both Weyr. His own knew his abilities, but that still did nothing for his stung pride.

As usual, all it had taken was one sultry glance and one of her titillating smiles for his ire to dissolve. It was nobody's fault she was so adept at finding ways to finish their competitions and win. He was proud of her, and he would never again let envy or anything else cloud his emotions, especially when it came to her and their relationship. She was his Truemate, the one and only love of his life. She had also saved his useless hide, for which he would always love, cherish, and respect her.

In five long strides, Mazar made his way to his Truemate. Enjoying the way she watched his every move, the way her bright-green eyes darkened to a deeper shade. His lips curved up into a sensual smile that spoke a million words, without him having to speak at all. Leaning to her delicate ear, he licked it, then kissed her neck. "You are becoming a menace, my love. I must figure out a way to best you at least on our final day of competitions," he huskily whispered into her already sensitive ear, and growled low in his chest. Moving to face her, his eyes sparkling with mischief, he smiled his best heart melting smile knowing what it always did to her. When his lips glided gently over hers, he felt her shiver and caught her soft moan in his mouth, and deepened their kiss.

After only moments, or so it seemed, Gemma cleared her throat rather loudly. Glancing up to her seated next to Iax and looking so innocent, his scowl quickly transformed into a real smile. How could one be upset with this female? She was his female's 'bestest,' and even though he did not know its meaning, he was sure it was a positive thing for them.

"Yes, Gemma, did you need something?" Still smiling, his hulking size hovering over Iax, it took a moment for Gemma to realize she was staring at him. Shaking her head, she quietly laughed at herself.

"I only meant to finish our discussions of when we leave here, which, by the way, is two-days from now. We never did finalize our plans." She beamed a smile back up at him and then shot her gaze to his Iax, flushing as though she had done something wrong. His female merely winked, patted her friend on the arm, then laughed and resumed her lively speech.

****

After a hearty repast in the Hall, all three of them felt as stuffed as a Thanksgiving Turkey, according to his Iax. Although Mazar had no knowledge of this thing, he was quickly learning to nod and simply smile at his love when she spoke her unfamiliars to or around him. She knew he did not understand, which is why she always winked one of her lovely eyes at him; eyes which he could gaze into, fall into, and stay within for several eternities.

Mazar leaned back, stretched out his long, muscular legs and, crossed his ankles, then folded his large, strong arms over his rock-hard chest. Unaware that he was openly ogling his Truemate, hanging on her every word, he flushed a little when he realized someone was calling his name. Straightening in his chair, he noticed a male-young standing at his side who was also flushed and out of breath, obviously from running to get here. Giving Iax a smile—a promise of things to come—he turned and gave his full attention to the seemingly nervous male-young.

"What may I do for you, young one?" Even speaking to the male and female-youngs, he always showed patience and kindness. They were the future of this Weyr, after all. The only outward sign that he would rather be elsewhere was the fast up and down shuffling of his left heel on the wooden floor. Out of a mutual respect they had quickly developed, Iax stared down into her lap to hide an unbidden smile, which made him soften even more toward her.

"Yes, um, that is, Chief would speak with you." The male-young could not look Mazar in the eyes as he stood wringing his hands. Iax stiffened next to him. Reaching down, he took one of her hands into his and squeezed it; he knew she needed to relax and hoped that would work. *What could be so awful?* He did not want her to worry before there was even cause to do so.

"Where would our Chief be at this time, and what are you called?" He quirked a brow at the male-young.

"I–I am called Nollum, and our Chief be out front," the young sputtered.

Before he could thank Nollum, the young respectfully bowed just before he turned on his bare feet and ran like the wind. *Odd. What would make him behave so strangely?* Mazar wondered.

Turning his attention back to his Iax, he tenderly smiled, gave her a long, slow kiss, then strode away to see what the Chief needed to speak to him about. Hoping along the way, there was nothing amiss. They had all been through enough, thanks to him, of late.

****

So deep into her and Mazar's flirting, Iax sobered when a male-young came up to announce the Chief wanted to speak with Mazar. Worried that something terrible may have happened, her heart threatened to sink. *No, not today. We're so close to being done and leaving. Can't we catch even one break?* she silently pleaded to any God or Goddess who would listen. She kept her concerns to herself after he kissed her, then turned and walked away.

Gemma had excused herself while the boy delivered his message to Mazar, so now Iax sat alone in the Hall glancing around. She observed the others still in the huge room; some eating, some visiting, some cleaning up, and clearing the long tables from their loads of leftover foods and dirty dishes.

Sinking back into her chair, she leaned her head back, closed her eyes, and sighed long and loud. *What now?* she wondered to herself, *Surely, we won't have to put up with more shit and end up stuck here even longer?* She didn't dislike this place, but she was the type to deal with things and move on. She knew traveling back to

Earth, dealing with her folks, straightening out her affairs, and getting on with their journey to the Amethyst Faerie Dragon Realm, would take patience and time she didn't have.

The sound of someone softly clearing their throat brought her out of her musings. Opening her eyes, Iax glanced up to see Yoren standing in front of her with a beautiful smile on her lips. She couldn't help but return one of her own as she straightened in her seat, and motioned to a chair for Yoren to use.

"Iax, I have come to offer you my thanks and gratitude. I learned only today of the reason for your presence, and I am deeply in your debt." She bowed and then claimed the seat.

Iax was stunned that this female, who looked more like a Goddess than anything else, would bow to her. Not something she saw every day, but it was kind of cool. "You're welcome, it's what I do. I only wish our trip hadn't been rife with so many other things. Maybe we could've gotten you outta here and back home a bit faster." She winced as she realized, if that had been the case, she wouldn't have met Mazar.

As if she read Iax's thoughts, Yoren flashed her a knowing smile. "Regardless, I am in your debt. I can see it in your eyes, you are very happy with your male, and I believe all has happened as it should have. No one was truly injured, and now you and Mazar are Mated. I am pleased for you both. Even though I know he most likely wanted to stitch my mouth shut all the way here, he was not mean to me." She giggled as Iax blushed.

"Yeah, I am happy; never thought I'd get married...er, 'Mated,' as you all call it. He is really pretty amazing, isn't he?" she finished on a dreamy sigh. Catching herself daydreaming, acting like a damn girly-girl, Iax cleared her throat and sobered her expression.

"Do not worry over what I think, I am happy for you. Now, I would show you something, if you would come with me?" Yoren clasped one of Iax's hands in her own, as her smile widened.

Brows furrowing in confusion for a moment, Iax narrowed her gaze on the golden beauty holding her hand, radiant about whatever she wanted to show her. "Yeah, sure. Lead the way," she replied. Apprehensive as she was, she went. Another thing *Iax don't do well; surprises*.

Chapter Twenty-six

Day seven was finally upon them and they were so tired, hurting, and just worn out, Iax could've stayed in bed under the covers, and nestled into the down-filled mattress for days. "Dammit! I sound like a pussy again. I gotta get my head on right, this is stupid. I've been through worse, been tougher, this ought to be easy as pie," Iax tried to garner herself.

Sighing, she slowly sat up feeling every muscle, joint, and everything in between protesting each movement she made. *Ugh! This sucks. Well, it's nothing compared to when I thought I could fly—right? Right. Get up. Get moving. Get done,* she sternly scolded herself. This would be the last day of the physical shit, and then tomorrow—the last day—will be a kick-ass party. It all sounded heavenly to her.

She wasn't sure if Mazar had come to her bedchamber last night, or if she'd gone to his, but she did know they spent most of the night together. Even though they had only cuddled and quietly spoken to each other, it had been thoroughly relaxing, even intimate. Who knew such an innocent thing could be intimate? They had both nodded off around the same time, and slept until sunrise. Whoever had gone back to their own chamber was either extremely quiet as not to awaken the other, or the other was sleeping so soundly that nothing could have awoken them, anyway. In any case, they had both awoken in their own bedchambers, alone. That was fine with her, since they had snuck into each other's bedchamber every night, so far. Iax honestly wouldn't have minded a few nights of uninterrupted sleep, with or without Mazar. *With. Yeah, definitely with. But only to sleep. And cuddle.* She smiled. Nothing against her hottie-warrior-hunk, she was just that tired.

Iax luxuriated in a steaming hot bath full of soothing herbs. She only thought she missed her neat bath stuff from home, but this was the shit! All natural and all healing; she soaked and enjoyed how the water and herbs took away most of her pain, helping her feel better and stronger. First she washed her body, then her long, golden hair, then rinsed. Rising from the now cooling water, eyes closed, she was startled as she reached for a *drying cloth*—as they called them here—when her hand brushed up against a rock-hard surface.

Whipping her head around, her eyes snapped open to see what was doin' and a slow, sensual smile spread across her lips. "Hey you, what're you doing in here now? I get our sneakiness at night, but aren't we supposed to not be together, alone?" She turned to fully face an almost naked Mazar, and shivered when he dropped to his haunches with the drying cloth in his large hands. He began at her feet and dried her with a tenderness that left her breathless. When he dried between each toe, alternating the cloth with tender kisses to each one, she couldn't help but giggle. She'd always been ticklish, and since he'd figured out her secret he had been using it all the time. She didn't mind one bit.

After a thorough, torturously slow drying from her toes to her hair, they stood facing each other. Only outstanding problem was, she was nude, but he was still partially dressed. And my-oh-my, he rocked his killer, tanned-leathers, which fit him like a glove. She literally ached to have him naked and under her, or over her, or, well, just anywhere as long as he was *inside* of her. She squealed in excitement when he lifted her bare form and walked them to her bed.

****

Still thanking God and the Goddesses for Mazar's visit, her magnificent bath, and the kick-ass herbs, Iax stretched and sighed in contentment when, for the first time in days, her muscles didn't knot up and ache as she rolled her arms and neck around in slow circles. "Ah, I love that stuff. I hope they have the same or better when we get to the other Realm," she declared to Gemma regarding the herbs.

"I am quite certain what they have there will be as good if not better, as their soils far surpass all others in the Dragon Dimension. It is nice to see you feeling well, I was growing concerned as you have been so tired and stiff for a couple days now," Gemma offered with a smile.

"Yeah, I haven't been feeling well, but I'm all good now." Bending at her waist, she did a few toe-touches. "I wonder what the hell they have planned for us for today? I'm pulling for fun; the other days have been okay, not really *fun,* I wouldn't say, except for the scavenger hunt, but they've just been okay. I wanna do something different and enjoyable. It's been too long, and this whole hop-scotching-it-through-time has been fucked up. I think I'm due, don't you?"

As Iax bent over backwards touching her fingertips to the ground, doing small bobs to limber herself up, Gemma looked on. She craned her head to one side, and grimaced at Iax's agility before straightening and shaking her head. She smiled again.

"Yes, I feel you are due some 'fun,' as you say. I wish you both much of it this day. Do you know of tomorrow's events, yet?" Gemma asked, a sparkle gleaming in her violet-eyes. "Because I do, and I do not believe you are supposed to be aware, and that is all I will supply on the matter. I will say this; I think you shall find it goovying," she finished. Crossing her arms over her chest, she turned up her nose and feigned her best haughty impression, fighting the laughter that tried to bubble up inside.

"Yeah, 'goovying,' is exactly what I was thinking, chicka." Iax laughed. "I don't know exactly, but I do know it's gonna be a big-ass party. Who knows what the hell they have planned, though? These peeps are fucking nuts, and just as Uncle Fred told me before, the less I know, the better off I'll be. Now, that's what I call 'groovy,' and I love groovy!" she excitedly exclaimed. "It's a perfect day, and I'm tired of being inside. So c'mon, race ya out front!" she threw over her shoulder as she laughed and took off in a blur.

Gemma stood there for a moment still shaking her head and smiling. "Oh, Iax…I can only hope to feel your happiness one of these days," she whispered to herself. Giggling, she took off after her bestest. They had to go down three-flights of stairs, careen around the many long tables in the Great Hall, as well as a few shifters, and make it out the large, heavy-wooden front doors. *I will win this, my friend.* Gemma smirked.

One of the coolest things about Iax's new abilities was, even if she ran miles and miles, she'd get to her destination not even winded. She was just opening the heavy doors when she felt a wisp of air brush past her. A wisp, she already knew, named Gemma. *Damn, not fair.* Gemma had been doing this her whole life, Iax was new at it, still trying to figure out all the little details and such. *Oh, well...next time,* she told herself. Yeah, next time, she'd beat the female.

Iax was a bit surprised at how many of the villagers were outside, apparently waiting for her to show up. *Yay, just what I always loved; making a scene.* "Hey, what's going on, why are there so many here, and what's on today's agenda?" she quietly asked the Chiefs, who appeared quite the item lately.

Grinning like a couple of fools, they didn't say anything. Instead, they chose to set their gaze first on Mazar, then on Iax, then back and forth a few times. She was just getting irritated and was about to say something probably rude, when Chief Zarckael finally spoke up. "Many thanks to you all for gathering here this fine morn! As we all know, Iax has been quite the victor thus far, with Mazar having only one win under his belt," he loudly announced to the crowd, holding his long, muscular arms up in the air. The extremely animated Chief then clapped his large hands, and everyone laughed and cheered for the Mated pair. Iax had to admit, it felt kind of good. She'd never had such a large group pulling for her.

"Alright, settle now. Settle, everyone. This day will be another of endurance, ability, and wit. The wit portion being of the utmost import." Reaching down to his left where Mazar stood—looking better than anyone should have a right to—Chief Zarckael joined his left hand to Mazar's right, then his right to Iax's left, and held them up high in the air. "They will each have to brave the elements once more, only this time there will be a few…surprises along the way."

After a rowdy bunch of cheering and boisterous laughter, the crowd quieted. He brought their hands back down and released them, then took a couple deep breaths before he continued, "As we all know, I cannot speak of any details. I will simply say it will be interesting, to say the least. I believe they will both enjoy this day, though if they make a wrong turn or any mistakes, that can always change. Are you both ready?" he asked. Turning first to Iax, who nodded, then he turned to Mazar, who did the same.

"Alright then, let the games begin!" he boomed as the crowd excitedly roared, agreeing with their Chief.

"Let the games begin! Let the games begin! Let the games begin!" they all chanted and clapped, while Iax blushed to her roots. It was a bit much; she just wanted to get the hell outta Dodge and get going.

Chancing a quick glance behind Chief Zarckael's large form, she noticed Mazar doing the same thing. He winked, she smiled, and they faced forward again, ready to get it on.

After practically having to fight their way through the masses and out of the village, they made their way to the foot of the mountain she had been perched on when she'd first laid eyes on Mazar. Smiling, she sighed.

"What brings you such contentment, my love?" he asked in her ear.

"Oh, not much. But I have a fondness for this particular mountain. It's where I was when I first spotted you, just before you came after me. You looked like a golden God come to life, and good enough to eat." She winked at him.

"Ah, a God, you say? Well, I do not have Godly powers, but I can certainly keep you satisfied for a very, long, time," he emphasized the last three words with a wicked gleam in his gorgeous, emerald-green eyes. Iax wanted to melt. *Lord, please give me strength. He's too hot, and I don't know if I can survive life with him,* she silently prayed.

Smacking her on the rump, she jumped in surprise, giggled, and they both went their separate ways, armed with only a sharp knife and their heightened senses.

She was to take one side of the mountain, while he took the other. This day, they would have to find natural foods; nuts, berries, flowers, things like that, and experiment on themselves. Although both of them had a basic knowledge of what you could and couldn't eat in nature, it was still somewhat foreign to Iax.

She was happy to find a well-worn footpath up the side of the mountain she had picked. Since Gemma had 'transported' them away from those Mr. Green Things, and landed them on the top of this mountain, and she was unconscious when Mazar had brought her to Chief Zarckael's holdings, she had no idea about the trail. Now, she was grateful for it.

The mountain was rather tall, and since they had agreed to walk up their trails instead of run, it took Iax about forty-five-minutes to make the trek. She didn't know about Mazar, but she didn't have time to think on him. She had a job to do, and Iax always took any job seriously.

"Okay, food; if I were you, where would I be, and what would I do to a person?" she queried out loud. Hands fisted on her hips, she turned in a slow circle, taking in every detail she could see, and there were many. About a dozen various bushes, some with nuts, some with berries, all at her immediate disposal. She also spotted a few bunches of vine growths bearing what appeared to be small fruits of some kind. Everything was so colorful and large, she had almost forgotten about that up here. There were also many different types of trees, some boasting fruits, some with only leaves; astonishingly humongo-sized leaves. Surely, at least a few of them would be edible? Yeah, they had to be.

After neatly slicing down a couple of the large leaves, she used some of the vines and made a bag of sorts. Within about thirty-minutes, she had filled the bag to capacity, and moved deeper into the densely wooded mountaintop. Finding a nice-sized hollow a few feet off the ground in a large, old tree, she stored her finds to make room to refill her bag.

Certain she was already doing quite well, she moved along gathering things here and there, and finally decided to take a short break. Sitting and leaning back against one of the many large trees, Iax carefully dug around inside her cool new 'leaf-bag' until she found what looked a lot like a peach. It was larger, of course, and more of a bright salmon in color, but it had fuzz on the thin skin and was the same shape. *I despise hindsight, dammit! I shoulda got some advice from the all-knowing Gemma.* She knew all of nature's safe edibles, and Iax knew quite a few, but many of these beauties were foreign, and foreign didn't sit well with her.

They weren't required to eat all their foods, one just had to collect more than the other. Some of her finds, which now rested neatly in her leaf-bag, fell into her 'Not So Sure' category. But most of the yummy-looking treats fell into her 'Hells, Yeah' category. They were too enticing, and she was sure, had to be edible.

Well, young lady, here goes. I seriously hope you're right. Rubbing it against her shirt while admiring the beauty all around her, now she knew why they hadn't been allowed to eat this morning. Shrugging a shoulder, she sank her teeth into the fruit. Oh, my God! It melted in her mouth! The succulent juices fired her every taste bud in a hundred different flavors of absolute yumminess! "Ahhh…" she audibly groaned. *This is amazing,* she mused and groaned again.

Because it was almost as big as a full-sized football, it took her a couple minutes to devour it, then she got out another. As many calories as they'd been burning up each day, she already knew she'd lost a few pounds. She didn't need to, though, 'cause she was in excellent shape, and her B.M.I. had always been spot-on. Besides, this was fruit, how could it be harmful to her figure? *It can't,* she decided, as she bit into the second treat. This time she ate slower; the first one had already appeased the rumbling deep in her empty belly, and she relished every bite.

****

Mazar had traversed and played on this very mountain since he was just a small-youngling. He knew everything that was or was not edible, yet some of the foods that grew here were remarkably deceiving. He only hoped Iax figured that out before it was too late. He had no troubles gathering what he needed, after making himself a satchel out of some large leaves from the native trees.

One of the best tricks in knowing what to, or not to eat from here, was to smell the food. If it had any bitterness in its natural scent at all, it was inedible. Although, much of what grew 'appeared' safe and even delicious, appearances were not a guarantee. The unsafe foods would cause one to see and hear things that were not truly there, and could drive one mad, if left for too long to their own devices. *What if she does not know this?* he worried, then quickly shrugged the concern away. This was Iax, after all, and she had been to so many places, that must have been one of the first things she had learned about nature.

After filling and refilling his makeshift satchel several times, he sat and took a much needed break. They neither were allowed to eat this morn, so he was famished and ready to dig into his finds. Mazar kicked out his long legs, lay on his side, leaned on an elbow, and rested his head in his hand as he ate a few choice pieces. "Ahhh…nothing has ever tasted so delicious," he groaned aloud.

Finally sated, he rolled onto his back, folded his hands behind his weary head, and allowed himself to relax. The day's beauty was breathtaking, and there was no threat of the weather turning on them. A small nap could do no harm. He was asleep in a matter of moments.

****

Her first sign that something was wrong when Iax opened her heavy eyelids, were the gigantic critters all staring down on her. Not realizing she had dozed off, she was now pissed at herself for the slip-up. *Damn. Who are these…things, and what do they want?* she speculated, eyeing them back. They didn't look particularly friendly, yet they hadn't bothered her, either. And, as with everything else around here, their size was not helping her comfort level, which in turn, hampered her efforts to come up with a plan.

The more she gazed up at them from where she lay on the unexpectedly comfy ground, the more their shapes wavered, roiled, and their eyes kept changing colors. She double and triple blinked, sure her own were playing tricks on her. Glancing away for a quick moment, she noticed the sun was going down. Fast. *Shit! I'm never gonna make it back in time,* she complained to herself, but she was unable to move.

Rolling her eyes back up to the giant things looming over her, she also noticed everything she saw was swirling and reshaping itself. *What. The. Fuck?* It didn't take long, even though she could barely concentrate, to figure out she was trippin' big-time. *The damn fruit! Figures, the one I pick has to be the one that fucks me up.* She scowled, or at least she thought so.

Peering slowly—'cause let's face it, slowly was the only thing she could manage at the moment—back up at the enormous things checking her out, she narrowed her gaze on them, hoping and praying for all she was worth that they weren't actually *there,* but were just hallucinations.

No such luck. They didn't go away.

There were—as far as her trippin' brain could tell—four of them. Each one was different but close in size. The one furthest to her left resembled a Mac truck-sized Praying Mantis. Next dude was a super-sized Moth. Number three was a ginormous, strikingly beautiful Butterfly. Last but not least was a big-ass—*Eagle?*—squinting and doing a triple take, it was definitely an Eagle. And holy hugeness!

Closing her eyes, shaking her head, she had to get a grip here. *They can't be real, can they? Shit, what'm I gonna do now? I have no clue. And watch, they're probably just gonna eat my ass, anyway. Ugh!* A slight groan escaped her before she could quell it. *There will be none of that, young lady. No. Sound. Got it? Good. Shit. Shit. Shit.*

She had to come up with a plan, but first things first; she needed to get up. Getting up would be beneficial, but her entire body felt like it weighed ten-times what it should. Her mind was so…just a mess, she couldn't concentrate. Her thoughts faded in and out and she had no control over them, so she just went with it. First, wondering what Mazar was doing led her to the memory of him trying to tell her his name; his sexy mouth popping open and closed making the M sound, and how she got all up in his grill.

Grill…hmm, a BBQ sounds like fun. I should do some honey-lemon-bourbon salmon on the grill, if he even has a grill, 'cause he's probably never had it before. Before…hmm, I've never felt like this, before coming here. Here…hmm, where exactly is here, she wondered.

Iax wasn't sure how long her mind went on its little field trip, and when she tried to reopen her eyes, they still felt heavy but not as bad. Afraid to make any sudden movements—though she wasn't sure what the fear was all about—she slowly opened them, and four humongous, freaky looking critter-dudes stood before her. Startled, she almost jumped and then quickly remembered already seeing them. *Whoa! This is some strong shit, whatever it is,* her trippin' brain informed her.

Her thoughts were still a mess, but she was able to focus a little more clearly. Noticing that the giant things still watching her hadn't so much as moved a muscle, she decided to check them out one at a time.

A huge, green Praying Mantis stood a respectable ten-feet-tall with its legs bent. It must be twice that when it stood fully erect. Large, round, glassy eyeballs bulging out on top of its green head swirled in a captivating combination of silver and an icy-blue. Fascinating.

Forcing her gaze away, Iax moved onto the Moth. It wasn't one of your run of the mill house-moths, this big guy was incredibly beautiful. All of the creatures were glittery and shimmering, just like those Mr. Green Things from the other day.

Making herself stick to the details of the Moth, it was taller than the Praying Mantis, but it was stretched up to its fullest height. The body was difficult to contemplate. It reminded her of a badass auto paint she'd seen that changed with the lighting and at different angles, kind of like a prism; a purple, green, and blue combo that seemed to glow. Its wings were silver, transparent, and glittered, and its eyes were a deep mixture of colors so dark, it was impossible to make them out.

She swallowed the hard knot stuck in her throat that was making her feel woozy, to peer over at the Butterfly, and immediately realized she'd have to come back to this one. It was so gorgeous and there was so much detail, it would take a while. With an effort, she ripped her gaze away and settled it on the Eagle, and holy gorgeousness! The thing was beyond spectacular; its shiny, pointy, black talons gripping the ground were at least three-feet long from front to back. Talk about sharp! Envisioning them ripping everything in their path to shreds, she shivered.

Also standing at its fullest height, just a little taller than the Moth, Iax could see the intricate outline of every feather cloaking the massive wings on either side of its mammoth body. All different dark shades in brown, green, and gold coiled together, giving it a remarkably striking appearance.

She couldn't be afraid of the Eagle; it was just too much beauty. Its shiny, large, pointy beak did look a bit scary, and certainly it could do some serious damage, if need be. Just above that, its eyes were round, black as black could be, and sharp as tacks. This thing would miss nothing, she knew, as it stood stock-still just like its friends. That it simply stared down on her, was slightly creepy and really weird.

Speaking of weirdness, why can I still not move yet? It was becoming increasingly frustrating. Closing her eyes, she tried concentrating on Mazar, to pull up an image of him to relax and hopefully get a better grip on reality. These were, by far, the strangest things she'd ever seen. When she reopened her eyes, nothing had changed nor had any of her visitors moved an inch.

As Iax now focused on the Butterfly, she was awestruck. It was fascinating—they all were—but this one was...difficult to describe. Long front and back legs rested easily under a thick, silver body, a pair of folded wings topping the gorgeous creature were so breathtaking. Not stretched to its fullest height, its weight was distributed so it had to lean forward a bit the way it was resting. Facing her at an angle, Iax could see the intricate, delicate design embedded in the large wings, yet she instinctively knew this magnificent, towering critter-dude was anything but delicate; none of them were.

Glancing up at its wings, she let her gaze wander over five sections outlined by thick, black, swirly veins; each section was filled in with different, vivid colors bringing the design to life. Even though Iax was most definitely still trippin' and muddleheaded, and maybe even for that reason, each color was more than crystal-clear. Three vertical columns made up the top half of each wing, from the outer edge to where it met with the body which began in deep aqua, the middle was bright purple, and it finished at the body in indigo.

The lower half of the wings consisted of two horizontal rows; an intense magenta rounded out the bottom row, an emerald green—reminding her of Mazar's eyes again—topped off the section. It was the brightest, most colorful thing she'd ever seen. Even though it would be difficult to make the color-combo work elsewhere, this thing rocked it, which made it simultaneously amazing and bizarre.

Glowing eyes sat on top of its body just below a long set of black antennae. She only thought the body was amazing, but those eyes...same as the body colors but swirling, churning, oddly mesmerizing, and distinctly reminding her of Mazar, again. *Why does this critter keep reminding me of him?* she puzzled. Furthermore, she suddenly felt safe yet more confused, almost like there was some sort of connection between her and the big critters. She couldn't think much on it now, as she suddenly felt like she'd been blanketed in a thick, lethargic cloak.

Iax attempted to fight the overwhelming urge to sleep, she shook her head and tried to force her eyes to stay open. She didn't want to fall asleep—that would just be rude—what, with her company looming over her and all. Who knew what they wanted, why there were here, and what they may do to her if she did nod off? Unable to resist a lengthy yawn, her eyes slowly drifted shut.

Chapter Twenty-seven

Every inch inside and out of Chief Zarckael's holdings was so brightly lit up, it was a wonder no one was blinded by all the raging torches, candles, and anything else anyone could find that would burn.

It was five-hours past time for the end of this day's competition. Five-hours since the sun had set, yet there was still no sign of Iax. Everyone, old and young alike, was out searching for her. Even the elders—as in over two-thousand-years old or more—who could barely walk unassisted had remained stoic, and demanded to join the search to help in any way possible. Convincing all just because they were no longer physically strong, did not mean they had lost their other heightened senses. They were determined and may be able to help find the missing female. No one was left out.

Mazar had already been all over the mountain they started out on earlier that morn to complete their competition, several times. He was certain something horrible had happened, possibly even an abduction. Having just done the same despicable thing to another Mated pair, he felt even worse and more guilty than he had before— which was saying much—when he had contemplated that taking his own life would be the only fair punishment for his sins.

How had Gordell managed his emotions and not simply gone on a rage? How had the male not ended up killing everyone in sight? That was exactly what Mazar wanted to do; if it were not for both of the Chiefs, many would be dead by his hand already. She was gone, and someone needed to pay!

"We will find her, Mazar. You must calm yourself," his Chief intoned and tried to calm him. He did not want help, nor did he want to be calm! He wanted his Iax back! "I will cover every inch of this territory until I find her, and if someone has done anything to her, they will die!" he roared, and made several of his own Weyr cringe in fear. *They should fear me,* he silently qualified.

"I understand your ire, Mazar, but you of all males should know that if you go into this full of emotions, those same emotions could easily defeat you. You need to clear your mind to focus, or you may miss the simplest of clues. Your warrior's mind knows this— yes?" his Chief softly reminded him with a comforting hand on his shoulder. *Damn, if the Chief was not right!* Still, he did not require comfort, nor advice.

"She is *my* Truemate, Chief. I should *know* her whereabouts no matter the circumstances. I. Should. Know," he said through tightly clenched teeth. As one of his large hands smacked the wooden surface of a table to emphasize his last three words, drinks spilled over, and females fled the area in fear.

Rubbing the same hand down his face, Mazar drew in a few deep breaths as he attempted to cool the blood that boiled inside every inch of his body. He could feel the change coming on, and the more he thought about that, the better it sounded. *Why should I fight it? My Dragon could find Iax much easier than my male-form,* he ventured. The other shifters who had already changed and had been combing their territory were no doubt trying, but he would be drawn to her. Their very hearts beat as one, now. *Why did I not think of this sooner?* he asked himself.

Straightening to his full, intimidating height, he gave his Chief a respectful nod, and quickly made his way outside. This left Chief Zarckael to heave a heavy sigh at the tightly strung, overemotional warrior's retreating back, and to wonder what his male would do now, as he prayed to *Meynix* that he would not do anything foolish.

Under the hot, midday sun, Mazar stood with his eyes closed. He leaned his head back, opened his arms out to each side, and allowed his Dragon-form to take over his body. Fire licking at his insides, his bones shifting and muscles reshaping, was a welcome feeling. Changing and taking flight always made him feel better; it allowed him to get a clearer perspective on all things which burdened and weighed heavily upon his heart and mind. He needed all the help he could get at this time.

It only took moments to complete the change, and even less time for him to take to the cool, open skies. Soaring and floating through the air, the caressing wind did wonders for his overheated form and roiling emotions. He had to find her, and let anyone who may have dared to lay a hand on her, beg for mercy when he found them. *My love, I must find you safe and well. Help me find her,* he sent out another silent prayer to *Meynix.*

After flying for a few minutes, his thoughts were more square. Mazar felt a faint pulse that should have matched his heartbeat. But it was lagging and unable to beat in perfect time with his, and it made him worry even more. It came from her image burnt into his flesh; even though he was in his Dragon-form and it was so small nobody would be able to see it, the image was still there. His spirit and hopes lifted, only by a degree. *Iaxsss, where are you, my love? You must guide me to you. Speak to me in your mind, and I will find you. I beg this of you, call out to me now!* he projected his thoughts and spread them out over the land, to cover as much area as he was able.

His head began to throb, but it did not matter. Nothing would deter him from finding his Truemate. He knew deep down, something was unequivocally wrong with her. Someone or something had harmed her, and he was more determined to find her than he had ever been for anything else in his overlong life. Hearing the slightest sound stilled him mid-flight. It was her! She was attempting to communicate with him! Still, he could not tell from which direction it came.

As his massive form was hurtling toward the canopy of the forest below at an amazingly fast pace, he swooped upward to avoid crashing. Then it came again, from down where he would have landed. *I am coming, Iaxsss! I am almost there! Hold on!* Pushing the thread of his thoughts out wide once more, he was frantic and desperate to find her.

An extremely faint, *Please hurry, Mazar. I'm scared, I don't know what to do,* made his heart lurch inside his chest, causing him to pick up his speed to a dangerous level. He must get to her. *What could have happened?* He was sick with worry and had to force himself to release his anger—for now—to find her and see with his own eyes what happened.

I am here, I am coming, hold on! he sent the words to her as he hit the ground running, changing back to his male-form and moving at lightning speed. "Iaxsss!" he boomed. "Where are you? Guide me to you, my love!" With no way of knowing which form she was in, he had tried their mental communications, and now he would speak aloud hoping she would hear him in either form.

He ceased his mad-dash in a small clearing in the woods. Turning in quick circles hoping to pick up on her pulse, his own coming from her image in his flesh rose to a searing heat. Slowing his turns, he felt the pulse quicken if only infinitesimally, in the direction opposite of where he had entered the clearing. In a blur, he raced toward the pulse that pulled at him.

"Iaxsss, say something! I am here, you must speak!" he entreated as his voice broke at the end. Air forced itself in and out of his lungs felt like fire, it burned and made it difficult to breathe at all. *Where is she?* he cried out in his mind that was such a swirling mass of emotions, he had no time to contemplate whether the mental communications would even work in his male-form. Moving through the trees and brush so fast his feet barely touched the ground, he came to a sudden halt in front of a towering tree that stood away from the others by a few feet.

He approached the ancient tree and suspiciously eyed it, then began to run his hands over its weather and age-roughened bark. Mazar rested his achy, weary head against it, unable to stem the hot flow of tears streaming from his eyes like lava. "Iaxsss, my love, are you in here? Help me, I must find you," he begged, unashamed of his tears and emotions. He loved her more than anything, and would do whatever he must to find and get her home safely.

Mazar, please...He thought he heard, but her words were so softly spoken, he was afraid he had imagined them. The bark began to heat under his hands, so he stood back, squared his shoulders, wiped away his tears, and made a slow circle around the tree. Rapping his knuckles over the bark, he tried to find a hollow area, or any possible way she had gotten inside, so he could get her out. "I am here, my love! Relax, I beg of you, hold on and I will find a way to get you out," he promised, his voice strong and sure once more.

Knocking on different parts of the tree trunk, he hit the hollow he needed. Without a care, he began ripping the bark away, bloodying his fingers as he threw pieces behind him in a frenzy to get to his female. *What is she doing inside this blasted tree, and how did she even get there?* he puzzled. Relief washed through his veins, cooling the fire that had been flowing inside him.

****

Iax awoke with a start. Wherever she was, it was pitch-black, more than silent, and she was only able to move in small increments. She'd never thought of herself as one of 'those' people, the kind with silly phobias...until now. It made her feel downright trapped, desolate, and despondent. They weren't feelings she had ever dealt with, moreover, she didn't care much for them. In fact, it was seriously starting to piss her off. *What did I get myself into this time, and why me?* Nothing made sense. Not since she had awoken to those freakishly large, gorgeous critters, which she hadn't seen any sign of for who knew how long.

She'd dozed back off, unable to stop sleep's claim no matter what.

Not knowing and not able to understand how much time had passed, she awoke again to find herself alone. Alone was doable; Iax did alone plenty and never had a problem with it before. Hoping she'd imagined everything, Iax was sorely disappointed when she found herself in the same silent darkness. She had absolutely no clue of where, or rather, what she was in, but it smelled musty. She also sensed a weird vibe, like, the place was half-bad and half-good. The 'good' was calming, but the 'bad' was almost sickening, as it threatened to evacuate the contents of her upset stomach. And her damnable headache wouldn't go away, or even die down.

Already resigned to the very real possibility she could die right where she was, she'd tried many things to pass her time, to make it less gloomy and depressing. She'd sang, hummed, recited rules and protocol from the O.W.O. Unit, even played computer games in her head, and lost. Now *that* was downright pathetic, seriously.

She'd gone over many of Gemma's attempts at her own aphorisms, hoping to find some humor so maybe she could laugh, at least for a while. And she did, for a while, still trying to pass the time. Time; something that had stopped being tangible. Time had always been just that for Iax; tangible. Always a deadline, an appointment, something doin' somewhere; time, more often than not, had always not only been her guide, but also her friend. Until now.

Unable to figure out where she was, she knew she was *in* something. But what? The darkened space was big enough to move around a little, but the walls were still pretty close together. Reaching out in any direction, arms fully extended, she could touch them, as she had in the beginning. They were constructed of something rough—*wood?*—who knew? And where she sat? Not so much a seat, but a surface seemingly supporting her weight without any problems.

After what felt like forever, Iax had become so tired again, she couldn't keep her eyes open. Even though something deep down was telling her that if she did sleep, she may never wake up again, at this point she wasn't so sure she even cared. She did, but still. Everything was a massive effort, and she could feel her once-steady heartbeat fading. Her tattoo was hot at first, but had cooled a long time ago. Even Mazar wouldn't be able to find her now.

Sleep's heavy pull was winning, no doubt, when slowly, Iax's head suddenly turned up and her dry, achy eyelids opened. *Oh,*

God…there was someone out there! They were finally out searching. *"…am coming, hold on!"* She thought she heard a voice call out in her mind, and it was the sweetest sound she had ever heard. "Yes, thank you, God!" she barely rasped out in her tiny, black prison. Realizing how parched her throat was, and that it was probably impossible for anyone to hear her feeble attempts to speak, her mind began to race as it worked to think of some way to communicate with him. *Her Mazar.*

As her tattoo began to heat again, it gave her an idea. It may not work since she wasn't in her Dragon-form, but against all odds, she'd take it. Closing her eyes, one hand over the other, she pressed as hard as she could over Mazar's Dragon image as she mentally cried out to him. *Please, hurry, Mazar. I'm scared, and I don't know what to do.* Sending her message with what little energy she had, she slumped at the drain from projecting just those few words; she was wiped out. *Oh, God, he'll never find me in time,* she quietly cried inside her quickly fading mind as she sniffled. Her heartbeat was still slow, not matching Mazar's like it should, especially since he was so near. And she knew it was him after hearing his voice pleading out loud, but when he spoke one last time, she was only barely able to hear him. "Iaxsss, my love, are you in here? Help me find you, I must find you."

Iax could no longer hold her head up, open her eyes, nothing. *But wait, that sounded extremely close. He's here, like, right outside these walls. I have to try again. Please help me, God. Please,* she silently pleaded. *Give me strength so I can live. I want to live.* Trying to gather the largest breath her lungs would hold—which already felt like they were closing up shop—she used every cell in her body to speak to Mazar, and let him know he was right outside of her little black prison. "Mazar, please…" Everything went deeper than pitch-black—if it was even possible—and she could no longer hold on. When all of Iax's organs ceased to function, she quietly slipped away.

****

Mazar was elated to have finally found his Iax. He could not believe she had been *inside* an old tree, yet there she was. Ripping off the last piece of the offending bark standing between him and his Truemate, without paying attention, he flung it off to the side so hard it embedded itself into another tree. He heard it, but cared not. His only concern was his female. "Iaxsss, oh my love. What happened? Speak to me, I must hear your voice," his own broke as he realized she was not moving, nor did it seem, was she breathing. *This cannot be. She spoke to me but a moment ago! What is this?* His body began to tremble with the force of his grief and anger.

Carefully—for she was the most precious and breakable item in all the Dimensions combined, to him—he reached into the whole he made in the side of the large tree, and tenderly gathered Iax into his arms. When he pulled her limp form tightly against his very alive and warm chest, his heart threatened to beat through the bone and flesh barrier that held it inside his body.

He fell to his knees and rocked her, as hot tears flowed anew and scorched his flesh in their free-fall. "*Meynix!* I beg of you to help her, now!" he roared with his head falling back, as he faced the sky and implored his Goddess. His agonizing plea carried on the breeze throughout the forest and beyond. Still, nothing. She would not move, breathe, or respond in any way. "*No!* You cannot take her from me! We only just found each other and I love her! I beg you, *Meynix,* I. Beg. You," his last words broke off in heaving sobs. He could not lose her, not now that he had just found her. How could he let her go? Why would he be expected to do such a thing? Nothing made any sense.

"Think, Mazar! *Think!* There must be something you can do for her! She spoke only moments ago, you can still save her!" he ranted aloud, wracking his brain to figure out how to bring her back. Then it hit him. "The healer. She is exceptional and lives in my own village. I can call on her, she even tended Iax once already. What was her name? Toralynn. Yes, that is it!" Gazing down at his Iax, he smiled through his tears as he spoke to her. "I will find her, and she will help you, my love." Stroking a few sticky, dirty strands of hair off her forehead, with an equally dirty and shaky hand, he placed a kiss there. Now, to keep the vow he had just made to the forest, himself, and Iax, who was still lying in his arms, and still not moving or breathing.

****

Well, if this is Heaven, I'm not sure what I think, were Iax's initial thoughts when her eyes opened. She expected to see at least a couple of her long-lost relatives, that's what everyone always says. But no, she wasn't seeing any of them. What she did see, though, was a middle-aged looking male and female, obviously a couple. And she was flat on her back, in an unfamiliar bed, in an unfamiliar place.

Great. So death imitates life? Am I destined to continue this absurd waking-in-strange-places thing, even in death? This shit is seriously fucked up. "Oops! Sorry, Big Guy!" She quickly glanced upward, immediately feeling ashamed for her speech. *And, in Heaven, of all places!* Shaking her head at herself, she tried to rephrase her previously spoken words, and cringed at the male and female shooting strange looks at her. Most likely confused and maybe even a little scared of her, an unfamiliar. *Another oops.* She didn't quite know what to think or do.

Okay, Lord, or God, sorry. I'm not sure of the proper protocol, so here goes. Please, forgive me for my mouth. I've done it so long, I don't even realize when it happens, and I'm sorry. Um... thank you? Uh, I mean, yeah, thank you for allowing me in here. In Heaven. I know I haven't been perfect, but I tried to do the right thing. So, definitely, thank you. Amen, she finished her silent prayer, feeling that it was nobody's biz what her and God spoke about. She felt better already, and that's all that mattered.

"Oh, no. She believes herself passed and gone. What do we do now, and where is Mazar? He would want to know. I mean, that she awakes," the female whispered to the male. But Iax still heard her.

Huddled on a bench against the wall to her left, Iax narrowed a suspicious gaze on the pair, the hair standing on her nape gave her the chills. "Where am I, and what are you trying to whisper about, ma'am?" speaking in quiet, soothing tones, not wanting to startle the already freaked out pair, she softened her gaze on them.

They kept fidgeting with their clothes, their hair, each other, and anything else they could touch, apparently trying not to look at her. *What. The. Hell?* she puzzled for a moment. Until she realized she'd just done it again. *Shit! Sorry!* Frustration doesn't always allow one to think clearly; she had to cool it, and now would be good. *God, sorry. Again. I'm working on it. Amen,* she silently prayed, feeling a heated blush from top to bottom.

This is so humiliating. Has my mouth always been this corrupt? I guess so, but when and why did I start talking like this? she rebuked herself. Shaking those thoughts away for now, she cleared her throat and refocused on the strange couple still seated on the bench, now acting even more freaked out. Suddenly, it hit her and she felt the worst sort of bad. All the 'inner-talk' and 'silent prayer' had been neither inner, nor silent. Iax had spoken all those words out loud. *Ugh! Awesome!* she thought, not sure what to say next.

Iax decided it might be best to start over; hopefully that was the answer to fixing the already bad situation she had so blatantly just made even worse. "Hi, my name is Iax. Who might you be?" She smiled her best, pretending everything was just peachy, but given the circumstances she probably wasn't fooling anyone. "I mean no harm. I simply would know your names–if that's okay?" she hedged, feeling uneasy and guilty for their bizarre behavior. She tried to use their speech patterns hoping to relax them, and maybe allow easier communications.

They squirmed more, and then the female finally decided to find her backbone. Iax sighed.

"Yes, Iax, we are aware of who you are. I am Toralynn, and this is my Truemate, Guillaume." She even smiled! A real smile that met her twinkling, onyx-eyes. Iax returned a meaningful one of her own.

"You would not recall, but I tended you recently after your first shifting." She gave Iax a sad smile, "I was called upon to come tend you again after you, well…" she trailed off, wringing her hands in her thick skirts and tossing a nervous glance over her shoulder to the male still sitting and fidgeting. Turning back to face Iax again, the female squared her shoulders, lifted her chin, and took a deep breath to bolster herself before she firmly spoke.

"You died, my dear. You ate some bad fruit in the woods you see, and, well, you died." With another sad smile, she came closer and patted one of Iax's arms.

Iax wondered if she looked as stunned as she felt. She couldn't speak now even if she tried. *Died? Me?* She couldn't even comprehend the words. Then again, when she awoke, right away she'd thought she was in Heaven. She guessed maybe hearing the words out loud was the stunning part. Mass confusion was taking center stage in her mind, making her foggy-brain work overtime trying to sort this mess out.

"You are recovering well, Iax. Do you need anything? I can help if you need to relieve yourself. Or, perhaps you would like a bath? Oh! That would be perfect! A bath!" The female's eyes lit up like a Christmas tree. Iax smiled at her excitement, trying to hide her own emotions. Maybe it wouldn't be so hard adjusting to things here, as long as this female was around, at least for a while.

But, wait–recovering well? Amazing, ain't it, how fast you can find your voice after hearing something like that? Iax briefly pondered. "I thought you said I died. What do you mean I'm 'recovering well'? Aren't I in Heaven? Isn't this the…the Afterlife, ya know, with God and all?" she tentatively asked, scrunching her nose in confusion.

The female hastily shooed the male out of the room, causing a slight giggle to escape from Iax without her permission. Funny how she was happy one minute, sad the next, then confused in the very next. "I'm sorry…I don't understand any of this." Her head felt heavier than an anvil the more she tried to think, so she reclined it on a pillow. Hopefully, she'd be able to get the nitty-gritty from the female, who had finally bucked-up and was now able to talk to her.

After getting the male out of the room, the female firmly shut and locked the door behind him, then turned to flash a motherly-smile on Iax. Suddenly, and unbidden, Iax was drawn into her own thoughts about her parents. She genuinely missed them; did they know she was dead? How would they take the news? And where was she? Furthermore, if she was still in the Dragon Dimension, how would her folks be able to attend her funeral? Too many thoughts and questions swirled around in her mind, and made her dizzy.

"Iax, dear, you must relax. You are thinking far too much on things which are not in your control at present. Chief Zarckael has appointed you a different bedchamber in his holdings, one you will share with your Truemate while you are still in this Realm. You should remain lying down. Try to relax, and I shall do my best to explain everything to you. Oh, you poor dear." She frowned, gently sweeping a few loose tendrils of hair off Iax's face and anchoring them behind her ear.

Iax smiled and nodded at the beautiful, motherly Toralynn. *What a super-cool name,* she thought hazily, waiting for the female to settle and tell her what the hell was doin'.

Chapter Twenty-eight

The moment Mazar was informed that his Iax was finally waking, he was up the stairs in mere seconds. Never had he felt such relief, the weight lifting from his heavily-burdened shoulders was a freeing sensation. One he was thanking *Meynix* for every other moment. *She lives!* He would shout it from the top of the holdings once he saw her with his own two-eyes.

Rounding the last corner that led directly to her door, his smile widened and his heart raced at such a speed, he felt it might exit his chest at any moment. It was a good thing her door was not securely closed, else he would have either torn it down or burst right through it. Coming to a skidding halt, he stopped when his shaky knees bumped into the side of her bed.

And there she was. His strong, sassy, beautiful Iax.

Kneeling almost eye level to her, Mazar was unsure of what to say. His emotions were such, he feared he would blather on like an untried-youngling. Although he wanted to be her strong warrior, he did not much care what anyone else presently thought of him.

With a small tears dripping from his eyes and a shaky smile, Mazar clasped his female's hands to bring them to his lips. Turning them over, he opened them and placed a soft, lingering kiss in each of her precious palms. Turning them back over, he proceeded to plant sweet, equally tender kisses on all of her adorable fingertips. "My love." He sighed as he leaned over to bury his face in the soft crook of her flawless neck, and his voice broke on each word.

He was positive he had lost her, yet here she was, alive and well. Closing his eyes, he silently thanked *Meynix*, and all else who had taken part in the saving of his Truemate. It had been touch and go for three full days. Three full days of feeling as though his heart would separate itself from his body. Three full days of thinking he would follow her into the Afterlife, even if he had to take his own life, and knowing full-well he would not have been welcomed had he committed such a sin. Three full days of absolute nothingness.

The loneliest, most heart-wrenching three-days of his entire life....

"Mazar, I–I—" she attempted, her throat tight and dry.

Snapping his head up, the sleepy, tender smile she gifted him with was all it took for the floodgates to fully open. With relief, he welcomed the raining of hot new tears combining with the old streaks on his face. Moving his shaky hands up to cup both sides of her glorious face, he wiped away her own with tender fingers. "My Iaxsss, you are here and you live. What did—" he broke off in a heaving sob, his heart filled to bursting with love and happiness, the likes of which he never knew existed.

"Shhh, it's okay now. We're okay now. You saved me, thank you. Thank you," she croaked out.

At the same time, Toralynn, who had been keeping watch over Iax, approached from the other side of the bed with something to relieve Iax's dry throat. She drank greedily, guzzling the life-giving liquid as if she had not drank anything for far too long. Knowing she likely had not, made more grief well-up inside of Mazar.

"Slowly, dear. If you drink too much too fast, it will come back up. You do not want that. There is plenty more, but *slowly*," the older female gently cooed, softly mopping sweat from Iax's face with a cool, wet cloth. Iax let out a soft moan, as they were both ecstasy.

Mazar glanced up at the female to whom he owed so much. "My thanks to you, Toralynn. I owe you everything, including my life. I can never repay you for what you have given to me. I know you do not think much of me, and I do not blame you." He looked back over at his Iax, smiled through his shame, then looked back up at the healer. "I understand you and your female-young are responsible for getting Yoren out of the cabin we put her in." He could not have looked more chagrined had he tried. He should never expect her, of all his Weyr members, to forgive him anything.

"You, Mazar, are not as bad as you would have others believe. Even the lovely Yoren spoke kindly of you, and would not allow her Truemate or his warriors to harm you. She was understanding of your plight, and had no desire to see you punished. She went on to say that you were doing a fine job of that, all on your own." With a sincere smile, she inclined her chin toward Iax. "Your female is strong and will be back to rights in no time. I am thoroughly honored to assist her again, and you are very welcome" She gave him a polite bow. "Now that you are here, perhaps you can tell her what happened, instead of me." She smiled again, and backed out of the room to allow the pair some privacy.

Iax nervously chewed on her lower lip, not sure what to say or where to even begin. She felt like even her male would think her crazy, if she told him all the details she could recall. Even though there weren't many, there were some, and they weren't going help her to look wholly sane. Pondering it longer than she should have, she released a long sigh before she spoke. "Mazar, were you able to hear me mentally communicate? I mean, I heard your voice in my head even in my female-form, yet I thought it wasn't possible, unless we were both in our Dragon-forms. I pressed hard on my tat with both hands when I felt you were near. I thought maybe it would somehow help our mental communications, but I wasn't shifted so I wasn't sure if it worked. And when I projected my thoughts out to you, I think that's what took the last of my–of me." She gazed into her Truemate's gorgeous eyes, and wishing she could climb inside and stay in them—in *him* and his safety forever—made her sigh.

After a short bout of coughing, Iax continued, "What happened, and where was I? I don't remember much, but I think there was a group of huge critters watching over me before I fell asleep, and more than once. Then I woke up in a small, dark space but didn't know where I was, or how I got there. How'd you even find me?" She was baffled, and only recalled small pieces of her trial. Still, nothing made sense.

Eyes level with one another, the smile he gave her was so real, so full of love, it took her breath away. He was too good to be true. *Wasn't there a saying about that? Something like; "If it looks or sounds too good to be true, it probably is." And wasn't that always the case? It sure as hell was, or at least, it had been for her.* She had learned that way early on in life. Glancing back at Mazar, he was just so much; male, determination, beauty, raw, not to mention the sexuality always that oozed from him. So overwhelming and impossible to ignore. As far as she was concerned, he was large and in charge.

Dropping her smiling eyes, she absently examined her hand on the opposite side of the bed from where her current source of sexual frustration was now comfortably seated, to hide her blush and sheepish smile. She wasn't physically up for *that,* yet. *But, damn! This really sucks,* she told herself.

Hearing his deep, sexy chuckle, Iax couldn't prevent her smile from widening. She turned to peer up at him through long, dark-golden lashes. Her eyes still felt a little bloodshot, but at least the swelling and itching had gone down from the ordeal she was finally coming out of. Not knowing what happened didn't sit well with her; Iax functioned best on facts, truths, irrefutable proof of what she was being told. But to now place her trust in a virtual stranger, and expect him not to lie to her? *Iax don't do trust,* never had.

That she was so willing to offer hers to Mazar now, spoke volumes, and was certainly a first for her. Besides, she had no choice, and she decided, he was trustworthy, had even saved her life, for shit sakes. Not to mention, he had even cried for her! Her big, tough warrior still had wet streaks running down both sides of his gorgeous face, and if that didn't tell her all she needed to know about his honor and intentions, nothing else ever would.

****

Hiding in the shadowed alcoves in the long hallway just outside Iax's bedchamber, Gemma stood stone-still listening to Mazar retell the tale. The same one he had been relaying since he found his no-longer-living Iax, three long days ago.

It was difficult to hear but she needed to know the details, and did not want to burden Mazar or Iax further by having to repeat themselves. The whole ordeal had been extremely hard on the pair, as it also had been for Gemma. She did not know what to make of the events her friend had gone through. Thinking Iax dead had been too much to contemplate. Too much, and too difficult to accept.

Hearing Iax mention the 'giant critters' she had seen in the woods gave Gemma momentary pause. *What were they, and why did they watch over Iax? Furthermore, how did she get stuck inside that tree?* Questions neither her nor Mazar could answer. It almost seemed as if they had been there to protect and keep Iax safe. *But, from what, or perhaps, whom?* Then again, it was quite possible they had merely been figments of Iax's imagination. Apparently, she had eaten enough of the bad fruits to make her hallucinate; that had to be the answer.

Finished with the story of rescuing Iax, Mazar was moving about in their newly appointed bedchamber from the sounds of it. Gemma had no wish to be discovered nor to interrupt, so she turned and quietly made a hasty escape.

Briefly, she realized she had not recently seen Skenyah. Where had the female been? She could not recall seeing her since Mazar and Iax had left the village, to complete their last competition. She needed to locate Skenyah, and find out where she had been and what she had been up to.

Finally reaching the landing at the bottom of the stairs, Gemma blew out a long sigh. Even if she did find Skenyah, it did not necessarily guarantee any answers. Not that she thought the female had any part in harming Iax, but she might at least know something of what had happened. She also thought it odd how, upon her initial meeting with Skenyah, such a peacefulness had exuded from the female. Now? It was still present at times, but it came and went, and the more Gemma pondered that, the less sense it made.

"Oh! Excuse me!" a melodic female voice exclaimed as Gemma was accidentally slammed into.

"No harm done." Gemma reflexively reached out to grab the female's arms to help steady the poor thing. She smiled at the beautiful female-young, and then recognized her as the healer's offspring, "Jolsynn, is it?" she asked brightly.

"Yes," the female replied, furiously blushing while trying to execute a clumsy curtsey. "I am called Jolsynn. And my mother, Toralynn, is the healer who tends your friend, Iax." Jolsynn straightened and offered Gemma a wide smile, her face lit with pride. "She is awake now and my mother says she will recover quite well. She also said this was difficult, something she has never seen before. What do you make of it?" she asked, as genuine curiosity etched her perfect features.

The details of Iax's run-in with the large critters—which Gemma was mostly convinced had not been real—were not yet common knowledge. Only Mazar, Iax, and now Gemma, were privy to that part. What was already known by all, was that he had found her stuck inside an old tree…dead. Refusing to dwell on it now that she knew Iax was clearly alive and would be well, she smiled back at Jolsynn. "I do not yet know what to think. But I do know she is a strong female. Between her and Mazar's love for each other, I believe there is not much through which they cannot survive, well and together." Jolsynn nodded her agreement, and Gemma continued, "Also, since Iax's body was so abruptly forced into changing, and twice, she will not heal as well nor as quickly, as shifters normally do. Unlike those of you born into it and raised as you were, having been taught how to change naturally with practice and guidance."

Jolsynn smiled. "I understand. We can heal from an injury as soon as one is inflicted upon us. Yet, for Iax to be forced as she was? I cannot imagine what she has been through, not knowing anything until it was upon her." The female-young sighed. "She is strong and everything will work out. I am as certain as my mother, who would allow nothing less." Her face radiated pride anew for her mother's abilities, and it made Gemma smile.

Gemma did not wish to be rude, but her need to find Skenyah was growing stronger by the minute. She kindly patted Jolsynn's arm, and then politely excused herself.

Where could Skenyah be? Surely, the female must have some knowledge of Iax's horrible events? Tapping a finger on her chin, Gemma tried to think like the elusive female. *If I were Skenyah and perhaps hiding, for one reason or another, where would I be?* she puzzled. Many pensive thoughts crowded her mind and for the first time, it pained her head. Another oddity. *When will they cease?* Shaking her head, she had much to do, and wallowing in her own trivial problems would get her nowhere.

Making her way outside, the sun's blinding brightness did not serve to help her already throbbing head, but rather, the pain worsened. She could hear small-younglings laughing and playing, grown shifters speaking to each other and chasing their younglings. Neither her sight nor her body were cooperating with the rest of her senses. Then, to make matters worse, while squinting and shielding her leaky eyes from the brightness bathing everything outside, she hit the ground with a hard *thud.* Embarrassed to her roots, she rolled over onto her back, spitting dirt from her mouth, thinking she must look like a drunken fool! *I do not imbibe! Damn all!* she declared to herself. *What is the matter with me now?*

She released a louder groan than she normally would have, but simply cared not about the unladylike impropriety. *Why should I? Things keep going wrong, anyway. Why bother caring at all?* she huffed to herself.

Blinded by the sun, she had tripped over something or someone. *Oh, no! I hope I did not harm anyone!* she silently worried. It was turning out to be a horrible day already, and they had only just broken their fast a little while ago. She had no desire to know what the rest of this accursed day may hold. No. She would much rather return to her bedchamber, crawl back under the warm, soft covers, and stay there until someone could tell her for a certainty it was safe to come back out.

Alas, no such retreat would be hers this day. Within only moments, she was gathered up from the ground by big, strong arms, lifted high in the air, and almost roughly pulled against an obviously male, overly hard chest. It all happened so quickly, Gemma had no time to protest. Whomever held her in his vice-like grip, she knew not. What she did know and strongly sensed was, it would be prudent for her not to speak. Even though she had a strong urge to do so, she sensed the male may take offense, whether it was her intent or not. Also she sensed that he was one of few words, yet strong of presence. And she could not tell if he was simply getting her—a clumsy nuisance—out of everyone's way, or he was worried about her.

Falling and bumbling as she just had, it was most likely the former. He probably thought her addled and did not wish to hear her words anyway, so she silently allowed him to carry her away. Her thoughts, though, refused to be quieted, and certainly had a mind of their own. His scent wrapped itself around her like a well-worn blanket; a sensation of comfort and safety ebbed over her every inch, making her skin prickle in the strangest, most delightful way. Yes, this male—rude or not—and the unfamiliar emotions he invoked in her, made Gemma realize she would not mind lying in his arms for as long as he would hold her.

What are you thinking, Gemma? she chastised herself when her brain suddenly decided to function. *Since when do I act or think this way? Iax is rubbing over me, is my only guess. I must speak to her, she will be able to help me. And, yes, she owes me.* She stopped herself from an unbidden, unladylike snort, remembering the few that had escaped her of late. Closing her eyes tightly, she tried to slow her breathing, her heart rate, her thinking, her everything. This was not her normal behavior; these were typical Iax actions and now more than ever, Gemma had to reach her friend. She had to try to get to the bottom of this…*affliction* she seemed to be suffering. All the symptoms occurring were new to her, and at present, their numbers were mounting too quickly to keep track of.

After carrying her inside—although the male evidently tried —he simply did not know how to be gentle. He half-roughly, half-gently deposited her onto a wooden bench in the Great Hall at one of the long tables. Wordlessly, he straightened to an intimidating height, turned on his booted heel, and walk back outside, leaving Gemma to sit with her mouth agape. *Who was he, and what was that about?* she asked her addled brain, but already knew she would get no answers.

Vaguely, she noticed the handful of maidens flurrying around her, bringing her foods and drinks, offering this and that. She did not hear most of their words, as her mind was still stuck on the strange male. The overlarge, somewhat chivalrous male who had just had a care for her well-being, or so she hoped. It was all so new, at least to Gemma.

Finishing off the last of the delicious, fresh bread in front of her slathered with fresh butter and honey, Gemma was still pondering the male who had carried her inside. She had not seen his face, but she instinctively knew he was handsome, obviously heavily muscled, and—as Iax would say—hot. She blushed.

Licking the scrumptious, sticky residue from her fingers caused images to sprout in her mind's eye. And what images they were; her lying in a field of soft, colorful flowers, and him striding up to where she lay, long legs displayed snugly in leather breeches that showed off large, defined muscles which rippled with his every step. He came to a stop and loomed over her with the sun at his back, and she was again unable to see his face. A face that had to be as gorgeous as the entirety of his body, which outlined by the sun, gave him a halo-affect. She was able to tell that his pate was hairless, as the sun's rays reflecting off his head lent it the same halo-affect. He was perfect, at least in her way of thinking. She sighed.

****

Stuck in a tree? Iax's mind was a swirling mass of confusion, and she was still unable to wrap her head around what all Mazar had told her. What happened to those huge critters, and what the hell had happened to her? *In a tree?* Shaking her groggy head, she sighed. "How the hell did I get inside a tree, Mazar? I don't get any of this." She gazed at him as if he held all the answers, and had a horrible feeling in the pit of her belly.

Well, at least she was still alive and not in Heaven, as she had first thought. *Good to know.* Not that she had anything against Heaven, of course not. But she wasn't ready to go there, just yet.

"I heard your voice in my mind but it was extremely faint, almost as if I had imagined it. My 'tat,' as you say, also heated quickly as our heartbeats attempted to match, about the same time. I suppose that means it worked, though I am unsure of how. I truly know not the how nor the why of anything that happened, my love. It was the strangest thing I have witnessed and I wish I could tell you more, but I simply know not. You are well now, and that is the only thing of import to me. We can leave here when you feel ready, and we will never have to return, if you do not wish it." His smile always tilted her heart and mind off their axis, and the amount of love always written on his gorgeous face melted her insides.

"Hmm, well, at least it sounds like the mental-speak worked, even though we weren't shifted. I don't know about you, but it's pretty freakin' cool to me." She gave him a weak yet real smile.

Once again, his heart wanted to break for what she had suffered. Clearing his throat in an attempt to prevent his voice from cracking when he spoke, she patted his cheek, and gifted him with another dazzling smile, before he could get his words out.

"No. You weren't there, so of course you wouldn't know. I just…I can't stand not knowing, that's all. And, you say you didn't see any sign of what I described? I mean the critters?"

He shook his head. "I believe them to be hallucinations. But who could truly know? Stranger things have happened." He shrugged.

She sensed his guilt over her incident, but it wasn't his fault; she just wished she could convince *him* of that. Hell, if it weren't for him she'd be dead. Like, really dead...forever. Deciding it best to change the subject, she plastered a bigger smile on her mug, and hoped it would at least appear heartfelt. She really was ecstatic to see him, but her mind and body weren't fully cooperating, just yet. "I feel pretty good, considering, so maybe we can leave tomorrow. You don't wanna ever return to your home? I wouldn't blame you if you wanted to, I mean, you're *from* here. But, we can make that decision later." She smiled, already feeling sleep's pull again.

Forcing her selfish needs aside, Iax would give almost anything for him to lie down with her and wrap his strong, comforting arms around her so that when she finally drifted off, she'd know nothing bad would happen. Not on his watch, she was sure. But, propriety won out. "I think I'll take a nap, 'cause if anything, I'm just worn out. Really, I'm good for the most part. That Toralynn knows her stuff. Whatever she's done really is working. Go on, go do whatever you need to before we leave. I know it's gonna take a while to deal with all my stuff back home before we're off to the other Realm. You must have loose ends to tie up here, so while we're still here and have the time, hop-to-it. I'll be fine," she insisted at his concerned expression.

Leaning to gently kiss her forehead, he pulled back to look her in the eyes, and smiled. "If you are certain, and yes, I do have matters to tend. I will fetch Toralynn so you will not be alone. If you need *anything*, you will send for me?" He gave her a stern look.

She smiled and thought, *What a tough guy.* Then she almost laughed, but was just too tired. Deep down, she wished they could give each other more. *It'll happen, be patient,* she reminded herself. Man, this love stuff was a distracting business! Cupping his handsome face in her hands, she whispered huskily, "You're the sweetest, prettiest, most wonderful husband in all the worlds combined. But I'm fine, and yes, if I need *anything,* I'll be sure to send for you. I promise," she declared, popping a noisy kiss on each of his cheeks.

Pulling a face in mach outrage, he pinned her with a heated glare. "Prettiest? Iaxsss, in case you have failed to notice I am a male, not a female. Males are not 'pretty' and it would please me if you kept that in mind." Softly tapping her nose with a finger, he grinned like a fool, gave her one more kiss, got up, and left the bedchamber.

Within all of two or three-minutes Toralynn was back, and from the looks of it, she was back for good. *Guess it could be worse. I honestly don't feel like being alone now, but she shouldn't have to spend her day in here, too. How should I tell her without sounding rude, that I honestly don't need her to stay?* she pondered as she watched the female straightening things that were already straightened.

"Hey, Toralynn. There's no need for you to stay in here all the time. Seriously, I'm a big girl and I can take care of me. Like I just told Mazar, I feel good enough. Thinking on maybe nappin' for a bit but otherwise, I'm good. So, please just go on about your biz, don't worry about me. But," speaking over the protest she saw coming, Iax rushed on, "If you would, please, can you maybe occasionally pop your head in the door and check on me? I think that would be sufficient." Beaming the female a compassionate smile, Toralynn's shoulders seemed to relax, and Iax knew her feelings weren't hurt.

She wasn't saying she *didn't* need her, but rather, she *did,* just not all the time. It was a win-win for everyone, and it looked like the female now realized it, too. *Perfect, chalk one up for me. Well, Iax, looks like ya still got your brain, that's something.* She blew out a contented sigh.

Coming to the bed, Toralynn reached down to clasp one of Iax's hands in both of her own, and gave her a proud smile. "I believe you are correct and wise, Iax, for someone so young. A true breath of fresh air, you are. Go on and nap, as I am never far. And I will be sure to 'pop my head in the door' to check on you oft as possible," she conceded with a wink. Then she turned to walk over and dig around in a chest at the foot of the bed. A few minutes later, she returned to Iax's side with something in her hands. "Before I leave, let me give you this." She revealed an ancient looking silver bell with a little handle sticking up on its top. "Here, if you have need of anything, do not hesitate to chime this bell. Someone will hear it and either tend you, or come and find me so I can. Promise me you will use this bell, if need be?" Raising an expectant brow, the stubborn, motherly female would not budge until Iax gave her solemn word, and Iax didn't mind at all.

Once she was finally alone, Iax re-fluffed her pillows, slowly stretched out all of her tightened muscles, hunkered down deeper into the wonderful bed, and closed her tired eyes. Within only moments, she was peacefully drifting on a fluffy cloud in a comfortable, restorative sleep.

Chapter Twenty-nine

Gemma was nervous to the point of almost throwing up, Mazar would not hold still no matter how hard Iax pleaded, and Skenyah, who until last night hadn't been seen by anyone, was tough as nails. The female stood stock-still, silent as a mouse, and had the resolve of a freakin' statue.

"Okay, please listen up. Since Auntie will be using her...*stuff* to take us to my home...er, my *old* home, we need to pay attention and do what she says," Iax ordered her troupes. "As for you, Auntie, please let's do this as smooth and quick as possible. And I don't want any mistakes. If I find myself somewhere I've never been and alone, I will figure out a way to find you, and it won't be pretty. Got it?" Not that Iax truly believe her auntie was afraid of her; that would be absurd. Skenyah could most likely kick anyone's ass.

The only outward sign of acknowledgement Skenyah gave was a stiff, slight head nod. *Was she even blinking?* Iax wondered. Always having to be on the move, she couldn't fathom Skenyah's ability to hold so still. It just wasn't natural. Realizing she'd snorted out loud, Iax shrugged her shoulders to convey that she didn't really care what anyone thought. Gemma and Mazar both shook their heads, but they also wore half-smiles on their amused expressions.

"Skenyah, what say we get this bus a'rollin'? What do you want us to do?" she questioned. Just fixing to give up on getting an answer, Skenyah finally spoke. Her soothing, feminine voice washed over all of them like a warm breeze on a cold day. *That's new, but not altogether unpleasant,* Iax admitted to herself, knowing this little 'trip' was going to be more emotional than anything else. Maybe Auntie could spare her some of the impending grief by doing that thing she just had.

"Mazar, you and I must wear these." Skenyah held up two choker-looking devices in her hands.

Iax scooted closer to get a better look-see. They were constructed of some soft, metal type of material; one silver and one gold. Both were adorned with a shiny, quarter-sized amethyst stone. As always, when Iax got a glimpse of anything shiny or sparkly, she couldn't tear her gaze away. "What are they?" Iax asked in an almost reverent whisper as if the beauties were enthralling her. Then she yelped in surprise when strong, sure hands gripped her around the waist, carefully picked her up, and moved her several yards away from the shiny-pretty things.

"You, my love, may not gaze upon such things. We now know it can be detrimental to your ability to function properly. We must all stay sharp–yes?" Mazar's voice brushed across her ear and ended in a low chuckle.

Embarrassed, and not a small amount of upset over being treated like a child, she wanted to scold him for being so bold. But, using that voice he used on her, and feeling his familiar hands wrapped around her from behind, she couldn't find the nerve or the words. She simply nodded, knowing he was right. It wasn't her fault those kinds of things drew her in. After Gemma and Skenyah had explained her Faerie blood was what pulled her to shiny, pretty objects, she'd been both relieved and pissed off. "It isn't fair," had been her full reply.

"This is yours, Mazar. They have been spelled and blessed by *Famista,* and will enable us to understand and speak the language of wherever we journey to. Here." Skenyah gestured for him to come forward. He did, and she put the choker on him, and clasped it from behind. The moment the clasp was secured, the amethyst stone lit up like a lightbulb. Iax gasped.

"Not so fast, Iax. You come over here and stand by me. We have much to discuss," Gemma softly chided, turning Iax around and moving them further away from what kept tempting Iax's good senses.

"What do we have to discuss? I thought we'd already been over the important stuff," Iax replied a little confused, as she glared at her friend.

"Yes–yes, we have. But I needed to capture your notice and get you away from those necklaces. Mazar is correct; we must all stay sharp and especially *you,* since you are the only of us who knows the ways of where we are going. And do not pout so, we are merely trying to help you," Gemma scolded for the petulance and the glare Iax was giving her.

"Fine," was Iax's only defense.

Just then, she noticed Mazar and Skenyah tucking the mesmerizing, glowing stones into the front of their shirts. She was grateful for the gesture, and felt a bit relieved knowing she wouldn't be acting like a fool over them anymore.

Reaching both arms outward, Skenyah gestured for them all to join hands and make a circle. Left to right, the circle went; Skenyah, Iax, Mazar, then Gemma who rounded it out holding Skenyah's left hand. Next, Skenyah instructed them to close their eyes and not open them. Period. The moment their circle was complete, a jolt simultaneously ran through them, and threatened to break the circle when everyone almost took an involuntary step back, but they held-fast.

No words yet were spoken, but Iax's curiosity was getting the best of her. She peeled her left eye open just a slit, and peeked all sneaky-like to her left at Auntie, to see what was doin'. To her surprise, Auntie was glowing and shimmering, as she raised their joined hands up a little bit at a time.

With her same spying-eye, she noticed everyone following Auntie's lead, including herself. The warm breeze was becoming stronger, lifting and swirling dirt and leaves off the ground all around them. Then she suddenly felt a comforting, humming sensation running throughout her body. From the looks of it, everyone was feeling the same affects as her. She didn't want to miss any of this, but she also knew she had to re-close her eye and keep it closed, or it would be full of dirt and such. Besides, who knew what may happen since, she wasn't supposed to have opened it to begin with? *Damn my curiosity,* she scolded herself.

The second she did, it felt like she was being sucked backward into a high powered vacuum. It didn't hurt, but the strength of the suction was overwhelming. Collective breaths gasped faster and harder as they all struggled to keep their hands joined. Their circle still intact, no one wanted to break it for fear their that journey might not happen.

Feeling her feet leave the ground was a bit disconcerting, making her feel out of control and, as everyone knew, *Iax don't do out of control.* Still, she knew she had to keep going; this was the only way to get back to her old home. With a twinge of sadness, unbidden thoughts hit her like a hard blow to the gut. How was she supposed to tell her family and friends goodbye? And not just 'till next time,' but forever. Realizing this was not the time or place to go there, she forced herself to stay in the present, out of control and all.

****

Sitting on her ass in the middle of the front yard facing her mountain cabin, Iax gasped at the raw beauty. The place always looked like a Winter Wonderland. *Magnificent,* was her first thought, until she realized she was sitting on top of a twelve-foot snowdrift. This made her next thought a no-brainer. *It's winter, duh. I need to get us all inside and build a fire, before we freeze to death.*

Glancing around, she didn't spot the others. "Mazar? Gemma? Auntie? Where all y'all at?" she called out. *Fuck! What if they're all somewhere else...a different, far-off somewhere else? I knew it was too good to be true.* Iax hung her head. Dread pooled in her belly, and mixed with a swarm of killer-bees, which almost caused her to puke.

Breathe, in and out, in and out. She tried to calm and strengthen herself 'cause no matter what, she still needed to get inside and make a fire. It was damn cold out this time of the year, and her ass was already wet and cold from sitting on the snowdrift. Carefully standing—as she knew from experience these snowdrifts could crumble under just the right or wrong circumstances—she made her way to where the drift tapered down closer to the ground, and jumped to the sidewalk that led to the front door.

When she tried to lift one heavy side of the solid, decorative Gnome on the porch to retrieve her hidden key, it didn't budge. "Damn thing's frozen, of course, and you expected...? Shit," she murmured out loud. Scanning the area for something to pry the Gnome off the wooden porch only took a moment, as everything was covered in various feet of snow, mostly hard-packed and, judging by the drift she'd landed on, she would find no help there. *Damn.*

"Well, Mr. Gnome, I'm glad you're tough and sturdy. I don't wanna hurt ya, but I need my key, so I'm gonna have to get violent. Nothing personal, you understand." She calmed herself before cranking her booted-right foot back, then propelling it forward to kick the poor, innocent Gnome right smack in his solid, ceramic potbelly. It didn't fall over or go flying, but it did move a tad. Not quite enough, though.

"Sorry lil' dude, gotta do it again. Close your eyes, it's always better when you can't see it coming. Ready? One! Two! Three!" With another swift kick to his poor belly, he still didn't go flying, but he did fall over backwards. "Yes! Thank you, God! Oh, and thank you, too, Mr. Gnome," she proclaimed gazing up to Heaven, then back down where poor little Mr. Gnome lay on the porch. At least he wasn't injured, that was important.

She reached down to pick up the ancient key, and wouldn't you know it? The damn thing was also stuck, frozen to the wooden porch. "You gotta be fucking kidding me! Fine!" she complained. "I got this. Think you've won? Watch this," she boasted to the door. After gently standing Mr. Gnome upright, she pulled her Swiss-Army knife out of her pocket, squatted down, selected the biggest cutting tool in her badass knife, and deftly pried the stubborn hunk of metal off the frozen porch.

"Ha! Told ya!" Victoriously smiling, she straightened and vigorously rubbed the frozen key on her pant-leg to melt the small layer of ice off both sides. It only took a minute, then she inserted the precious key into the lock in the doorknob and turned it. She smiled at the lock for not being frozen, 'cause that wouldn't have surprised her at this point. As she leaned in to push the stubborn old wooden-door open, she cursed again when the damn thing wouldn't budge. "Frozen shut, of course it is. And, this would surprise me why...?" she expressed in disgust as she gently and repeatedly smacked her forehead against her current bane of existence.

After a few deep breaths, Iax left the key turned to the unlocked position in the doorknob, took two-steps back, and using the method she'd learned in her training, threw her right side against the frozen door with all her might.

She wasn't sure how long, but it had to have been at least a few minutes, when Iax found herself sprawled on top of her ancient wood-burning cookstove; the first thing one would see upon entering the cabin. Thank God it didn't already have a fire raging inside, 'cause that would have sucked even more. Slowly, she pulled herself back, found the floor, and was standing upright as it dawned on her; she needn't use so much force anymore. For shit sakes, she had heightened everything, including physical strength. The only force she probably should have used would have been about one-tenth, or less, of what she just had. "Note to self: First things first, ya gotta tone everything *way* down, sister," she advised herself.

She absently rubbed her throbbing elbows and the right side of her ribs. The damn stove was solid, and she knew she'd live to pay for her landing. Taking a few steps around to survey the condition of the cabin, she was happy to see that other than the fact it was freezing inside, the place looked just like it always did when she visited during the summers. Except for the furniture being covered with white bed sheets, it was perfect.

Feeling nostalgic, like she'd gone back to her preteens, an immense smile broke out on her face at the memories of all the fun family times had here. She genuinely missed it, that was the reason she'd bought the place. All the upgrades and the addition made it different, but the main kitchen-dining-living-room area that made up the central downstairs space was still the same. She'd left that part alone, and it would always hold a significant place in her heart; the place where she'd spent much of her childhood summers growing up, having fun, and bonding with her family.

Not wanting her emotions to get a grip on her, she headed upstairs to the addition she'd had done a couple years ago. Reaching the top—her pains forgotten—her smile widened and her eyes lit up as she squealed. "Oh, my poor babies! I'm so sorry. I know you've been up here alone for all these months. Mama's back now, don't you worry. I promise to take good care of you," she placated and cooed over her tech-station while gently running loving hands over everything. Her fingertips gently grazed each component for an extra moment. "Mama's home, you're okay now." With one last affectionate glance at them, Iax turned and bounded back down the stairs to make the fire she'd been so desperate for a few minutes ago.

With four steps to go, highly excited as she was, Iax jumped the rest of the way down. The spectacular landing found her hitting her head hard on the floor, which was just the cherry on top. *Ugh, that sucked-ass.* But at least she was next to the old cookstove, and for that, she was thankful. Reaching up with her right hand, she grabbed a handful of cold, hard steel to steady herself. Her head felt like a herd of cattle was stampeding inside, which caused it to throb, and made her feel like she wanted to puke, again. *"Ugh,"* she loosed a pitiful groan, only to detest the action before she even finished. *What now?* she questioned her foggy-brain; it was preferable since speaking out loud was too painful.

All her new injuries coming to the forefront, joining the ones she just inflicted upon herself a few minutes ago. She wanted to just lie there and forget about everything else, but that wasn't how Iax did things. Pulling in a few deep, fortifying breaths, she attempted to think straight. Still holding tight to the stove with her right hand, she used her left to search out the problem with her head. With a start, she winced as her fingers located the newest source of her current conundrum; a colossal goose-egg right in the middle of her forehead. "Well, shit," she grumbled, which also hurt, but it couldn't be helped.

What's everyone else gonna think of this? she worried. *Great. Fan-fucking-tastic. Mazar's gonna run screaming the other way from me, Gemma'll try her 'healer' shit, and who the hell knew what Auntie would do? Guess that's what you get for using unnecessary force to break down your own door, not paying attention to your own stairs, and owning an old stove built for business.*

They used to make things to last. Now? Not so much. That was only one of the things she loved about her cabin; everything in it was built to last. She had made sure of it, only using and buying the best-of-the-best when it came to her new addition. Only down side was, would the stove have so much as a scratch on it? Hell no, 'cause it was built so solid. But her? Of course. "Alright, chicka, get it together. You need to make a fire, and apparently tend to a few injuries. Sitting here feeling sorry for yourself, ain't helping anything. Here goes," speaking through the pain, she tried to bolster herself.

It took much longer than she had anticipated with her new heightened senses and all, but Iax finally had a fire raging in the old wood-burning cookstove, and another in the smaller coal-stove in the back of the main living space. She'd also found a few fans and positioned them in all the right places, making the glorious heat recirculate in the main living space and around the pipes so she could use the sinks and tub soon. She hoped. She'd also gone down to the creek a few times, checking unsuccessfully for the three-lost souls who hadn't yet found her, but she was sure they would sooner or later. The several buckets of water she'd brought back now nicely heated on the cookstove. The steam and humidity they produced wafted all around the large room, and the much needed moisture it added to the bone-dry air, was just a bonus.

After a quick sponge-bath, Iax was wearing clean, dry, comfy clothes; sweat pants, an oversized sweatshirt she'd had since high school, and a super thick pair of soft wool socks. Reclining on her favorite of the two couches downstairs, she recalled from when she'd undressed, all the many bumps, bruises, and scrapes she'd found upon her person. She had painstakingly gathered a large mixing bowl full of pristine, white snow, then assembled five ice-packs, or rather, snow-packs to apply to her injuries. She now had one tied around each elbow, the snow resting nicely over the scrapes on the backs of each one. One tied over her right knee, which must have been injured throwing herself into the frozen door, possibly made worse by landing on the cookstove. Another long, wide, kind of skinny pack was snugly tied around her ribs, the snow doing its job and easing some of the pain on her right side. And last but not least, the fifth pack lie loosely over the awesome goose-egg on her forehead, as she rested the back of her head comfortably on the fabulously soft pillow.

To say she was thrilled when she found some Advil, would be an understatement. She also recalled from her last bout with the other stuff to be patient and only take two-pills every four to six-hours. Thankfully, the two she'd taken about an hour ago were doing a splendid job assisting the snow-packs, lessening the swelling where it was present, and dulling the pain so it wasn't bothering her much anymore.

Relaxing on the couch as she pulled a throw-blanket up to her chin, Iax wasn't at all surprised when she'd quickly dozed off. She was, however, surprised when she abruptly awoke to the sound of voices in the room. Eyes still closed, she used her amplified hearing to discern their source and location in proximity to her. "She looks as if she has suffered another accident. Poor thing, she truly never has had so many troubles on any job I have been present for. I wonder what happened this time?" Iax heard the female release an exaggerated sigh. "She appears to be comfortable, although seeing those cloths wrapped everywhere is rather bothersome. Especially the one on her head," the voice let out another sigh. "I do worry over her. As you can see, she needs someone to, as she obviously does not care properly for her own self at times."

Of course, that kind of concern would come from Gemma. Now Iax felt guilty, like an accident prone idiot, which she had never been. But now? Yeah, humiliated for sure. She was happy as could be that they were finally there, though. Auntie had assured her, if they became separated, they would find each other. Period. And, Iax was relieved she had been right. The next voice made her opossum-playing-self go weak-kneed—well, in one knee—and mushy-gushy inside.

"I must agree with you, Gemma. She has had more than her share of injuries, some self-inflicted, even if only by accident, which she seems to have a great propensity for. Though, I think I will wake her. I would check her head wound, as those can be tricky," he finished. She had to force herself *not* to smile.

Still snug-as-a-bug-in-a-rug, she snuggled deeper, faked a soft snore, and turned her face toward the back of the couch, away from the overly concerned peeps milling around in her cabin. She had always loved the couch; overstuffed cushions, and large enough for two adults to comfortably sleep on. They were busy, anyway, obviously giving her a thorough once-over while assessing her injuries and all.

Feeling the spot next to her right hip sink a little, she knew he had sat down next to her. Playing opossum was becoming increasingly difficult, with him sitting so close. He'd most likely be touching her soon, and Iax wasn't so sure she could pull off her fake-out much longer. Then, right on cue, her blanket was lifted with such care, had she been sleeping she wouldn't have felt it. The action was followed by large, strong hands gently probing and checking out all of her snow-packed areas.

"I fear she had a rough landing, otherwise I have no idea how she could have ended up with so many injuries. Whatever she has done to tend them seems to be beneficial, as I do not sense her suffering. Her training certainly must have taught her how to tend her own wounds. I am once more impressed," he admitted to the room.

Iax felt his eyes on her as he spoke, and heard his voice drop to a sexy, husky tone at the end. *Ugh. If I wasn't so tired, I'd kick the females out and have my way with him,* she pondered the idea, knowing it was impossible. *A girl can still dream–right?* Absolutely.

Everywhere his skin touched hers, she felt their powerful connection fairly crackling in the air around them, as her skin heated almost uncomfortably. And her mind, well…it just wasn't working properly at all. Realizing she'd probably better knock off her charade, she let out a soft-sounding yawn, stretched her arms and legs, then winced and yelped from the pain her actions caused. *Damn, that hurt.*

"Ah, she wakes. How do you feel, my love?" Mazar asked in her ear, leaning over to nuzzle the side of her neck.

The love in his voice sent a shiver through every inch of her, and brought a smile to her lips. "Hey, you. I feel fine, just kinda sore. Guess I had a crash-landing. What about you guys? I've been worried and didn't know where to even begin looking for you. What happened?" she rushed out in one concerned breath.

Softly tracing her lower lip with his finger, Mazar's gaze followed his own movements, as one side of his mouth hitched up into his super sexy half-smile, which always turned her into Jello.

"We landed only a couple miles away, but we were able to track you fairly easily. It took us longer because of all the snow. I only thought we had harsh winters, I do not know how you can survive this. It is so cold…*too* cold." He did a mock scowl, and Iax laughed. She'd never witnessed that expression on him, and it was one of the most adorable things she'd ever seen.

****

Proving herself a quick-study in this unfamiliar world, Skenyah—being wicked-powerful and all—had sped up Iax's healing time by setting her up with a mind blowing, innovative pain and antibiotic delivery system. She somehow had an instinctive, acute, and even downright scary knowledge of infections, pain, and all kinds of medical stuff indigenous to Earth. And who would Iax be to question anything after the shit she'd seen and been through, since she had landed in the Dragon Cove Realm a few days ago? Exactly; nobody.

In less than half an hour, Iax had what, by all appearances, looked like a stunning, not too big yet not too small tattoo of a Dragon: Iax's own Dragon, from what they'd told her. It wasn't like there were mirrors in the clearing where the change had overtaken her, and since she had yet to see herself in that form, she believed them.

The beauty began below her shoulder on the outer portion of her upper-right arm and ran halfway to her elbow. Try as she did, she couldn't stop running her fingertips over the intricate, flawless design that had simply 'appeared' out of nowhere. At first, they had all been mesmerized as they literally witnessed it taking shape. And watching it settle fully onto the surface of her skin was even cooler. It was like watching a moving masterpiece, a true work of art.

At first it slowly swirled and wavered, then hovered only a moment just over the golden-tan of her skin. Auntie said once it relaxed, it would lay smooth and then permanently embed itself into her flesh. Painlessly. She wouldn't feel a thing. *I could make a killing inking peeps like this,* Iax mused. *No time, no pain; simple perfection.*

And the Dragon wasn't the best part, not even close. The image was a profile angle, leaving a narrow, three-inch wide view of her Dragon-form's right side. The entire thing was raised and she could *feel* the tiny, soft shimmery scales. Each one was a pouch, wherein lie the sweetest feature, the whole reason for even having her stylish new accessory. *Seems Auntie is hella-awesome-brilliant, even here on Earth! Who knew?*

Altogether, there were fifty raised scales in two different styles, both of which were equal in circumference; one almost skin-level and barely raised, but she could still feel it, the other was raised a tad higher, and both held liquid medications. The first pouch was a pain killer, whereas the second was an antibiotic. The scale-pouch-things were much like blister packs in OTC medications. Big difference was, instead of depressing a blister to aid the pill in escaping its sad little foil and paper prison, these babies were calibrated to release the perfect measure of whichever medication her system needed at the time. The height variation was so she didn't have to look to know which one she was dispensing, she would know by touch.

She had been instructed, with no exceptions, to use it exactly how Skenyah had explained. Iax was grateful to her auntie, at least for this. She still didn't fully trust the nut-job, not completely, anyway. But this thing? Hells, yeah.

Another badass benefit; once all the little pouches were dispensed, the tat stayed, just without the juice. It would be smooth like a normal one, but not created by ink being painfully forced into her flesh. Instead, it was merely *on* her flesh, yet somehow permanent, and not at all manmade. Yep, this little work of art was all natural; another bonus.

"Whoa! This is the coolest thing I've ever seen! How the hell'd you do that? I mean, how'd you know what I needed, and where on Earth—" Iax had to laugh, it seemed like forever since she'd said 'on Earth,' because no one from anywhere else ever got it, "—did you get your hands on this shit?"

"Slow down, Iax. You must pace yourself," Skenyah advised. "With your first finger on your left hand, you gently depress one of the raised scales on your Dragon image. It will only recognize your touch, therefore, you alone can activate it. If you select a pouch for pain, that shall be released into your system. The same goes for the other, yet it will release the infection fighting medication. Having this unique medication delivery system will not only afford you relief, it will aid in your healing time, as well. I should think it may also make you more aware of your new abilities, your heightened senses, and perhaps serve as a reminder that you must have more care for all of these new changes your body is going through. Hopefully, it will also keep you more mindful of your surroundings, as well as your actions."

She turned to walk away, then stilled and said over her shoulder, "Also, Iax, your new powers, or however you refer to them, will not be at full strength away from the Dragon Dimension. Do keep in mind you are much stronger, faster, and many other things, than anyone truly of this world, yet you still are not quite at your best. Your recovery time is longer than it would be had you not been forced into your first change, and so brutally." Skenyah turned to look out the window to her right for a long moment, obviously recalling and feeling guilty over 'the event.'

She breathed and cleared her throat before continuing, "Partially due to your penchant for self-inflicted injuries, and partially because you are so young and new to the changes of your transition, you must exercise patience. All things in time, indeed, you would do well to remember all of what I speak." With a tight nod, Skenyah walked outside to think, Iax assumed.

"Holy freakin' wow! This is some amazing shit. More than amazing," Iax marveled to the shocked-silent Gemma and Mazar, and happily welcomed the affects of her first dose of pain medication as it suddenly kicked in. It made her feel all kinds of warm and fuzzy, inside and out. And giddy! She'd never felt so great! *Wow, this shit's like morphine! Auntie don't fuck around. We seem to have lots in common, guess she can't be that bad after all.* Iax smiled, silently praying she was right as she welcomed the smooth slide into a hazy sleep.

Chapter Thirty

This small, cold place had decidedly captivated Mazar shortly after he had gone outside to do some exploring. Iax had fallen into a deep sleep, one her body needed, and Gemma had offered to stay inside to tend her if need be. It was the perfect time to get a decent look at one of the places his Iax called home.

She was even tougher than he already knew, which was saying much. Enduring all she had at his home, and experiencing the bone-chilling cold she braved spending time here, he was impressed anew. She excelled even at that; always upping his level of awe regarding her. Not that she need worry, in any case, it was impossible for him to ever think badly of her. These things only added to her many considerable attributes.

Leisurely strolling along a path made in the snow, taking in every detail he could, Mazar enjoyed watching the frigid water lazily flow down the small bed of dirt, rocks, and other underwater growth in what Iax had called a 'creek.' Studying its frozen edges, he had never seen such a small flow of water so clear, that he could see every tiny detail clear down to its dirt-bed. With a quick glance back toward her cabin, he smiled at all his gaze touched upon, and the sheer, breathtaking beauty he saw in this peaceful place.

He eyed the small yet spectacular creek once again, only to wonder for a moment how the water flowed at all. Recalling the rivers from his home—for they had no creeks—their flowing waters were large and raging most of the time, only ceasing for a few months when they froze solid during the cold season. Yet, theirs was nothing compared to the cold season in this world.

With so much else to take in, his gaze was roaming before he realized it. Skies much bluer and clearer than at his home, had him wondering how the same such things could be so different from one another? Everything here seemed clearer, brighter, more crisp, and... something he could not yet name. Even the freezing air was refreshing, as it filled his lungs and kept his thoughts more focused. Something he had been in desperate need of for some time now.

Too bad, he thought, that they had to leave this place and journey to the Amethyst Faerie Dragon Realm. Beautiful as all the Dragon Realms were, none of them could possibly compared to his Iax's Earth. He sighed, longing to have the choice of where they would live out the rest of their lives together.

Alas, it was written, prophesied, and decreed that his love would be Ruler of her own Realm. Blood of her own blood.

And their younglings...surely they would have several of their own. He certainly hoped so. What would she look like heavy with his youngling? She would be radiant, he was positive. How could she be anything else? As beautiful as she already was, there would be no other outcome.

Their younglings, as long as they favored her, would be equally stunning. Female-youngs would undoubtedly have her fair looks. He would also love to have at least a couple male-youngs. Though, he never had considered his own looks one way or another, being with Iax these past couple weeks, had made him ponder the matter a few times. He supposed he was handsome, at least *she* certainly thought so, for she spoke of it oft enough. But he was not entirely convinced. Perhaps, if they had male-youngs who favored him, it might not be such a terrible thing, as long as they resembled her at least somewhat.

When he kneeled and cupped his hands to scoop up a mouth full of the clear, refreshing water, Mazar was surprised to feel just how cold it was, and still amazed at how it flowed at all. In any case, it was even more delicious and reviving than it looked. Releasing another sigh, he let his gaze roam further, taking notice of the mountains framing either side of the small valley they were in. It was sort of similar to the valley he had taken Yoren from, but much smaller, colder, and covered in several feet of snow.

She had explained to him how her family came here in their 'summer seasons,' the warmer times when she had been a young.

Seeing it as it was now, he could only imagine the attraction the place held with everything blooming, growing, and teeming with wildlife. Truly a fine sight to behold.

Straightening to stand, he stretched his coiled muscles. He had not, nor would he ever share with Iax, how afraid and worried he had been when he and their other female traveling companions had found themselves here, in this strange new world, without her. Skenyah had assured him that Iax was nearby, and though he had felt their connection he had still worried. It had taken some time to locate her, and when they did, he wanted to take her into his arms and hold her forever.

Seeing her on her 'couch,' as she had called it, looking so small, helpless, and covered in injuries, had almost been his undoing. Had Skenyah and Gemma not stayed him from rushing to her side with the grace of a wild animal, he may have accidentally caused her further injury.

And thank *Meynix* for Skenyah's powers, abilities, or whatever it was she had called upon to tend his love, as he had no such abilities or knowledge. He knew he had much to learn, and that it would serve him well to listen and take knowledge from these amazing, capable females. Although he did not plan to ever be parted from his Iax, there could come a time when it may happen. Even if not, he would know how to tend her, himself. What if none of the females were available when he or his Truemate was in need? No, it would not do to sit back and expect others to tend her from now on. He would know these things, too.

The sound of dried twigs snapping, brought him out of his thoughts. Silently, Mazar hid behind the tall, thick, leaf-bare tree nearest him, to discern the identity of the intruder. After only a few moments, Skenyah appeared as she walked on the same trail he just used, but coming from the opposite direction.

Stepping out from behind the tree, he revealed himself. "Skenyah." He nodded in acknowledgement.

"Mazar," she returned. "What do you think of this place? It is quite cold, is it not?" she asked, absently waving a hand in the air around them.

"I believe I like it here, and I can see why she thinks so highly of it. But yes, it is quite cold." He did a mock shiver and made them both laugh. For the first time, he realized he was coming to truly like Skenyah. She was a mighty female-warrior and obviously loved Iax, or she would not be here now, nor would she have assisted his female as she had, and on more than one occasion.

"Are you headed back to her cabin now?" he asked, hoping they could walk together so he could speak to her for a few moments.

"Yes, I am. I would have words with you, too," she softly replied, as if she had read his thoughts.

Narrowing his penetrating, emerald-green gaze on her, he crossed his muscular arms over his considerable chest, and assessed the strange female in front of him. "How do you always seem to know everyone's thoughts, before they even voice them? I do not much care for this...talent—if you will—which you seem to possess," he ventured, one brow raised.

The innocent shrug of one shoulder and her answering laugh washed over him like a welcome balm. Once and for all, this convinced him that she truly was there for her niece. "I cannot explain some things, Mazar. They just...are," she replied, turning to walk back to the cabin.

Mazar presented her with his elbow, and smiled while waiting for her reaction. Not at all surprised now, that his smile widened when the fierce-female accepted, and he tucked her hand into the crook of his arm. As they walked in companionable silence a short way, he realized—excluding his Iax's injuries—how pleased he was with the outcome of their journey, thus far. Hoping the rest of it would be at least as favorable, he patiently awaited those 'words' she would have with him.

****

Gemma was pleased to simply sit and relax in the cozy building Iax had called one of her homes. Hearing the popping and crackling of wood burning in the stove across the room for where she sat near a peacefully sleeping Iax, was immeasurably comforting to her soul.

"Oh, Iax," she whispered to her slumbering friend. "This is even more lovely than you described. I wish we could stay here. I do not want to deal with any of the other Dimensions or Realms any longer." With a watery smile and a gentle pat on Iax's arm, she got up to go to the door when she heard voices approaching. She already knew who it was without looking, and opened the door with a smile on her lips.

There stood Skenyah and Mazar, their arms intertwined. *What is this?* she puzzled to herself, as her smile faded. Everyone who had ever been around the two had known immediately, they did not get along at all. *Yet here they now stand, touching and laughing?* Not wanting to cause a scene or make assumptions that may cause unnecessary problems, Gemma kept her thoughts to herself. She was well-aware that Skenyah had a way of getting into other's minds, but Skenyah did not know that Gemma was as adept at keeping such intruders out of hers. If only she could keep the female out of Iax and Mazar's minds, too.

"Skenyah. Mazar." Gemma gave them a stiff nod, backing up and allowing them space to enter the warm building. "You both seem…cozy. Did you have a nice time out in the freezing cold?" Piercing Mazar with a lethal glare, she forced herself not to laugh when he visibly winced at her tone, and what she had not-so-subtly implied. Her smile returned.

Skenyah, on the other hand, was either an expert at hiding her emotions, or she truly did not catch Gemma's meaning. Perhaps she did but simply cared not, which could be. Ironically, neither did Gemma. The two had butted heads several times, and would most likely continue to do so for the rest of their time together. She saw no reason to hide her feelings, or be anything other than herself.

Arching an accusing brow at Skenyah, Gemma knew she need not give voice to her thoughts, all she needed to do was allow the female access to her mind, so she did. It only took a moment, and Gemma had to stifle a giggle when the female winced and took a step back, as a result of the thoughts she had just skimmed from Gemma. *Ha!* she thought, *That is what she gets.* A bigger, real smile formed on her lips as she quickly made certain her mind was closed. That was all the female needed to know.

She almost felt ashamed, but quickly dismissed it. She had come to care for Skenyah, even respected and had some understanding of the trials plaguing their Weyr. 'Breaking Iax,' as Skenyah had so politely said, was not going to be as easy as she assumed. In fact, knowing Iax as she did, Gemma was quite confident no one could 'break' her friend. Iax only did something if she wanted to, as long as it was in her control. Still, she wished the Weyr much luck and patience. They needed all they could get of both.

****

After sleeping for a shocking three full days, Iax refused to self-medicate any longer. Enough was enough already, dammit! She had shit to do. Important shit. They could all kiss her ass, if they thought for even a second that they could gang-up and strong arm her into using more of the stuff that made her sleep like the dead. *And what the hell is it with me sleeping for three-days, every time something happens?* she wondered, then dismissed it.

"We are only concerned for you and your well-being, my love," Mazar cooed in his damnable, sexy voice. If he wasn't so yummy and mouthwatering, she'd kick his handsome ass!

"I know, but really I'm fine. Look," she said, as she sat up and twisted each way, wiggled her fingers and toes, and just for extra measure, rolled her ankles and arms in circles. She genuinely did feel much better than she had in…a long time. "I'm fine, but if I lay here any longer, I won't be. My muscles are cramped from not doing anything. I need to get up, have a bath, and join the land-of-the-living, before I lose my mind," she declared, and pasted a smile on her face as to not offend her staunch little band of health-caregivers.

After assessing Iax for several long moments, Skenyah walked toward her. "I believe you are well and able, Iax. Come, I will tend your bath," she announced, turning toward the bathroom.

Shooting Mazar and Gemma a smug grin, she leapt up to her feet, and instantly wished she hadn't when she fell back onto the couch.

"Easy, my love. You will only cause yourself further harm if you do not take things slowly. We do not want that, now do we?" He winked, and held her still when she tried to sit forward and rise again. "I will assist you, whether you like it or not." He tapped her nose with one finger, gave her another wink, and as always, she melted.

"Fine, you can 'assist' me, but don't coddle me. I'm not a baby, for crying out loud. You're all a bunch of worrywarts," she grumbled, letting Mazar help her stand. She wouldn't admit it, but she was grateful for his help. She would've done a nice face-plant on the floor, otherwise.

Wrapping both hands around one of his rock-hard biceps, she closed her eyes as she felt their usual spark bounce between them. When she reopened them, the damn fool was grinning like the proverbial cat that ate the canary! *I gotta get my hormones under control, this male's gonna be the death of me! Death by hotness. Who knew?*

"I believe I can persuade them to give us some privacy, if you would like?" he whispered huskily in her ear, making her already weak knees weaker. Shaking her head at herself, she had to laugh when his expression instantly sobered and he stiffened. She couldn't help smiling at her hunk.

Looking at her as if she were insane, he shook his own head. "First you reject me, then you cause insult by laughing at me? You should have more care, my love. I will get even," he whispered, then winked at her again once he realized she hadn't been mocking him, but herself.

"Even, huh? I think I can handle you, my love," she whispered back as they reached the bathroom door. "I suppose this is where we part ways. Thank you," she offered, using the wall and door to help steady herself while entering the bathroom. She knew he'd much rather be the one tending her, and even though she felt better, she was still more achy than she would admit. Besides, if they were alone—which they weren't—it'd probably be a long while before they came back out.

She had shit to do. Important shit–remember?

****

It took longer than Iax would have liked, but finally after another four days, she had wrapped up all of her business on the Colorado front. Her lawyer thought she'd thoroughly 'lost her damn fool mind,' as he'd told her, when she'd called him to will her cabin to Fred and Dana. They had small kids, after all, and would get much use out of the place. The kids would make lifelong memories there, which was what she wanted. *And that was that.*

She had spent all of the fourth-day *trying* to convince Mazar, Gemma, and Auntie that flying in a plane would not kill them. Even after researching on the net and trying to prove that flying was considered one of the safest ways to travel, they still scoffed. She'd tried to get them to understand it could be an enjoyable experience. There was no way she wanted to chance another debacle, like landing in different places again, if Skenyah transported them. That happening in a small, remote, mountain town was one thing; having it happen in the always-hopping Manhattan, was quite another.

Utilizing the private jet she'd requested from Fred after calling him the day before, they had taken an evening flight after driving to a small airport in Gunnison, Colorado. But not until after they'd taken care of their first order of biz; hitting some local shops and buying modern clothing for her three companions.

It had been such a disaster, she had to laugh. If one of them wasn't putting something on wrong, another was grumbling. None of them understood the concept of 'wait until you pay before you walk out the door,' and had all set off multiple alarms in various shop doors. Iax had apologized more in those couple hours, than she ever had in her lifetime.

At least now they would fit in, even if they were all squirming and fidgeting like children. Iax was already worn out and exasperated, before they'd even made it to the small airport.

The best part of their shopping experience, for her, had been seeing Mazar in jeans. The moment he came out of the dressing room wearing a pair of semi-faded Levi's, Iax's jaw had dropped. She wasn't sure how she'd missed walking all over her tongue, when she walked over to have him turn in circles. A few times. She already knew he had a magnificent ass, and, well, a considerable package, but she hadn't been at all prepared for how it would all look encased in some good old fashioned American jeans. One of her best decisions to date, she had decided. *God Bless Levi Strauss!*

They touched down at La Guardia Airport in New York at ten p.m. eastern time, and Iax wasn't feeling particularly well by the time their plane rolled to a stop. Talk about a long flight. A long day. A long everything, when it came to her company. The three and a half hour trip had felt more like twelve-hours. Her every nerve was thoroughly frazzled.

Before their jet had even taken off from Gunnison, all three of her companion's faces were a pasty green color. Not ten-minutes into the flight, Iax was sure they'd all get sick. Though they were on a private jet, it wasn't fancy, just meant to get one from point A to point B without the hassles of dealing with airport security, and all that fun stuff. It was rather small, and with the four of them and all the stuff Iax had brought from her cabin, there was barely room to breathe, let alone to get up and move around.

It didn't help that they were all bigger than the average human, either, as they had tried to move freely about. Keeping them seated and buckled in had been an enormous feat. Keeping their attention off of themselves and on other things, had been damn near impossible. Iax spent the whole time explaining things of her modern, technological world to them, hoping they would catch on quickly, and not get too freaked out in the Big City.

She'd had trouble aplenty explaining electricity to them back at her cabin. All three of them had jumped, then hit the floor, the first time she'd asked Gemma to flick a switch, and an overhead light had come on. Of course, her laughing at them hadn't helped, but it had been freakin' hilarious!

Showing them her computer station had been even more humorous. They all kept shooting her fierce scowls, acting like monsters would jump out at them at any moment, even *after* she had explained in detail what all her equipment did, and what she used it for. Checking her email had never been so much fun!

Still, none of it compared to what they were about to face. She was worried, but knew if she could just keep their minds busy, keep explaining things in a way they'd hopefully understand, everything would go more smoothly. *Hopefully.*

After ensuring her belongings would be delivered to her home, and a long, crowded taxi ride to Greenwich Village where Iax lived, they were all exhausted, in need of food, and time away from everyone and everything of this world. She didn't think it could have been a worse time to bring them here, as Christmas was only a week away. Of course, the city was bustling with more people than the normal masses.

They had all calmed down at least enough to ask questions, and Gemma even got excited at all the sights and sounds on their taxi ride. The female fairly shone with awe. Who could blame her? Gemma had never seen anything like this. "Iax! Oh, my! I know you have told me of this place, and you were correct; one must actually see it to understand the magnitude of such beauty!" Her face pressed close against the window as to not miss anything passing them by, Gemma let out a long, whimsical sigh.

Skenyah had immediately claimed the front seat, leaving the others to sit in back. Mazar was in the middle, Iax to his right, and Gemma was to his left next to the door with a window. Iax knew this area with her eyes closed, so she finagled, scooted, and at one point, even straddled Mazar, trying to put him on the right side window. She wanted him to see the view like Gemma was.

"If you do not cease this mauling, my love, we will embarrass everyone in this…moving contraption," he whispered in Iax's ear as she straddled him. She giggled then wiggled on his lap, which had warmed so much, she felt the heat radiate through both of their clothes. She shivered.

"It's not my fault you're a horny-dog! Stop thinking about *that* all the time, and you'd be much better off. Why do you think on it so much, anyway? Seems you have a one-track mind, just like all males," she laughed. "You need to find a hobby, or someth—" She was abruptly silenced when Mazar cupped the back of her head with one, large hand, and pulled her mouth down to meet his. He caught her gasp in his mouth, and she felt his laughter rumble deep inside his chest—his awesome, sexy chest—as she melted into him.

It felt like a long time, but apparently had only been a couple minutes when their cab came to an abrupt stop. Thank God he held her in such a strong embrace, or she may have rolled over into the front seat. At least it brought her back to reality; the reality that they'd just pulled up in front of her Manhattan Brownstone.

Attempting to jump off Mazar's lap in her excitement over being home, Mazar held fast, his gentle hands keeping her firmly rooted in place still straddling him. "Unless you wish for everyone to see the proof of my desire for you, it would please me greatly if you sat still. I am in need of a moment to…relax. Got it?" he intoned, veins and muscles visibly working as he tried calming himself. Poor thing, much as she wanted to help him relax, she wasn't sure how. The whole situation was kind of comical. Unable to help it, she snorted, then sobered at his serious expression.

"I'm sorry, and we can wait, but only a minute or two. I can't wait to get inside! You're all gonna love this place, my other pride and joy!" she excitedly exclaimed, oblivious to the fact that she wasn't holding still, therefore, making Mazar's problem even worse. It wasn't until she heard him groan, that she realized her mistake. "Shit, I'm sorry! Again! Dammit, I'll sit very still and…and I'll talk about stuff, and it'll help *that* go away," she said quietly, motioning to his groin with her chin. His brow was covered in sweat, and it made her feel guilty. But, only just a little bit.

"Here, let me help." She reached up and dabbed at his brow with the bottom-front portion of her thermal pullover-shirt, not realizing what a colossal mess she was creating for him. His groan was much louder this time, his expression pained. "Shit!" She jumped off his lap, realizing she'd given him an up-close-and-personal 'hey, how are ya,' of her braless and considerable chest while trying to 'help' him. *Awe, poor baby. I'm gonna accidentally kill him from sheer stupidity.* She sighed.

Skenyah and Gemma had already exited the cab, thank God, which allowed them to sit in silence for a couple minutes as they awaited his 'problem' to ebb. After scooting over and exiting through the left door, Mazar walked around to the right and helped her out. At least he wasn't sweating anymore, but his jaw was clinched so hard, she feared it might shatter. Smiling up at her sexy, testosterone-ridden male, she tossed him a wink and jumped up at a run, excited to reach the front door of her Brownstone.

Leading them up the stairs, Iax took some keys out of her jacket pocket, flipped through them until she found the one she needed, unlocked the door, and then welcomed them all into her home. "Well, here it is! What'cha think?" she proudly asked everyone with a bright smile. Turning back to them, her smile began to fade. None of them had moved an inch to cross the threshold and enter her home. *What the hell?* she wondered.

"This is, um–it is…" was Gemma's initial reaction. Not too surprising, really, but Iax had hoped for more.

"Yes, it is–it is…" was Auntie's initial reaction. Not a real shocker there, either.

"This is where you–reside? Here, in this, this…" was Mazar's initial reaction, as he absently waved an arm in the air.

None of them appeared to be disappointed, but they weren't quite as impressed as she had hoped. Not even that, truly, but Iax had hoped they would at least smile and show *some* excitement.

"Mm-Hmm," was Iax's response.

****

"Stubborn damn people," Iax grumbled to herself, chopping veggies for a salad to go with the spaghetti she was preparing for dinner. It had taken damn near a half hour to get them to actually enter her home, and another half an hour to get them to sit down and stop gawking at everything in utter confusion. "Guess the saying's right; you can lead a horse to water, but you can't make it drink." Shaking her head, she narrowly missed chopping off the tip of her finger, deep in thought as she'd been. "Shit!" she yelped, sucking on the tip of her now-bleeding forefinger. And wouldn't ya know it? All of her company appeared at her side in a heartbeat.

"What has happened, my love?" Mazar asked, pulling her finger from her mouth.

"Nothing, I just cut myself a little bit. Don't worry, I'm fine," she snapped, trying to free her finger from Mazar's vice-like grip. Not that it hurt, he always managed to be gentle and would never harm her, she knew.

"You need looking after every moment of every day," he muttered, making her blush.

Why can't they stop babying me? I'm not usually a klutz, I just wish they *knew that,* she complained to herself. Enough was enough, already. She couldn't walk through a room without one or all of them jumping up, expecting her to disable herself in one way or another.

She hadn't noticed the others leave, but suddenly Iax realized it was only her and Mazar standing in her spacious, hi-tech kitchen. Leaning back against the counter, his head bent to get a close look at her finger, he peered up at her through long, dark lashes. Her heartbeat picked up, causing his to do the same. His delectable lips hitched up one side into his sexy half-smile, and he slowly brought her finger to his mouth. Her knees went weak, then her whole body followed.

"You poor thing," he whispered, licking the throbbing tip of her finger. "I am more than happy to look after you, always." Sucking her finger into the heat of his magical mouth, a soft moan escaped her. She had to force her eyes not to roll back in her head. What was he doing? Didn't he understand yet that when he touched her, she couldn't think at all? *Totally not fair,* she decided, still trying to keep her breathing pattern even, but miserably failing.

Shaking her head, she gained a small sliver of control as she quickly pulled her finger to her chest. "You need to knock it off, if any of us wants to eat anytime soon." Spinning back to face the counter, she snatched a Kleenex from a nearby box, wrapped her finger, and finished chopping the veggies. The last thing she heard was Mazar's deep chuckle as he left the kitchen to join the others in the living room.

They were all much more relaxed by the time she served dinner on the table, from where the television could be seen. She'd laughed at Mazar's reaction to that bit of technology. She had a fifty-inch flat screen with every channel ever imagined. True to his gender, he had become engrossed in the boob-tube, and picked up surprisingly fast on how to work the remote.

A male from any time or place was still a male. Go figure.

"Oh, Iax! This is delicious. What did you call this exquisite food?" Gemma exclaimed, her eyes closed as if she were having an orgasm. Iax laughed.

"Well, thank you, but it's just spaghetti. I've always loved Italian, Mexican, and of course, American foods. And I try to have salad with my dinner every night. My mama—" Slanting her gaze to Auntie who was seated to her left, she didn't want to make this awkward. Seeing no reaction there, she continued, "She always grew big veggie gardens, various grapes, some melons, just all kinds of stuff. I never did understand those moms who couldn't get their kids to eat veggies, 'cause even as a kid I always macked on all of them I could get my hands on. Still do, when and where it's available." She resumed stuffing her face.

Mazar was scarfing it down like there was no tomorrow, keeping the tube in his sights all the while. Iax smiled and shook her head.

"What about you, Auntie, you like?" she asked, paying more attention to her plate than to anyone.

"Yes, Iax. It is delicious. I did not know you could cook," she replied with a smile.

"I love cooking, but I don't get to do it very often. It's kinda hard to when I'm almost always gone on an assignment. You know, out there saving the world and beyond." She smiled back, tearing off a large chunk of her sour dough French bread. Ah, it melted in her mouth! Like Gemma, she thought she might have an orgasm. A food orgasm. She had slathered the bread in butter, fresh garlic, and a couple of spices before toasting it in the oven. She really, really missed her favorite foods while she'd been away.

They all sat and ate in a companionable silence for a while, before Iax decided to nudge Mazar's leg under the dining table with her socked-foot to get his attention; the male's eyes hadn't left the stupid flat screen! Still, he gawked as he ate, not giving any sign to acknowledge her foot-nudge. Now she understood why her folks had always insisted they eat with the television turned off. It was kind of rude and, funny as it was in Mazar's case, it was beginning to annoy her.

"Yo, Mazar! Wanna join the rest of us?" she asked, slightly louder than she normally would have. But for shit sakes, there didn't seem to be any other way to get his attention! *Seriously?* Even hollering at him did nothing. "This is absolutely fucking ridiculous," she said under her breath as she got up, walked across the wooden-floor, and turn the damn boob-tube off. "Jeesh!" she grumbled again.

"Whoa! Why did you do that?" Mazar had the nerve to ask her, his expression a little freaked out and shocked. Next to his chair —the side he'd been leaning to so he could watch a Wild Kingdom show—Iax stood firm, hands fisted on her hips, with a decidedly irritated look on her face. She would not put up with this. Not now. Not ever. Even if their stay was only short-term.

"Why did I do that–really? You haven't taken your eyes off the damn thing since I first showed it to you. I only meant to give you something to do so you wouldn't be bored, but I draw the line when you completely ignore everyone around you. This is *my* house, and *I* make the stinkin' rules. Ya don't like, then leave. Ya like, then follow the rules," she huffed, walking back to reclaim her seat and finish her now-cold dinner. She shook her head in frustration.

Busy eating her dinner—even if it was a bit cold—Iax realized after a moment that all eyes were on her, and nobody was making a move. Resting her head on the high-back of her chair, she closed her eyes, counted to ten, and resisted the urge to give them all lessons and notebooks they could scribble notes into. Unable to stop herself, she laughed out loud at the thought. Not a one between them could write, not in English anyway, so it would serve no purpose. *Well, it was brilliant, in theory.* She sighed.

Chapter Thirty-one

Even though his love had thrown quite a fit, Mazar had still enjoyed the scrumptious sup prepared by her own hands. After a blissful eve's slumber, waking in his Iax's home pleased him. He was further pleased at how it had felt to lie in her bed, his body wrapped snugly and protectively around her lovely form. They had no need to fear a battle-interrupted slumber here, in fact, it was quite the opposite as they had slumbered the whole eve with nary a sound to stir either of them. He had never slept so soundly, peacefully, and contentedly.

Although this world was new and inexplicably strange to him, he understood Iax's wish to be done with her business and away from here with haste. Yet, after only a mere glimpse of her dazzling world, he could also see why she would have difficulties saying goodbye. He would aid her in any way possible, to speed up their journey to the Amethyst Faerie Dragon Realm, sooner rather than later, he hoped.

It had taken more time than the last, but his Iax had prepared a mouthwatering meal to break their fast which was simply called, 'breakfast,' in her world. He supposed it made some sense, putting words together the way her kind did. Still, he preferred his ways better; there could be no misunderstandings as long as they paid proper mind as others spoke. Always, they would speak each word separately; it had been the way of his kind since long before his time.

As delightful as last eve's sup had been, this meal was overlarge with almost too many delicacies from which to choose. Eggs; 'any way,' she had offered. Bread, of which she had several types to 'toast' in a strange contraption—there was no cease to her strange contraptions—aptly named a 'toaster.'

In this case, his Truemate's toaster had 'settings,' but first, you placed sliced bread vertically into the thing, then chose a number—of which he had no knowledge, and her letters were equally unfamiliar—depress a lever, and after a short wait the sliced bread popped up from the toaster, and it came out...toasted. The mechanics of the contraption truly were ingenious, not to mention the toast had been delicious. But it had still been a lesson in patience for everyone, except his Iax, as it only toasted four slices of bread at one time.

She had also offered a variety of meats; the first type was 'strips of bacon,' and then three types of 'sausage,' in links, patties, or ground; the latter being small, loose pieces which cooked quite fast in her frying pan. There were two more items—personal favorites of hers—over which she had gushed; the first was 'corned beef hash,' which, she had insisted, must be served with her second favorite, 'hashed potatoes'. After several servings of the grand feast, Mazar understood and had even agreed with her choice of favored foods. In truth, he had enjoyed all the tasty treats.

In addition, she had offered several drinks; an array of juices she had prepared from the succulent fruits she 'bought' at her 'store.' Cow's milk, and something called 'coffee,' a drink she apparently had quite a liking for as long, as it was dowsed in her 'creamer.' It had taken over an hour for the meal to digest, so full were their bellies, before any of them could get the events of the day underway. Not that he was complaining. Never that.

When she had stacked all the dirty dishes into a noisemaking, self-cleaning contraption in her kitchen, it had been too much for him. She had explained to him that her 'dishwasher' was one of the quietest-running and best on the market. Yet, the humming, popping, and other noises the contraption made, had him jumping at every turn. It was pushing on his last nerve, but it may have been due to his overly sensitive hearing, too.

He had become petulant and perhaps even a bit grumpy. It had only made matters worse when she had commanded to him—quite sharply—that he was no longer 'allowed' to view her magical-flat-box which hung on her wall. It was one of her better contraptions, bringing living, colorful pictures right into her living-chambers. He knew none who would ever believe such a tale.

Digressing over the matter, he admitted to himself—somewhat begrudgingly—it probably was best. There was much to do this day, and him dallying with her magical-flat-box, coupled with his pouting—which he did not realized he was even capable of—would only serve to put them further behind with everything his Iax needed to do on their journey.

After expressing a strong desire to bathe, and be away from her many contraptions, she had showed him how to work her 'shower,' something he had quite enjoyed. It was incredible, unlike anything he had ever seen; water falling from the overhead spout which continued to run hot, and by itself for long amounts of time. He wondered at the possibility of assembling such a device, when they got to their destination. His Iax had promised to help him figure it out.

She had cleaned up from their morning meal, and they all helped her pack some of the things she wished to bring with her on their journey back. Before they knew it, it was time for another of her magnificent meals, this one she called 'lunch.'

He would have never guessed of all females, his Truemate could prepare such tasty foods. She was talented in so many ways, it made his head swim. Hoping she would continue to bestow these delightful favors upon him forever, he could only nod, thank her, and accept all of her offerings with a genuine thrill. He had never eaten such scrumptious foods in his life. A female who could cook, fight, and everything in between? He never knew one existed, let alone that he would someday have one for his own.

She prepared what she called 'grilled cheese sandwiches,' and soup. Indeed, the sandwich had been so delightful, he had eaten five of them before she refused to serve him more. He knew what soup was, yet hers was far better than any to have ever graced his taste buds. It came in a strange container called a 'can' and was labelled 'New England Clam Chowder.' Something he assuredly wished for more of in their future, which he had expressed to her, along with all of her other scrumptious cookery-concoctions. Her reply had been, "I don't think I can cook enough to keep you full, even if it's all I ever did. You're either gonna have to learn how to cook, or find someone in the Realm to do it for you." She had even called him a 'bottomless pit' at one point, shaking her head and smiling, as she oft did. He truly loved her more than the air he breathed.

Hearing her voice brought him back to the present, and he quickly realized she was in her commanding mode. He had never seen a female give orders, yet she was fully capable. All the females standing in her living room were wholly capable of much.

"Okay, I've got everything taken care of for this place," she sadly announced, lovingly caressing the wall beside her. He knew she would miss both of her homes, yet she had remained stoic and dealt with everything uncomplaining. He had already vowed to her and himself that he would make certain wherever they lived, would be a grand place. It was already a 'grand' place, she had reminded him, in fact, it was probably more of a 'fancy' place. As long as she was happy, that was all that mattered to him.

After a sentimental moment with her wall, she gave them all a weak smile, pointed down to the few boxes and bags of her belongings on the floor, and said, "Let's be off, then." They had each chosen what they could carry, then walked out the front door, and loaded her belongings into the trunk of the taxicab, leaving her beloved home behind, forever.

This one, she informed them, had sold between the two meals they had eaten this day. Apparently, others had been interested in purchasing her home for quite some time, so she had no trouble finding a buyer. The proceeds would be donated to her choice of 'charities,' whatever those were. She had explained it to them but at this point, it didn't matter to him. In the end, it seemed to make her feel better, in turn, they were relieved for her and glad to have been there to offer her support.

****

Iax was happy to have both of her hella-cool digs dealt with, even if it had been a bittersweet situation. She found some comic relief recalling her vow that she'd become one of those 'flame-throwing-Dragon-fuckers' before this day ever came. Well, be careful what you say, 'cause you never know what life will throw at you or what changes may take place, before you even realize it.

As for now, she was back in the position of caregiver, regarding her three-traveling companions. "You just need to relax and breathe," Iax advised them, drawing out each word. "We'll be there soon and everything is fine, I promise." Mazar and Gemma were both green since they had boarded the private jet again, much like on the flight here. *Big babies,* Iax grumbled to herself. At least Auntie had adjusted pretty well.

Trying for all she was worth to breathe evenly and slowly, poor Gemma was still having a hard time. They all kept saying the speed was making them nauseous. Or, they agreed, perhaps it was the height. Probably a bit of both, Iax guessed. It made sense, but she'd grown up traveling in cars and trucks, buses and planes. All just a means to an end for her, but these peeps were wound way too tight, she thought.

"We'll be seeing my folks in a few minutes, so please, try to relax. Mama's sweet and really laid back, but even she may become a little unglued if anyone gets sick in their car," she tried joking with them. It didn't work.

"You find this humorous, my love?" Mazar groaned, eyes closed. "Perhaps I will take you on a journey in a manner of which you are not accustomed, and then we shall see where your humor lies, and if you can find your clever quips." Squeezing his eyes even tighter, the poor male scooted further down in his seat. Iax covered her face with both hands to hide her laughing expression, and suppress any sound that may further upset him. She should feel a little worse for him, but it was too funny.

Deep breaths for you too, chicka. She sobered after realizing her own words about her folks; this was not going to be easy. The reason she'd brought everyone with her was so her folks would believe their crazy story, and so her companions could meet and understand her emotions over her folks, not to freak anyone out. Besides, she'd been through this with herself several times already. Her dad and mama knew of these beings, maybe not in the same way, but still.

Their flight took less than an hour to Dover, Maine, the adorable East-coast town her folks had been living in for the last few years. Iax had purchased a house and an easily manageable property for them; after her dad had retired and his medical bills had skyrocketed, it left them all but broke. She figured since they'd raised her and never let her go without anything—but never to the point of spoiling her—she owed them. She made killer money now, so why not?

She'd been to their home several times for Christmases, a few birthdays, stuff like that. But this visit? She wasn't sure how to broach the subject that she may never return, may never see them again. And damn if her eyes weren't leaking now, before she'd even seen them.

One of the sweetest things about a private jet was, you landed, they put the stairs down, and you deplaned. Plain and simple. Another sweet thing, especially in a small town, your ride could drive right up to the plane. No long airport walks, no security checks, none of the pain-in-the-ass stuff you were legally required to do on commercial flights coming and going.

When the jet came to a full stop, Iax looked out the window and saw her folks standing outside their car. More specifically, her dad's Mustang. And what a beauty it was. They wore welcoming expressions, but she knew them and knew it was only to save face.

"Shit! Fred told them, and now I'ma have to kill Fred!" she bit off, irritated at Fred's perfidy. Well, maybe not perfidy, at least, not on *purpose,* but still! Dammit! Oh, and there was that thing, too; she honestly had been working on her mouth. Really. Kinda of. Sort of.

"What did you say, my love?" a green-faced Mazar asked with thick concern in his still liquid-sexy voice. Slumping back down into her seat, attempting to bolster herself for a minute, she glanced to her right and saw his color quickly return to normal. Apparently it was only while he was inflight, that he had such an adverse reaction. Flicking her gaze to Gemma, she supposed the female's deal was the same. Smiling, Iax reached over to squeeze Mazar's hand. He returned the smile and the squeeze, and rubbed comforting circles over the back of her hand.

"Nothing, I was just spewing nonsense. Don't worry 'bout me. There they are." She turned and pointed out the window to the parents who raised her. The only parents she'd ever known, and ever *would* know. "That's Dad, Special Agent David Conifurr, and Mama, the ever quiet, always formidable Elise Conifurr," she proudly owned, respect and love for them shining in her watery eyes. She held her gaze on them, grateful they couldn't see her, and jumped a little when Mazar gently swiped tears from her face with his thumbs.

Giving him a weak, soggy smile, she tried to wink, but it just didn't hold the same charm when the one giving it was, well, weak and soggy. Still, the look he gave her always made her melt. He was incredible, and probably much too worthy a male for her. Probably.

****

Seeing his Iax in this condition, he wanted to weep for her, but he would not. She needed him to be strong for her, and he always would be. He could see that need in her watery eyes, and his heart almost split in two, but not now, and especially not here. He was a warrior and Truemate, in truth, they were each other's everything. After all she had done for him already, he could do no less than support her through this emotional time in her life. "You, my love, are going to be well. Do not worry overmuch, as we are all here for you. Besides, if they are anything such as you have said, they will be well, too. Have faith, my love. Have faith," he whispered in her ear, after pulling her tenderly against him. Rubbing large, strong hands down her back, he willed as much of his warmth and strength as he could, into her. One of only a few things he could do for her at this time.

Melting against him, her arms tightly twining around his neck, he almost broke anew when he felt the small racking of her silent sobs. Closing his eyes and resting his chin upon her head, he blew out a long sigh. She was correct, this would not be easy. In fact, it was seemingly becoming more difficult by the moment for her. Anything that brought her pain, made him hurt for her. *What should I do? What can I do?* he silently beseeched *Meynix*. He had no experience in matters regarding delicate female sensibilities. Not that he would ever think of his Iax as 'delicate,' yet he was discovering that perhaps she was a bit, more so than even she knew, or would ever admit.

At least he was better now, and no longer felt as if he would lose the contents of his previously-filled stomach. Gemma also looked much better. However, they could not, nor did he wish to remain in this death contraption any longer.

Giving his love a gentle, comforting squeeze, he pulled back to look her into eyes. "You, my love, are the strongest, most capable female I have ever met. You will make it through this, and we are all here for you." With a sad smile and a firm nod, he released her, stood, and then helped her to her feet, "Let us do this," he teased, using one of her phrases. In truth, he was becoming quite fond of some of her words and sayings. Not all, but some. This one made her smile, which was what he had wanted.

"Thank you. All of you. I think I may need your support, even if I don't like to admit it," she replied with a half-smile. "Guess we'd better get off here and get the hard part over with." Turning and grabbing a couple of bags out of an overhead compartment, she walked to the door, and with the style only his Truemate possessed, Mazar watched with pride as she took a deep breath, and descended the length of stairs to greet her parents. He saw her chin lift higher with each step she took. His heart melted, and he did not realize until he wiped tears from his own face, that he had even loosed them.

Luckily, nobody had witnessed it, which is how he preferred his weaker moments in life; unnoticed.

Iax's 'mama' was extremely beautiful, just as Iax had promised. Not quite as tall as his female, yet her mama still stood proud, mere inches shorter than Iax. Her long, wavy blonde hair was perhaps a shade darker than Iax's golden tresses. But, where Iax had bright-green eyes, her mama's were a breathtaking hazel, both as mesmerizing as the other. She was physically toned, and in an overall healthy state by all appearances.

The female's 'husband,' just as Iax had counseled them, stood at about six-feet-tall. His brown, all-knowing eyes and solid, muscular build was more than Mazar had expected of the male. Thick, dark hair showed a fair amount of aging with silver and gray streaks running through the sides of his once evenly-darkened hair. It gave him a distinguished look, though, not at all elderly. He looked to be a capable male; one of worth.

Iax had explained what had happened to her dad, and they all expected to see a smaller male, perhaps slightly broken, physically. He had a massive heart-attack a few years ago and almost died. Thankfully, they had been able to get the best cardiovascular specialist—a well-qualified heart doctor, Iax had explained—to tend him. After offering much prayer, spending many monies, making several journeys to where the specialist lived, and even more prayer, her dad had recovered well. Although, she had indicated that he never did fully rebound and was not quite his old-self since the attack, he appeared to be as formidable as Iax's mama, which was saying much. The female was the picture of perfect health and worth. Mazar smiled at the scene unfolding before him.

"Mama! Dad! It's so great to see you!" Letting her bags carelessly fall to the ground, Iax ran and threw herself into the waiting arms of her parents. Seeing the threesome tightly embrace each other, such a display of love swelled the hearts of all who witnessed the reunion. Swell with happiness for the family, and a deeper, unfamiliar emotion Mazar and his two traveling companions had no name for. Nonetheless, they stayed back, giving Iax and her family the time and space needed to reacquaint themselves. It was a truly touching sight.

"Baby girl. Look at ya," Mazar heard her dad's greeting, his voice gruff and full of emotion. "It's been too long, ya lookin' real good, kiddo," the male added. He was larger than Mazar had expected. Watching the emotional, private moment made Mazar's respect for the male grow. He already had nothing but respect for him; knowing what a handful Iax was now, she positively had to be nothing less, as a youngling. Most likely giving her parents fits much of the time while growing up in this strange, somewhat scary world. Anyone who could raise her and still be whole and hale, most certainly had his fullest respect. Sliding a glance to the other two females still standing a few paces back and to his left, Mazar saw as much in their all-knowing gazes.

After what felt to be a long while, Iax came running back over to Mazar, still standing in the same spot he had allotted himself when he first got off the jet. Slamming into him with such a force, had he not been paying any mind and not been so large and strong, she would have knocked him over. The way she acted, laughing and such, he did not think she would have cared had they both ended up on the hard ground.

"You," she began, but sighed, not speaking for so long he thought she may not finish, yet he knew she was strong. She would endure and get her words out, after she took a moment to gather her wits. He smiled at her as he waited.

"Yes, you, thank you. I'm so glad you're here. All of you," she exclaimed, gesturing over his shoulders for Gemma and her auntie to join them. Including them went a long way; everyone always appreciated that. "Here, let's go meet my parents. I promise, they're the nicest people you'll ever know, and they definitely wanna meet all of you. Okay! Let's go!" Seeing her act so much like a young, made Mazar's heart melt as she tugged on his arm, reached for Gemma's hand, and used her odd eye language in an attempt to get Skenyah moving to meet her parents. A moment later, they were all gathered around Mr. and Mrs. Conifurr. Somewhere between middle-aged and elder in their years, stunning, was the 'wife,' and handsome, was her 'husband.'

When Mazar extended a hand to the male, he was surprised at the strength with which it was met. He would have never believed an aging male who had been through all this one had, and one with no powers—shifter-lineage or otherwise—could have such physical strength. His respect for the male grew tenfold, perhaps more. His Iax had already schooled them all on how her people would greet one another, and thank *Meynix,* he remembered everything she had said. They all remembered.

"Mr. and Mrs. Conifurr, it is a pleasure to make your acquaintance," Mazar said, reaching for the female's smaller, softer hand. With a head nod, he gently raised her hand, and dropped a soft kiss on the back. She beamed him a smile, which he wholeheartedly returned. Even though the obviously proud female did not birth his Iax, he clearly saw a strong resemblance between the two.

"Oh!" Mrs. Conifurr exclaimed, as a slight pink blush flared on her cheeks. "Thank you. A lady is never greeted in such a chivalrous fashion nowadays, I am honored. Quite a gentleman you are, and it's my pleasure to meet you, too," she finished, and the light blush on her beautiful countenance deepened to a fine red. The female certainly did not appear her age, as many in this world he had already noticed, did. Many appeared even more than their true age.

Someone clearing their throat grabbed Mazar's attention. Turning back to the male, he could have kicked himself! *'Quite a gentleman,' I think not,* he berated himself for ignoring the male he so respected. "Apologies, sir. I was simply taken by your female's beauty and kindness, I forgot myself." Giving the male a chagrined smile, he faced him. "I am Mazar, your young's Tru–" Suddenly, his Iax was standing between him and her dad, face fully-flushed, and a hand resting on each of their chests.

"Sorry, Dad. His kind speaks a little differently than we do. I met him in the Dragon Dimension, he and his Weyr reside in the Dragon Cove Realm." She waved a negligent hand in the air, then brought it back to rest on Mazar's chest. "He is very…old fashioned, you could say, compared to our modern ways." She smiled at both of them.

Mazar had a sinking feeling she was keeping their love a secret. *Why would she do such a thing?* he puzzled to himself. He would allow her some secrecy, for now. They were Truemates, after all, and as such he would not be denied, shamed, or expected to stay silent on the matter. Not for long, anyway.

"I know, kiddo. No worries," her father assured, kissing her forehead. "Ya really do look different, but in a good way. What ya been doin' differently?" He smiled wide, pride written on his face for everyone to see.

"I haven't done anything different, Dad, just been staying busy and trying to take better care of me." She smiled back. "Now, I'd like you to meet my other two, um…friends." Turning to Skenyah and Gemma, she waved them over. They closed the small gap between the group, and suddenly Iax wasn't sure how to introduce her new auntie. *Hmm, this is awkward,* she silently admitted. But as she looked at Auntie, she noticed her neutral expression. Hopefully, it meant she wouldn't mind being introduced as a 'friend,' at least for now. This was not the right time or place to break all the news to her folks.

"Mama, Dad, this is Gemma, and this is Skenyah. I met them both on my assignment. They're amazing friends, both of whom have saved my ass and been super supportive of me." Iax clasped Gemma's hand as she pulled her forward, and then gave it a small, reassuring squeeze before introducing her. "I met this one a few months ago. She's the one who's always there when I get to all of my away assignments. You know, the *far* away ones? She's awesome, and I just know you'll love her as much as I do," she finished, meaning every word.

Shaking hands with her dad, then her mama, Gemma bestowed one of her killer-smiles on each of them. In turn, Iax's folks both looked to be in shock for a minute; Gemma had that kind of affect on everyone. Iax had always known, if her friend ever came here—to Earth—it would only intensify; her beauty wasn't the kind anyone could simply look past.

"Gemma, our baby girl has told us about you a few times. We thank you for being there to help her, and apparently save her life on more than one occasion." Iax's dad kept Gemma's hand in his for a long minute before giving her a slight bow.

Whoa! He's taken by her. Why doesn't that surprise me? Iax smiled. Still, this was her dad, and she'd never seen him act like this over any woman, except for his wife, of course. He wasn't flirting, it was just that pull Gemma had on everyone, unbeknownst to her. She'd probably be mortified to know, but she was so pure, so innocent in these matters, Iax would never tell her what certain reactions actually meant. She smiled at her friend.

"There is no reason to thank me, sir, I am grateful for the friendship I have with your youn–daughter. I would do anything to see her safe and well, with pleasure," Gemma replied, giving Iax's dad a small bow. "It means much to finally make your acquaintance, and in person, sir."

He smiled even bigger, Iax shook her head in amusement and slid a glance to her mama. No signs of having been offended, she wasn't surprised; her mama knew better, and was ever-the-lady.

Gemma turned to Iax's mama and bowed lower, as she held both of her hands in her own. "You are exquisite, Iax's…mama. I would thank you most graciously for being such a wonderful example to her. You both have done well, she is a wonderful, worthy female and friend. I thank you." Bowing her head again, Iax could feel the affection rolling off of Gemma's body. She almost broke down, but stopped before it started.

Skenyah must have noticed the tension in Iax, as she came forward and introduced herself, first to Iax's dad, then to her mama.

A female of few words and always sporting a closed-off, guarded expression, she made quick work of her greetings. She merely stated that she had met Iax only days ago, and as a 'friend,' was traveling with Iax to assist her, if need be. Iax was so shocked and touched, she damn near broke down again! *Ugh! I will not cry. Especially not here,* she scolded herself.

Although Skenyah was polite and didn't linger, Iax's folks reacted much differently to her. Not in a bad way, just different, kind of like they weren't sure what to make of her. Iax understood, she still wasn't sure what to make of her new auntie, either.

Grateful to have the introductions over with, Iax was eager to get the hell out of there and to her folks' home. "Everyone ready? I'd like to shower and freshen up, if that's okay with you all?" She gave them all pointed looks and a small smile. She wasn't eager to have the discussion she'd come here to have with her folks, but she would. In time. But for now, she would revel in their company and make the best of each moment as the precious gift it was.

They all nodded. "Heads up, kiddo," her dad said as he tossed her his keys. "Ya wanna drive her every time you're here. I'm supposin' now's as good a time as any, don't ya?" he asked with a sad smile and a dull-but-there twinkle in his eyes. *They obviously know.* She'd call Fred when she had a moment alone. *He knew better, dammit! Telling them was my responsibility, not his.*

After everyone had climbed into her dad's badass, newer model Mustang, Iax started the engine. Hearing her roar as she came to life made Iax smile and shiver. Her dad bought the Mustang, his pride and joy, two-years ago, and he was right; every time she was here she had asked, begged, and pleaded with him to let her drive it. Knowing the reason he was finally allowing it, gave her goosebumps, and she swallowed past the large lump that had formed in her throat.

I will stay strong, and we'll all get through this, Iax kept chanting her new mantra to herself, as she drove off the airport's small tarmac, then turned onto the main road on their way to her folks' quaint, beautiful Maine home.

Chapter Thirty-two

Smoothly shifting through the gears of the Mustang's five-speed, manual transmission, Iax deftly maneuvered the streets like a professional driver. It was cold outside, and even with the heater on high she still felt cold all the way down to her toes. Cold and numb. Hearing her mama speak brought her out of her thoughts.

"Honey, I wanted to thank you for that music CD you sent me. I can't believe I'm admitting this, but I really enjoy it. The whole thing is so much fun! I find myself singing along every time I put it on, and though I can't quite make out all the words, I still enjoy it," she said, smiling at Iax from the front-passenger seat. "I get strange looks from other people when I'm driving and singing, but I don't care. I think it's funny and I keep doing it. It's in the player, if you'd like to have a listen now." Her mama inclined her chin to the CD player on the dashboard.

Her dad groaned in the back seat.

Iax smiled, but on the inside she felt like she was being torn in two, knowing her fate in the extremely near future. One more thing to confirm her initial suspicions that Fred had already told her folks; first, her dad letting her drive 'The Stang,' as he called it, and now, her favorite CD already in the player of said car? Yep, just more confirmation.

Well, she thought, *we're all here now. May as well make it fun as possible for everyone.* Just thinking about what she'd play first, Iax knew her eyes were twinkling with mischief. She'd play a couple of the songs she'd broke out into on that long, crazy day only a couple weeks ago—although it felt like months now—the day she first laid eyes on her Hot-Dude, now stuffed in the backseat. She sighed, and then shook her head not wanting her mind to go *there,* she would concentrate on the here and now. It was safer.

"I would love nothing better. Thanks, Mama, and I'm glad you're enjoying the CD."

Reaching over, keeping her eyes on the road, Iax pushed the power button and waited for the CD player to engage, and the awesome music to start. The second it did, she quickly changed it to track ten. The whole CD was kind of intense, but as a few songs could be considered sad and even a bad influence to some, Iax just loved the beat and the sound of the singer's voice. It spoke of contemplating not existing anymore, yet she'd probably even screw that up, somehow. The sadness in the singer's voice was tense and real, but the feelings it evoked in Iax were those of strength in solidarity; the total opposite of the song.

Humming along to part of the cool tune, and even though she'd turned up the volume more than she probably should have, Iax could still make out the conversations in the back seat. All of those still-new-to-her heightened senses, like her hearing, still blew her away.

"No, you are not making me uncomfortable. I am well, thank you, sir." Iax heard Gemma's ever-proper words. They were probably squishing each other back there. The backseat wasn't made to hold four, full-grown adults, not to mention they were all larger than the average bear, so-to-speak.

Feeling guilty over having a seat all to herself but unable to do anything about it, Iax turned her attention back to the song. Sooner than she preferred, it was over, but now she could have some fun. Laughing to herself, she found track eleven. *Let's see what Gemma thinks of it now.* She waited for the song to start, and made sure she could see Gemma in the rearview mirror.

Peering into the rearview again as the song began, she saw that they were positively crammed too close, making them all squirm and fidget. They only had a little while longer till they arrived at her folks' home, so she waited and smiled, watching for any telltale sign that Gemma would recognize the song. When it finally came, Iax couldn't hold her laughter inside.

"This would be what you attempted to sing, is it not, Iax?" Gemma's face brightened, and her lips curved into an excited smile.

"I can see the allure, yet I must say the singer does sound much more...pleasant than you did. I like this." Iax could see Gemma's head bobbing, just a little bit. Always the proper-lady.

"Yep, this's the one, and I love it!" Iax owned. Then she realized her parents were both laughing. A lot. *Now that's just mean.* She scowled. They'd heard her 'attempts' at singing her whole life, so they understood Gemma right away. After a minute of reconsideration, Iax joined their laughter. She had no problems admitting she had an awful singing voice and understood their mirth, but they didn't have to laugh out loud at her! *And I most certainly shouldn't be doing it, too! I must be tired,* she wearily thought. Everyone's laughter slowly subsided, as the CD ran through a couple more songs.

Mazar and Skenyah hadn't laughed, and she appreciated that. It had struck Iax as odd that Mazar appeared to enjoy a couple songs on the CD; the softer, more mellow ones without guitars or drums. The faster paced, more lively ones, however, were a different story. *Silly male.* Iax smiled. He was a big, tough, strong warrior, yet a little music totally freaked him out? A few times it had practically brought him to his handsome knees. She had noticed every time there was a guitar solo on any of the songs, Mazar would dart a concerned gaze all around them, obviously thinking the sound was a portent to some kind of attack.

Knowing how it felt to be laughed at and mocked, quite recently even, she held it inside. He was obviously struggling with many overwhelming things of this world, and it wasn't polite to make fun of stuff like that. It didn't hurt that she was so in love with him. Or, that he was so hot. Or, that she couldn't stop thinking about his glorious, nude, rock-hard body. A shiver ran from her head to her toes. Then she blushed when she noticed her mama's all-knowing expression from the passenger's seat. *Ugh, just kill me now,* she silently groaned.

By the time they finally got to her folks' home, everyone, including Mazar, had settled into a peaceful, companionable silence.

They were all tired, and the drive had almost taken longer than the flight. Having eaten two large meals already, Iax was surprised when her tummy rumbled. She hadn't even thought about food, what with the emotional reunion, the introductions, and all. She was just glad to finally be at their destination, and that she wouldn't be traveling by any mode of transportation, at least for a couple days.

Her muscles were already tight, and groaned in protest as she exited the car. Only then did she recall her folks' hot-tub. *Oh, Lordy! That's gonna feel sooo good,* she agreed with herself, bending and twisting, as she tried to work some kinks out of her tight, achy body.

Mazar could join her. Later, after everyone else had gone to bed. She smiled.

****

Iax had to admit, Fred telling her folks about her situation had probably been for the best, after all. The fact that he didn't seemed surprised in the least, hadn't quite dawned on her when she'd called him to see about arranging for their private jet. They both would've preferred to have such the discussion in person, but since he, his wife, and their kids were vacationing with his family in his home state of Montana for the Christmas Holiday, it hadn't been an option. He had promised to do everything in his power to make it to her folks' place before her visit was over. She genuinely hoped they could make it.

As for breaking all the crazy news to her folks; she didn't plan to blindside them, but she definitely thought it was her place to fill them in, to break it to them softly as she could. At least knowing beforehand, they'd had a little time for things to sink in a bit. Not completely, and it hadn't made it any easier for them—or her—but it had helped. So, she supposed, she wouldn't kill Fred. Good old Uncle Fred, Auntie Dana, and their kids. If she didn't get to see them and say goodbye, it would break her heart for sure.

She still needed to contact a few friends and coworkers to… say goodbye. *Iax don't do goodbyes well.* Thank God for e-mails and phones. She knew she couldn't tell them she'd probably never see them again, or the truth of why. Some of them were also visiting family for the Holidays, so with no other means to get ahold of them, she'd have to be a chicken-shit. Only chicken-shits broke up with, or said goodbye to people in e-mails, or over the phone. But, she didn't have a choice, nor did she think she could handle doing it in person. It was already hard enough dealing with her mama and dad.

Iax had already come up with the perfect explanation for them; her job was sending her to some small, faraway, remote village on the other side of the world. For a long time. They all knew she traveled a lot, and her work was precarious at best—most of the time—so it wouldn't seem at all far-fetched to any of them. Still, she would miss them all like a phantom limb.

Turning her thoughts off, she glanced across the dining table to her dad. He hadn't said a word about any of what she'd told them. Yet. Hadn't even looked at her. He didn't even speak when she'd explained the whole 'Truemate' thing between her and Mazar, though, she did notice his assessing gaze landing on Mazar for a few long minutes. He didn't look disappointed by her male, just thoughtful. Now, he just stared down at his food, absently scooting it around on his plate. She knew it was just his way, trying to digest the info and not show any weakness in front of the others. He would most likely ask her to take a walk with him after dinner was done, and the kitchen was cleaned up. A walk she would gladly go on.

Her and her mama had always enjoyed the chore of cleaning up after meals, whenever Iax would visit. It gave them private time to talk about whatever they wanted. This night would be no different, in that regard. It would, however, be much different in that it would be their last time doing so together. *Do. Not. Cry. Dammit!* she ordered herself. This was the most emotional, heart-wrenching thing she'd ever gone through. As much as she knew being in the Amethyst Faerie Dragon Realm would keep her together with Mazar, Gemma, Auntie, and all the others there, and she'd be super busy with her mind on other matters, it still wasn't helping much at the moment.

There was a gaping hole in her chest where her heart was supposed to be. At least, that's what it felt like. And a heaviness suppressing the rest of her physical being, all of which literally hurt, and made her feel like she might not survive the next couple days she had planned to spend here. Together. With her family. *How the hell is this supposed to go?* she wondered, *How do people simply sleep, get up, eat, drink, talk, and whatever else, acting all the while like nothing's wrong? Like everything's just right, and life will go on normally? That's insane. Impossible.*

Now she was letting her anger drive the crazy-buggy. *No, you don't,* she scolded her anger. As much as she wanted to give her anger its head, let it run like a wild stallion, it would only serve to make matters worse. Tamping it down, she let her emotions reclaim the reins. They seemed to handle things better.

Again, she tried to understand how they all acted as if everything was fine, just went on pretending no one knew what was about to happen. Yet, there still was no damn way she could see it ending well. No way. At the very least, Iax, her mama, and her dad would all be heaping masses of nerves, choking emotions, and God only knew what else. *What a mess.* She sighed.

Try as she did, it was impossible to *not* think about all the stuff wearing on her, on them all, like a ten-ton weight sinking them down emotionally, and somewhat physically, further and further. Drawing a full breath was becoming increasingly difficult. She had to get out. Unable to wait another moment, and knowing there were two other fully capable females here to help her mama clean the kitchen, Iax beat her dad to the punch. "Hey, Dad, wanna take me for a walk? I could use a big dose of fresh, cold, salty air, and a stroll on the beach. You down?" Waiting with a watery smile, she kept her face angled so only he could see her.

Watching the relief flow over his still-handsome face, her smile grew when he stood and smiled back at her. Jumping up so fast his chair almost tipped over, made everyone laugh for a minute, and it felt fantastic. "I'd love nothin' more, kiddo. Get your jacket, it'll be cold out," he said over his shoulder, walking to retrieve his own jacket and stuff his socked-feet into his boots by the back sliding glass-door.

The view beyond the door was spectacular, and the sun hadn't fully set, so the colors shooting through the sky over the ocean's horizon were magnificent. The angle at which the house sat, the glass-door faced mostly east on their finger of land that jutted a little ways out into the ocean. It ran north and south, parallel to the mainland, and was positively captivating. Iax was grateful, and hoped it would help make their walk and talk a little less sad, as it were.

****

The walk on the beach Iax shared with her dad had been phenomenal and extremely enlightening. He'd finally cleared up several things she had been recently wondering about, from early on in her life. The reason they moved so much, according to him, was so they could keep her from the crazies—as she'd already contemplated—and to literally *keep* her, as if her own true kind wouldn't be able to track her down. He admitted it would have been a futile effort to hide Iax, but it made his wife feel better so he indulged her, and they had moved, a lot.

He also had revealed the details of the day he and her mama had been called into his office, and how Uncle Fred had told, or rather, showed her to them. The whole tale had made Iax cry like a baby, though her tears were those of happiness, for them. She couldn't have mail-ordered better parents.

Growing up listening to other kids constantly complaining about their own parents had always confused her. And as they got older, those constant complainers had pissed her off; most were spoiled rotten, and they just wanted more. Of everything. Iax had always been fully content with her fate, and thanked God for her parents. They truly were and still are the best.

She couldn't believe how well they were taking her news, having expected a lot more turmoil, emotions, and who knew what else. It could've been much worse, she knew, but it really hadn't been so bad. Now she was simply enjoying every minute she had left to spend with her mama and dad.

Uncle Fred, Auntie Dana, and their kids had showed up the day after Iax and her bunch. It was like a mini-family reunion, having all of them together. They all tried to keep things on the light and easy side, telling humorous stories from their past and such. Iax had forgotten many of the experiences they now spoke of, but laughed until she'd teared-up at each one. It was fantastic, and the best way to spend the last of what little time she had left here.

"And that time you took to the archery field at only eighteen-years old. Every other Agent stood slack-jawed, watching you in awe as you hit dead center on every target out there!" Fred recalled, laughing so hard tears streamed down his face.

She remembered that day, too, and yes, slack-jawed they all had been, as well as jealous. But she had learned to ignore those ugly traits as a child. She'd always been above proficient in everything she did, even her academic studies throughout all of her school-years. And the weapons thing? Yeah, she'd always kicked-ass in that department, too. She laughed and sniffled at the same time.

Great memories. Great, and bittersweet, because memories would be all these incredible people would have of her for the rest of their lives, and vise-versa.

She'd decided not to mention anything about leaving the cabin to Fred and his family. She also knew he wouldn't mind her folks using it whenever they got the chance. It had been theirs first, after all, and she couldn't see Fred not sharing. So, yes, it had been the best decision. Her lawyer had been instructed not to inform Fred of his new real estate until the first of the year. She'd be gone by then, and wouldn't have to go through those uncomfortable emotions. The ones she knew she would've been subjected to, once everyone found out.

After spending one-on-one time with everyone, they'd all cried their fool hearts out. Iax couldn't recall ever crying so much, or so hard. Nope, this was, indeed, a first. Always one to fight those types of emotions, she still hadn't stood a chance, and quickly gave in when the two most influential males in her life—before Mazar—had let loose their own tears in front of her.

Who knew crying was so calming? So freeing? She thought maybe she'd do it more often. Not all the time—never that—but at least occasionally.

Everyone was in and out of the hot-tub still telling tales, laughing, drinking, and simply trying to have an enjoyable time. They were doing a superb job of it, too. So, why couldn't she possess a more pliant humor tonight? Most likely, because tomorrow was her last day here. On Earth. She barked out a short, sarcastic laugh, but quickly coughed to cover it up. Who didn't know that saying? '…last day on earth' was in so many jokes and barbs, if they only knew. As for their departure, they'd be 'poofing' out sometime in the afternoon, according to Skenyah.

Speaking of, that female had been super quiet the whole time they'd been here, often disappearing for hours at a time. Nobody questioned her, figuring maybe she needed some alone time, or whatever. Iax had noticed an unusual sadness on Auntie's beautiful face, and thought she probably felt remorseful for taking Iax away from the male and female who had raised her. Iax had overheard a short-and-to-the-point conversation between Skenyah and her folks. She had thanked and plied them with flattering compliments on how well they'd raised Iax. She also pledged her never-ending gratitude for keeping Iax safe, healthy, and not trying to interfere with her natural abilities, when they began to surface.

It had made Iax smile 'cause it was true. Her folks never tried to hold her back, and now she finally knew why, or at least most of why. They knew she wasn't of this world, and she'd have to one day leave. They truly were the most loving, unselfish people she'd ever known, and she'd love them for all of her days.

Her many, many days, according to her three travel companions.

Apparently, she was almost fully cooked, or as her Dragon-peeps said, 'physically matured.' They'd all informed her that she would live at least a couple thousand years, maybe even more since she would be a 'Ruler.' The best part was, she'd wouldn't physically age much past what she looked like now, until she was over one-thousand or so years old. Which, she agreed, was a pretty sweet deal.

She'd also found out with quite a bit of prodding, that Mazar was three-hundred and twelve-years old; try as she did, she just couldn't find it creepy. Skenyah was six-hundred and thirty-seven-years old, but apparently her kind—some sort of half-breed species, which Skenyah had revealed, made her only half-sister to Iax's birthmother—lived even longer than Iax and her soon to be new full-blooded family.

Gemma, Iax already knew, was four-hundred and fifty-two-years old. Her kind lived longer than the average Dragon-shifter, too, since she wasn't one. She didn't shift at all, just lived an incredibly long time.

Coming back to the present, Iax let her gaze rest on each of them for a couple minutes; she just couldn't comprehend living so long, nor could she fathom always looking young and beautiful. Not that she was complaining, it was just unbelievable.

December's biting cold, and the crisp scent of saltwater hanging thickly in the air on the East Coast didn't hamper anyone. They all spent a couple hours sharing the hot-tub, as they exchanged places so everyone got a few turns. After the therapeutic soaks and storytelling, everyone was showering and getting ready for bed.

Everyone except for Iax and Mazar.

They did shower, but they didn't go to bed. Instead, they went back outside to sit on the porch, and watch the inky waves slowly rolling onto the beach a couple hundred feet away. The full-moon cast plenty of light to see well, even if one didn't have extra cool, heightened eyesight, making the living scene before them a breathtaking one. One she'd never see again.

Iax leaned back in a lounge chair between Mazar's muscular legs, and melted against his firm body. Between being wrapped firmly in his strong arms, and the heavy blanket he'd nabbed off the couch, her body drank in the warmth his offered. Eyes closed, she smiled when he gave her a firm, full-body hug. "Are you thinking about not returning here, my love?" he softly asked in her ear.

Trying to swallow past the giant lump that had wedged itself deep inside her throat, she couldn't answer him verbally, so she squeezed his arms instead. The only thing keeping her from crumbling into a dark, hollow mass of nothingness, was knowing she'd still at least have him in her life, as well as Gemma and Skenyah.

"My apologies, Iaxsss, for your heartache. I would do anything to help soothe your pain, and ease your burdens. If you simply speak the words, I shall do whatever I can," he whispered in her other ear, sending shivers down her back. Hearing his sexy, deep chuckle helped. Some.

She knew he wasn't making light of anything, but rather, he was well aware of what his deep chuckles did to her. And he was right; the results were always the same, and always good. Smiling, she moved to get up, and then reached for his hand so he could join her. "Let's take a walk, shall we?" she offered, giving him what she hoped was her best fake smile.

After rising and wrapping the blanket around her, he pulled her against his chiseled body. So tender was his embrace, she lost the ability to speak again, afraid she'd have to fight through the sobs that threatened to wrack her entire body. This, too, he must have known, as he continued to say and do all the right and most comforting things. And he proved it when he replied, "A walk is something I am well-able to do, my love." Standing back, he clasped one of her hands in one of his, and gently pulled her toward the beach for their walk here.

Her last walk—on any beach—ever.

Chapter Thirty-three

Waking up the next morning brought horrible news; an awful storm was quickly moving in, and Iax wanted nothing more than to stay and help her folks batten down the hatches, and prepare their home. They insisted she not worry, claiming they had friends living further inland who they would stay with until the storm broke, or moved on.

"Are you sure? Dammit, you know I worry about you guys!" she strongly protested. "If you're lying to me, I–I—" Realizing even if they were lying, she'd never know, and that there was nothing she could do about it, she blew out a frustrated sigh.

Standing before her in the living room, Mama and Dad stepped forward and pulled her into a fierce embrace. *This is it. This is our goodbye,* Iax's mind told her. Her heart, on the other hand, refused to accept it. Feeling like a little girl in the secure arms of her parents, she broke into heaving, gasping sobs, unable to stop the maelstrom of her churning emotions. Her insides felt much like it sounded outside; a wild raging storm.

There were so many things she wanted to say, to hear from them, but this was it. *God help me. Please, give me strength,* she silently prayed, not knowing how she could survive this day. She still hadn't made up her mind if she would accept those Goddesses, or just continue to worship the one and only God she'd always know and trusted. But, that matter was for another time. For now, she would pray to Him. Her God. Her Jesus. Her Lord and Savior.

It was time for them to leave; Mazar, Gemma, and Skenyah were standing by the front door, trying to give the family a modicum of privacy while also staying sheltered from the howling storm outside.

But that was nothing compared to the storm inside of Iax. She could hear the wind as it snapped smaller branches off the trees, screaming the same way she wanted to. The roar of swelling waves crashing on the shore, was equal to the force she wanted to throw herself onto the floor and never leave. It was all too much.

Too intense.

Just. Too. Hard.

"Honey, we'll be fine, I promise. We're not lying, either. This isn't the first time we've taken refuge at a friend's home. We're fine, you hear me?" her mama tried to convince her as she pulled back to look her in the eyes. Swollen, red-rimmed, tear-filled eyes she couldn't do a thing about.

"Mama's right, kiddo, we'll be fine. Ya don't need to worry 'bout us. Ya got more of a journey than we do, and ya don't wanna mess it up, do ya?" her dad asked, looking into her eyes. Gripping her by the arms, he gently squeezed, trying to comfort her a little bit. "Ya gotta go now, before it's too late. Skenyah said there's only a small window of opportunity for ya all to make it to your destination. Don't cry. Don't do that, please, or ya gonna make me cry, then Mama will make fun of me." He gave her a watery smile. A forced one.

At least he made her laugh through her sobs. Suddenly, Iax began to hiccup, which made her laugh again, and her parents couldn't help but join in. They all had tears in their eyes, but this was better. A little bit.

Iax straightened and gave it her all, as she attempted to bolster herself. Her dad was right; they needed to get going. All of them. "Okay, long as you're sure. I guess this is…it. I love you both more than you'll ever know—" she broke off in ragged sobs, unable to stay strong. Being pulled back into their arms helped, but it also brought on more tears.

All of a sudden, strong hands came around Iax's middle from behind, gently coaxing her to back away, to leave. *No!* her heart roared. *Not yet! I'm not ready! Please!* At the same time, her brain knew this was necessary, she had no choice. Her parents stood firm in their living room, while Mazar lifted her off her feet, her knees had already given out.

The walk to the front door seemed to go in slow motion, everything was so surreal, yet once they finally stood outside under the front porch where they were still protected by the overhead eaves, time slipped away. It felt like it had already been forever since she'd stood in the living room with her parents, during their heartbreaking goodbyes.

Iax still couldn't stand on her own two feet, she knew. She also knew that Mazar held her shaking body close to his warm, muscular one. Words were being said, weird feelings were swirling through her mind and body, and the last thing she remembered was the loud crack of thunder, as another tree branch broke only a few feet away from where they stood.

****

Voices, many of them shouting, yelling, some screaming, and loud clanking sounds assaulted Iax's overly sensitive hearing. It made her already-achy head throb to the point she wanted to scream, too. With enough wits about her to know that would be a bad move, she lay silent, eyes closed, breathing even, and listening for a few long minutes.

The cacophony sounded like it came from far away. *Maybe outside?* She wasn't sure, but a deep, controlled voice issuing crisp, clear orders, sounded much closer. And, it was getting closer, still, to wherever she was.

"You up top, gather more males and make extra arrows!"

"You, whoever you are, clear paths to every bolt hole with all haste!"

"Pay mind! You cannot be underfoot hampering our efforts! Move it, now!"

Shit. I know that tone of voice. What the hell's going on, and why's he so freaked out? Iax puzzled. Fully awake, she sat up ramrod-straight in the bed where she'd been sleeping. She wanted more than anything to call out to her male, but something told her to be patient. And lo-and-behold, Mazar entered the room two-breaths later. His handsome features morphed into harsh, bold planes as he was in full-warrior-mode, yet to Iax, he was still hotter than ever. With a stern mental slap, she scolded herself, *Not the time or place.* Shaking her head, she gave him her full attention.

Before either could speak, he was sitting next to her on the bed. With one large hand, he tenderly cupped the side of her face and she leaned into his magical touch, breathing in his male scent. Closing her eyes to take in the heady combination that was *him,* she wanted to revel in it for just a moment.

"My love, we are preparing for an attack. It would seem *Famista* has deemed it so, and shortly after, the lookout guards spotted a large army making their way here. I know you are supposed to be in charge, but you need more rest. If you would allow it, I can command. I know how to do this, and we will not falter. I will not allow it. They will not approach for a few days yet, so think this through. And know we shall prevail, but I would hear the words from you," he said, resting his forehead against hers. His breathing was a tad heavy, obviously from running around trying to do everything, all while she slept. *An army attacking us? What the hell did we do, and to whom?* she puzzled.

"Why didn't you wake me? I'm fine, and no I don't need more rest. I can also command. Let me get up, I'll be ready in less than five-minutes. I can kick some serious ass, and I'm well-trained to do this, Mazar. You wouldn't believe me unless you saw, but I don't miss my target, no matter the weapon. Surely Gemma's bragged about my mad-skillz? She always does. Here, move, lemme up!" she rattled on quickly, wanting him to move so she could rise and join the action, she pushed at him. This is what she loved! What she apparently had running through her blood; her warrior blood.

She watched slowly him move down to the foot of the bed, giving her room to get up, as he skeptically eyed her attempt to vault herself into a standing position. *Oh! Big mistake!* Of course he knew that would happen, which is why he remained sitting on the bed. It was a good thing, too, 'cause he's all that saved her from falling flat on her face. Feeling herself blush like a fool, she groaned in frustration as his strong arms wrapped around her, and eased her back onto the bed.

"Now, will you listen to me? I do not say thus to vex you, my love, I speak only truths. After all you have been through, you need more rest, and food. You have slumbered deeply for a couple of days with little to eat, it is no wonder you got dizzy. You need nourishment. I will go fetch you something to eat and drink. No, *stay,*" he firmly protested as she tried standing again. "Please, stay here. You are more stubborn than anyone I have ever met. I shall return anon with a plentiful repast for you." Looming over her, Mazar chuckled low, then leaned down and feathered loving kisses over her forehead. "I shall be right back." He winked, just before he left the room.

With all the grace of a Billy goat, Iax flopped back on the bed, narrowly missing the pillows. Reaching back in frustration, she gave them a somewhat rough re-fluffing, and then situated her head to get more comfortable. It was obvious she'd be here for a while.

Damn! She wanted to argue with Mazar, to tell him that she was solid, and she could fight. But he was right, she was about as useful as a newborn. And, truth tell, she was ravenous. *A couple days?* It sure didn't seem like it. Then again, it kind of felt even longer. She released a long, audible sigh.

Awaiting Mazar's return with the promised food, she held up her right hand to admire the 'surprise' Yoren had given her the day the female had introduced herself, then asked Iax to come and see a surprise. Out of gratitude for Iax journeying all the way there, and for Yoren's sake, Iax was floored at the beauty snugly nestled on her right ring-finger.

She wore a different one on her left ring-finger, the one Mazar had gifted her with on the final day of their Mating Ritual.

Even though Iax hadn't been awake, he still came to her sickbed and slipped the incredible work of art onto her resting finger. She hadn't noticed it until the morning they were leaving the Dragon Cove Realm to go to Earth, and when she did, she had busted out crying again. She'd turned into a big-whiny-baby.

A few tears were also shed when Yoren gave her the other ring, but not by Iax. She refused to cry then, and especially in front of a virtual stranger; just another someone she was supposed to have located, saved, and then safely returned home. Still, the ring the female had given her was extraordinary. The band looked like regular gold, but the stone was like none other. It was large, and a deep turquoise in color. Yoren told her it was—in other words—a good luck kind of stone, and she had wished for much fortune and happiness to come her and Mazar's way. Iax loved and always wore it.

After young Nollum had delivered the message to Mazar about their Chief wanting to have words with him, Mazar had returned practically glowing later that day. His Chief had gifted him with a ring also, but it was a large, bulky, manly one. A thick, golden band with a square on top, and atop the square was a Dragon symbol, kind of like a coat of arms for the Dragon Cove Realm. He was beaming with pride and joy; it wasn't every day a Weyr Chief gifted one of his warriors with such a grand piece. They guessed it was probably because Mazar would most likely never return to his home Realm, and Chief Zarckael wanted to gift him with a visual and sentimental reminder from whence he came. It had worked, as Mazar had yet to remove it. He wore it on his right ring-finger, just like her, while wearing the ring her dad had given her for him, on his left ring-finger. They both were thrilled at the generous gifts, and even more so at the tokens of their joining as Truemates.

Chief Zarckael had also gifted Mazar with something he called a handy-band of warriors, assuring Mazar this Realm would be in need of their assistance. It had been totally unexpected and Mazar tried to turn his Chief down, but no one ever turns down such a gift, and most especially not from one's Chief. In the end, the 'handy-band of warriors' ended up totaling over two-hundred extra dudes to help the Amethyst Dragon Faerie Realm. Even though they were technically 'on loan,' everyone knew they were here indefinitely.

So far, they all had fallen for the breathtaking Amethyst Faerie Dragon Realm. A few had taken a liking to some of the females, whereas many had completely fallen for others, hopeful that they, too, would find their Truemates. After what had happened between Iax and Mazar, they all agreed and prayed that it could happen to anyone, anywhere.

Even Gemma had been spying on one of the largest, most handsome males who had come with them from the other Realm. Iax's heart warmed at the thought of her bestest finally finding love. She truly hoped for all their sakes, that they would end up finding their Truemates, and be as happy-in-love as her and Mazar.

Speaking of, he kept his word. In no more than five-minutes, he returned carrying a tray heavily laden with all kinds of goodies, and interrupted her ogling the shiny, sparkly baubles on her fingers. Everything looked fabulous, and smelled even better. Right on cue, her empty stomach let loose an embarrassingly noisy growl, to which Mazar simply gave her an 'I told you so,' smile. That was fine, she was too hungry to worry about her own hang-ups, so she'd give him a pass. Just this once.

Iax sat on the bed unceremoniously stuffing her pie-hole faster than was safe, yet unable to make herself care. She knew she needed to eat, but man this was bad, even for her healthy appetite. Everything was perfect, and each bite melted in her mouth. She knew she'd eaten too much too fast, but she forged on and devoured every little morsel the food. She'd rather be full than hungry, any day of the week.

Mazar was the best. He'd brought her roasted meats, piping hot fresh bread, fresh, real butter, veggies, both raw and steamed, along with some 'safe' fruits. To drink, whatever he'd given her was the best she'd ever tasted, but she was unsure of its name. It was frothy, kind of like beer, but flat with a strong honey-flower flavor, and served at room temperature. Strange and different as it was, she was surprised at its pleasant taste.

After downing every bite, Iax lay back on the pillows again, patted her now-full-belly, and closed her eyes as she released a contented sigh. "Thanks, Mazar, that was amazing. Maybe a little too much, but you were right. I didn't realize how hungry I was. Whoever made the food is who I want to make all of my food. Do I have that kind of authority here?" she wondered out loud, popping one eye open to glance at him. She was already half-asleep, feeling much like whenever she would have a whopping Thanksgiving meal, then become so tired she had to take a nap.

Suddenly, she remembered a question she had for him. "You never said, but who's attacking us, and why?" she pressed. Opening both eyes, she leaned her head up to look him in the face, hoping she would feel more in control. Somehow, she was a little more awake than she had been a minute ago.

His expression instantly sobered, making her worry even more over what was doin' with the attack. But he schooled his handsome features so fast, if she hadn't already seen it, she would think she imagined the whole thing. "Of course, my love. You have every authority here." He smiled, obviously unwilling to answer her latter, more urgent question. *He'd better not start that shit. If I'm supposed to be the boss, nobody better ignore me. Especially when I ask fundamental questions!* she silently fumed.

"And, my Iaxsss, you are more than welcome. I did not know you could eat so much, yet your beauty astounds, and you continue to amaze me," he whispered, leaning over to kiss her neck, then her eyelids, her nose, and ending on her mouth. *He's good, too good. But–no!* Fighting the clash of her mind and body, she pushed at his chest, needing to know what was doin' outside.

"Answer me, please. Who attacks us, and why?" she boldly pressed harder, staring him down when he remained unmoving and unwilling to answer. Releasing a ragged sigh, he pushed a hand through his unbound hair, turned to face the window, and stood gazing outside trying to figure out the best answer. *Fine, as long as he does, that's my only care.* She patiently waited.

Before he could string the words together, Gemma burst into the room as if the hounds of hell were nipping at her heels. Out of breath—which should have been impossible for Gemma—her face was sheet-white, eyes large, and she looked utterly terrified. Iax had never seen her friend in such a state, and it scared her.

"What the hell's going on, Gemma, and why are you such a...mess? Someone better tell me something and soon, before I really get pissed off." Raising an expectant brow, she crossed her arms over her chest, tapping her fingers on her elbows. "Well?" she repeated as Gemma and Mazar secretively regarded each other.

Then, wouldn't you know it? Before she could get an answer from Gemma, Skenyah entered the room. Albeit with much more grace and not physically taxed, she still looked extremely troubled.

What. The. Fuck! Iax was about to scream, when Auntie came to her bedside. "Iax, I need to do...something. It is of the utmost import and I should have done it sooner, but we are out of time. Will you allow me this?" she asked, her expression firmly set.

Iax could feel heavy emotions emanating from Auntie's body. *This isn't good,* she thought. *Not good at all.* Whatever it was, Iax figured it was crucial, but she wanted to at least know what Auntie was talking about. "What is it, and why now?" she asked.

"It is a vision, as well as a bonding-thread—if you will—one which will tie your blood to that of your kin, your Weyr. The bonding will cause all the blood of your blood to call to you, to connect you to us all. It is imperative to your position here, and now it must be done without further delay. May I?" Skenyah pleaded once more.

Quickly, before she could reply, Mazar was at her side. "My love, you should allow this; it is of the highest import, as she claims. I must go, but I will return soon. They will give you the answers you desire. Remember, all will be well, and I love you," he admitted, and then reined more soft kisses over her face.

As much as she may have wanted to kick the females out of the room, keep the mood light, and take his kisses to a deeper level, it wasn't an appropriate time. Besides, she felt herself fading again, her eyelids felt like lead-weights, and she couldn't keep them open much longer, let alone, do anything physical. She allowed herself an inner-smile, and his low chuckle reminded her that he could sense her feelings. *How does he do that? It's wartime, and he still makes me mushy-gushy. Something I always vowed never to be.* She sighed.

"I love you, Iaxsss," he repeated. "And all will truly be well. This, I promise. You rest, and I shall return to keep you updated. Do not worry yourself," he finished and smiled as he pulled her covers up, took the empty tray, and left the room.

"I love you, too!" she yelled after him. *I love you, too,* she silently communicated to him, reaffirming the depth of her proclamation.

The purposeful strides that carried him away told the stark truth of the matter; there was a battle raging on the horizon, and he meant to be victorious and prove himself to her. Not that he needed to—not at all—for she totally trusted him and knew he was more than capable. But still, it was her job, and she genuinely wanted to be in on it. Yet, as always, he was right, and she had to leave it up to him since she was in no shape to man a war.

"Okay, Auntie, whatever it is, let's get it done. I'm confused and having a hard time staying awake, and I'm already feeling like a shitty leader. I should be out there helping with what's doin'. Oh, but wait! I don't know what's doin', do I? No, 'cause no one's told me a damn thing! What. Is. Happening?" emphasizing her last three words, she leveled a stern gaze on Gemma, then on her auntie. Enough was enough, already! "Oh, and one more thing, please, don't hold back. I want only truths, nothing but truths, got it?" she directed at her auntie.

"You believe I speak non-truths to you? Oh, Iax, can you not feel the pull between you and I? It would be our blood recognizing each other, calling out, as is your birthright. If you are so unsure of my words, allow me to show you," Skenyah spoke in a soft, almost scary voice, making Iax think of those who, the madder they got, the quieter they became. But, she wanted to see whatever Auntie wanted to show her.

"I never called you a straight-up liar, but maybe I don't believe all you've said. How the hell ever it is you that can show me, please, by all means, impress me." She gave Auntie a weary grin. Over their travels, and due to their proximity, the time they'd spent together had brought the two closer together. Iax still had a few reservations about her new auntie, and she finally trusted her a little more, but not wholly. It wasn't Skenyah's fault; pure and simple, *Iax don't do trust.*

Since 'arriving,' if that's what one would call it, in the Amethyst Faerie Dragon Realm, Iax had been approached by so many of her 'followers,' her head had been spinning. Some left her sacrificial gifts such as various animal heads—apparently quite an honor here—along with all sorts of foods, and even ornate, handmade jewelry pieces.

She'd only been here for a few days, and after sleeping for the first couple, everyone wanted her blessing, or some such shit. She didn't know which end of her was up, down, or sideways. What she did know was that she had an awful headache, was bone-tired, and more confused than she ever had been in her life.

Her birthday had passed her by while she'd slept. And talk about a transition, this took shit to a whole 'nother level. Everything looked, sounded, smelled, and felt different, more so than the heightened senses she'd come into after shifting in the Dragon Cove Realm. Apparently, she was now a full-fledged Dragon-shifter, as well as the proud new Ruler of the Amethyst Faerie Dragon Realm.

It was turning out to be quite the responsibility.

Mazar, Gemma, and Skenyah had all ganged up on her and made her go to bed, finally, after being up and unendingly hammered at for four straight days. She'd protested for all of about ten-minutes, capitulating much faster than she was proud of. But, she'd needed the rest, and apparently still needed more. Skenyah's voice brought Iax out of her thoughts.

"My pleasure," Skenyah returned. She was well-aware that Iax was only barely beginning to trust her, and some of what she said. It hurt, but she tried to be accommodating to the female-young; blood of her blood. "You will have to stand, I am afraid, and we must face each other while keeping our hands tightly clasped together. We must also concentrate deeply on each other's eyes. If one of us looks away, the link will be broken, and it will be painful for us both. Are you certain you wish to do this? Make *very* certain." Her eyes held a clear warning.

Pushing her exhaustion aside and already feeling better from eating, Iax slowly rose to her feet. She was determined to be strong, and didn't want anyone to think otherwise. "I'm as ready as I'll ever be. Let's do this." She gave Auntie a firm nod. At Skenyah's unconvinced gaze, Iax straightened herself and lifted her chin, "Really, I'm fine." She nodded again. Facing her auntie, their hands firmly clasped, they looked deeply into each other's eyes.

After a few moments, Iax was becoming agitated. "Well, what's the deal? Thought you were gonna show me someth—" Iax's mouth clamped shut, and every inch of her body tensed when Skenyah squeezed her hands. Both of their bodies rigid, eyes uncompromisingly glued upon the other's, neither would break at this point. One was curious, the other eager to impart knowledge of which only she possessed. Suddenly, and almost too fast, Iax was bombarded with visions of everything that had happened from just before her birthparents were killed, until this day.

She saw it all, was spared nothing.

Her birthparents being cut down by some ugly fuckers who seemed to be some kind of shifters, but not from the Dragon

Dimension. They were bulky, ugly, ogre-looking fat dudes. Looked like none of them had showered in, well, an awful long time, and none of them had probably ever indulged in a real shave a day in their lives.

Hideous scenes, wailing screams, blood everywhere. A big, solid, human-looking male was gravely injured, though it didn't stop him from carrying out her parent's orders to the T. There were two females; Skenyah, and another who looked so much like her and Iax's birthmother, the three must be sisters. The females firmly attached Iax, only a small infant, to the human's chest with some weird looking cloth they had ripped into long, wide strips.

They were all working and moving so fast, everything was a tremendous blur, but she could still see it all. Iax's birthmother—who was the most beautiful female Iax had ever seen, even more so than the one who raised her—with barely any life left in her, was still able to dictate a note for her other sister to pen with an inkwell and quill on a piece of parchment. Oh. My. God. That's about me; my prophecy that Auntie spoke of.

Iax watched in utter terror, all the sights, sounds, and even— smells?*—definitely smells. It was too weird, but not wanting to break the connection, she quelled her curiosity and stuck with it, while Skenyah's memories on that long ago, fateful day were unleashed.*

Suddenly, she was gone from the Amethyst Faerie Dragon Realm, and the visions continued as if she was watching everything on a monitor. Would've been nice to have a filter, but she was getting it all. Every ugly detail, and then some.

Her and Mazar's Mating Ritual played out before her, and she recognized those humongous critter-things. She saw herself lying on the ground checking them all out, taking in their beauty and details. The vision faded in and out, much like how she had during that time.

Then, like an aerial shot, she saw herself floating through the air and slowly going down into the top of an old tree. It 'appeared' that someone or something was physically holding her, but not. As her body was somehow being gently guided into the tree, she caught movements off to the side of the area where the tree stood; it was the critters.

They witnessed her body go into the tree, nodded like they were satisfied, and then they all disappeared. Just, poof...gone. *She heard the word 'Guardians,' whispered in the air, but wasn't sure where it came from. Nobody else was around, that she could see, and she knew that she had been fully unconscious during the whole bizarre event.*

As the vision faded, her mind wandered for a moment as she tried to puzzle it all out. She felt Skenyah's hand squeeze hers, not hard, just a comforting feeling. Then the vision was back, but she was in the Faerie Amethyst Dragon Realm again. The major difference this time; she was an adult.

She remembered this Realm from a few months ago, when her and Gemma had been here. Iax's mad-skillz were such at the time that she'd been able to locate, eliminate the threat, and be back home—on Earth—all in the space of a couple hours. Now it all made sense.

The vision changed again, to when her birthparents had been so callously slain in cold blood. Over, and over, and over...she continued to witness their vicious, ruthless murder.

Why isn't the vision changing? Is Skenyah 'stuck,' or what? Iax seriously considered, only momentarily, before she broke eye contact, and gasped for air as she pulled away. She noticed Skenyah's eyes were swirling, and her body hadn't moved at all, as if she was still back there.

What the fuck! Not a question. *Seriously, what the fuck! Why is this happening to Skenyah?* Suddenly, she felt the need to vomit, probably all over herself and Auntie. Iax was livid, confused, and about ten other intense emotions, all connected to whatever the hell had just happened. *What do I do?* She didn't know. Skenyah wasn't moving, and was barely breathing.

Just when Iax was about to make her move and shake her auntie, the female's eyes went back to normal, her rigid frame slouched forward, hard and fast enough to send her to the ground face-first. Iax reached out and caught her before she managed the face-plant, which probably would have injured even her; the always-tough-Skenyah.

Facing each other again, Iax more in control this time, she thoughtfully gazed into her auntie's eyes. She easily detected sadness, torture, and something beyond her comprehension. Wanting to be supportive, she wrapped Skenyah in a fierce embrace. "I'm so sorry. You were there, you saw everything happen, and you still had to care for me. I'm so sorry," she finished, fighting the shakiness in her voice while she rubbed comforting hands over her auntie's back.

Steadying herself and needing to change the mood, Iax grabbed both of Skenyah's hands, moved just inches away from her mesmerizing eyes, then she went off. "That was dangerous – I mean, look at you. Just, *please,* don't ever do that again!" She instinctively knew Skenyah was okay now, so Iax released her hands and took a few steps back, feigning a bravado she didn't truly feel.

With a sincere smile, Skenyah reached out and gave Iax's arm a gentle squeeze. "Apologies, Iax, I did not know it would go that way, it never has before. I am well, and my thanks for your concern. It pleases me more to me than you could ever know." As she made to leave the room, she glanced back at Iax, she obviously had more on her mind, but wasn't sure how to say it, Iax assumed.

"What? What's wrong? You can tell me whatever, ya know, I think we're good now. You and me." Iax encouragingly smiled.

"I hope you understood much of what you witnessed. And yes, those 'critters,' as you refer to them, are your Guardians. They sensed trouble, and were correct as you had eaten the bad fruits and needed to be hidden. There was a threat heading in your direction, another crazed male, and they willed you inside the large tree so the male would not find you." Skenyah turned to gaze outside. "They never meant for it to turn out the way it did, and had returned here.

By the time your circumstances had turned dire, it was too late. Also, because you were...you died, the link was inactive, so they no longer sensed the threat. That is what led them to believe you were well." Her head slumped forward. It was clear to see this tale was difficult for the female.

"You see, the Guardians can sense a threat, but not always from the emotions of their charge. The male who was almost upon you, had vile thoughts, and with them came a strong, evil sense which your Guardians easily picked up on. They assumed you had awoken and got out of the tree, or someone else had found and helped get out. They feel as though they have shamed and undoubtedly failed you, therefore, none of the other Guardians have heard from them. It is only possible for them to be seen by the one they are to protect—which in this case, would be you—as well as other Guardians. Even then, they can cloak themselves with invisibility to all, except for you. Yet, by the critical time when you needed them, they were here. As I said, they thought you were well, but they still remain unseen to all." She gave Iax a sad smile. "Either way, It will be up to you, should they receive absolution for their negligence as they see it. When you are ready, all you need to do is be alone, firmly concentrate on them, and they shall appear only for you. They will have no choice, Iax, as you are their Mistress for all of time." Reaching out, she patted Iax's upper arm.

"So what, I just think 'em up, and they'll show for me? Now I feel bad," Iax muttered, staring at the floor. "Hmm, guess I'll have to git 'r dun, won't I? Oh, but shit! Shouldn't I do it now? If we're having a war, shouldn't I have access, or whatever you call it, to my Guardians in case I need them?" She looked expectantly at Skenyah, all the newness and unfamiliars hitting a nearly overwhelming level.

"Yes, you may want to do it, and as soon as you are able since—as you said—you may need their assistance. It is up to you," Skenyah confirmed. Then she turned around and walked away; shoulders back, chin up, and truly looking like the powerful, dignified female she was. Iax fully caved, allowing feelings of respect and others she had no name for, to fill and wash over her for the first time. So many emotions she now had for this formidable female, Auntie Skenyah.

Blood of my own blood.

Now she was awake and fully bolstered, as fierce determination coursed a scorching swath through her veins. She was ready to take on anyone or anything. *Bring it, bitches!* She smiled inside and it felt good, almost too good. But damn, she still felt a little guilty. She'd treated her auntie harsh. *Too harsh?* Who knew? What she did know was that Auntie was tough and could handle anything–right? *Right?*

"Oh, Iax! I believe what you just said to your Aunt Skenyah was perfect. I mean, she did deserve a stern talking to, but you did not go too far. Please, do not be upset with yourself, you had to tell her how you felt. She knows your intend held no malice, only concern. You both have much to deal with, and what just transpired between you was wonderful." Gemma smiled at her. Although it was only barely, she was visibly a little less shaken than she had been a few minutes ago.

"The army which protects your Realm is all but nonexistent at this point. However, the warriors Mazar's Chief gifted him with are formidable, and will be of great assistance. Skenyah still has much stress, as she is always trying to fix everyone's problems. Those responsibilities now include you, though she is grateful you are finally here." Gemma gave her friend a pat on the back, remembering her initial reaction to Skenyah; peace and comfort. No, the female could not be all bent. It was simply not possible, Gemma concluded. Too bad, though, she thought, as it may not matter for much longer.

Everything Gemma just said reminded Iax that she still hadn't been offered any answers to whatever was doin' with the impending attack. The attack she, too, had all but forgotten about until just now. Joining Gemma, who now stood in front of the large glass windows, she noticed her friend was looking out over the horizon, her eyes leaking. *This doesn't bode well.* Iax frowned.

"Gemma," she softly began. "What is it? What makes you cry?" Rubbing her right hand in comforting circles over her friend's slumped back, she kept one eye on Gemma, and the other on the horizon. She almost missing Gemma's soft, almost imperceptible words when they finally came.

"It is him. My brother has figured out my plans not to return home, and has come for me with his full army." She breathed out a trembling sigh.

Beside her, Iax tensed as her hand stilled on Gemma's back. "What?" she whispered in shock.

"He will arrive soon, and he is terribly angry," Gemma whispered back.

About the Author:

I live on the beautiful Western Slope of Colorado, and enjoy a moderately quiet life with my husband and our two-year old English Springer Spaniel, Stryder. Our three-grown kids and all their furry four-legged kids live nearby. I'm doubly blessed to also have in the area my parents, my brother and sister in-law, my sister and brother in-law, as well as my three-nieces, my two-nephews, and my two brand new great-nephews. Writing has become my passion over the last couple years, and self-publishing—as much of a trial as it's been —has also become quite the learning experience! I have several more books in the works, which I hope to have completed and released very soon. Thank you.

For more about me, please check out my blog at http://ressaempbra.wordpress.com/ Find me on Facebook at http://www.facebook.com/RessaEmpbra, become a member of my Facebook group—this book's namesake—at http://www.facebook.com/groups/206315256073749/?ref=ts. Then, hop on over to Twitter and follow me at https://twitter.com/#!/RessaEmpbra. Comments are not only welcomed but encouraged, and I answer every comment, post, and email personally….

Thank you for reading my first published novel!

~Ressa~

Acknowledgements:

Foremost, I thank my handsome husband, Shannon, for being patient even when it went totally against his grain, lol, and when I'm sure we both thought I'd never finish this novel. He was supportive and allowed me writing time when it should've been mealtime, or some other such important thing. Next, I thank my beautiful daughter, Monica, for always listening to me prattle on like a loon, lol, and being one of the best sounding-boards a writer could hope for. Whenever I got down on myself and didn't want to finish, she was there pushing me. Additionally, I thank my dashing boys, Matt and Josh, for also being supportive, running errands, or even coming up with a dinner or two while I worked at trying to make the words in my mind make sense in print.

Most importantly—even though I can never give enough thanks—I'll still try; I thank Mama and Dad, the best in the world of course. Mama, for being supportive even before you read this novel, and sticking by me throughout. Dad, for your encouraging words occasionally when we talked on the phone. Also, for bringing me into this world and raising me with so much love, and the ability to freely give it to my own family. I Luv You All!

I give extra thanks to two very special friends of mine, both of whom I dubbed my 'secret readers' while writing this novel. Elise Cooley, sister of my heart, and Judy Leavell, a family friend. You're both precious and I can never thank you enough for reading every excerpt, chapter, or whatever I sent you. You're both amazing and I'll never forget your kindness, time spent reading my work when you probably had much better things to do, and your feedback; all of which was invaluable. You'll both always hold a special place in my heart. Just remember my super-sweet words while I'm writing my next novel! *winks* You'll be the first to know!

I have many others to include in my eternal thanks: To Scott D. Muller; thanks for helping me when I was stumped. Your suggestions—few words of wisdom though they were—got me over my stump and back to the business of writing the moment I read them. I appreciate your kindness and ingenious ideas. I can't leave out the man who helped me through one of the most trying and difficult parts of the 'self-publishing' process; SJB Gilmour, you saved me and my book! I don't know why the e-book formatting gods hate me, lol, but they do. Luckily for me, they think the world of you…and so do I. It's been one nightmare after another for months as I've tried to get the formatting just right, but after you introduced me to the correct program, it only took me a few hours. Thank you a million times over for being a genius!

To the world's most FAB beta-readers: Sinead MacDughlas, Monique James O'Connor, Elizabeth Anne Lance, Iris Blobel (if I missed anyone, I am so sorry—you all know that I can't remember five minutes ago, lol): You're all talented, creative, fun, and working with you has been a pleasure and a true joy. You're also spectacular, beautiful woman inside and out. A very special thanks to all of you, because not only have we become friends, but without your assistance, this novel may not have come to fruition. Even if it had, it would not have been half as great as it is now. I Heart You All!

In general, I have so many family members, friends, and e-friends, I could never list you all. Please let it be enough that I thank you for your love, kindness, words of encouragement, your loyal, never-ending support, and your gentle guidance a time or two.

Now, for one of the most important people to this novel (and of course, to me) because we all know that the cover can be our biggest initial asset; you know, that perfect moment when people see your novel in a bookstore and say, "Oh, I love that cover! It *must* be a great book!" And they buy it solely on that basis. I'm really hoping for that scenario, and for that possibility I give a ginormous thank you to the man who created my outstanding cover-art; Dave J. Ford, you are a Rockstar, as well as one of the most talented people I know. I was impressed anew with each new proof—I already knew you did great work—and while you were creating my amazing cover-art, you never failed to blow me away! So, Dave, I thank you profusely! And yes, I heart you, too. You can find him at:

David J. Ford - Photography & Art , www.davidjohnford.com *or* www.printsbydave.com

Last but certainly not least, I thank my fans. I worried the whole time I was writing and preparing this book for publication, that I wouldn't sell even one copy. Although I haven't yet sold as many as I'd have hoped, lol, I am selling. My fans have been loyal and amazing, and as I write the next installment in this series, your words of kindness is what keeps me going.

Thank you all from every corner of my heart....

Praise for the Author:

Reviews and praise for The Dragon Dimension: Caught in the Dragon Cove. Look at what reviewers are saying about Ressa's adult fantasy fiction novel, and please feel free to visit the links to learn more!

"Caught in the Dragon Cove by Ressa Empbra was a fantastic example of storytelling. From the very beginning I got lost in the story of Iax and Gemma. The fact that this was only a partial manuscript tells me that author Ressa Empbra has a gift for storytelling, and creating fantastical worlds where mythical creatures, such as dragon shifters, exist. I hope that I have the chance to review Caught in the Dragon Cove when the book is completed."

http://speedyreader-allthingsbooks.blogspot.com/2011/07/dragon-dimensionscaught-in-dragon-cove.html?spref=fb

Partial Review By Tanya Contois

"Ressa Empbra's, The Dragon Dimension – Caught in the Dragon Cove, is a unique and suspense-filled paranormal read. Her characters, though supernatural, were ironically real and easy to connect with. It was compelling and forward-moving, keeping this reader's interest at every twist and turn. I commend Ressa Empbra for fabricating such original and refreshing characters, as well as unparalleled story lines. Ms. Empbra makes the impossible seem possible, and in an ever-increasing market for the paranormal, I see her rising to the top with her characters emerging as the next TV series/movie franchise ensemble."

Review By J.P. Grider

"Having had the pleasure of beta-reading 'Caught in the Dragon Cove,' I have to say Ressa's done a hell of a job! Regular readers of Fantasy-fiction are in for a rare treat. I love the movies ˇin your head, Ressa! Keep putting them into words!"

By Sinead MacDughlas

www.ingramcontent.com/pod-product-compliance
Lightning Source LLC
Chambersburg PA
CBHW071220250626
47163CB00001B/50